FIERY LITTLE THING

AVINA ST GRAVES

Fiery Little Thing by Avina St. Graves
Published by Avina St. Graves
Contact the author at author@avinastgraves.com
Copyright © 2024 Avina St. Graves

ISBN Print 978-0-473-70792-7
ISBN eBook 978-0-473-70794-1

Cover by Maldo Designs
Chapter art by DesignsbyCharly
Character art by ekilateral.art
Editing by Nessa's Lair
Proofreading and sensitivity reading by Havoc Archives

AUTHOR'S NOTE

There's no simpler way to put it: Kohen is a dick. A massive dick (he's got a big one too—not the point). He gets handsy, and says stuff that makes you want to knock his teeth out. But then he'll do debatably cute things, so we'll bat our eyelashes and call him misunderstood. #icanfixhim

You might want to knock Blaze out too. But as Lady Gaga said, "I don't believe in the glorification of murder. I do believe in the empowerment of women."

Which leads me to the next point: This book is a dark romance that touches on themes that are difficult for some people to read about. The full list of content warnings is on the following page. Please read responsibly.

This book is set in a fictional reform school created by Avina St. Graves. This means liberties were taken with the setting, and is not at all what occurs in real modern-day reform schools.

PS This book is a work of <u>fiction</u>. It does not mean I condone the characters' actions.

TRIGGERS

Degradation, sex, questionable use of medical equipment, BDSM, clamps and rope play, orgasm denial, dub-con, medical latex, consent nonconsent, biting, forced breeding, air play, blood play, pyrophilia, pyromania, kleptomania, trichophagia, drug abuse and addiction, reference to overdose, alcohol and drug use, substance abuse, death of grandparents, bullying, trauma, death, mentions of suicide, profanity, mental health issues, parental neglect, reference to off-screen emotional child neglect and abuse, financial abuse, financial manipulation, reference to off-screen dissection of animals, police, institutionalization, medical torture, nonsexual choking by the MMC, the FMC has sex with someone other than the MMC (while they aren't together), manhandling by the MMC, graphic violence, domestic violence, childhood trauma, toxic characters, arson, attempted sexual assault, victim blaming, hydrotherapy, electroconvulsive therapy, blood, gore, murder.

Please read with caution. Your mental health matters.

PLAYLIST

"My Medicine" – *The Pretty Reckless*

"Habits (Stay High)" – *Tove Lo*

"Girl With One Eye" – *Florence + The Machine*

"Kill Of The Night" – *Gin Wigmore*

"Kleptomaniac" – *DEZI*

"High Enough" – *K.Flay*

"Play With Fire" – *Sam Tinnesz, Yacht Money*

"Arsonist's Lullabye" – *Hozier*

"Control" – *Halsey*

"Bang Bang!" – *Nessa Barrett*

"Crazy Girls" – *TOOPOOR*

"Demons" – *Hayley Kiyoko*

"Decode" – *Paramore*

"Gasoline" – *Halsey*

"High School Sweethearts" – *Melanie Martinez*

"Ptolemaea" – *Ethel Cain*

"Desire" – *MEG MYERS*

"Flawless" – *The Neighbourhood*

"Okay" – *Chase Atlantic*

"Sippy Cup" – *Melanie Martinez*

"House Of Balloons / Glass Table Girls" – *The Weeknd*

"Hayloft II (SMASHUP)" – *Mother Mother*

"as good a reason" – *Paris Paloma*

To the girl who wants a man to treat her gently, burn the world
for her, and fuck her like a whore.
This pyromaniac is exceptional at multitasking.

KOHEN

PROLOGUE

Kohen: Age 7—Blaze: Age 6

She's going to love this. I just know it.

Blaze always uses her weak little arms to hit the other boys on the playground, but she never does much damage since she's all skin and bone. I'm scared she might break something if she keeps attacking people and climbing trees when she thinks no one is looking.

That is why this is the perfect gift for her. I spent all week thinking about what to get her after she bruised herself punching a kid three grades higher than her.

My skin grows colder and prickly the closer I get to her house. I didn't even know she lived so close to me. Hopefully, she's home—I mean, I at least hope this is where she lives. Last week, I saw her walking down a long gravelly driveway and guessed it led to her house.

Mom was driving so fast that I missed the house number, but I saw her. I'll always see her, even from a mile away. She's so pretty with her messy red hair and tiny fists. It's annoying though. She still hasn't figured out her thumb needs to go *over* her fingers. Not under. Maybe I can teach her how to throw a proper punch tonight.

Mom and Dad left at five to have dinner and watch a show with my brother, Kiervan, and they'll be gone for hours, so I'll have plenty of time to spend with Blaze. They wouldn't be taking Kiervan to the movies if they saw what he did to the dead mouse last week. But if they find out I'm doing this, they'll ground me for life. Then Kiervan will laugh and blame more things on me so our parents can pat his head while locking me in my room.

Chewing on the inside of my cheek, I eye the sun that's setting way too fast, then look both ways before sprinting across the road, carefully holding the backpack to my chest so I don't drop her present and ruin it before giving it to her.

The last time I gave her a gift, she took the pencil case with her trembling hands. She didn't say thank you or anything, but didn't give me her dead eyes, which was super cool.

This time, I'm *sure* she's going to smile at me. And then once I know how to make her smile, I'll make her do it over and over until she's sick of me.

She'd better not smile at anyone else but me.

My chest feels all funny as I tug on the collar of my sweatshirt. This was such a stupid idea. Yesterday, we didn't have to wear a uniform, and Blaze came to school wearing a red top. This hoodie is the only red thing I own, and I can't even fit in it anymore; it's too tight.

It's too late. I'm here now—I think.

The trees surrounding her house seem bigger up close. They aren't nice and cleanly cut like where I live. There's no way my family would ever let this many leaves sprinkle over our driveway. Blaze should really get a better gardener.

Music pulses through the air, a low vibration that grows louder and clearer the closer I get. Then it stops, only to be followed by someone droning through the speakers about a sale going on for a pair of tires. Do Blaze's parents let her listen to the radio this loud? That might be why she's always yelling.

My eyebrows knit together when a building comes into view, and I stop midstep.

This can't be right. This can't be where Blaze lives.

But I *swear* this is the same driveway I saw her walk up.

The house looks like it's from a scary movie. The paint is stripped away from the edges, and planks have fallen to the ground. The ground is littered with empty wrappers and glass bottles. Vines grow up the side of the house, and one of the windows on the bottom floor has a big crack going through it. The wood holding up the deck roof is splintered, poking out of the house at an angle, looking like it'll snap at any second. There's even a small fire in the middle of the lawn. What even is this place?

Narrowing my eyes, I spot the red-haired doll she brought to school last year sitting on the windowsill. Maybe this is like a pool house or something.

A man stumbles out the front door that is broken off its hinges. He takes two steps, then tumbles down the stairs, falling face-first onto the grass. A groan passes his lips, but he doesn't get off the ground. Gripping my backpack, I edge closer to the house, watching for any sign of movement between the surrounding trees. It's hard

3

to tell how many people are inside because all the curtains are closed, but I can hear the adults talking and laughing.

I hear glass shattering and I freeze. Shaking my head, I shuffle closer. Will her parents kick me out? They could be having a dinner party, and they may not want guests. Mom doesn't let Kiervan have any of his friends over whenever they do. Blaze's mom might not want that either.

A branch snaps to my left, and I whip my attention toward the noise, catching sight of a dash of red. I take in a deep breath as my blood rushes to my ears. I knew she wouldn't be in the house when so many people were there.

"Blaze," I call quietly.

Jumping off the main path, I wipe my sweaty hands on my jeans. I have to lift my legs higher to cut across the grass to get to the part of the forest where there are only weeds, trees, and mud.

I call her name again, carefully pulling out the gift from my backpack. I've had to hide it from everyone in my house all week.

My clammy fingers tighten around it. What if Blaze doesn't like it?

No—there's *no way* she won't like it. I spent so many nights under my blanket, flashlight on, trying to make it special for her. It's going to be her favorite thing. Ever. She might even ask for another. Maybe a bigger one—one that isn't plain brown but has big red and black stripes.

"What are you doing here?" Blaze's voice carries through the still air and tickles my ears. She isn't much of a talker, but her voice is my favorite sound.

I open my mouth to speak just as I turn to look at her, only for nothing to come out. She pales to bleach white as her bright blue eyes swing from me to my hand, then back to me. I dig my nails into my palm.

I don't think she likes it.

It's like watching an action movie with how she transforms, going from soft, wide eyes to an evil villain who could cut me with her glare.

"I got you something." I grind my teeth together. Why does she have to keep looking at me like that?

I fumble with the gift for a moment, gnawing on the inside of my mouth. *She's going to like it—she* has *to like it.* Once she holds it in her hands, she'll never want to let go. She just—*Come on, Kohen.* I need to be quick before she runs back into the house. Or worse—she tells her parents, and they tell *my* parents, and I can never see her again. I've heard them say how much they hate her parents even though they keep mentioning the mansions her grandfather has. If her parents kick me out, how will I give her this so she doesn't keep hurting her arms?

Her wide eyes stay fixed on me. My chest expands, and all my worries melt away. *See, she likes it.* Instead of coming forward, she takes a step back. Then one more. And another. She casts a quick glance at the baseball bat in my hand, and sprints toward the house.

"Blaze!" My sneakers pound against the forest floor as I weave between rocks and jump over exposed tree roots. I have to hug my backpack and lift the bat in the air so it doesn't hit the ground and wreck the words I've engraved on it.

She almost trips over her feet as she looks back at me, but she rights herself too fast for me to catch up. "Leave me alone!" Her shrill voice echoes against the muffled music.

"Stop!" Blaze breaks through the tree line and into the yard where the firepit has died down. I push myself harder, running faster than I've ever run before. "Come back!"

I keep running, watching as she leaps over the man sleeping on the grass, clambers up the steps, and quickly dives into her house, disappearing out of reach. "No! Get back here!"

Stopping short by the last tree—before I get too close to the house and the man—I hunch over and heave in lungfuls of air, searching each window for signs of her. I stumble back to the tree line, hiding behind the thick trunks in case she rats on me. When no one comes out after what feels like hours—but is probably only a few minutes—I dash from tree to tree around her house. It doesn't matter how many times I circle the house; I don't catch even the slightest glimpse of red hair.

She hates my gift.

She hates *me*.

Stupid. Stupid. Stupid.

Kiervan would've known what to do. He would have picked the right gift, and she wouldn't have run from him.

Each time I hear footsteps, I hold my breath, hoping it's her. But it's not. It never is. People come in and out of the house, barely able to walk, laughing or grunting, even if they're the only ones around. One person comes out to throw things into the fire, then hobbles back inside.

By the time I move from my hiding spot behind the trees, the sky is navy blue. The only light left outside comes from the moon that's hidden behind blankets of clouds, and the fire that's slowly dying.

The bat shakes in my hand as I run my fingers over the words one last time before I drop it into the fire. There are only eleven letters, but I took the time to measure each and every one of them properly so they span the entire bat.

BLAZE & KOHEN

BLAZE

CHAPTER 1

Present

"Asshole."

Both a noun and an unofficial adjective—such a versatile word. Just like *cunt*. For example, Kohen Osman is a psychopathic cunt.

Those are the two words that immediately come to mind when I see him leaning against the tree, carving into his lighter with a switchblade.

Kohen Osman doesn't necessarily look like an asshole, but he's the biggest one in this city.

"Klepto." The aforesaid bane of my existence pushes off the tree and pockets his switchblade into his uniform, taking up the entire footpath with his unwanted presence.

"Fuck off, Pyro."

My head is pounding, and I'm two minutes away from turning my teeth to dust. His company is making my hangover worse.

Kohen always hangs around the school corner, leaning against a tree on a street I have no choice but to take. The only other option would mean adding an extra ten minutes to my forty-five-minute walk home. I figured I'd rather deal with the human embodiment of a cold sore than endure ten more minutes of this freezing weather.

I keep shuffling along. Paying no attention to the asshole by my side, I quickly check my phone to see if my granddad has decided to transfer money to fix my bedroom window after one of Dad's friends threw a rock at it two nights ago.

Nothing.

Great. My T-shirt taped to the window frame isn't exactly keeping the winter chill out.

Digging half-moons into my palm, I glare at Kohen. Every day, I wrongly assume he'll leave me alone if I have headphones in or a shiv ready to pull on him.

But no.

Whether he's risking giving himself hepatitis B with a stick-and-poke tattoo, or lighting something on fire, every day those disgustingly pretty golden-moss eyes of his collide with mine, and every damn day, he opens his equally disgusting pretty mouth to turn my mood from bad to worse.

He falls into stride beside me, twirling the lighter between his fingers and then flicking the spark wheel. It's brand new, with a dazzling gold surface and a skull he personally engraved.

It would look great on my shelf.

Give me another week, and I'll probably pocket that one too. Lord knows how much of his shit I've stolen after thirteen years of enduring his insufferable presence.

I'm pretty sure he knows I'm the one who keeps stealing from him. One day he's going to try burning me alive for all the shit I've done. I just know it.

The pyromaniac kills the flame and then lights it again, on and off, on and off, on and off. He pulls the lighter away before I have the chance to snatch it from him.

We both look out of place while walking through this part of town—him with his tattoos and fire fingers, me with my *reputation*. The caliber of most students who attend and live around St. Augustine is beyond the type of suburbia with white picket fences and homey-looking buildings with children playing on the front lawn. The top ten percent reigns around here.

Each house we pass ranges in the millions, surpassing the term *house* and sitting comfortably within the category of *mansion*. Some are hidden behind tall trees or long, winding driveways. Others are open for all to gawk at.

A couple properties have the words *manor* or *estate* on big wooden signs by the entrance to their driveway. Maybe I'll ask Grandpa to send me money to put a plaque out front of our house that says *Crack House*. Hell, I'll even let them put the sign in place of my window as long as I can stop worrying about snow in my room or worse, someone climbing through.

A car pulls up ahead in front of one of the homes, and a lady clad in Louboutins and a Burberry coat glides out of the back seat of a Maserati, pushing her Fendi glasses up her nose as the car drives away. She's blissfully ignorant of the world around her as she adjusts her open bucket bag in the crook of her elbow.

And just like that, I'm not queasy anymore.

Kohen shakes his head and slows his walk, knowing what comes next. He folds his white shirt sleeves up to his elbows, so I have an unobstructed—and unwanted—view of the muscles in his forearms bulging against the tattoos. Except it isn't enough to distract me from the fact that we're a few feet away from the grab bag in thousand-dollar shoes.

Stealing Nicholas's laptop bag yesterday didn't give me nearly the same thrill as this. *A stranger.* It's an urge more profound than getting to the metal container behind my bed frame. An itch that needs to be scratched or else I'll die. And why die when this woman makes it so damn easy for me?

Blood rushes through my ears as I near her, keeping my steps even and steady. She keeps buzzing the gate that won't open, while my eyes are on the abyss of goodies hanging off her arm. Then I see the corner of a wallet, and the itch turns into a full-blown need.

Jackpot.

I love rich women; they can be so wonderfully oblivious.

My shoulder collides with hers as I pass, and I quickly pull away, making my stomach turn unhappily.

"Sorry," I mumble, holding up a hand when the woman tears her attention away from the gate long enough to sneer.

She turns around without a word, too busy with the buzzer to notice the wallet-sized bulge in my pocket. I keep walking with a steady pace, innocently tucking a lock of copper hair behind my ear as Kohen mumbles something under his breath.

"Are you going to spend another night alone in your shitty house?" Kohen doesn't spare me a glance, saying the words as if they taste like bile he's been forced to swallow.

Great, it's a talking kind of day.

"I was thinking of inviting your dad over, actually," I snap, then chide myself to reign in my temper. My teeth chatter as I pull my blazer tighter around myself, even though it's a record-hot day for winter. I need another hit so all this shit is more bearable. I can't be hungover if I never stop.

The entire Osman clan is blessed with ungodly good looks that make the other mortals look pathetic—even their mom is bangin'. Their family shares warm, deep brown skin that practically dazzles in the sun because they probably eat gold for breakfast. Kohen is the only one who likes to keep his black hair cut short on the sides with soft curls on top, and just like Kiervan, he has staggeringly broad shoulders, thick legs, a thicker wallet, and the type of smile that makes everyone in the PTA give their life savings for a share in their pharmaceutical company.

They—not including Kohen—have the charisma that thaws even the coldest of hearts. I was ready to risk it all when I buddied up with Kiervan for a ridiculous charity project a few years back. And, I'll be honest, I was suddenly a reverent humanitarian during those three hours he was charming my panties off.

Kiervan is everything Kohen is not; namely, he doesn't piss me the fuck off. This particular Osman wakes up every day and makes my imagination run wild with all the ways I could kill him with a pen.

"I like them older," I tack on, because mentioning his father dearest always pisses him off.

The dark cloud beside me darkens further, but I couldn't give a shit. No one is making Kohen talk to me. He's always been better seen from afar anyway.

Kohen scowls, then schools his features into an annoyingly nonchalant look. It does nothing to hide the fact that he wants to strangle me. "Funny, last night your mother said the opposite about me."

Kohen's father would never deign to look at the dirt on his shoe, especially my specific breed of dirt. On the other hand, my mother would mount anything that glanced her way, as long as she could score at the end of it.

I snap my fingers, pointing toward him. "So *you're* who she got HIV from? It all makes sense now. Your father will be happy to know you do have manners with all the sharing you're doing."

It's getting harder to hold my stare when my stomach feels like it's wringing itself out. I catch the muscle feathering in his perfectly sculpted jaw. How dare he be easy on the eyes. More than easy. He's an Adonis—the most attractive man I've ever seen, with hazel eyes from his mom and a condescending stare he acquired from his Turkish father.

Not that I'd ever tell Kohen, but that pyromaniac's been featured in my dreams one too many times.

Too bad I want to deck him.

Finish him off in more ways than one.

"It's called multitasking. I'm disappointing my family and ruining yours at the same time." Kohen's voice pierces through the momentary satisfaction of scratching the itch before a cold sweat starts on my spine.

"With a brain like that, it's a wonder why they held you back a year." Now *that* was the biggest disappointment. With how the tendons in his neck tick, I'm sure he knows it too. "I guess Daddy couldn't buy your grades."

At the end of the last school year, I thought I would finally get rid of the fucker, but he failed all his exams and showed up in my class the following semester. I could barely stand him when we were in different grades; sharing classes is a testament to my patience.

The only other thing Kohen and I have in common is that we're still at St. Augustine High because of our families' money and name. However, our families have different ideas about their reputation. His parents are building their fortune; mine are snorting, smoking, injecting, or fucking it.

Kohen lifts a tense shoulder and drops it, even though I can tell he's not exactly pleased about being a nineteen-year-old who still needs to put on a uniform every morning and pretend to sing hymns in assembly.

The corners of his lips curl. "At least I saw my dad this month, Klepto."

Well played, dickhead.

I sway in my steps when my stomach twists, threatening to push out the little bit of water I consumed today. I need to get rid of Kohen. Pronto.

I swallow the spit forming in my mouth and look straight ahead. "How's Kiervan, by the way? Still on track to getting summa cum laude?"

Kohen's annoyance vibrates off him in waves.

He opens his mouth, but I cut him off with a swift "don't care" and a wave of my hand.

I pull out my earbuds from my pocket, press play and turn up the volume of my music to drown out the sound of the blood rushing through my ears.

He yanks a headphone out my ear, and I slap his arm out of pure reflex, then snatch the earbud back.

The distance closes between us, and I'm unsure if it's because he moved closer or if I'm getting hit with another wave of vertigo.

Either way, I stumble back, only to be pulled closer by the solid grip around my bicep.

"Why the fuck do you always have to be such an insufferable bitch?" His voice sounding like gravel, inches from my face.

Lethargy holds its sharp teeth in my muscles, weakening my attempt to shove him back. "Maybe because you're an annoying piece of shit."

They say the devil looks hideous up close. I wish I could say the same. Somewhere underneath my exhaustion, I'm hit with the disgusting thought that Kohen would look stunning underneath me.

He twists us around. The air punches out of my lungs as he pushes me against the wooden fence. Before I can make up from down, his fingers curl around the column of my throat, and his thumb presses against my pulse point, placing just enough pressure to keep me put. "I haven't done shit to you, and all you do is—"

I scoff. "Do you even hear yourself?" My voice raises to a pitch too loud for my ears, and my stomach churns one pace faster than my heart rate. "You're so goddamn delusional."

My body struggles to escape. No amount of shoving, hitting, or kneeing is doing any damage other than winding me up and solidifying the hatred that's boring down on me from his hazel eyes.

His body presses against me, forcing me to push as far back to the fence as I can, making me keenly aware of every firm ridge of his body that's touching me—a toned thigh wedged between mine, chiseled abs brushing against my chest, strong fingers wrapped around my throat. If I hadn't already been lightheaded a minute ago, I would be now.

Hazel eyes burn into me, taking apart every inch of my soul like he's trying to figure out how I'm getting it all wrong.

16

"Typical *Blaze*." He spits my name out the same way my grandparents do. "Always playing the victim when this is all on you."

"You're the one who started all this shit—for fuck's sake, you lit my hair on fire in second grade!" I screech. "You stole my bag. Pushed me into a pool. Took my clothes from my locker at the gym. Showed up at my house—*in my room*—in the middle of the night. And that's not even the half of it."

I told the teacher, the cops, and cried to my grandad, thinking he'd do more than just throw money my way to shut me up. But every week, Kohen kept coming after me in one way or another. He's the only consistent presence I've had in my entire life, and he looks at me like he can't wait to snuff my light out.

His eyes harden into steel, and the words that follow slice worse than the real thing. "You look just like your mother right now."

My palm cracks against his cheek. He doesn't wince or even twitch. He does something far worse: he smiles. It's all teeth, with a crazed glint in his eye to match.

His scent wafts over me, patchouli and mint, like the candle beside my bed, as he lowers his lips to my ear.

"Did that feel good?"

My eyes dart to the hand-shaped welt blossoming on his cheek, and my brain doesn't register what it's doing fast enough to stop myself from slapping him again to turn it crimson. "Better."

His nostrils flare, but he doesn't move away. He almost looks... *pleased*. So I do it repeatedly, hitting his cheek and arms. Wrapping my fingers around his throat only makes his eyes brighten, and bucking my body against his widens his malicious grin. But it all makes my body feel worse.

I still, panting into the space between us. I just need to get home and get to my stash, then everything will be fine. "Let go of me, you freak."

His breath fans my cheek; the upward curl of his lips slowly turns down as if my actions have only just caught up to him. "One day, you'll stop fighting me."

"Is that a threat?" I ask through gritted teeth.

"Always."

"You can die trying."

He leans down until his lips are next to my ear and tightens his hold around my neck. "Oh, Blaze," he says mockingly. "I already know you burn so pretty. And if it isn't by me, you'll just do it to yourself. But your death is mine, Thief."

I suck in a sharp breath when he pulls away, and my legs give out from under me.

Fuck, fuck, fuck.

I shouldn't have taken so much last night.

The white wooden fence scrapes against my back as I slump onto the ground, silently heaving. I don't think he's out of earshot when my stomach decides to give up. A prickle sinks into my palm as I keel over on the grass, liquid acid stinging my throat before spilling onto the earth.

I stay down, pulling my too-tight blazer around my torso and letting myself have a minute before resuming the remaining thirty-minute walk. My heart stutters as my hands dig into my pockets in search of the lady's wallet, coming up empty each time.

"Motherfucker," I grumble.

Like I said, Kohen is an asshole.

18

She was home.

Of course, my mother chose today of all days to show up. She returns every once in a while for food, to sweat out a withdrawal before snorting another line, or to steal my shit. The sight of the open cupboards is a good enough distraction to make me forget about the human stain that was taunting me.

I have to hand it to her though, she's late. Grandpa's grocery delivery came three days ago, and another box won't arrive until tomorrow—or three days from now if he's feeling especially vindictive about our existence.

Now, all that's left are broken bits of pasta and an expired packet of instant noodles. I growl and slam the raided cupboard closed. The sound echoes through the empty house, and I try not to think about what other messes she might have left behind. This is the reason I have to lock my fucking door.

Grabbing the trash, I sweep Mom's empty wrappers and crumbs off the counter and into the bin. I only have thirteen dollars to my name, and that's meant to last me until the next delivery. My stomach turns, and I massage my temples like it might make this shit show go away. If I want to put food in my stomach, my only option is to cook.

It's a damn good thing I don't have an appetite then.

I'm going to kill Kohen the next time I see him for taking my shit. Whatever goodies I might have found in the lady's wallet could have set me up for the week so I wouldn't need to rely on my grandpa Jonathan Whitlock Sr.'s good graces to send me my fifty-dollar "emergency" allowance.

I can't blame the old man for being an intelligent businessman. Who else would have thought of sending their addict daughter to the other side of the country to hide their greatest shame? Pay to

19

put a roof over her and her fucked-up offspring's head, cover their insurance, send them food once or twice a week, give the responsible one—somehow that's me—some money in case of emergencies, ship her to a fancy school, weaponize it all to keep her in line, and no one will be any wiser.

Except, of course, Kohen figured it out and has held it over my head ever since.

He discovered that if I skipped school, Grandpa "accidentally" misses a grocery delivery and "forgets" to send me my allowance. If the school calls about my behavior, he halves the amount of food he sends, and that's another allowance I won't be seeing. Any money I get now will go straight toward fixing the broken window, and there won't be anything left to buy groceries with if he decides not to send any.

Sure, our house is nice enough from the outside after the remodel. It's lower-upper class, suitable to pass as an acceptable residence for a Whitlock. It's secluded enough that neighbors won't complain about the woman walking down the main street with her flavor of the day. Thick curtains ensure that the stains and a seven-inch rip on the three-seater couch remain hidden from prying eyes. No one will notice the coffee table, precariously balanced on a granola box; the circular dining table with just one seat, barely held together by duct tape; or the dried blood in the grooves of the tile floor and the shattered mirror in the downstairs bathroom—evidence of an incident where one of Dad's friends tried to kill him.

I'm so goddamn sick of living here and under my grandfather's thumb. I'm sick of praying Mom doesn't come home and that Dad won't come knocking trying to grab cash or a couple grams of anything I have. And fuck Jonathan Whitlock Sr. for leaving me in this godforsaken place with these horrendous people.

I drag my feet out of the kitchen and up the stairs. I can hear my bed calling me. Every cell in my body screams for sleep, nutrition, and more of what Tony gave me yesterday—in no particular order. But the last thing I want to do is sleep while Mom still remembers she has a house she and her friends can come back to.

The dirty wooden floors creak beneath my weight while I use the walls for support so I don't go tumbling down the stairs. *Left foot, right foot. Left foot, right. Left, right.*

I don't look up from my feet until I reach the door to my bedroom, and my stomach sinks into the ground.

It's unlocked.

The handle is broken.

Oh fuck. Oh fuck. Oh fuck.

I tear into the room and take stock, heart pounding in my throat. Everything looks untouched—at least, I think it is. It's hard to tell. My collection of stolen items that ranges in the hundreds covers every inch of flat surface—watches, pencil cases, glasses, books, jewelry, hair clips, creams, a couple of thimbles. I turn toward the shelf beside my bed where everything I've ever taken from Kohen sits.

It all looks fine. Mom wouldn't have come in here unless she wanted something. The last time she was here, she took my warmest jacket and best boots. The time before that, she grabbed a couple pieces of jewelry to pawn off. Before that, she found my stash of—

I lurch into motion, crashing down onto my knees beside the bed to reach behind the frame. But I don't need to squeeze my fingers to get to it because the metal container is on the floor. Open.

Empty.

Fucking. Empty.

21

I snatch the container off the ground and hurl it across the room. It hits the hallway wall with a vicious thud, the sound echoing across the frigid room. The breeze from outside filters through my T-shirt covering the window, forcing a shiver out of me as tears sting my eyes.

"That bitch!" I rip my lamp away from the wall, letting it join the empty container.

That was meant to last me a month.

A whole fucking month.

It would have lasted longer if I didn't get carried away with Tony last night. Last month, he discounted a couple grams for me to sell so I could make some cash. Does she realize how many wallets I stole and how much shit I pawned just to get all that?

Fuck her.

Fuck Kohen.

My eyes catch on the black T-shirt taped over my broken window. And fuck Dad too.

I collapse to the ground and slap the floor. *Fuck*!

I can't stay here and wait for morning to come when there's nothing to do at night. Dad stole the last TV we had, and one of Mom's dates for the night broke the modem. I can't even afford a fucking laptop. I also don't know what I might do if Mom comes back tonight. Yell? Scream? Shake her until she gives me back what she took?

I drank my body weight at Tony's house last night, and it's only Wednesday.

Fuck it. I've got nothing better to do, and I need to forget this shitty day. Snatching my phone off the floor, I call the only person I've contacted this month.

Tony picks up on the third ring. How pathetic is it that my drug dealer is the only person who hasn't let me down?

"I need a hit. I'll owe you one."

BLAZE

CHAPTER 2

"Chug. Chug. Chug. Chug."

The cold liquid goes down my throat without effort. I haven't got a clue who's chanting or how this drink ended up in my hand, but what I know is that I well and truly owe Tony one.

And Duke.

Whoever the fuck Duke is.

Oh, he's the one who's chanting. Wait... *That* Duke. I think he sits behind me in history class. He has a funny nickname... What was it?

Something tightens around my thigh while I tip back onto the hard chair to finish off the strawberry flavored... vodka? Gin? Fuck knows.

Who cares? This is the most fun I've had in... ever.

Slick sweat glistens across my body, sticking my uniform to my skin as my pulse hammers harder than the bass. My nose twitches with a numb tingle. I wouldn't mind another bump right about now.

Or two.

I drag my eyes up as the faint sound of chatter rings all around. Everyone looks blurry yet completely clear. Other than Duke, I don't think I know anyone else here, except maybe the girl in the green ripped jeans who's flashing her phone in people's faces. I think she's in my history class too.

Have I been here before? Maybe. It looks like the living room of every college flat I've ever been to. Beer bottle caps litter the floor, drinks are on every flat surface, and random sporting items hang on the wall.

Vibrations hit my back, followed by tumbling laughter. I blink once, swing my gaze to the hand sliding up my thigh, then to my warm chair—chest?

Duke's chest. When did I end up on his lap? Wait—isn't it a school night? How many hours until I need to get ready for it?

God, how much have I—

"Come on, baby," he purrs against my skin.

I barely feel when the ridge of his nose runs down my neck or when he takes control of my hips to grind me against his slowly hardening cock. I turn my head into him, and I can't help the laughter that bubbles out of my chest. Didn't I think he had bad BO when I first got here? He doesn't smell so bad now. He doesn't smell like anything, actually.

After I called Tony, he picked me up and drove us to this party he knew about. Then he gave me a couple lines on the house and followed it up by thrusting someone else's box of drinks in my face. Next thing I knew, Duke was my best friend because he had a bag of pills with my name on it.

26

His blue eyes flash to mine, lips splitting into an excited grin, showing slightly yellowed, crooked teeth. He looks wrong. His eyes should be hazel, not blue. And he's so skinny and he doesn't have an ounce of muscle on him.

I jolt when his teeth scrape against my jaw. "You owe me some fun, Blaze."

My brows knit together. I don't owe him anything, but I wouldn't mind some fun. It's been months since I've been laid. Maybe longer. I can't remember. I don't like anyone in Tony's crowd—and you should never screw the crew—but we're at some college student's flat, so who gives a shit?

I definitely don't. Not after the shit Mom pulled and all the fuckery I'll have to deal with up until I graduate—and Kohen *Fucking* Osman. How dare he steal the wallet from me.

"I've been wanting to get a feel of that—"

"Stop talking. You're not hot enough to open your mouth too." I slam my lips against his, effectively shutting him up. For a couple seconds, at least.

Duke chuckles, moving out of time with my lips. My eyes close, and golden-moss irises and black hair flash through my vision, and I push my ass down against his groin. Cool air kisses my legs as he pulls the skirt of my uniform up to sink his fingers into my bare flesh, kneading it uncomfortably. My head swims as his other hand fists my hair to deepen the kiss.

"You like what I have to offer," he mumbles against my lips, pulling away long enough to take two pills out of a bag. One ends up on my tongue, the other on his.

I snicker to myself because I definitely didn't end up on his lap for his personality. *This* is what I needed. I'm three sheets to the wind and couldn't give a shit if he's just offered me cyanide. I'm not missing out on anything if I die.

My equilibrium shifts when Duke yanks me back to his lips. Either he's an awful kisser, or it's my fault there's so much teeth going on right now. I bet Kohen's kisses would be all pillowy and bruising with all that anger and his thick, kissable lips.

Duke keeps kissing me. And kissing me. And kissing me. It's a dizzying cycle that tips and turns.

I'm distantly aware of someone hooting in the background over the music playing. I think I hear a giggle as well. Nothing makes sense because I blink, and the music becomes muffled, and a door slams somewhere around me. The room is dark with only the yellow light of a lamp to illuminate the unmade bed and clothes on the floor. We're in someone's bedroom.

He yanks off my uniform top and grabs my tit. "Fuck, Blaze," a head of blond hair groans around my nipple. "I knew these'd be good."

A whimper drags out of my throat when he—Duke?—squeezes my free tit. My eyelids feel so damn heavy.

I gasp, and the next time I blink, I'm on something soft. Glazed blue eyes bore into mine from above me, blond hair swaying in time to the jolts going through my body. God, he's ugly. Is this what my life has come to? Sex with men whose best lighting is no lighting?

A strangled moan comes out of me in the next blink. My fists curl around the sheets, and I watch the wall inch closer and closer from the force of his thrusts. He might not be good to look at, but his dick game isn't half bad.

My head hits the wall, but I barely feel it. I laugh—it feels good. At least it should feel good. I can sense the stretch and the slap of him

28

against me and the heat of my skin against the sheets. But it's pressure without the sensation. I feel nothing, and it's fucking *phenomenal*.

I'm *free*. My body is weightless and numb; my brain free of all problems. Just this moment. Just sweat, heavy breaths, and the muffled sound of the world around.

I cry out for the sake of crying out and arch my back to meet his thrusts. Another laugh tumbles out, and it feels better than anything else. *This* is why I do this, to feel exactly like this. Soft snores fill the air somewhere by my ear in another blink, and a heavy weight lies over my middle. Then everything plunges into total darkness.

"Fuck," I groan, slapping around the bed to stop the incessant beeping noise.

"Stop hitting me," another voice rasps.

I freeze.

I peel my eyes open and shut them straight away.

Oh fuck. I moan into the pillow and fumble around for my phone that's somewhere in the sheets. The alarm stops when I press a random button.

On top of the killer hangover from the copious amount of alcohol I consumed, I'm coming down from who-knows-what. But above all, *that* is what I'm waking up next to? Kill me now. It also smells *horrendous* in here. I thought rock bottom would at least smell better than this.

I've done walks of shame before, but *shame* isn't an adequate enough word for sleeping with Duke Morrison—one of St. Augustine's resident drug dealers, and—rightfully—nicknamed Shitcake after what happened when he ate the food he made in cooking class. Nothing beats this kind of low.

I push myself onto my elbows.

Uh oh.

"Where's your bathroom?" I stumble out of the bed and scramble for the door. My head spins, and my stomach does the same thing double-time—Jesus Christ, why is it so bright?

"What?" He sounds as shit as I feel.

"*Where's your fucking bathroom?!*" Bile lurches up my throat.

"Uh…"

Fuck his response. Whipping the door open, I sprint to the only open door down this hallway. If it's someone's bedroom, well, tough. Everything I consumed last night is coming out—and it's all coming out *now*.

I crash onto the floor in front of a toilet and throw my head forward just in time for everything to go hurtling out. The acid burns its way up my throat as I empty my stomach into the bowl. I'm never drinking again.

Shivers rack my naked body as the cold of the tiles sinks down to my bones. Over and over, I hurl until my throat is swollen and my cheeks are soaked with tears. I clutch my stomach as cramps radiate out from every nerve ending in my body.

Somewhere in the distance, I hear someone having the same reaction as me. The two-night bender wasn't my brightest idea. I wish I could say that it got out of hand, but last night was exactly what I wanted. I came here to forget about my shitty mom and the theft of my vice, and I did. If Duke has anything on him, neither of us will have to deal with the second part of our hangover. The aftermath never gets easier, no matter how many times I've ended up at this point over the years. I never seem to get used to it either.

When there's nothing left to come out of my stomach, I stay put, staring at the bowl and wondering how many more mornings like this I can take before one day I don't wake up at all.

I leverage the door handle to pull me onto my unstable feet, my fingers tightening around the metal as the room spins with the motion. It feels like an impossible feat, but I manage to find mouthwash before sitting back on the floor.

After a while I leave the bathroom, my bare feet shuffling along the carpet as I try to locate the shithole room I've been sleeping in for the past however long. Both of our cell phones blare with the alarm, and I rush as much as my body will allow to shut it off. Why on earth would I set an alarm this early on a weekend—

Shit, I forgot.

"Want a ride to school?" In front of me stands the unmistakable embodiment of regret, butt naked at the foot of the bed, and the urge to repeat last night's mistakes surges within me. *Gross.*

I stare at him. Dear God.

Hmm, being seen walking with him into school, or walking solo from who-knows-where to school, risking who-knows-what fate along the way. The latter sounds more appealing, but if I skip a day of school, Grandpa's punishment will be far worse. That's another week before I get my allowance, or money to fix the window, and an extra day before my grandpa sends groceries.

Incentivizing me to stay in school is his way of keeping up with appearances as if everything in our life is all pixies and butterflies.

"Yes." I'm a goddamn ray of sunshine today; why not let everyone see that Blaze Whitlock fucked Shitcake. "Got anything to make today bearable?"

He shakes his head.

I doubt Duke is disappointed about last night's events, but we are both well and truly hating ourselves right about now as we take turns showering, and then shrugging on our itchy, used uniforms. Neither of us speak during the drive or when we park and go our separate ways—me with my head down and sunglasses on, and Duke mirroring me down to the way we both clutch our stomachs.

I'm better than my parents—I *am*. Drugs don't control me. I still attend school, show up to all my classes, get sent to detention, and pass over 70 percent of my papers.

Hell, no one is—or will be—getting hurt by me consuming my vice of choice. I've got no kids or a partner I need to stay loyal to. I can stop drinking and taking drugs whenever I want. It's just a bit of fun—of course, until every step taken feels like a fight not to run to the closest trash and throw up.

A few people give me the side-eye, and a lot more whisper when they see me walk inside the class. I must look like one of Satan's experiments. I'd scream at them, but I'm worried I might pass out if I exert any more energy than necessary.

Chatter fills the air as I enter the classroom. I keep the shades firmly on my nose and sink into my seat, dropping my head toward the back and rhythmically tensing and untensing my jaw. To say I feel like dying would be an understatement. I need to sleep for a solid forty-eight hours, and if my hibernation starts in first period, that's fine by me.

The shrill sound of the bell indicating the start of the class makes me wince, and I slump lower in my seat, trying to hide behind my chem book.

"Miss Whitlock." A woman's voice breaks through the haze. *Fuck.* "May I speak to you outside?"

No, not particularly.

I take a deep breath and force myself onto my feet, leaving behind my sunglasses on the table to follow my teacher Mrs. Yang into the hallway. My stomach swims as I step forward, fighting the urge to use the desks as support. The last thing I need is for the school to complain to Grandpa so he has another reason to delay sending me food or money. But fuck it. Let's just get this over with.

As I scooch between tables, a hand lands on my arm, and I whip my head around. "What?" I snap.

Cindy Masterton—an overly friendly girl whom I have yet to figure out completely, unable to tell if she's fake or not—snatches her hand away and plasters a pitiful smile on her face that, frankly, grinds my goddamn gears. She doesn't know shit about me.

"I'm sorry about what happened. If there's anything I can do to help, please let me know." Her voice is candy-sweet, but not in the condescending way everyone else says it around here.

"Right," I mumble, pulling a face. "Thanks." I don't know what on earth she's offering to do for me, but I might as well keep it civil until she makes it out of my good book.

Mrs. Yang's downturned lips greet me the second I step outside. Why is everyone looking at me like I'm a charity case? Seeing her so softened up is weird when she usually doesn't hesitate to slap a ruler on someone's desk when she doesn't get her way.

Don't tell me she's about to stage an intervention about how I've been showing up to school lately. I've only gone to school hungover twice this week, and once last week. It's hardly a problem.

"Look," I start, feeling my temper rise up my throat. "I just have a cold and—"

She cuts me off. "We didn't think you would come to school

today."

First of all, who is *we*? Second of all, why wouldn't I come to school today? If I'm absent, they'll call my grandfather, then there go my groceries right out the broken window.

"Uh, okay?" What else am I meant to say to that?

"It's okay to feel upset about what happened. None of us can begin to imagine what you are going through." I glance around, trying to see if there are cameras on us, or a bunch of cops ready to snatch me up for possession of drugs. "It's never easy when something so traumatic happens." Wait. *What*? "Think of it this way"—my eyes fall to the hand she places on my arm—"at least no one got hurt."

Is this some sick joke? I knew the socialites of St. Augustine were proficient at mind games, but no one's laughing now.

I rip myself out of her bony hold. I can barely handle her weaponizing a ruler and attempting to embarrass me in class with questions she thinks I wouldn't know the answer to. This is a whole other level of bullshit I refuse to put up with. "What the fuck are you talking about?"

Her face hardens at my choice of words before her brow line drops in confusion. "Your house?"

"What about it?" My temper laces those three words. If this is a trap, I'm going to be giving Grandpa another reason to starve me and cut me off from affording Tony's goods.

She gapes at me like *I'm* the one who's fucking with her. "Your house... last night? Don't... don't you know?"

I cross my arms, even though the added pressure on my stomach is less than ideal, and wait for her to continue.

"Blaze... It burnt down."

I blink. "What did you just say?"

She shifts her weight. "It was on the news," she explains. "Your house caught fire around dinnertime last night, and the firefighters... they couldn't salvage it."

Blood rushes through my ears. *No.* She's lying. She has to be.

I spin on my heels and storm down the hallway. Mrs. Yang calls after me, but I can't find it in me to react. There's nothing wrong with my house. It's completely fine. All my things are completely fine. This is a prank. My collection is untouched, and my room looks exactly the same as I left it yesterday.

The sound of my footsteps bounces along the empty corridors, echoing against the rows of metal lockers and glass cabinets filled with trophies. The exhaustion I felt before is hidden somewhere beneath the blanket of adrenaline.

If Mrs. Yang were telling the truth, I would know. Someone would have called me. My phone would have exploded with missed calls from my grandpa, or my grandma would have contacted me for the first time in my life. Maybe my uncle would have touched base to see if the scums of the family had finally been killed off.

My breath rushes out of me, and I stumble backward until my back hits a locker. I grind my teeth as I make out the face of my attacker.

"You mother—"

"Fucking bitch." Kohen presses his forearm against my throat. The venomous look in his eyes makes me stall for half a second too long, giving him enough time to put more pressure on my windpipe. "You deserve everything that's coming for you."

Rage emanates from him in violent waves, and I can't make sense of it or why it's even there. What if he's the one who's setting me up? He's making this one big practical joke because he somehow knows about the power Grandpa lords over me, and Kohen's using him to exact punishment against me for skipping out on school and acting out. That's probably why he was asking me if I'd be home yesterday. Fuck if I know. I'm so sick of everyone's bullshit, and I have to see the lies for myself.

I shove him off me and duck under his arm. "Stay the fuck away from me, or you'll pay for it!"

I whirl around and charge out of school. He yells something at my back, but I'm too far away to hear.

Once I finish high school, my house is the only thing I know for certain. Maybe I find a job, maybe I make it to college, but either way, there's somewhere for me to go back to. I have a room with everything I've ever owned—clothes, books, a torn blanket underneath my pillow that I've had since I was a baby.

All the trinkets and bits and bobs along my dresser and shelves tell a tale. Like the thimble I pocketed the first and only time I visited my grandparents' house. A fraying Michael Kors wallet that I took from a woman who yelled at me in the grocery store.

Tucked away in the corner of one of the shelves is a single AA battery and a stone from the Dollar Tree that says *Live, Laugh, Love.* Dad gave it to me at Christmas one year and tried to make it seem like a life lesson that I have to "stay solid and power on." It was the smartest thing I've ever heard him say.

I can't pinpoint the moment I got to the start of the long, winding driveway leading to my house, but it's as if I blinked and found myself here. The nausea that lurked in the back seat since I left school comes to the forefront. My stomach isn't just a passenger now; it's the one calling the shots, steering me toward a nearby tree where I double over, dry heaving, wishing I could be anyone but myself.

Mrs. Yang was right.

I don't need to trek down the path to know that fire touched the only solid thing in my life. Smoke and ash clog the back of my throat, spreading char down to my lungs. The distinct pattern of large tires has left black imprints on the once-gray concrete. I can hear it too. The slight groaning of what was once my home.

I force my feet forward. I have to see it with my own eyes. I could be imagining the rest. The smell is from a bonfire, the sound of chatter is from my parents' friends. My shitty beat-up house will be at the end of the driveway. I'll be able to see my shirt taped to the window, and broken pot on the front porch. I'll walk up to my room and crawl into my bed and pretend this was one big joke.

But my delusions come crashing down when I see the fallen, charred remains of the place I've lived in since I was old enough to string a sentence together and not need a nanny to reach into the cupboard for me and drop a slice of bread into the toaster. All that's left are the bare foundations of the only solid thing in my life.

I stumble back and gasp for air as a heavy weight presses down on my chest.

Two voices play in my head. The cracks in my own voice whisper, "They were right."

And the second, much more sinister voice, is of a pyromaniac who makes every muscle stiffen and my veins flood with another burst of adrenaline.

"Are you going to spend another night alone in your shitty house?"

"I'm disappointing my family and ruining yours at the same time."

"You deserve everything that's coming for you."

Kohen did this.

He fucking did this.

That building is the oldest place I've ever known. There isn't a single inch of it I haven't explored. Not a tree around it I haven't climbed. It is the *only* thing that hasn't let me down. Every single day, from the moment I woke up to the moment I fell asleep, the only certainty I had was that there would always be a roof over my head and a place for me to rest. I could be sober or out of my mind, and the shithole of a house would still be there.

Tied to the broken headboard in my bedroom is a dirty piece of ribbon and a smashed-up chocolate bar Mom gave me as an apology when I was five after coming home from a two-day bender. It was the only memory of my mother where she acted like a mother. She sat me down on the steps and braided the ribbon into my hair. Granted, she forgot to brush my hair out first, which she blamed on her "migraine," but at that moment, I remember thinking *this is it*. Mom's coming home for good. We'd finally be a family. Then I didn't see her for another two weeks.

And I'll never see any of my things—my *memories*—again.

It's gone.

Hatred courses through my veins, drilling down into my bones and turns the world into shades of black and red as I charge down the street, getting farther and farther away from the graveyard of my memories. Somewhere along the way, I feel wetness slide down my cheek as I run from my nonexistent home. It isn't until the Cape Cod–style mansion is in front of me that I realize thunder has cracked through the sky and rain is battering the ground, soaking through my uniform and saturating my hair.

Kohen is going to pay for what he did to my house.

I barely feel the wrought iron fence dig into my skin, or the trickle of blood that runs down my stomach. The liquid fire coursing through my veins turns my body numb. It doesn't hurt when I kick down their $100K outdoor sculpture, using its remains to break the tail off the mermaid fountain. I hardly even register the splinter sticking out of my finger as I grip a shovel and bring it down on their marble pavement. I flip off the security cameras before grabbing a rock and throwing it at the window beside the back door to unlock it.

Each movement is another drop of gasoline to my wrath.

I need him to pay.

The alarms don't go off when I step into the kitchen. Instead, an older woman wearing a stained apron meets my stare with wide parted lips. I grab the knife on the kitchen counter and look her dead in the eyes and mouth a single word.

"Run."

She scurries out another door and into the rain. I pick up my pace, running up the stairs and into the room I know *he* sleeps in.

I throw the door open, and a wave of patchouli and mint crashes into me, making me stall for a second before fury rears its ugly head, and my hand goes flying, intent on ruin. His room is covered in junk: ripped up magazines, half burned posters, a hoodie that looks just like the one Mom took from me, buttons and knick-knacks, and the wallet he stole from me yesterday. There's no rhyme or reason to my path of demolition, stabbing into his bed, slashing into his pillow and his stupid fucking Egyptian cotton sheets and waffle duvet.

My vision is a violent, pulsing crimson as I scan the room for something that looks like his soul would perish at the thought of losing it. I need to find a keepsake. Something sentimental. His old boxing gloves fall victim to the blade next. Then, his championship belt and signed shorts. The rage courses through my veins, intensifying as I destroy Kohen's things, one after another.

I exchange the knife for the bat leaning against the foot of his bed, taking it with my trembling hands to bring it down on his computer, then the walls and windows. I can't stop even if I want to. Nothing is free from my wrath. Not Kohen, and sure as fuck not his parents. They're the ones who let their pigheaded son get this way. *They* taught him to shit on anyone who isn't him.

Their grand bedroom is easy enough to find. Designer dresses and suits become torn, and their lamps and fancy ornaments are broken, along with the hideous modern art hanging above their bed. Mrs. Osman's jewels and Mr. Osman's expensive watches find a home in my pocket.

My heart races and sweat beads along my forehead as I picture my bedroom and everything I've lost. In the bottom drawer of my bedside table—my *destroyed bedside table*—there's an empty instant noodles wrapper from the first time I successfully used the stove without burning myself. On my bedside table, sunglasses I saw my dad wear one day, even though they didn't belong to him. In a porcelain jewelry box, there's a hairpin from my cousin whom I've only met once—I don't even remember her name. And there's the very first thing I stole from Kohen—an empty green and red BIC lighter.

I will never see any of it again. It's all fucking gone.

Fiery goosebumps explode over my flesh as the rage burns hotter. The sound of a shattering mirror isn't enough to calm the beast that's left its cage and has no intention of going back in. Nothing is soothing it. Not the antique vases in the hallway, their wedding photos, the expensive cars in the garage, the various sculptures and art pieces that look as hideous as the family, or the dents and holes I'm leaving throughout the house.

I can just imagine their faces when they see what I've done to their precious art. I bet the rich assholes around here would call the pieces one of a kind. I bet they argued over who would buy each one and paid more than they're worth at an auction filled with more pretentious rich fuckers. They probably cracked a $5,000 bottle of champagne afterward and laughed as they watched the help struggle to carry the pieces through the gigantic house.

Their pretty art is gone now. They'll never get it back; nothing from their insurance payout. The artists are probably in their graves, turning with the knowledge that the Osmans will pay a run-of-the-mill artist to replicate each piece for a tenth of the price they bought it for.

Fuck them. Fuck them. Fuck them.

I hate them all.

I fucking hate this place.

Red and blue lights flash behind the curtains, but I don't stop. The china cabinet groans in protest as I push it forward, sending each delicate item flying to the ground in a symphony of shattering pieces. A resounding boom reverberates throughout the room while I aim for the cupboard stocked with liquor worth more than I could earn in a year, and—

"Stop! Put your hands up!"

Of course I don't listen; I haven't caused enough hurt yet. My grandparents need to pay for sending me here. The Osmans need to pay for treating me like shit. They all need to suffer like I did—like my mother and I did.

Arms trap me before I can take a broken chair leg to their bay window, but I still manage to kick my leg out to send cracks radiating outward from the point of contact. Another officer manages to wrangle the chair leg out of my hand while the one holding me sends me sprawling onto the floor with my hands locked behind my back.

"You have the right to remain silent. Anything you say can and will be used against you in a court of law—"

I throw my head back and laugh. "Tell Kohen I'm not done yet."

BLAZE

CHAPTER 3

Two Months Later

"What do you have to say for yourself?" Mr. Fifth-Divorce asks.

"I'd do it again."

As a matter of fact, it's been scientifically proven I'll do it again. Kleptomania is quite literally written in red ink on my file, and the school shrink circled ten out of ten on the "likelihood to reoffend" scale.

Anger management is also in red, but in my defense, I acted appropriately and reasonably to the situation. I'd steal my phys ed teacher's diary again, the same way I'd destroy Kohen's house again.

"You can only get better if you want to be better." The headmaster of Seraphic Hills Reformatory Academy for the troubled rich brats has been in denial since the day I got here. "If you don't take your well-being into your own hands, then your grandfather and I will be forced to make decisions concerning your future—and for Christ's sake, stop picking on Sarah."

I roll my eyes and slump down my chair. Wrinkles over there has been singing the same tune for the past two months. I'm bored of hearing the same thing every time I get dragged into his office by the stun gun–wielding security guards. And, unfortunately, there's no way to slip one of those bad boys out without someone noticing and throwing me back in here with the man who wears cheap cologne.

"Speaking of my grandfather, how's his gout? Is it any closer to killing him?" I ask hopefully.

His white beard twitches as he slaps the table, then puts a hand over his beer belly like nothing happened. It's a wonder how these pretentious parents trust McGill with their beloved brats. The guy is 30 percent mustache, 5 percent people skills, and 65 percent incompetence.

"Your grandfather is one of the finest men I know. You should show some gratitude to him for reaching out to me, rather than sending you to juvie."

I stick my bottom lip out. "Awww, then how would he and I have our weekly grandfather-granddaughter bonding session?"

In the past two months, I've seen my grandfather for a total of twenty-three minutes. He walked into the holding cell, told me what a disappointment I was, then tried getting me to beg him not to send me to juvie. Joke's on him; I'm not stupid enough to not realize that landing my ass behind bars wouldn't look so good on Jonathan Whitlock Sr.'s portfolio when he's bankrolling an election campaign.

When I asked him where my mother was, he gave a stern, "Taken care of." When I questioned my father's continued existence on this earth, he looked at me blankly and asked, "Who?" Then he turned around and threw over his shoulder, "There won't be a next time, Marie." I bristled at his use of my hated middle name. Unsurprisingly, my prim and proper grandpa isn't impressed by my junkie mother naming me *Blaze*.

He ended the entire interaction with, "If you don't clean your act up, this is the last time you will see me." Which was funny because by that point, I hadn't seen him in a year and a half.

Headmaster McGill leans forward in his seat. "Do you know what juvie does to girls like you?"

"The same thing the history teacher does to the boys here?"

His eyes flash and his entire body twitches like he wants to slap the shit out of me. In a show of superior self-restraint, he surprises me by saying nothing, just taps a single finger on the armrest of his big, fuck-off wingback chair. Flattening a hand over his fake designer tie, he gives me a smug look that wipes the grin off my face.

This can't be good.

McGill hums, and I butt in as soon as he opens his mouth. "Oh, another question. Did the third Mrs. McGill finally take the kids, or are you still fighting to have a 20/80 custody arrangement?"

And I wonder why he hates me.

I'm not the first student to get under his skin, but I'm probably one of the select few students he can *let loose* around because no one will care about what happens to me.

Oh, I also may have punched him during my first week here.

And threw a chair at the douchebag security guard, Boris.

And got caught with rat bait before I got the chance to put it in the star quarterback's food after he asked me whether the curtains match the drapes.

Needless to say, McGill hates my guts. Knowing good ol'

Whitlock Sr. probably has Mustache over here by the proverbial balls, and that's why McGill hasn't gone to a judge to throw my ass in prison. All I know is this asshole got the green light from the big man to treat me like shit.

Headmaster Bad Cologne cocks his head to the side like he has a secret he knows would well and truly ruin my already bad year. The heavy chair scrapes along the rug as he rises to his feet. "Come."

"I'm good." He doesn't usually escort me to solitary. Normally, he'd push a button, and security would come drag me to my time-out room, either while I'm kicking and fighting or half comatose from a syringe or taser—I'm not sure if either of those are legal to use on students.

I bite down a hiss as he yanks my head back with a fist around my ponytail. "I will repeat myself one more time, and one time only. Come, or I will report that you attacked me. Do I make myself clear?"

"Crystal," I say through gritted teeth.

The first and only time I attacked him, he let Boris, the sexually repressed security guard, do to me tenfold what I did to him. I'm pretty sure he broke my rib when he yanked me down by my tit, kicked his boot into my side twice, then threw me into solitary without food for forty-eight hours.

Of course, Whitlock Sr. knew and consented to the punishment. I overheard the two old men talking about it over the phone, and my dear, loving grandfather suggested they should take more extreme measures next time.

McGill releases my hair and claps his hands together, pleased with himself, nodding toward the door expectantly. I glare his way as I push myself onto my feet, grab my backpack, kick the chair away for good measure, and hold his stare until my fingers wrap around the brass door handle.

I don't break eye contact until I push the handle down. The last thing I see on his face is an excited grin that shows off his bleach-white smoker's teeth.

My foot crosses the threshold into the foyer, and every fiber of my body stiffens when I hear the voice that's been haunting my dreams ever since I was young.

"Long time no see, Klepto."

My eyes catch on hypnotic hazel. I falter for only a second, trying to rationalize the sight before me, and then each atom that makes up my being explodes.

"You motherfucker. I'm going to fucking—" I lunge for Kohen, ready to throttle him, but two security guards catch me before I can. "Let me the fuck go!" I kick behind me and thrash in their bruising grip. "You're a fucking dead man for what you did!"

One corner of his lips lifts in a victorious smirk. "Didn't think you could look any worse for wear, Blaze."

I grunt when Boris elbows me in my side and tightens his grip around my arm. Kohen's stare drops to my aching ribs, and I start yelling before he gets the chance to slap a shit-eating grin on his face. "You've got a lot of nerve coming in here, you goddamn fucking pyro. I'm gonna do the same thing to your skull until your dad can't even recognize you!"

"*One.* Settle down, Marie."

I swing my lethal stare to the piece of shit headmaster who brought me to this walking horror show. "*You,*" I growl. "You call me screwed up for my habits when all those wives and beer bottles you're going through are making you even dumber." I laugh humorlessly. "If you want a campus murder, I'll give you a murder."

Kohen huffs behind me, and I flip the dickhead off without looking at him.

I can tell McGill is biting back a smile. It makes me want to sucker punch his ugly mug. *Especially* when he shrugs so innocently. He starts talking in that self-righteous tone teachers always use that screams *I'm better than you.*

"The first step to healing is facing your demons. Then you shake their hand and call them old friends—"

"I'm going to shiv my fucking demon in his sleep and call him a cunt if he comes within ten feet of me." I throw my arm back, trying to catch one of the guards in the face, or loosen one of their holds enough to get at least one hit at Kohen's face.

"Two—and trust me, Miss Whitlock, you do not want me to get to three." McGill's tone holds patience, which I know he doesn't have.

My eyes widen wildly, and I give him a smile that's all teeth. "Oh, I'd love to see what happens at three."

He raises a brow, unamused. "I suggest you appreciate your limited freedom while you have it. Prison is far less accommodating for your *habits.*"

"Why?" I tip my head to the side and jerk in the guards' hold, only to still when a taser presses into my side. I scoff and pout, fluttering my eyelashes. "Will a decrepit old man drag me into his room and *punish* me for my misbehavior?"

A tendon in McGill's throat flexes, and I watch as he curls his fingers into a fist and folds them behind his back. Finally, a proper reaction. "There are worse fates than what could happen in that room, Miss Whitlock."

My lips peel back with a scowl, and I stomp onto Boris's foot and spit in his face. He whips me backward and shoves the taser painfully deep into my spine. "I'd rather be put in solitary than be in the same room with that cunt."

McGill stands straighter. "Three strikes, Marie."

I lift my feet off the ground so the two security guards hold all my weight. "You can take your strikes and shove them up your—"

"Careful, Blaze. He might be into that." Kohen finally speaks up.

I jump, trying to throw the guards off-balance. "Shut the—"

"You are to be Mr. Osman's buddy until he settles in."

Why the fuck is he in here? I roll my eyes and point to the firebug who torched everything I've ever called mine. "The only thing I'm going to be—"

"Do you remember the option I gave you in my office?" McGill says with eerie calm.

I slam my mouth shut. "You can remind the class," I say, raising my eyebrows in the arsonist's direction.

Cooperate, or the guards will have their time with me.

"Perhaps you've mistaken me for being weak." McGill steps toward me, and I draw my shoulders back in response. I refuse to ever look weak in front of a man who hangs around children but can't keep a woman. "Or perhaps you've simply mistaken my complacency for kindness, Miss Whitlock. I can assure you that my patience has run extremely thin, and it is in your best interest to ensure you do not see the bottom of it."

"Or what?" A beating is only a scary threat if I haven't had one before. What does he think my father does when he returns with beer instead of gear?

McGill looks me dead in the eyes. "I may decide to take up Dr. Van der Merwe for alternative forms of treatment."

I narrow my eyes. "Drugs? I can't wait."

"Give Mr. Osman a tour of campus, Marie." His tone indicates finality. Mine sounds a lot closer to brutality.

"He burned my house down!"

Headmaster Cheap Suit sighs. "Your delusions are getting to you." *Here we go.* "How many times do we have to tell you that *you* started it while you were high on whatever drug you could get your hands on, and you don't remember what you did."

"I have an alibi!" I screech.

I am *not* insane. I know what happened that night, and it sure as hell wasn't me who started the fire.

"We all saw the pictures, Miss Whitlock. They were *very* telling." His condescending tone grates my spine. Not only does everyone think I'm a drug addict, but they've also labeled me as a "slut" as well. "That boy doesn't have any memory of you coming into his bed."

My cheeks heat. I don't want Kohen to hear about any of this. He has enough ammunition he can use against me. He doesn't need more. Everyone at St. Augustine probably thinks I started the fire as well. Hell, my own mother probably does too. I wonder how long it took her to realize that her hovel burned down and food wouldn't come without effort anymore.

This conversation won't get me anywhere except in solitary or paying the fines for a false report. Either I deal with this shit head-on or go into a negative balance with my dignity.

At the end of the day, no one is going to believe my version of the story. The worst crime the son of the legendary Yusuf Osman has ever committed—well, as far as they know—are a couple speeding tickets, and jaywalking. God forbid anyone thinks that the kid who stick-and-poked a flame on his middle finger and a match on his inside wrist would ever do anything like commit arson.

Also, why would they trust the junkie? The blood tests they took when they arrested me came back off the charts for basically every drug known to man. On the other hand, the full-time bad boy and part-time goody-two-shoes that's the youngest member of the Osman family just flashed some cash, and the pearly gates were open for him once more.

Ask not what you can do for the system, but what the system can do for you. "If I become his *buddy*, I won't be locked up after dinner," I barter. I don't spare the fucker a glance. He isn't worthy of proper acknowledgment anymore.

"Fine." McGill signals for the security goons to release me, and I have to fight the urge to rub the pain away from their firm grip. "But a single misstep and *all* your privileges are revoked."

I give myself two days before they lock me up straight after class, only to be released for class or piss breaks. "Fine."

I roll my shoulders back, take my backpack off the ground, throw it over my shoulder, and walk out without checking to see if Kohen is following. "Look at me, touch me, or so much as breathe in my direction, and I will throat punch you."

"I'm counting on it."

My insides twist as if they're hosting a parasite tuned only to *his* voice. I wish he were ugly or short or had a terrible voice that grates on my nerves. But he's the epitome of my ideal type—save for being an asshole who, oh, I don't know, *burned down my house*—and he ticks every box on my list.

He doesn't talk for once as I show him around campus. A couple times, the side of my face burns from the weight of his stare, but not once have I let myself turn to check.

Suppose I keep staring at his face and imagine what he's packing underneath the green uniform blazer, white shirt, black tie, and pants. In that case, I might forget about his numerous sins—unlikely, but he's never been this quiet or followed any of my requests before, so I'm worried this is all a trick. Or who knows? Maybe he's all melancholy from being trapped here too.

The people in here suck, but I'd be a damn liar if I said this place looks as depressing as it feels, given how eerily stunning it actually is. A gothic, mid-century church is on the outskirts of the grounds, right by the cemetery. The rest of the school buildings sit somewhere between 1600s convent and modern contemporary—depending on which part of the school you end up.

The modern part was joined to the gothic a couple years back, and now the entire Science and Social Science Departments are in there.

There's a state-of-the-art gym at the back of the campus—but no pool. Wouldn't want to have any drownings. Apparently, death by lake isn't a concern though. There's also a running track, tennis court, and football field, and they're currently building an ice hockey rink. I'm not sure how the hell they have the budget for any of it, but I definitely won't be enjoying the perks of anything but the back of the church.

My new friend, Charlie, told me that back in the day they used to run this place like an asylum, doing all sorts of dodgy treatments. I guess it's not that much different nowadays since we have mandatory sessions with the shrink, along with getting medication shoved down our throats, if ordered.

I give the lake in the middle of campus a wide berth, hoping that the jackass doesn't notice I've intentionally avoided the little bridge even though it would make our walk faster. I don't know how anyone enjoys swimming or Jacuzzis. The thought of being submerged underwater with no certainty of when the next whiff of oxygen will come is unappealing, to say the least.

In hindsight, maybe if I learned to swim, I'd jump off a wharf thinking I could take Poseidon on.

The water aspect of the lake makes me more uneasy than the prospect that there are a bunch of dead, evil nuns rotting at the bottom and that the Sacred Lady of the Lake will come out to drag naughty students into her depths.

Me and the Lady can throw hands out on land if she intends to kill me. What happens after is none of my concern.

The door slams shut behind me as we enter the corridors. My eyes cut to Kohen, imagining storm clouds following him to every beach he visits. I'm itching to know what he's in for. To find out what kind of strings his dad pulled to get him in here instead of prison when he should have graduated already. I was lucky since I "celebrated" my eighteenth birthday in this shithole last month, so I *just* missed the cutoff to be tried as an adult. So what's his deal?

I glance at the camera above his head as if I can see if someone will come running if I try to murder him. But none of the cameras are recording because that's a premium parents pay extra for—the less damning evidence against their spawns, the better. Honestly, I don't even know if it's working.

"Where's the girls' dormitory?" Kohen ruins the peaceful silence, filled only by our footsteps on the marble floor.

"Wherever the boys aren't."

I bare my teeth at him when he pushes me against a hidden crook right next to the janitor's closet. He encroaches on my space, towering over me as his hot breath brushes against my skin. "Don't touch me."

His eyes are prettier than I remember. Deep brown rings merge into moss green before a burst of gold. I can't believe I imagined the pyromaniac's eyes when I was with Duke. I wish I found his appearance abhorrent so my brain wouldn't think of stupid things like what his lips might feel like.

All the expressions he lacked before are loud and clear now, from the downward curl of his lips to the tight lines around his eyes. "Answer the question, or I'll tell Principal Beer Gut that you didn't show me around."

"I don't give a fuck. Tell him."

He tips his head to the side and says condescendingly, "Oh yeah? Should I also tell him about the fountain pen you took from his office, Thief?"

"I didn't—"

He holds up the pen.

Fucker.

My gaze darkens on him, and I'm trying not to think about how close he is. Or how this is the first time I've smelled patchouli and mint since I nuked his room. Or the fact that his hand is right beside my head, leaning on the wall behind me.

"Why do you want to know? Planning on coming over to watch *10 Things I Hate About You* and touch toes underneath the blanket?"

He sneers at me. "I don't want hand, foot, and mouth disease."

My jaw drops in disbelief. "You're saying you look like that *naturally*? How about we go on that walk back to Principal Fifth-Divorce, and we can see about giving you shingles instead."

"Please," he scoffs. "I'd probably catch chlamydia just by standing next to you."

Temper grows its own valve inside my heart, releasing a rush of scorching red that has me curling my fists to bring them down on him. I am *not* my mother. "Wow. Big words for such a little brain. It's truly a wonder why they held you back a year."

His hand grasps my throat, and he presses his thumb against my pulse point. The touch is oddly… gentle, with threatening undertones.

"You shut the fuck up." The words come out beneath his breath; I'm taken aback by his lack of aggression. He's never been the simmering type of angry—or the boiling type.

"Or what?" I get in his face, so close that he can feel the warmth of my breath just as surely as I can sense his. If his proximity is going to get on my nerves, then I'm damn well playing the same game. "You'll torch my house again?"

Kohen scoffs.

"What?" I snap. He's been here all of two minutes, and I already want to kill him. It truly is a talent.

A pinch forms between his brows, and he looks down his nose like he's better than me. "Here I was, thinking you'd be less of a bitch after spending some time in here." The betterment and entitlement seeping through his tone remind me that he is his father's son. Charming looks, sweet in his smile, and lethal in his words.

"Here I was, thinking you'd be in prison. Guess we're both disappointed."

I gasp when he shifts his leg and it brushes against mine—and the parasites in my stomach are at it again. My body is fucking ridiculous. I need a new one. The disconnect between my brain's hatred for him and the barest touch sending sparks up my spine is going to send me to a ward with all the conflict going on.

I swallow the lump in my throat. "All the drills they make us do in the morning means I can pack a punch. Happy to demonstrate."

His next exhale flutters through my hair, and he looks at the movement. There's something about how he watches it that has the fifth, angry valve in my heart relaxing its beat. Then his eyes harden, and I'm back to imagining all the ways I could put him in a grave.

"Doubtful. The only thing you do is run as fast as you run your mouth." His gaze briefly drops to my lips before his own twists into an even deeper scowl.

"Don't pay attention to my mouth, Pyro. It's gross."

"You wish I were paying attention to your mouth, Klepto." He sneers.

I'm sick of this. I shove Kohen in the chest, but he doesn't move an inch. I breathe in the hatred-tinged air until it fills my lungs. I haven't felt this alive in weeks, and it kills me that Kohen is the reason for it. "Why the fuck are you here, you absolute maniac?"

I hate that when his lips turn into a mischievous smile, my lungs forget how to work. "Haven't you heard?"

I square my shoulders. "Don't flatter yourself. No one willingly talks about you, Kohen. Only about your brother."

The muscles in his jaw tick. "I'm as crazy as you say."

I roll my eyes. "Don't pretend that you listen to anything I say." My words are a lie, and I know it. I'm sure he takes what I say home to dissect it and throw it back in my face. "Did you finally get caught lighting children on fire?"

He doesn't react to either of my comments. "No. I sent someone into a coma."

"Why?" I push off the wall and close the distance so our chests touch. I feel him stiffen as I look him straight in the eye. "They called you stupid, Osman?"

58

"He touched something that didn't belong to him." A dark look settles on his face, as if he's seconds away from killing someone. There's no hesitation when he says it, just steel resolve and the promise that, given the opportunity, he'd do it again.

Still, he's an asshole. Nothing he can do will change the fact that the damage is already done, and there are no broken pieces for me to pick up.

"Boys and their toys." I slip out from under him and point to one of the many doors down the hall. "Your class is there. Stay the fuck away from me, Kohen."

The last thing I hear before I hide in the closest bathroom is the deep tenor of his voice, echoing down the hallway. "You wish, Thief."

BLAZE

CHAPTER 4

"He's kind of cute."

I glare at Charlie, stabbing the restaurant-quality asparagus with a wooden spork. "I'm going to pretend you didn't just say that."

"He's just so... big." She bites the inside of her cheek in a poor attempt at hiding her blush, gazing at him as he stands in the cafeteria line with his arms crossed, eyes narrowed, balancing his tray with a single hand. But Charlie is most definitely right. He *is* big. I mean, the white button-up uniform is literally straining to contain his bulging biceps.

I'm clearly not the only one who's noticing, because Sarah and her posse of pretentious bitches haven't torn their eyes off him and his stupidly handsome face since he showed up this morning. Scratch that; the entire school hasn't stopped staring—boys included. But I'm not sure if the guys are eying him up to gauge whether he's a threat, or if they're questioning their sexuality.

"And his face?" Charlie whistles.

I clap my hands in front of her face to stop her from ogling the literal bane of my existence. "He's a fucking pyromaniac, Charlie."

She pulls on her box-dyed black hair five times, then pops it in her mouth and sucks on it, giving me an innocent glance. Her eyes wander back to him, and she goes all dreamy. "I'm sure he has redeeming qualities."

"Zero. Nada. None." I shake my head. She's the only person I tolerate in this hellhole, and right now, I'm about to reconsider whether sitting with this loose cannon is a good idea.

"Did you hear me when I said he's abusive? Pushes me around? Keeps trying to choke me?" Not to mention he lit my hair on fire when we were kids, broke into my house and started going through my stuff, and left me a dead bird on my front porch then had the audacity to ask if I liked his present. Let's not forget the time he stole some of my clothes after PE and left a knife in my locker a couple years back. Oh, and also all the horrendous shit that comes out of his mouth every day.

"Really?" She whips her attention back to me, and her eyes widen with... fucking excitement? Jesus Christ, clearly that wasn't the deterrent I thought it would be.

A string of extra bad boyfriends landed her in this place after the last one convinced her to start dealing, and then she tried gouging his eye out when he cheated on her in her own bed.

Her reaction was justified, if you ask me.

I'd love to see her try to fight Kohen, but unfortunately, she's the size of my pinky, and her mood swings aren't her only issues. On the bright side, when we blow up at each other and she lashes out at me,

I can hold her back by putting a hand on her forehead.

The only reason we keep coming back to each other is because we're both broke, and she's not a recluse by choice. Apparently, her ability to cry and go berserk just because someone looks at her weirdly doesn't make her the most popular person.

"You think he knows where we can score?" Charlie whispers.

If I'm being honest with myself, this place isn't all bad. I'm fed, I have electricity, running hot water, and security that no one is going to steal my shit. Plus, I'm not about to run into either of my parents or their equally screwed-up friends.

On the downside—or up, depending on how you look at it—I haven't had a proper bender in two months. *However,* where there are spoiled, rich kids, there are drugs. Except this whole cashless-campus "bank transfer only" is cramping my style.

But where there are people with drugs, there are dicks and pussies that want attention.

I'm inclined to either.

"The motherfucker is clean," I grumble. Even if Kohen knew where to score, it would be a cold day in hell before he recommends anything.

As if he senses my stare, he turns my way. My heartbeat stutters before I flip him the bird and mouth, "Asshole."

Boris shoots me a warning look, and I send him the same message I sent Kohen. Except Boris leaves his supervisor's post by the cafeteria door and walks toward me, reaching for the taser at his side.

Oops.

I jump up, ready to gap it, but both of our heads swivel toward the commotion at the lunch line. The guy ahead of Kohen has managed to spill his entire tray onto the person behind him.

There's something to be said about the predictability of ego and testosterone. Naturally, punching said spiller is the only possible conclusion to restore one's prespilled food status. Before any security guard can take two steps, someone yells, "Food fight!"

A heartbeat later, chaos erupts from every corner of the dining hall.

The food part of a food fight here is optional. There's one of these every month, from what I gather. The benefit of court-mandated attendance at a rich reform school is that bribery is the lifeblood of this place. So why would McGill want to shrink his pockets by running to the judge to spill the beans about his inability to control the student body? He'll just piss off parents and lose their "donations."

I want to say it's a pity to see tomato sauce plastered all over the three-hundred-year-old stone or spaghetti hanging from the chandelier, but it's what puts the *reform* into *school*. And I've gotta admit, I almost prefer Seraphic Hills over St. Augustine, because here?

We love a good fight.

But I'm above such childish behavior, because me? I stretch my fingers out and eye all the unattended backpacks. My pockets need filling, and after the encounter with Kohen, what better way to satisfy my cravings than by stealing from the rich.

The cold night air feels crisp in my lungs as I button up my woolen coat, watching clouds of condensation form and disperse with each breath I take. God, I missed this.

McGill hasn't let me out past dinnertime in almost three weeks. He thought locking me up would teach me a lesson about keeping my hands to myself. It did the opposite.

Without the chemical highs, I've been clawing for anything to make my heart race or make me temporarily forget about everything. Stealing lost its thrill when the worst thing about getting caught is being stuck in a room with McGill. Sure, getting shoved into a room with next to no stimulation except my homework is bad enough. But honestly, my grades have never been better.

Even sneaking off like Charlie and I are doing now isn't fun when there's a chance we won't find what we're looking for on the other side of the spear-tipped fence.

I grunt as I pull back the loose bars, allowing Charlie to squeeze through the gap. Once she's on the other side, she pushes the bars towards me. As high as Seraphic Hills's budget is, they don't monitor the fences as closely as they should. Or the church. It works in our favor.

Under the harsh glow of the moonlight, vines snake around trees and between gravestones. The bottom of my long coat catches on shrubbery and skims the top of the grass. Walking through the cemetery is risky, as the roots are a tripping hazard. We tread carefully, trying to be as quiet as possible. Security rarely makes it all the way out to the church, but it doesn't hurt to be careful.

Rain drenched the campus earlier, and the cemetery is known for its bone-breaking mudslides. We remain silent as we take each step, ensuring we stand on even ground before shifting our weight.

The faint sound of chatter fills my ears as we trek further away from campus. Eventually, the trees clear, and the church of Saint someone or other emerges behind the safety fencing that was erected five years ago.

I glance back, checking to see we aren't being followed, then we climb over the chain-link fence, landing ungracefully on the other side with an *oomph*.

Like the campus, the church has the same gothic structure, with pointed arches and flying buttresses that are hanging by a thread. Moss and mold cover the once sandy-colored stone, creeping through carvings and covering the boarded-up windows and doors, as if slowly eating the church alive.

I tried breaking in once when I was hopped up on Molly, but like my predecessors, my attempts failed. Rumor has it the roof is unstable, and some pillars have crumbled away. A couple of the windows are smashed, but whether by divine will or coincidence, the stained glass of Mother Mary remains untouched.

Actually, it's probably because the artist gave her a BBL, and that's the only thing the guys around here would worship.

I can still recall when I was tweaking and was convinced she was talking to me. It was concerning because she sounded like my mother but looked like Meryl Streep.

I look over at Charlie to see if she made it over the fence. She stands back, tucking her hands into her armpits, waiting for me to walk first, even though she was the one who introduced me to this place. I stall as my attention snags on the gold chain around her neck, and my veins buzz with the need to liberate it from her.

Swallowing, I shake my head. *She's my friend*, I remind myself. I can't just steal from friends. It takes monumental effort to look away and keep hiking through the forest, attempting to push back the urges by focusing on the fact that another one of my cravings will be met tonight.

Someone laughs, causing me to tense up before the adrenaline kicks in, and I move faster with a slight bounce in my step. Without even seeing them, I can smell the devil's lettuce permeating the air. Weed isn't my usual drug of choice, but it'll do. Unless Elijah decides to be generous today, but I won't hold out hope since I've been holding out on him. Seraphic Hills has really messed with my mind because I haven't spread my legs since that night I spent with Duke. My fucked-up brain is convinced that *I'll* be burned alive this time.

I round the corner, and half the group groggily shifts their attention toward us, all with dilated pupils. Elijah is the first to make a noise, wolf whistling and rising from the stone steps leading up to the church. "There she is."

I plaster on a coy smile when I make eye contact with him. It's not a substitute for letting his dick near me, but my dazzling looks are all he's getting until I get desperate enough to beg on my knees, which I'm nearing. Elijah will chase as long as he believes he's the only male I'm putting on a show for.

I don't acknowledge the other two guys and one girl who are all sharing a joint. Charlie gives them each a timid smile but stays close to my heels, sitting a foot away from me as I all but sit on Elijah's lap—and throw up a little in my mouth when I touch his greasy, mousey-brown hair.

He wraps an arm around my shoulder and tugs me closer to his side—*too* close for comfort. If I weren't trying to get something out of him, I'd gut him for how touchy he always gets with me.

"We missed you out here." His hair tickles my face as he presses his head against mine.

"I bet my right tit that's a goddamn lie."

Elijah reeks of weed, and I'm praying to that Virgin Mary window that I'll get high off the smell alone. Otherwise, I'm breaking his hand for trying to reach for the tit in question. The only reason Duke—or any other guy I've been with—has gotten anywhere close with me was because I was impaired and willing. If I had all my faculties in place, I'm sure I'd still be a virgin.

"You got anything for me?" I ask, stopping Elijah's hand in his tracks.

If you want to touch, you've got to pay up.

One of the other guys—Aaron, I think—looks at Charlie warily when she gives him her crazed "fuck me" eyes. Whatever she's doing, it works, because he sidles her way and pulls out a ziplock bag of pills.

Damn it. Every guy knows she's going to put out. Elijah is the idiot for trying to bark up my tree, and it's only a matter of time before he realizes. Then I'll be shit out of luck.

"You know I do," Elijah whispers, kissing a path up the side of my neck while grabbing my tits. I'm so glad my thick coat is enough of a barrier to stop me from feeling the full impact of his hands.

The telltale clang of someone climbing over the fence makes me freeze. The metal clang sounds again. "Someone else is here," I say.

Elijah shrugs, reaching for my boobs again, but I swat his hands away. We're still sitting hip to hip, so that will have to be enough contact for the time being.

I turn toward the spot where we came from, waiting to see who else shows up. I haven't been caught leaving school grounds before, and I'm not losing my freedom as soon as I get it. If I'm the most sober person here, chances are I can gap it and let everyone else take the fall. My heart hammers as two people walk around the corner, and it takes me a second to figure out who the newcomer is.

"Oh, for fuck's sake." I throw my hand up and point to the dickhead I've been chaperoning all day. "Who the fuck invited you?"

Specifically, who the fuck let Kohen wear something other than his school uniform? The guy makes the shitty green blazer look good, and now he's out here in a leather jacket, boots, and a pair of black jeans that are making his thighs look downright illegal.

The man in question pins his gaze on me, then the piece of shit glued to my side.

"I did," Liam, the scrawny kid who's freakishly good at calculus, says matter-of-factly before dropping down on the steps by Charlie, who is blushing like crazy at the bane of my existence.

Traitor.

"Get lost, Osman," I growl.

Kohen looks me dead in the eye, drops his gaze to where Elijah and I are touching, and then looks down his nose at me as he says, "I think I'll stay."

"Get me that joint." I slap Elijah's chest with the back of my hand and do the universal sign for "gimme."

Kohen and I don't stop glaring at each other like a couple of prepubescents as Elijah grabs my medication. I narrow my eyes at Kohen when he pulls out a lighter, and the flame comes to light, reflecting off the silver rings on his fingers and the chain around his neck, and I momentarily forget about our budding fight.

I want it. I want all of them. I wonder if I can get close and try to slide a ring off his finger. Or I can try to break into his room when he's not looking. Any one of the rings will do, but if I had a choice, I'd want the signet ring with the—he catches me staring, and I snap my attention away and snap my fingers at Elijah.

"Hold up a second," he says, all stupid and drowsy as he fiddles with the latch of a tin container.

"Give me that." I snatch the container away and open the lid. I grab the fattest joint I can see, then drop the rest on his lap.

He ungracefully tucks it back into the pocket of his puffer, then slides his hand underneath my coat to place it on my thigh, and a fresh bout of nausea lurches up my throat. My skin itches with the burning intensity of Kohen's stare, and it takes physical restraint not to squirm.

I fight back the bile and slip the joint between my lips then call out, "Anyone got a light?"

"Nah, babe." Elijah is the first to respond, squeezing my thigh like it'll soften the blow of the fact he gave me something I can't consume. Then he leans back on the step and gawks at the cloudless sky.

Charlie gives me a sympathetic look. The guy who offered her pills doesn't notice me. The other three people don't respond.

Useless. All of these idiots.

I repeat my question again, and no one but Kohen speaks up. "You deprived me of information," he says as if it's the most obvious thing in the world. What information he's referring to, I wouldn't have a clue.

My lips twitch. "I'm going to deprive you of your balls if you don't give me your lighter." Childish insult, but whatever. Fuck him. He's not going to ruin my first night of restricted freedom.

He scoffs, nodding at Elijah, who's rubbing my leg—I have a feeling he's doing it for the texture of my jeans rather than to touch me. But that doesn't make the sensation any less disgusting.

Kohen sneers down at me, even though he's the one who's two steps below me. "They'd shrivel up and fall off if you go near them."

"And I would be doing mankind a favor in the process," I add, seeing Charlie swing her attention between the two of us. That bitch really does love drama. "Ending the Osman line? Call it charity."

"In one night, I could have taken out your deadbeat parents."

My skin turns cold. He's fucking admitting it. I was right. *He* burned my house down. "You keep my mother out of your mouth," I snarl.

The corner of his lips tips up in a cruel smile. "Does that woman know how to keep things out of her mouth?" He huffs a humorless laugh as his eyes burn into me, then the hand beneath my coat. "Seems to me the apple doesn't fall far from the tree."

I lurch forward, but Elijah must have regained some consciousness because he latches onto me before I can jump to my feet. "Get the fuck off me," I screech, knocking him back.

I can't be in the same area as these two assholes, or else I'm going to lose my mind. I pocket the joint and storm up to Kohen, who looks at me with the same vapid hatred I feel. His lips twitch as he scowls back at me, mirroring me in every way.

I want to make him pay for everything he did, but I don't know how. It's so fucking pathetic. There's nothing I can do that would put any kind of dent in his world. Everything I can take from him can be replaced. No one would believe a thing I say, truth or lie. No one would care about any kind of impact he has on me. I have a jammed gun with no bullets. My only option is to throw it and hope for the best or sell it for parts.

"I don't know what your fucking problem is or why you've been up my ass since grade school. But I know one thing." My voice is full of malice, and my heart rate spikes with the adrenaline I've wanted to feel all night. "You will never be as good as your brother. No one will ever notice you, even if you were the last Osman." I edge backward, toward the fence. Lowering my voice, I say, "You're nothing, Kohen. You're less than trash, just like the rest of us. You just don't have drugs to blame for it."

KOHEN

CHAPTER 5

"Kohen Osman, there's a phone call for you at reception," the lady's voice drones over the library intercom.

My jaw sets into a hard line. You'd think the librarian would take the concept of "quiet place" seriously, especially since the stained glass windows along the gray stone walls look like they're going to shatter with the slightest vibration.

There has to be some rule about getting calls during our designated study time. I tighten my grip around my pen and stay in my spot in front of the fireplace, waiting to see how long I can make him wait.

It won't be Mom; she has her day down to a *T*. She has penned down Tuesdays from 5:15 p.m. until 5:30 p.m. and Fridays from 4:00 p.m. to 4:30 p.m. to talk to me. If I'm five minutes late, my "appointment time" is gone.

Such a pity. I *really* want to speak with the woman who always tells me to sit down, shut up, and let my brother do the talking.

Father isn't patient enough to hold the line for me unless one of his secretaries is calling for him. He doesn't have time for anyone anymore since *Oskadine*. The breakthrough cancer drug is in the third phase of clinical trials. The medication was my grandfather's passion, and my father's third child. The drug's success is making Osman Pharmaceuticals' shareholders froth at the mouth.

Settling deeper into the couch, my attention shifts away from the textbook to the golden dance in front of me. The fire licks up the walls of the fireplace; it's such a shame there's a padlocked safety grate in the way of something so hypnotic. There's something soothing about the wild crackle and whip of the flames, the way they can taper into blue tips that the human eye can barely see, though the skin can feel their agonizing burn. The smell of smoke alone has a faux calm settling over my body.

Fire is hated because it's considered chaotic and an element of destruction. But people are foolish, so utterly close-minded because they refuse to understand anything beyond the box they put themselves in.

Fire cannot start from nothing. It needs life and *air*, only created by nature or man. But fire is everything. We can't eat most of our food without cooking it over a flame, or drink safely without boiling the water first. Metal is molded by flames, and technology is pieced together by sparks. Everything starts from fire.

I rub my thumb over the lighter hidden in the pocket of my dress slacks, barely feeling the cool metal surface from the nerves that were burned off when I was eight. I was stupid thinking I could control fire, that it wouldn't harm me if I only tried hard enough.

It's untamed, out of control, ready to burn if I get too close. But that's what people always forget about fire; it can be contained in its space if nurtured just right. But fire is the way it is because it's a matter of sacrifice. Nothing can give without pain.

"Paging Kohen Osman. There's a phone call for you at reception. I repeat, there's a phone call for you at reception. Please head there immediately."

My fingers tighten around the lighter, and I count to ten. By three, the heat in my body is a dull simmer, nowhere near as violent as the flames before me. By seven, it heightens to a boil. By ten, I slam the book shut, then almost rip off the safety grate and shove *Molecular Medicine: Genomics* into the fire.

I can't believe I'm stuck in school for another fucking year—and for what? To be treated like dog shit?

"Kohen Osman, this is your—"

"I'm coming," I bark, throwing the strap of my backpack over my shoulder.

The librarian peers down her nose at me as I storm out, disturbing everyone with the sound of my boots hitting stone and the murderous energy that's coursing through my veins.

Jocks, nerds, cheerleaders, loners, junkies, and blue-collar criminals in the making all look up at me as I pass. One girl bites her lip, another waves, a couple guys glare, and some avert their eyes as quickly as they look up. I've been here a whole week now, and I've determined that it's the exact same shit as St. Augustine's but at a different school.

Usually, people fall into two categories: they want good grades or they don't.

When it's a school filled with nepo babies, there's a subcategory:

they don't give a shit which way their grades swing since their last names and trust fund will ensure they'll end up in the same place within society.

I keep my gaze forward, jaw clenched so hard, almost grinding my teeth to dust. My muscles tense further with each step as I navigate the maze-like structure. Blaze said with total seriousness that it's hard for people to find their way around the school because everything looks the same with its dull stone and brick walls. She also added that she hopes I get lost and end up in one of the dungeons this place is rumored to have.

Just like the first time I had to find my way around, I get to my final destination without the slightest slipup. It's no surprise she has no sense of direction, both literally and metaphorically.

The woman sitting at reception could have been taken out of one of the fashion magazines Mom likes to keep in her office for show. This area is the most modern place in the entire school, with the ridiculously sleek black leather couch only parents are allowed to sit on. There's a disgusting amount of art all around the room and a giant ball-shaped sculpture in the center, all donated by someone's family. Bribery is my guess.

In my pocket, I flip the lid to my lighter open and closed, feeling the six sides of the object. I'm itching to see the blue flame shift to copper in my hands.

Following the hallway to the side of the reception area, I pass one of the two entrance doors into the headmaster's room. Then I'm in front of the student access door I should have come through to begin with. This particular area of the school is straight out of the 1980s, completely opposite to the reception, with worn wooden floors, yellow-tinted windows, and one too many different patterns around the place; floral curtains, maroon paisley cushions, and a green chevron vase that reaches my sternum.

It's where Blaze had so excitedly agreed to be the worst tour guide known to mankind—the kleptomaniac couldn't even figure out how to exit the building when the door was right in front of us. She's going places; far just isn't one of them.

The same woman from the last time I was here sits behind her desk, typing with a single finger. Spiderwebs crease her leathered skin, making her look as ancient as the structure most of this school is made out of.

"Who is it?" I say while approaching her desk.

"Pardon me?" Administrative grandma's tone is just as sour as her face. The deep divots of her wrinkles leave her with a permanent frown.

I give her a blank look. "I have a call."

None of us are meant to have cell phones here, but it's safe to say that at least 90 percent of the students do. Myself included—a privilege earned by my father's *generous* donation to the Science Department.

Her loose skin moves as she gives me a mocking once-over. "Use your words."

I turn to walk away but only make it as far as the door before I hear her sigh. "You've got ten minutes." I glance over my shoulder at her as she gestures toward the phone on the wall, the spiral cord long since lost its bounce.

The only reason I've made it this far is because I'd rather make my ears bleed for a couple minutes listening to my father than be stuck in solitary where anything could happen.

"I only need two," I mutter and begrudgingly whip the phone off the receiver. "What?"

"Hello to you too, Kohen."

Irritation slices up my spine at the sound of his voice.

Fucking Kiervan.

The lighter digs into my palm so hard I'd be surprised if it doesn't bruise. "What do you want?" I gripe.

"Can't a man talk to his little brother?"

"Yes, but not you."

"You wound me. What would you do without me?"

"A lot more."

"Please." He chuckles. "Give me a break with that attitude. I took the spotlight while you ran away at night to ruin your life. Dad would know about everything you get up to if it weren't for me." Kiervan uses the same taunting tone every time we speak. He wants a "thank you" he'll never get from me. "The type of people you associate with. Specifically, *a person* you associate with." Kiervan tacks on the last part and receives the exact reaction he hoped for.

"What the fuck do you want?" I bark into the phone, fighting the urge to whip out the lighter. Whoever had the gift of foresight must have anticipated people like me because half this place is fucking fireproof.

"Language," the administrator hisses, but I don't pay her any mind.

"If you've got nothing better to do than talk shit, I suggest you never call this place again," I hiss into the receiver.

"So hostile, baby bro. Aren't they teaching you manners over there? Maybe I should suggest to Dad that he send you to the military. If you don't come back trained, then hopefully you'll come back in a coffin. Then you'd finally be doing something good for this family."

I slip my hand into my pocket to flick the cap open and roll my finger over the wheel. The urge to see the flames or slam my fists into something tangible snakes beneath my chest and winds its way around my lungs.

I can't do either of those two things when the son of a bitch guard is watching me. "Let's add Dad to the call, and he can hear about your extracurricular activities," I say.

"Don't throw threats when there's a bigger one around." Kiervan sighs, and it only pisses me off more. "I guess that's why they have me to think and for you to stay out of the way."

"No, you pay other people to think for you." My brother's intelligence isn't about understanding and implementing theory; his talent for manipulation is where he shines.

"Careful." His tone turns dark.

But I know something he doesn't. Call it a kill switch that will make every single Osman fall. Kiervan isn't the only one who knows how to play the long game.

"Right." I scoff. "*Blackmail* is the more appropriate term." Kiervan wasn't always perceived as intelligent. Rather, they called him bright and intuitive but not *smart*. He knew how to talk and play the act of a kid who understood what he was doing, which led people to believe he was wise beyond his years.

My brother's gifted in his own way. A real charmer, just like our father. Two peas in a pod. While I'm no psychiatrist, I believe the medical term for the people I share my genes with is *psychopath*.

The laugh that crackles through the static line sends my blood soaring. "You can tell them if you want. They'd never believe you."

Kiervan wasn't always this way. We were friends at one point—and I use that word loosely. I was the one they called smart. I was the rising star on the way to the very top. Except they didn't use the term *bright* or *intuitive*. They named me *trouble*, and my brother is the reason for it.

Why believe the son who was shit at communicating, when the boy who hadn't been caught in a lie said it was my fault? It started off with broken toys, ripped-up pages, and dissected animals. Eventually, I was being blamed for the drugs they found in *his* bedroom.

Kiervan knows about my fire-related tendencies, just like he knows about what I've kept from my parents for years. The day he realized I had a weakness, was the day he learned he could have it all.

It doesn't matter how much I try to get rid of my weakness or lessen the blow; it doesn't happen even though I hate its very existence.

"How's my assignment coming along?" he asks.

"I was in jail two weeks ago. How do you think it's going?" I roll my neck, trying to loosen some of the tension. I stayed there for all of sixteen hours after beating that kid up before our father's lawyers got me a deal so I'd attend Seraphic Hills.

He clicks his tongue. "Better get to it then, champ."

I can hear my pulse pound in my ears. I'm sick and tired of being his bitch. Once we graduate, there won't be shit Kiervan could say to our parents that would matter. "What do you think is going to happen when you accidentally kill someone because you didn't get your biology degrees yourself?"

I pull the phone away from my ear when he whistles. "Bold claims. Rein it in, little man. You make it sound like I didn't think this through. What do you think the business major is for? Why mess with biomedicine when I could sit behind a table and order people around? You could never see the bigger picture."

"Then do it yourself." If I spent less time doing his assignments, I'd have more time for shit I want to do.

I'm about to hang up when he tsks. "There are so many things that could happen while you're all boarded up in there, don't you think? Imagine all the things Father could do..." The dreamy edge to his voice hides a sharpened blade within. "Don't be stupid, Kohen. The assignment is due in two days. I'll hear from you then."

He ends the call before I can.

The old woman gasps when I slam the receiver. My breath comes out in short bursts as I thunder through the halls and into the frigid air. Tugging at the collar of my shirt, I spin the wheel on the lighter and imagine what its golden hues look like.

I survey my surroundings, checking no one is watching as I stick to the edge of the school grounds until I get to the loose part of the fence that leads into the graveyard. I don't go deep into the forest, only so far until I reach a spot where the canopy is thickest to put a damper on the smoke.

My backpack hits the wet ground, and I yank out the three books that have been weighing the bag down all day. *Theoretical Hydrodynamics and Aeromechanics* makes contact with the earth first, then Kiervan's course materials fall next to it. The last to come out is a notebook filled with useless scribbles.

The lighter is in my hand before I register it, and I have half a mind not to set fire to the textbooks. Yet in the next breath, the orange flame licks the corner of Kiervan's book. It's slow to start, but I watch it swallow the book with a roar. The plastic cover bubbles before it turns to charcoal and withers away into ash. I could watch the flames for hours, hypnotized by the vermillion and gray.

Fire is chaos at my fingertips, something I can harness and lose all control over, neither of which can happen unless I strike the match.

Throwing the second book on top of it, the flames stretch upward until the smoke touches the back of my lungs. It's better than nicotine or weed because seeing the dance of yellow and copper is enough to push the phone call further to the back of my mind.

Maybe one day, I'll do to my parent's house what I did to Blaze's. Maybe next time, it'll go out with a bang.

God, she's such a little shit.

It's no surprise to hear that Mommy doesn't love her and Daddy's gone walkabouts. She defines the word *irritating*, and all she's doing is sitting there, not making a sound or moving.

Yet for some screwed-up reason, Blaze is the only thing I've been able to see in over ten years. From her roaring attitude to her name and copper hair—*Christ*, her hair—her entire presence commands attention. All she does is scream *"look at me,"* and I can't fucking look away no matter how hard I try.

The worst part of it all is that she's the biggest bitch around. Since the night behind the church, she's been avoiding me as if I were the damn police.

I twirl a blue pen between my fingers, ignoring whatever it is the teacher is talking about—it doesn't matter; I've already learned all about it. My fingers graze over the dented surface of the pen; I wet my lips as I pull my attention away from the thief, to the perfect little teeth marks decorating the top of the plastic casing. The clip has been bitten off, and the spring is long gone. To continue to call it a *pen* is a stretch of imagination.

I tuck it behind my ear and cast my eyes over to her as she chews on the lid of a different one. She's antsy. That much is clear. Blaze has a bad habit of needing to keep her hands and mouth busy whenever she's on edge—biting her nails, fiddling with the rosary beads she recently stole from somewhere, engraving the desk when she thinks no one's looking. I could be the cause of it this time round. Or maybe it's the fact she can't call that fucker Tony to get her fix.

Who knows who Blaze stole either of the pens from, but out of the both of us, she's the one who can't afford to luck out with her schooling. If she doesn't pass and continues getting caught for everything, then she has a one-way ticket to jail now that she is eighteen and considered a threat to public safety. Blaze is an idiot if she's considering prison as a valid life option.

Her eyes find mine, and she mouths, "Get fucked," before looking forward with her shoulders tensed. A minute later, she dismantles the pen, tucking the spring and case into her bag and leaving the ink chamber on the desk to doodle in her book.

Blaze makes a point of sitting behind me in the next class, and it takes every fiber in my being to ignore the cut-up eraser she throws at my head. My jaw ticks when a marker cap hits my ear. I'm woefully disappointed if this is her pathetic attempt to get back at me. I expected more.

When the third object collides with me, I whisk around to face her. "For someone who wants me to fuck off, you're sure trying to get my attention."

She's so fucking infuriating all the goddamn time.

Her wild, sterling-blue eyes flare, and my lungs catch, just like every other time I see them. The world can have Prometheus; I have Blaze, the girl with the fiery attitude—completely and utterly unhinged. The girl with hair and eyes the color of flames: blue, copper, orange, red. Blaze *is* fire.

She leans forward in her seat. I'm sickeningly aware that closing the distance wouldn't take much. It wouldn't even take a full second. "Don't think so highly of yourself. Your attention is the last thing I want," Blaze whispers, and all I seem to notice is the way her chapped lips move.

I'm hit with a bolt of rage at the memory of what she looked like in *the* photo. That motherfucking photo. I can still picture what she looked like sitting on Duke's lap with his tongue down her fucking throat.

My shoulders stiffen, and my hand shoots out under the table to grab her knee as I shoot her a glare. Her skin is the softest thing I've ever felt, and the contact hardly puts a lid on my urge to pull her across the desk. But then I remember one crucial fact.

She's never fucking chosen me.

"You have a funny way of showing your disinterest, Thief."

My eyes cast to where our skin is touching, and tension instantly starts beneath my pants. Blaze has no idea how easy it would be for me to push my hand up her leg and slip my fingers into the tight cunt she's been keeping from me. It's a colossal show of self-restraint that I'm not driving her thighs apart just to finally know what it feels like to have them open for me.

Her lips curl into a sneer. "Disinterest? You came to *my* school. I want you gone."

This is precisely what I'm talking about. We're a little over halfway through the school year, and she thinks I'm so awful she'd risk getting thrown in solitary every day under some misguided pretense that she might be able to get rid of me. Then, once she's out, she fucks pieces of shit like Duke and who knows how many others.

For what? More importantly, *while* on *what*?

I pissed around after school for the past four years to walk her home because half the time she's plastered, coming down, hungover, or simply unobservant. Not once has she thanked me or shown a modicum of appreciation.

The dumbest thing I've ever done was to assume she wouldn't just fuck any guy who waves a bag in her face. I don't care if that's her mom's MO or any other woman's game; that shouldn't be *her* game—not after everything I've done for the ungrateful shit.

"Miss Whitlock," the teacher snaps.

Blaze glares at me one last time before averting her sharp eyes to the English teacher. "What?"

Mrs. Nauly cocks a brow and crosses her arms. "Anything you'd like to share with the class?"

Everybody turns our way, and Blaze's cheeks flush the same shade as her hair—fuck, if she doesn't look hot like this. If I had known being in the same class as her would get her this wound up, I'd have done it years ago.

When Elijah turns to look at her too, I quickly do the math on whether it would be worth spending a night in solitary if I got the chance to crack his skull. I bet he's fucked her as well.

Fuck.

I ball my hands into fists. Blaze prefers everyone but me.

"Yeah, there is, actually." Blaze sits straighter up in her chair and crosses her arms, mimicking Mrs. Nauly.

She truly does astound me. She's either so delusional and has no idea how much verbal diarrhea comes out of her mouth, or she genuinely aspires to do everything possible to get her ass kicked.

I sigh and settle back in my chair. This is gonna be good.

"Go on," the teacher says.

"Kohen was feeling me up and trying to look up my skirt."

I scoff. She wears it so short there's no looking *up* when I can just look *at* it. Her lack of hand-eye coordination has benefited me too many times to count. The girl has never heard the concept of "bending at the knees," and every male in this school is too aware of that fact.

The teacher sighs. "Miss Whitlock, I doubt Mr. Osman desires to do such a thing. Stop crying wolf." She gives Blaze a condescending look people seem to reserve especially for her. The one that says *why should I believe you?*

It almost makes me want to step in. I turn my head just enough to see her wrap her fingers around her pen in an iron grip. Her blue eyes swing my way, and the hatred I notice in them makes my blood burn. All of this is her fault. I'm not coming to save her. She created the mess; she can clean it.

"He attacked me the first day he was here," Blaze adds.

Mrs. Nauly shakes her head. "I, along with every person in this faculty and classroom, have no desire to continue listening to you spreading lies. Frankly, we've all had enough of hearing it."

Blaze throws her hands up and slams them on the desk. "I'm not ly—"

"Another word out of you, and you will be sent to Headmaster McGill's office." Mrs. Nauly turns back to the whiteboard, then stops. "Your attitude is equally unwanted, Marie."

"My name is Blaze," she grumbles.

The teacher sends her a warning glance, and she doesn't bite back, slumping down in her chair and crossing her arms like a petulant child.

People like us can cry wolf when there is one, and no one would bat an eye even if we never lied. The only difference between her and I is that my father will step in to protect the family name, and hers will step in just to score some cash from her.

Blaze is silent for the rest of the class—apart from her incessant tapping and leg bouncing. But I can feel the rage radiating from her in waves. It only fuels my own. I'm in here because of what *she* did. If anyone has the right to be angry, it's me. I'm the one who's pissed. I'm the one who was betrayed over and over again.

If there's one thing that will never disappoint me about Blaze, it's her predictability; right now, she's stripping down any walls she has. Whatever shred of control she's got is being incinerated. All that remains is pure, unfiltered compulsion. It's only a matter of time until she acts.

I glance at the clock above the whiteboard. Pulling out my ring from my blazer pocket, I drape my arm off the side of the table, twisting the ring between my fingers. My grandfather gave it to me when I was eight. It was the last gift he ever gave me before I found him on the floor of his estate, dead from a drug overdose while I was staying for the summer. He told me that one day I'll be a man worthy to have the *O* in my initials. My grandfather was a good man and the only person who ever saw Kiervan and Father for the snakes they were.

So when I was fifteen, I used my allowance to engrave my name into the band. As I see it, the Osman name died with my grandfather.

I fidget with it just long enough to get the klepto's attention before letting it clatter onto the edge of the desk. The artificial light reflects off the silver varnish and glints off the small sapphire stone in the corner of the square-shaped signet ring. If I look hard enough,

I can see the *K.O.* I engraved on the back, and my first name wrapped around the inside of the band.

We're dismissed as soon as the bell rings, and I wait five seconds before grabbing my books and stationary. Once I hear the chair behind me scrape against the floor, I lean down to shove my belongings into my bag, and a pair of long, pale legs and knee-high socks walk past just as I do.

When I sit back up, Blaze is gone, along with my ring.

The tension lining the fibers of my muscles ease. Since I got here, she's been acting like she's better than the things I own. Back at St. Augustine, she would steal something from me on a weekly basis. The little thief had a whole shelf in her room dedicated to everything she thought I didn't know she took *and* the things I let her take—not that she knows any of this.

For the better part of the past two weeks, I've been trying to coax her with the bait she used to always fall for, like scribbling random shit on drink bottles, fidgeting with a lighter in front of her and leaving it out just enough to make it look like an easy challenge, as if it's just begging to be stolen. Or "accidentally" leaving my backpack half open, or dropping something and looking for it in the opposite direction.

But the little shit hasn't fallen for any of it.

She hasn't taken a single thing from me, and it pisses me off to no end.

We both know she isn't miraculously cured. She isn't above petty theft either. She's debatably worse than the macaques at the Monkey Forest in Indonesia.

I didn't want to part with the ring, but I had no choice. She's been leaving me no other options for years. *Now* she's acting above what

I have—like she's better than me. As if there are different guys she'd rather wrap her fingers around.

I yank the zipper of my bag down, remembering the picture of her sitting on Duke's lap, and all the times Elijah touched her right in front of me.

I bet she's stolen from that asshole. I bet she's swiped from every unassuming person in here *but* me.

I'm fucking sick and tired of waiting for her to stop being psychotic for two minutes for once in her life so she can open her goddamn eyes. I'm done being patient, and I won't sit by and watch her show non-homicidal interest to everyone but me. This shit is going to end. She's going to get in fucking line, or else she's going to see what happens when I feel cornered.

Until then, my son of a bitch Father has signed me up to play football, guitar, and fucking *chess*, and I'm about to spend the next two hours surrounded by a group of men who have all lost 80 percent of their brain cells.

"Hey, Kohen."

I snap my head in the direction of the voice.

Fucking hell, what does Sarah want?

"We haven't been formally introduced—well, you know, we talked in history the other day, but that wasn't *formal*-formal, if you know what I mean." She laughs at her joke and waits for me to do the same. I don't. "I'm Sarah." She sticks her hand out, and I just stare at it.

There isn't a single thing on this earth that will make me have any desire to touch her or even speak to her.

Sarah clears her throat and fumbles for the piece of paper behind her. "I meant to ask you a question." The answer is going to be no.

"Our annual ball is in a month, a couple weeks before finals, and we've all been preparing for it for *months*. It's going to be—drumroll, please." She taps the desk beside me. "Haunted House themed! We spent *forever* deciding on something, but figured we'd make it spooky with smoke machines and spiders."

She places the flier in front of me. Sure enough, it says Seraphic Hills's Annual Ball in big, bold letters and a punch of spiderwebs in the background. Fitting for an old nunnery.

I look blankly back at her.

Her smile falters for a second before she slaps it back on. "I was actually wondering..." Sarah's cheeks flush red, and it looks unappealing on her. "You know, everyone needs a date for prom?"

I blink.

She chews on her bottom lip. Does this actually work for guys?

"I was thinking... since you don't have a date, and Finn and I just broke up..." All this hesitation isn't cute. I'm just bored. She steps forward, and my skin crawls from her proximity. "Maybe we could go together."

I throw my bag on and leave her with one parting word. "No."

KOHEN

CHAPTER 6

She's wearing my ring.

She's wearing my ring, and she's looking smug about it. The little thief thinks she won this game we're playing, as if she's somehow in control of what's happening.

The ground was laid for us, but I was the one who set the kindling and struck the match. Blaze keeps trying to escape the parameters I placed for her; she almost got away once, but didn't get far enough. She never will.

It's more than just that.

Blaze woke up this morning, and every morning for the past seven days, looked at my initials on the back of the ring, and slipped it on her thumb even though it's two sizes too big for her.

Blaze woke up, put it on, and walked around *wearing my initials*.

The thief twists the ring around her thumb as she walks across campus, completely unaware of her surroundings. We've been at each other's throats daily, which is unsurprising. But she's been growing increasingly jittery, starting fights with anyone who looks at her for longer than a heartbeat.

Blaze wants a fix, and it seems the girl who has no money and nothing but her legs to trade for drugs is doing exactly what I thought she would do: find the dead man named Elijah.

She beelines between the throngs of students, all trying to stay out of the rain and leave to enjoy their few minutes of freedom before we're all forced to attend our mandatory after-school study session or sports training. She tightens the scarf around her neck and starts shouldering her way through the crowd. It doesn't take long until she reaches Elijah, who's leaning against the wall and talking to a couple of other people who hang out behind the church.

I watch the scene unfold from behind one of the stone pillars on the peristyle surrounding the courtyard, safe from the elements. The church crew all leave Elijah a few seconds after Blaze arrives, and he looks down at her with a self-satisfied smirk when she closes the distance and rubs her hand over his chest.

Her lips curl into the perfect smile, and her blue eyes soften and round as she looks up at him like he means everything to her. My skin heats as I watch her twirl a lock of hair around a slender finger. Why the fuck does she never look at me that way? She's known that fucker for what? Five minutes? And she's looking at him in the way I could only dream of.

Since day one, she's only ever thought of me with disdain. She's only ever seen me as an inconvenience. A nuisance she wants to get rid of. Blaze hates me, and I've done everything possible to change that. Yet she goes and throws it all in my face.

My fingers curl around my lighter, and I'm hit with the sudden urge to test out how flammable Elijah's school uniform is. It'd be a win-win for me; hurting him and sating my demons at the same time. I need to smell the smoke and watch chaos unfold in a dance of vermillion and yellow.

Nothing about what she's doing to Elijah is genuine. It's not about him, but what he has. The only thing that makes her smile is the same thing that will kill her, and I won't stand for it.

My heart hammers against my ribcage as I watch their interaction, the smile on his face growing with each word she says. I inch closer to the edge of the pillar to eavesdrop on their conversation, but the rain and howling behind me are louder than the echo of their whispers.

He raises an eyebrow when he speaks to her. Whatever she says makes his eyes widen with excitement, then he reaches behind her and grabs her ass.

I start walking before I can weigh the pros and cons of smashing his head against the stone until he becomes unidentifiable. My knuckles go white with how tightly I'm clenching my fists, but dick for brains doesn't notice the warpath I'm on, too distracted by Blaze to realize he's about to fucking die.

I stop short before I reach them because she turns around... and there's white powder on her fucking nose. When did either of them pull that shit out?

"What the fuck is going on here?" My feet start moving again, and I yank her away from him.

"Let go of me!" she screams. How many times have I heard her say that? Ten times, give or take? Probably more.

"Dude, don't touch her. Chill." Elijah's two brain cells clearly are too busy fighting for first place to work, because he steps towards us and *reaches* for Blaze.

"There are twenty-seven bones in the human hand. Breathe in her direction again, and we'll find out whether I can break them one at a time." He's mad he isn't receiving payment for fulfilling his end of the bargain.

Elijah holds his hand up and points to Blaze, who's struggling in my grip. "I'm just saying she obviously wants nothing to do with you, dude."

I tighten my grip around her. She isn't going anywhere. "I've always wanted to see what a real human heart feels like in my hands. Keep talking, and I'll get to find out."

"Stop being such a psychopath," Blaze growls.

I'm so amped up I don't so much as grunt when she elbows me in the ribs with every ounce of energy she has. Without waiting for Elijah's response, I drag her down the corridor, scaling the courtyard, barely aware of how she's kicking and screaming for me to release her.

I throw her into the first open, empty classroom, slamming the door behind me. I feel like I'm burning alive, and it's all her fault. Only she can set me off like this.

"Stop," I roar when she launches for me.

She doesn't.

Of course, she doesn't.

When the fuck has she ever listened to me?

I tell her not to cross the road because there's a car speeding our way, and she'll cross it. I ask her to sit still so the teacher doesn't rip into her again and run to Whitlock Sr. about her behavior, and she does the exact opposite. Nothing I've ever done is enough for her, but *everyone* else is as long as they give her a temporary escape from this shithole.

"You're the one who's manhandling me, you Denisovan!"

I hate what she does to me. I despise how fucking simple it is for her. It's a pathetic insult. Yet, here I am, grinning like I've just inhaled nitrous oxide because she paid attention in biology class.

My grin twists into a scowl, my hand finds her neck, and my thumb searches for her pulse. Her blown-out pupils meet mine as I back her against the wall.

"How much did you fucking take, Blaze?" My voice is lethally calm. The way her lips part tells me she knows I'm seconds away from losing it. Still, she bares her teeth at me.

If Blaze could kill me with a single look, I'd be dead a thousand times over from the daggers she's shooting my way.

"What I do is none of your business."

She's wrong. And it makes me fucking wild.

She thrashes under me. It's not remotely hard to control her whole body with one hand to her throat. I put my hand on her arm just to feel her skin against mine. Even when her eyes are harsh, her skin is always so soft. I can't help but appreciate that her bones aren't digging into me the same way they used to. Back then, she was skin and bone and had lifeless, fiery eyes.

Now, she's using nowhere near as much as she used to, eating at least three meals a day, and putting on muscle. Her eyes are also sharper, and her skin has color. She's even lost the bags underneath her eyes. Christ, if I don't appreciate what this place has done to her.

"What's your end goal, huh? Are you planning on using so much you blow your lights out? Do you want to end up like your *mother*?"

She jolts forward but winds herself against my hand instead. Her back crashes against the wall, eyes watching me with the hatred I'm so used to. "What's yours, Kohen? Where are you going once you get out of here? Back underneath your brother's shadow? Playing bitch for the rest of your family?"

Wrong again. I have a plan, and the only part my family will play is to release the trust fund that's waiting for me when I graduate. After that, Osman is just a name.

I add more pressure on my thumb, feeling her pulse fluttering against my numb flesh. I can't feel hot or cold, smooth or coarse, but *that* I can feel. "All you do is talk about things you don't understand."

Her face twists with challenge. "Making my life your business won't change your own."

"Using won't change yours."

"If I wanted to stop, I would." Blaze raises her chin, exposing more of her slender throat. "Besides, none of this has anything to do with you."

"Then prove it," I say. "Stop."

"I don't need to prove *shit* to you."

"I know one thing you want more than powder to snort."

"You think you know me so well, don't you?" She sneers. "You think you have me all figured out because you've been looking down at me from your gilded tower, throwing dirt my way just because you have the money to do it."

"You tell yourself you use and steal because you like the high of it, that it makes you feel alive, but that's a lie. You do it because that's the only time you feel you have control over your life." Two sentences. That's all it takes for her chest to expand as she takes a deep breath. "You act out because you want the attention—at least, that *was* the reason, wasn't it? Maybe Mommy will come home if she hears you need help, and everything will return to how it was. Now you act out because no one listens to you. I am the only person in your life who hasn't turned their back on you, and you know it too." Her eyes mist over, but she only raises her head higher. "And I know you want me to pay."

Her throat bobs beneath my hand. "Don't look so proud of yourself, Osman. Anyone with eyes can see I want payback for what you did."

"Not just for your house. You want me to pay for everything," I say, hating the following words. My father was my alibi that day because the entire Osman line knows my parents never let me leave the house unless it's for school and practice. Kiervan is the only person who's aware that I snuck out of my window at night.

"You made my life hell!" she yells, shoving my chest.

Blaze is still fucking alive because of me. How many times have I saved her now? I don't understand how one person can be so difficult. This girl wakes up every day and chooses to be a pain in the ass.

I take a deep breath to reign in my temper. Blaze has no idea how patient I've been with her, and still she continues to test me. "Don't use *anything* for two months, and my entire trust fund is yours."

She blinks once. Twice.

"I think I'm tweaking. Say that again."

I grip her chin and angle it up so there isn't an inch of her face that I can't see perfectly—the same face I saw shoved against Duke's. I run my tongue over my teeth, then say, "There are two more months left of school. If you last until graduation without any drugs or alcohol, I will give the entirety of my trust fund to you."

Her lips part, and her blown-out eyes widen. "You're shitting me, right?"

"If you so much as inhale a speck of that shit or get a secondhand high, it's over. You lose."

"I don't believe you," she whispers, searching my face like she's waiting for me to say it was all a bad joke. But I don't.

Seconds pass while we do nothing but breathe in each other's air. Blaze's pulse is going rabid against my thumb, and her violent blue eyes stay on mine, not breaking the connection for a second. This is all I wanted from her: cooperation. But then she ruins it when she rolls her eyes and shrugs me off. I step back, letting her get away.

"Yeah, right. Good one." The thief scoffs, shaking her head. "You're such a fucking cunt, Kohen." Blaze opens the door and gives me one long, pitiful look. "You're going to die alone."

She's wrong about that too.

I follow her out of the room to find Elijah waiting against the pillar in the courtyard like a slimy creep, jacked up on whatever it is he gave Blaze, and ready for his payment—and I hate her more for it. He looks my way for a hesitant second before wiping his hands on his pants, moving to follow her down the hall.

I grab him by the strap of his backpack and throw him out from the peristyle and into the rain while I remain beneath the shade. Curling my fists until my knuckles hurt, I watch as he falls back on his ass, soaking his uniform in mud and water. The confused daze lasts a second until he scrambles back onto his feet, but I push him back into the rain, where any chance of burning him alive is gone because of the elements.

"What the—"

I square my shoulders and draw my lighter, flicking the spark wheel to let the flame dance over the silver metal. Then I say with eerie steadiness, "You don't want to see what happened to the last person who got too close to my fire."

His face falls. "Look, dude, I don't mean to—"

"I'm going to say this once, and only once." I take a step forward, and he skitters back, eyes bouncing around the place, searching for help before they land back on my lighter. *"Run or burn."*

BLAZE

CHAPTER 7

Subtle shivers rack through my body despite the heater running on full blast—and I'm pretty sure I'm seconds away from breaking my jaw from how tense it is. My entire body is sore as shit, and my head is pounding, but at least the nausea is gone. I guess that's why they call it *Suicide Tuesday*. I would much rather die than go through the shit I went through yesterday again.

I tried seeking Elijah out yesterday, because why go through a comedown when you can keep going? But the little coward ran in the opposite direction. I was even willing to give him a handjob in the bathroom for it.

His loss.

Just kidding, it's my fucking astronomical loss.

So, I had to suck it up and try to live through the comedown, and almost died choking on my own damn vomit. It's not as bad today because I'm running on pure rage. Elijah is two seats to the right of me and hasn't looked up from his hands since the history teacher hid herself behind her desk so we can have "study time."

Just in time, the person between us gets up from her seat to go to the bathroom. And who am I to look a gift horse in the mouth?

"You've been avoiding me," I growl under my breath as I slide into the seat she occupied. He's not attractive enough to be treating me like this.

His frantic eyes cast to mine, and then he twists his entire body to look at the table behind us before jerking straight upright. What the fuck?

"I wasn't."

Read the room, jackass. I flick his forehead with my index finger. "Don't insult me with a shit lie. You've been avoiding me. Why?" By the time I finish talking, my face is two inches from his ear.

Can't avoid me now, bitch.

He whips his head toward me, whisper-yelling, "You didn't tell me you were with that psychopath."

I rear back. "Which psychopath?"

One comes to mind, but there's no way we're thinking about the same person.

"Kohen."

"Are you insane? I wouldn't touch that man if he were the last person on Earth." Mentally, at least, I wouldn't go anywhere near him. Physically? This slut likes whatever it is he's packing. My ovaries see him, say "wow, so strong," and think he's a suitable mate to procreate with. "Why would you think we're together?"

Elijah throws his hands up. "Because he shoved me and threatened me!"

I snort. I'd do the same to Elijah too. "For what? Wait, let me guess, you looked at him for too long? You made a joke about him being held back a year? Ooh, ooh, I know. You called him Kiervan." It's gotta be one of those. Not that he knows who Kiervan is. That man only reacts that strongly when either of those things are mentioned. My house is evidence of his tantrum.

"No, *you*." At the face I pull, he explains, "He practically pissed all over you."

"Never say that shit again." I blanch. "The only thing he'd do is pour gasoline over me. Now, how about we pick up where we left off yesterday, huh?" I glance around to ensure the teacher isn't looking our way, then place my hand on his thigh. "What have you got for me?"

He stiffens. "Are you sure nothing is going on between you and the new kid? He made it seem like you guys were an item or something."

I scowl at the imagery and the fact that it doesn't bother me nearly as much as it should. My reaction to my thoughts about that crazy hunk of a man should be visceral and make me throw up on the spot. Instead, my head goes a little light thinking about having all that muscle beneath me and having his golden eyes tear into me in an entirely different way.

"The man has a few loose screws," I purr. "Don't trust a word that comes out of his mouth."

I can't say Elijah looks any more at ease about my admission than he was a minute ago, but eventually, his shoulders slump slightly. "I'm out, and my guy won't have anything for a couple more days. But you still owe me for yesterday."

It's my turn to tense. Now, *this* reaction is near visceral. There's no way I'm going anywhere near his disgusting penis unless I'm hopped up or he's waving a more figurative carrot in front of my face.

I've never done any kind of sex sober before, and I don't intend to start now. The lights would have to be off, and even then, I couldn't stomach it. Especially when I know for a fact it will end with me feeling unsatisfied and in desperate need of a shower. I definitely will not die a virgin, but my fingers would have racked up considerable mileage before then.

I snatch my arm away and glare at him. "I was ready to pay up with my hand, but you were nowhere to be found. *You* fucked *me* around."

Elijah frowns. "I told you that lunatic tossed me around."

Welcome to my life, bud. I roll my eyes and then frown, feeling my face heat. "Fine. Next time you have something to give me, come find me."

"You think a handjob is enough after all the shit you've leeched?" His nostrils flare as he speaks.

Throwing caution to the wind, I palm his cock and hold back bile. He snaps upright, gaping at me but hardening all the same. *Gag.*

The hair at the back of my neck stands on end like I'm being watched. "Harsh words, Elijah." I lean in closer, so my chest brushes against his arm. "Get me something worth my time"—and will make me lose all sense of reality so I'm not aware of what I'm doing—"and you might find something... warm and wet in return." My voice is silky smooth even though acid is rising up my esophagus.

I pull away and pat the top of his head like a dog, then slide back into my chair, unable to get comfortable. It feels like all the oxygen has been sucked out of the room. My head slowly inches toward the source of the vacuum, and my mouth goes dry.

My eyes meet Kohen's, and all sense of disgust evaporates out of me. He feels like a real danger for the first time since I've met him. The pyromaniac isn't just looking at me like he's going to eat me alive, he's looking at me like he's about to commit murder. The question is, who's the victim?

I whimper and press my face into the pillow, all my muscles protesting. A solid eight hours, zero bathroom breaks, or soul-altering dreams might solve all my problems.

After flipping my pillow over and beating it half to death, I lie back down, the faint whiff of the weed I scored earlier reaching my nose. Maybe if I didn't constantly feel like I'd been hit by a truck, I would get an epiphany about the course my life was going down, and then everything would suddenly be in order.

The shitty sleep has everything to do with the shit Elijah gave me two days ago, and smoking a joint has done nothing to make sleeping possible. Come to think of it, I need to change tact and go right to the source. Take out the middleman and see if Elijah's dealer can score me some vitamin K and give me a bump; then Bob will most definitely be my uncle.

A couple more minutes pass, and I turn over, tangling the sheets and ratty blanket between my legs as I do. My exposed leg skirts the edge of the bed, and not for the first time, I'm loving the central heating this place has. It's a fucking Christmas miracle that I haven't needed to sleep in a coat and hoodie to survive the colder months.

Now, even though it's freezing outside, I'm in here at risk of a tit falling out of my singlet, and the bogeyman getting an eyeful of my ass. This really is the life. If only I were born into a wealthy family.

Oh wait.

Sighing, I rub my leg up and down the cotton sheets and smile to myself. Grandpa was forced to buy me a new set for school. It's cheap, but it feels damn good not sleeping in something threadbare or ripped. At least once I'm out of this place, I'll have semi-acceptable bedding—*and* a goose down. I've always wanted one of those.

"I'm so sick of your shit."

My eyes snap open.

I'm tripping. I did not seriously just hear that.

I notice movement from the shadows in the corner of my room. I don't get the chance to make a sound before the man is on me, trapping half my body beneath the blankets. How does that saying go? Strike, scream, then run? Fuck it, screaming is my first instinct anyway. He doesn't cover my mouth fast enough because a strangled cry leaves my lips before his hand is on me.

"*Shut up*, Blaze," the man growls, fisting my hair to keep me steady as he moves his face closer.

My mouth snaps shut. I blink, adjusting to the darkness and making out the beautiful deadly features of the man on top of me.

"Kohen?" I mumble against his hand.

Oh, this motherfucker has a death wish.

Three questions race to mind: how did he get *in* here, *why* is he here, and how do I get him *out*?

I don't let myself think about the sudden burst of desire that rips through my core at the realization his hips are nestled between my very bare legs, and that he's lowered himself down to his elbows on either side of my head.

His hand slowly moves away from my mouth, and that's when I strike. Pain radiates from my forehead as I whip my head forward, colliding with his nose. In the darkness, I can just make out his widening eyes.

Good.

His creepy smile as he touches his nose is a little *less* good.

I leverage my arms and wiggle my hips to throw him off me, but he's back on me before I get that chance.

Not good.

Thick thighs straddle my waist, and his strong hands wrap around both my wrists, holding my body captive against the bed. I buck my hips and attempt to sock him with my head again, but everything about him is overpowering.

"Why the fuck do you keep fighting me?" Kohen snarls, tightening his hold on me.

I swing my legs up because they're the only free part of my body, except he easily holds them down by shifting his legs over mine, and the next thing I know, the only brutal thing I have left is my tongue. "Because you're a psycho pyro who won't leave me the fuck alone."

"I bet you fucked Elijah just like you fucked Duke."

My jaw drops. How the fuck does he know about Duke? I narrow my eyes. I bet his parents told him about it after they heard it from the police.

"And you, what?" I huff. "Wanted a slice of the action? Wanted to see if your balls fall off, you creep?"

His hold around my wrists goes painful for a split second before he uses one hand to put my throat in a steellike grip. "Don't you dare put me on the same level as those two dicks-for-brains."

The rough material of his jeans scrapes against my lower stomach, and I tense. I'm going to need to check myself in to see Dr. Van der Merwe, because my heart is slamming against my ribcage for reasons other than the threat to my safety. The pale moonlight sneaking through the gap in my curtains highlights his cheeks and the path along his nose, accentuated by the shadows that fall on his face and dip beneath his jaw and down the column of his throat. For one very concerning, very unsettling moment, I want to know whether he tastes the same way he smells.

Enough of this shit. This creeper behavior is not okay—maybe just a little—*no*. Fuck, I hate that it turns me on a little that Kohen could have done anything to me if I were asleep when he came in. He probably got an eyeful of me for however long he stood in the shadows of my room.

I try thrashing around again, and shifting my elbow. But nothing works. This guy has a better grip than the security guards.

"Careful. You're starting to sound jealous," I say. The accusation even sounds ridiculous to my ears, but Elijah mentioned he thought the pyro was acting territorial.

"I'm not!"

There goes the painful grip again. If I wake up bruised tomorrow, I'm definitely snitching. No one will believe me unless I have proof, but I'm sure McGill and every other person in this school will spin it in a way to say that I somehow did it to myself.

My entire body is protesting from all the movement, and the added strain tells me that it's going to hurt like a bitch tomorrow. I try to whip my head forward to knock his nose, but he dodges it easily because his grip around my throat stops me from getting very far.

Frustration slices through my spine, and I snarl. "Then why the fuck did you sneak into my room to rape me?"

"I fucking wasn't!"

"Someone's throwing a tantrum. Do you need some crayons to help you express your feelings?" I mock in the same tone I'd use to talk to a child.

I involuntarily flinch because his hold is getting a little too painful for my liking. Either he realizes the same, or I'm doing a terrible job concealing my expressions, but he eases off in the next heartbeat.

Kohen's eyes harden. "You're such a bitch."

"Hmm, I wonder why I might be acting like this. Oh, maybe it's because *you broke into my room and burned my fucking house down!*"

"It was your fault!" He gets right in my face when he yells it.

"Victim blaming, asshole? Really? Uncool."

"Shut up."

"No. I'm sick of you acting—"

"Stop talking."

How *dare* he? "Don't interrupt me when I'm speaking. You think you know me so well? Fine. It doesn't take a genius to know you started lighting fires the day you were born because it was the only way you'd be seen in your brother's shadow. Your impulsiveness wasn't something hardwired into your brain. You kept feeding it so you could see how long you could get away with it until your parents started giving a damn about you the same way they did Kiervan. The bigger the fire, the more the attention, right? *Wrong.* Nothing worked, so now you're an angry, bitter, spoiled—"

I don't get to finish because he gets me to do exactly what he wants: I shut up. I don't make a single sound when he kisses me—whether in shock, disgust, confusion, or a wave of lust, I stay completely still.

Until I don't.

It doesn't matter how much I yell at myself to stop, to pull back and spit in his face; my lips keep moving with his.

My suspicions were correct. Kohen tastes like mint and patchouli.

His lips are the softest things I've ever felt, giving me a headier feeling than any drug I've ever taken. I had no expectations about kissing Kohen, but I always imagined it would be exactly like this: searing hatred that makes the air so thick with tension, feeling as if he's lit a match between us and we're being enveloped in smoke.

Nothing about this is loving. It's packed to the brim with poison and cinders that make my veins boil with need. This is the first time I've been kissed sober, and I've never felt more intoxicated.

I'm unsure what happens next, because this high has seeped into my marrow. One second, he's gripping my hair to deepen the kiss; the next, his tongue pokes out to battle mine. Suddenly, he moves away from me and cold rushes through my body as he ends up on the other side of the bedroom.

Kohen shakes his head and runs his hand down his face, pacing the short space between the width of the room, pissed off beyond comprehension.

It doesn't matter how hard I try to understand it; I can't figure out why *he's* the one who's angry. *He* snuck into *my* room. *He* mounted *me* like a caveman, then shoved *his* tongue down *my* throat. None of this is my fault.

My lips feel bruised, like I've just gone ten rounds in the ring. One thing's for certain: if I thought the ache in my muscles was terrible before, it's nothing compared to the throbbing that's started between my legs. If he hadn't been straddling me, I would have died from embarrassment over what my body would have done against my wishes.

He runs a hand over his head, paces back and forth twice, then hits the wall. The sound stirs me to my feet, and I somehow find the decency to drape the sheets over my shoulders.

I lick my lips, tasting the remnants of him as I swallow the lump in my throat. "Alright, settle down, Kyle." My voice lacks its usual lethal touch.

The pyromaniac whips toward me. "What the fuck did you just call me?" The rage that carries with his voice rumbles down my spine and has me swaying backward.

What the fuck is his problem? I've never seen him so distressed before.

His gaze drops from my eyes to my chest—where I'm certain my nipples have come to say hello, and have only become more enthusiastic in their greeting now that they're getting attention. I'm only wearing a tacky, shoestring tanktop, and the air is already kissing the top half of my tits. I can only imagine just how much cleavage he's getting.

My stupid, traitorous eyes do the same thing he did. They fall from his face to the heavy rise and fall of his chest, down to his jeans. I suck in a sharp breath and try to get the image out of my head, but there's no unseeing the tent in his pants. Holy Mother Mary, there must be a monster living under there.

My tongue slips out to wet my bottom lip, and his inhale is so audible I squeeze my legs together in a useless attempt to alleviate the tension.

I bite the inside of my cheek, and I hate that his eyes drop to my lips. I have to stop this. *Now.*

"It's not funny when I have to explain the joke to you, dipshit. All the Monster-drinking, wall-punching dudes are named Kyle—" Wait. Why am I explaining this to him? "You know what? *Get the fuck out of my room!*"

Kohen moves faster than I do, cornering me like I'm a caged animal. The chill of the wall seeps into my back, and the sheet I had draped over myself lies discarded on the floor. I press my palms against his chest to stop him from getting closer, but it's as if I'm Sisyphus pushing the boulder—minus the strength, endurance, and will—because Kohen keeps coming closer.

His hand goes around my neck, thumb feeling for my thundering pulse, his preferred position. Our combined ragged breaths settle over my skin like I'm in a sauna. Unlike all the other times he's had his knee wedged between my legs, the only thing stopping my pussy from making direct contact with him now is the pair of thin cotton panties I'm wearing—my very *drenched* cotton panties.

The differences don't end with the uneven division of clothing between us. It spreads to how his eyelids have gone heavy, even though the rest of him oozes disapproval.

The worst difference is what's going on below our waists.

His thigh isn't just wedged between my legs; the thick fabric of his pants is touching the only material I have on the bottom half of my body.

If I thought the ungodly thing warring in his pants was impressive a minute ago, having it pressed against my stomach feels akin to having a gun pressed against my head; a little horny at what could be done with it, and a teeny bit uneasy about the prospect of death.

But fuck me sideways if I'm not tingling all the way down to my toes imagining what this pyromaniac looks like without clothes. Better yet, what all that muscle will feel like under my fingertips. And like a damn frigid virgin, I squeeze my legs around his thigh—which is the worst possible thing I could have done because my lust-addled brain doesn't catch up fast enough to stop me from moaning.

If Kohen looked like he wanted to eat me alive earlier this afternoon, right now, he's ready to splay me out to feast on me like I'm a Sunday roast, and he's been starving all week.

I try to save face by curling my lips into a scowl, but then his hand on my hips—something I hadn't realized until now—grips me tighter, guiding my hip into soft rolls. The feeling of my throbbing core against the rough fabric of his jeans has my eyes rolling to the back of my head, and I'm done for.

I've lost before the rules of the game are even set as I whimper—I fucking whimper like I'm touch starved, and he's the only person alive that has touched me like this—and he's done absolutely nothing to me. This is the first time someone has touched me sober, where I feel electrified instead of repulsed.

I see why people seek solace in external sources like God to get over drugs, because right now I'm seriously considering turning to sex. It's almost the same; the body tingles, the lightheadedness, feeling like I'm on top of the world, reaching for the stars like I never have to worry about falling. Nothing matters but what's going on within the parameters of my skin.

Kohen does it again, dragging my center over his hard thigh, pressing his cock harder against me when he brings me up. My head falls back against the wall while his dips down to watch me with more scorching intensity than the sun.

This is wrong. Fucked up on every level. But I've always been a sinner, getting turned on by the things that are bad for me.

Kohen's stare brings me back to earth, and it takes extreme effort not to move my hips again to feel his cock and alleviate the pressure that's ready to explode. "What the fu—"

"No." My eyes widen as I gasp when he closes his fingers around my windpipe, depriving me of my oxygen and rendering me silent. "I'm sick of hearing shit come out of your mouth."

If he notices the subtle movement of my hips in response, he doesn't let on. He doesn't react when I slip my hand over his broad shoulders to the back of his neck or when I sink my nails into the knotted muscles that ripple beneath the surface of his skin. Blood pebbles beneath my nails, and I do it again in a different area while focusing on keeping my damn hips still.

"You—"

He tightens his grip around my throat, cutting me off. My eyes roll to the back of my head as another moan builds in my chest.

A trip to the shrink isn't enough. I need to be put down.

I make my muscles go rigid when he tries moving me again, but all it does is make him flush his body against me, dragging his thigh along my pussy so there isn't an inch of space between us. The simple gesture tells me everything I need to know: I don't need to comply for him to get me off.

He does it again and again until my body becomes putty in his hands, grinding against him like I'm an animal. The vein in his forehead throbs as he watches me from beneath his heavy lids. I can see him cataloging every minute response and saving them for later—probably to use against me. I fruitlessly try to push him away. I do it partly for show and to assure myself that I tried.

"Fuck you," I manage to breathe out of my burning lungs, grinding up and down his thigh.

His hot breath fans my ear as he roughly nuzzles the side of my face, tilting it so he has better access.

"Don't pretend you don't like it, Blaze. You're looking at me like you hate me, but you're riding me like you love me."

The deep cadence of his voice sends a shot of liquid fire straight to my core, and I press myself harder against him with the next grind. The sound of his harsh breath is nearly muted from the blood rushing through my ears.

Stars dance behind my vision as I try to push him away. We both know I could make it happen if I really wanted him to stop. I've kneed him in the balls plenty of times. Mostly, he knows just as well as I do that if he keeps going, I will make an even bigger mess of his jeans.

The fingers gripping my hips dip beneath my panties and dig into my ass, holding it like he's about to fall off a cliff. A barely noticeable sound rumbles at the back of his throat when he skims my soaked center, and my eyelashes flutter. The combination of sound and touch forces me to bite my lip to keep from whimpering for more.

He rakes his teeth along my jaw, eliciting a shudder. "You don't want to be good. You don't want to be broken. You want to be loud and mouthy because you want someone to notice you. You want to choose when to hand over control, and it makes your pussy wet that it's me making all the decisions."

A muffled groan is the only response I can give him. It's becoming impossible to keep my eyes open to watch how he looks at me. It's even more impossible to hold my body up on my own. I need to tap out or get him to ease his grip. Somehow, I know he'd do it if I gave his arm the slightest nudge. Except I can't bring myself to do it.

If I tap out, he wins. If he lets go, I lose the headiness I itch for every time I look for my next hit. The blood rushing through my ears, the slowed thoughts, the fuzzy vision. A part of me—some sick, twisted part of me—wants to see how far he'll take it. Whether I'll pass out and wake up to his lips around my nipple or my underwear pushed to the side as he lines us up.

117

"Look at you, so needy and helpless. It's pathetic—you hate me, and yet you're about to come on my thigh when I haven't even touched that pretty clit of yours."

Our grip around each other's neck loosens incrementally, and slowly, my head drops against his chest, and my eyes fall closed. There's no fight in me to stop him from moving my hips, and without my restraint, he rolls my hips even faster until my hiccupping breaths stop, and nothing comes in or out anymore.

Kohen lets my throat go before my lights go out, and I gasp for breath as strength returns to my body. My hold on his shirt is the only thing keeping me upright as my lungs fight a battle between moaning and getting more oxygen.

"Fucking hell, Blaze. Are you trying to die?" he growls under his breath and yanks my head back with a fist in my hair.

"A murder charge would look good on you," I sputter between strangled gasps, staring up into his disgustingly beautiful eyes.

I wish I could say I was only disappointed that he stopped, and there wouldn't be big purple bruises around my neck for me to stock as evidence. Instead, the bar must be somewhere in hell, because my heart goes gooey knowing he let go before he could do any damage. It's crying a pathetic tune under a misguided perception that Kohen might care for me.

He pulls my hair harder. "You think you can get away that easily? Haven't you figured out there's no separating us?"

Huh? "You're delusional."

"Is that why you've soaked through my jeans?" He makes a sound between a huff and a snarl—whatever it is, it does things to me. "Fuck, you're a dirty little whore."

Feminism? Out the window.

My hips buckle on their own. "*Fuck you.*"

"I'd be careful if I were you. I'm this close to fucking you into the wall." He palms my ass. "Think I could fuck the brat out of you then, Thief?"

He releases my ass for a moment to flick my nipple, and out of pure reflex, I slap him. He has my arm above my head in the next heartbeat, and it kills me that my eyelids flutter. It shouldn't turn me on how easily he overpowers me. I guess I'm a simple-minded girl who wants a strong man; none of his other qualities matter. The fact he ruined my life? Nope, my pussy doesn't give a shit about any of that.

I grin. "Others have tried and failed."

I know my answer would only piss him off more because what person wants to hear about the other's sexual escapades when condensation coats the windows from their heated encounter.

Kohen's lips peel back, and each one of his movements becomes painful, from the pull of my hair to the grip on my ass, to the coarse fabric of his jeans. "Only I get to make you come. Only *I* get to feel your thighs around me. You burn for me. *Only* me."

His fingers drift past my ass to skate over the entrance to my pussy, and I bear down on his leg, riding his thigh because *fuck him.*

Kohen isn't the winner here; *I am.* I'm the one using *him.* I'm the one who gets to come at the end of this, for once.

I let my hips loosen, let him move me faster than I'd be able to move myself as I claw and hit him like I'm the brat he knows me to be. I let myself moan without restraint, and I look him in the eyes as I do it. Helen of Troy had the right idea, because this is how she sank a thousand ships.

He's not in control. I am. He thinks he's broken my spirit, taken from me when I didn't want to give. This isn't humiliation. This is liberation. He wants the fight, and I want the feeling of ecstasy. *I'm the one who wins this war.* I don't need an army to take him down when he has holes in his armor.

So when I come, there aren't just fireworks and overfilled champagne. The earth rumbles, the ground opens up, hellfire tears through the sky, and I throw my head back to scream his name.

Not his.

His.

Kiervan's.

Checkmate, asshole.

KOHEN

CHAPTER 8

I'm going to fucking kill her right after I kill my brother.

Kiervan.

Kiervan?

She humped my leg like a dog in heat, she kissed my lips, she soaked through *my* clothes, and Kiervan gets the fucking credit? He isn't even here, and he's in the spotlight.

I release the band around my wrist, and the sting that follows the snap isn't nearly as calming as it should be. I've been pissed off at her before, but last night I was ready to strangle her. I couldn't even look at her, let alone touch her.

Kiervan? Fuck.

Blaze had to open her mouth and ruin it. Everything about her up to that point was intoxicating; the sounds she made, the curve of her waist, the feel of her ass in my hands, and the way her nipples looked through her poor excuse of pajamas—thin black fabric taunting me.

Then she touched me—well, she slapped me.

But she chose to put her hand on me. *Me.* And god it makes me giddy to think she willingly put her hand on me.

She *chose* to slap *me.*

I expected her lips to taste smoky or as sour as she is, but I've been tasting cherries since I kissed her. Blaze doesn't appreciate the gravity of what I told her last night. A thread is sturdier than the shit I was hanging on to last night.

My cock was hard the second I stepped foot in her room, and then she moved and all but shoved her pussy in my face while she was half asleep. Then her little panties shifted, and I wanted to fuck her until she felt like she was choking on my cock, then spank the cherry tattooed on her ass.

But I was good. *Patient.*

I wasn't sure what I expected by entering her room—I definitely wasn't planning to kiss her. Not by a long shot.

I found her room, then stole an access key from one of the security guards last week, and I didn't think I'd do anything with it. But then Blaze went and touched dipshit Elijah in the middle of class, and I was ready to do worse than just sneak into her room to make her come.

Seriously. *Kiervan?*

Fuck.

I was half tempted to break out of here to get home where I've got everything I need to bring him down, then push the big red button.

The klepto had the nerve to walk into class this morning looking smug. It did make me feel marginally better to watch her deflate when the teacher returned her paper, and there was a big *F* in red marker at the top of the page.

Squinting, I managed to make out what she wrote for the creative writing assignment and spotted the words *dark, gloomy night, as fast as a cheetah,* and *branches like fingers,* as well as two typos in the first paragraph alone, then decided I didn't need to read any more.

An *F* seems accurate.

Writing isn't in her future.

The only thing that's stopping me from pulling her aside and making her scream the correct name this time is the fact that there are red marks along her neck where I choked her. Blaze can feel as smug as she wants, but she's walking all around school carrying the marks that came from my hands. Not Kiervan's.

The thief opted to pick the seat furthest away from me when she arrived late to our next class. I snap the band around my wrist again as I watch her causing mayhem at the other side of the classroom.

The school made two fuckups this morning. The first was thinking it was a good idea to pair Blaze up with Sarah. The second was trusting us around Bunsen burners. Or specifically, trusting *her* around one.

As soon as Sarah steps out of the classroom, Blaze snatches a piece of paper covered in Sarah's handwritten notes and holds it over the fire until it all burns into ash.

Blaze isn't stupid; she just lights her notes on fire. She's got to use something as a starter, and nothing spreads like knowledge. My fiery little thief is a pyromaniac in the making.

I glance at her, then the flame, then back at her. It's Bunsen burner day, and here I am, consumed by her instead of the flame. What a waste.

There's a glint in her eyes that isn't usually there. It makes her all the more mesmerizing and all the more dangerous. She's not concocting a plan, but her unmade hair and wide eyes scream with a wildness that goes beyond what I'm used to.

She's antsy, looking for a fight rather than a hit.

I rub my thumb over the band around my wrist and drop my gaze to the strands of copper hair tangled around the tie. I snap it against my wrist again and look back at her. I'd be a liar if I said watching her play with fire doesn't make my dick hard.

Blaze keeps glancing back at the teacher to make sure he's not watching, and because she has no concept of first aid, when she burns her finger, instead of running it under cold water, she sticks it in her mouth.

She's beautiful, violent, vulgar, and batshit fucking crazy.

The bench is cleared of evidence by the time Sarah comes back, and Blaze plasters an innocent look on her face as Sarah rummages around the bench in search of what I assume is the piece of paper that is now ash. Blaze shrugs and ignores her, heading to the front of the class to clean up, leaving behind black skid marks on the floor from her shoes.

I shake my head. They're the same pair she's had for the last two years. Jonathan Whitlock Sr. is unbelievable. He's more of a scum than my own father. My dad would never let his own granddaughter wear shoes with holes in them.

"Pyro." She sneers when she catches my stare.

"Klepto."

She's right; I am a pyromaniac—not that I've been diagnosed. But she's called me that enough times that I've looked into it. I might as well figure my problems out myself rather than paying some old person to do it and then report back to my parents. We're both looking at the DSM-5 either way. Some parts of it make me doubtful; people like me usually have mood disorders and addictions, but I don't believe I have either of the two. Either way, my self-diagnosis still stands. It's apparently manageable, but incurable.

Her, on the other hand? The only test she's ever passed with flying colors is the one that makes her the poster girl for kleptomaniacs. She's a therapist's wet dream; the easiest diagnosis they've ever done.

I remember watching her steal the janitor's cleaning supplies to tip out the contents on the lawn and keep the bottle. Or when she stole someone's phone just for the case, even though she didn't even have a phone. Or that time she took some kid's eraser that was torn in half and mutilated by a pen. Hell, she's taken at least twenty of my lighters in the past year alone.

When the bell rings, she heads out with Charlie in tow. Sarah's face brightens when she sees me, as if she has me cornered, but I sidestep her before she can open her mouth. I have the misfortune of spending the next hour with the headmaster, and I'd rather not make it worse by talking to her as well. I slowly walk through the hallway, hoping to shave off the amount of time I have to spend with him.

I veer into the bathroom, then wait for everyone to empty out before drawing out my lighter to watch the flame. The orange hues flare as threads of smoke billow into the air. Even though I know better than to reach into my pocket and take out the piece of paper, I do it anyway. I flatten it out to watch the fire climb up the sheet, eating it up faster than I'd like. The sight of the flame's rage and the smoky taste that follows soothes the pounding in my chest.

The paper and its ashen remains flutter into the bowl before it reaches my skin. I watch as the last fire flickers out and the urge to grab another piece of paper hits me. Slamming my palm against the wall, I shake my head and whip open the stall door, heading to the sinks. Turning the tap all the way to cold, I splash the cool water onto my face, taking slow, deep breaths.

Control. I have control.

Gritting my teeth, I storm the rest of the way to the headmaster's office, pushing away thoughts about all the flammable objects in my bag.

McGill's assistant nods, signaling for me to go into his office once she hangs up the phone with him.

I'm late because I didn't want to come. McGill doesn't seem to care about that particular fact because a smile explodes across his face, but all I really notice is his filthy mustache.

"Good morning, Kohen," McGill says, bright and cheery as he tucks his notebook into the drawer. He's so full of shit. "How has your day been?"

"Fine." Let's get this over with.

His brows pinch together, accentuating his wrinkled face. "When someone asks you that, you're meant to ask it back."

I give him a blank look. "Okay."

This isn't my first interaction with the headmaster; I doubt it will be my last. The first time we spoke, he was getting his feelers out for me, and that hasn't changed. He's still trying to figure me out. Soon, he'll realize he doesn't care about getting to know me—just like every other adult in my life.

As long as the checks come in and I don't do anything to ruin Seraphic Hills's squeaky-clean reputation, he doesn't give a damn about what I do.

"Sit." He motions to the chair in front of the table across from him. I oblige only because the less I hear from his mouth, the better.

"Your father did say you have difficulty talking to people," he muses. "He also warned me that your emotional regulation often gets the better of you."

He's dancing around stating I'm prone to outbursts. The only incidents Father knows about are the one that landed me here, and the one where I gave Kiervan a black eye because he had too much to say about the girl who moaned his name last night. Every reaction I've had has always come down to one or both of them. And, as far as they're aware, I ended up here because the fucker from school started talking shit about the fire.

But fine, let's call it issues with emotional regulation. I'll bite.

McGill sighs. "How are you fitting in?"

"Fine."

The excess skin around his eye twitches. "Do you like your classes?"

"Sure."

The headmaster sucks in a sharp breath. "I hear *Oskadine*, the miracle drug, is currently waiting for FDA approval."

I shrug. It's all over the news.

He leans back in his wingback chair and folds his arms over his gut. The buttons on his crisp white shirt strain to stay together, and I can just see the slightest brush of pink staining the collar. Lipstick, I assume. Specifically, the receptionist's—not to be mistaken for the secretary.

He tilts his head to the side like he's trying to study me. "You're not a man of very many words, are you, Mr. Osman?"

He said this, word for word, the first time we met and suggested buddying me up with Sticky Fingers.

Shrugging, I cross my legs to hide the fact that I've slipped my hand into my pocket to feel the smooth surface of my lighter. "I have nothing to say."

He hums to himself, pinching his brows together as if bemused. His flare for dramatics rivals Blaze's. "I received the same feedback from your teachers. In fact, they had some interesting things to say. Do you know what they're saying?"

My father would crush a man like him without even moving his pinky. His poor attempt at playing politics is laughable. "You're going to tell me anyway."

He purses his lips but continues, "They tell me there is only one person you interact with inside the classroom—but I've been advised she has been the one picking on you. Also, they find your relationship with Liam outside of class interesting."

"Okay."

"Tell me, how did your friendship with Liam start?"

"He asked to hang out. I said yes." That's quite literally the start and the end of the story. The skinny, ghoul-looking kid saw my tattoos, glanced at the lighter, and asked if I was a snitch. I said no; he said he and some friends hang out off campus to *chill* if I wanted to hang out. Leaving school property to get high sounds precisely like the klepto's thing to do. So, after a prompt "yes," we were behind the church, and I was face-to-face with Blaze. He's been my "in" ever since.

"Yet you turned down Sarah when she asked you to prom." He says it like a question rather than a statement.

Sarah Lawrence is a snitch. Noted.

"Your point?"

He narrows his eyes just a fraction before adopting a more blase composure. "How's Miss Whitlock treating you? Outside of class, that is."

After class? He doesn't want the answer to that one. Neither he nor Blaze needs to know that last night wasn't the first time I found myself in her room. So, I settle for an easy "Amicable."

"You and I are both aware of what she's been accusing you of."

You and half the school.

I nod.

He scrutinizes every inch of me, and I do the same to him, analyzing his crow's feet and the knockoff Givenchy tie. "Do you have anything to add about it?"

"Do I need a lawyer?" I counter.

Any semblance of friendly comradery disappears from his face and tone. "Your father expressed concerns about you and Marie's acquaintance. He was unaware that you had some kind of relationship with her, and is rightfully worried about the influence someone like Blaze might have on you." Everyone's persistence in using every name but her first irks me—her grandfather's doing, I'm sure. She's Blaze when she needs to be demoralized, and Marie or Miss Whitlock when they need to feign respect. "I'm sure you understand that men your age can be very impressionable to beautiful young women."

Keeping my features neutral, I grip the lighter in my pocket. I don't like this degenerate's choice of words to describe Blaze, and I *especially* don't like how he says them.

I haven't figured out why he has an interest in Blaze, though I understand the logic in linking me with her *accusations*, as he puts it.

Something about it doesn't sit right with me, and I can't pinpoint why. I don't trust McGill, and that's the only reason I haven't done anything to land Blaze's ass in solitary, where he has easier access to her. There, no one would care if she screamed.

The silence stretches between us when he finally says, "I was willing to give your lack of response a slide the last time I asked you. Now that you're settled in and the first day jitters are gone, tell me more about your relationship with Marie."

The lighter digs into the palm of my hand. She isn't an old fucking woman, and that's not her goddamn name.

"Nothing to tell."

His exhale reaches me from across the desk. "That's clearly not the case, now is it? You may have had your parents fooled, but nothing happens in this school without me knowing. I hear about the way you watch that girl."

It's becoming increasingly hard to stop from lunging forward and slamming his head on the table. He needs to keep her name out of his mouth before I do it for him. "In case you missed it, she threatened to shiv me."

"And you believe it?"

"She thinks I burned her house down," I explain. The man is like a bloodhound.

"That may be so, however, we both know that wasn't the look I was referring to."

"Spell it out."

"You two are more alike than I realized," he says more to himself than to me. "It appears I need to ask frankly because you're so insistent on going around the question. It's clear the house fire has made her rather aggressive toward you, which begs the question: did you and Miss Whitlock have a relationship?"

"No."

"Claims were made by teachers at your previous school that you were often seen walking together after school. Miss Whitlock herself confirmed it. Other than that, you weren't interacting with the other students. I have to ask, why were you walking when you had a car, Mr. Osman?"

"Fresh air," I say through gritted teeth.

I spent years walking her home because I didn't want her to get run over by a car because she was too hungover to notice her surroundings, only to risk killing her in the fire. She could have been passed out inside and I missed her. Or she could have crawled in just before everything went up in flames.

If she had died... I grip the lighter tighter, knuckles turning white. Blaze's near-death is the only thing I'm sorry for.

I won't apologize for what I did because that house held nothing but trauma, but I deserve what she did to my place.

It's pathetic actually; the first thought that went through my head when I came home to see the damage was disappointment. Blaze was finally in my bedroom and I hadn't been there to see it.

I bet it was a sight to see. All that red making its way through my room, breaking everything in its path—chaos unbidden.

However, the scales are still nowhere near even.

McGill's nostrils flair. "It's my job to know my students and understand everyone's relationship dynamic to ensure they get the most out of their time here. Individuals like Blaze tend to... *negatively* impact your growth and progress." He leans forward, resting his forearms on his desk. "You'll forgive me if I find it difficult to believe that a recluse such as yourself would choose to make that wild child your only acquaintance."

"What's your point?"

"We are simply trying to get to the bottom of the situation. There are certain standards and expectations from our students, just as there are from your family."

This.

This is exactly why I've kept my mouth shut. It's why I only ever interacted with Blaze outside of school. Social standing is everything to these vultures, and money can go far to achieve it. My father could take Blaze out in a single swipe; send her to prison, kick her out of school, or move her to an entirely different state. There is no end to the lengths he would go to protect the Osman name.

An Osman and a Whitlock are fine. Blaze is just the wrong Whitlock.

She is the start and the end of the reason why I've turned into my brother's bitch. Kiervan knew what my father would do, and by second grade, I had already decided it was worth it to do everything he said.

"What did Blaze say?" I ask.

"She says a lot of things." He takes a sip of water, pausing for dramatic effect. "She claims you asked her if she would be home the day of the fire, then the next morning, you told her she deserved it."

I grind my molars together. That's not what I meant by saying she deserved what was coming for her.

"I'm curious why she would make such accusations against you. My theory is that she was smitten by you, and you rightfully turned her down because she's too much of a liability. Then she decided to get back at you—correct me if I'm wrong."

That's the running theory held by everyone who's heard her story. As McGill said, I'm a loner. The only person I speak to is Blaze. So, with their small-minded logic, it's the only plausible justification.

I don't need her smitten by me. I don't need her fawning all over me and falling to kiss the ground I walk on. Fire has no master. Blaze is no different. If I wanted a dog, I would have gotten one.

McGill looks at me, waiting for a response that never comes. "Fine, have it your way. Don't answer. I'll figure it out eventually." He lowers his voice as if telling me a secret. "I will give you this one piece of advice, son, and you'll do well to heed it: stay away from Miss Whitlock."

"Fine."

Not a fucking chance.

BLAZE

CHAPTER 9

Who the fuck thought group therapy was a good idea? None of these pretentious assholes are going to spill family secrets in front of ten other people. And I sure as hell don't want any of these people knowing shit about me—especially Kohen, who's sitting directly across from me in our circle.

We've been glaring at each other since we sat down, and I can feel myself becoming increasingly amped by his presence. Even though I felt like I had the upper hand before, I now think I've lost it. He could tell them about the church as retaliation for what I moaned last night. He could open his mouth and say that Elijah is giving me drugs, and I'm whoring myself out for them. What if he catches me stealing and reports me? I don't want to lose my privileges. I've been too careful for him to throw it away, and I've enjoyed having a pillow and a blanket.

I don't trust him one bit, not after he said all that shit about how much he apparently knows me and now, can access my room whenever he wants.

But he was wrong. I don't want or need people to listen to me. I'm perfectly content on my own. Here, no one is letting me down or pissing me off. No one is calling me a liar or belittling me to the point I start to question my own sanity.

Alone is where it's good.

Alone is where it's safe.

Drishti, one of the counsellors, has her "active listening" face on as Liam regales the group about the time he was so high, he broke into a mom-and-pop store to beat up a mannequin because he thought it was an alien.

Aaron speaks next, talking faster than I can comprehend and answering more than Drishti was asking him.

Their voices echo through the room, bouncing against the vaulted ceiling, making each word sound ominous and foreboding. Centuries-old paintings hang on the walls between posters of bumper-sticker-type quotes like "Be the person you want to be." The heating has been cranked up to full blast to stave off the perpetual chill of the stone structure, but it does nothing to warm my frozen bones and chattering teeth.

Kohen shifts in his seat and I glare at him. Seriously, what the fuck is Kohen doing in this school?

There are two fancy reform schools in this country where all the rich people send their kids: Seraphic Hills and Westwood Grove, a couple states away. Word on the street is desperate parents and the state sends the real crazies to Seraphic, and the students at Westwood get hand massages instead of a slap on the wrist. I hear they also have this wild concept that isn't practiced here. It's called *free time*. The pretentious kids at Westwood don't have to attend group therapy sessions or wake up at five in the morning to do military drills either—which went wonderfully yesterday morning when I "accidentally" threw up on Sarah's $4,000 backpack. Such a shame, really, because I hear stomach acid doesn't mix well with dyed leather.

Fuck Face keeps crashing these group sessions. I'm really not sure which part of Kohen screamed "I'm an addict" to Drishti. They never said as much, but this is the addicts' group. Every person who frequents the back of the church is here, either feeling as hungover as I did yesterday or keyed up like I do now. Ergo, Kohen doesn't belong here since the only thing he is addicted to is being a prick and lighting things on fire—and for the love of God, why would I talk about my problems when the reason I'm in this place is sitting right in front of me?

"Blaze." Drishti, the only semifriendly staff member in this entire school, drags my attention away from Kohen.

At the same time I look at her, Charlie starts sputtering on a cough from beside me, choking on her hair. I reach over, yank her hair out of her mouth, grab her single-use drink bottle, and shove it in her hand. Might as well empty it now before she turns it into a bong later. The simple movement makes me wince as my muscles scream in protest like they do after every comedown.

Kohen is right about one thing; I'm turning more and more into my mother, and I hate it. No wonder my grandfather couldn't care less if I live or die. He's probably rubbing his hands together, cackling menacingly, waiting for the day Mom and I eventually kill ourselves off so he can stop bleeding money for us. That's why he refused to pay to fix anything around our house.

I bet my cousins know what his smile looks like and what my grandma's baking tastes like—if she even bakes. They all hate my mother because of what she does. They hate me because I'm my mother's daughter.

"Blaze," Drishti repeats, setting her scrupulous attention on me. "Why don't you tell us how your week has gone?"

"Not interested."

She purses her lips. "There was a lot on your mind last week, and your answer was the same. These sessions enable open discussion and mediation, free of judgment. It benefits you and the rest of your peers so that they can better understand you. If you feel this sort of structure is not suited to you, I and Dr. Van der Merwe can look into how we might be able to support you in being the best young woman you can be."

Translation: You used your *get out of jail card* last week, and you're going to start talking or else you're in with the doc doing whatever treatment he recommends.

Aka, they're either shoving CDC-approved drugs down my throat while forcing me to talk to old bones Van der Merwe for an hour, or they'll give me a lobotomy. I'm doubtful about the last option, but you hear rumors. Who knows what happens in the basement near Dr. Van der Merwe's room—or, as the students call it, the Dungeons.

"Good to know," I gripe.

Charlie chokes again. I whip my attention to her and roll my eyes. Drishti runs over to pat her back like it might do something.

Honestly, it's probably a hairball. She'll cough it up eventually.

Come to think of it, maybe if Charlie starts choking for real, I'll suggest she requires the Heimlich maneuver, and then we can all leave on account of being traumatized by her near-death experience.

Unfortunately, she recovers too soon, so I have no choice but to settle back in my seat and cross my arms.

Drishti resumes her position within the circle. "Blaze, how about you tell us how you've been feeling lately? I hear you've been having more trouble staying focused in class." Oh great. What's next? Is she going to start sharing my grades too? "What do you think is the cause of the change?"

"Hmm, I wonder." This chick is either daft or the biggest snake at this zoo. She's read my file. "Couldn't be... oh, I don't know. How about the fact that the asshole who burned my house down is sitting right there?" I point to Kohen and raise my voice at the last sentence.

He just watches me. He doesn't flinch or smirk. He doesn't hold his breath or show even a shred of remorse over what he's done. Nothing. He looks at me like I'm not worth a single thought in that screwed-up head of his.

"Blaze, please sit down and lower your voice," Drishti says. I didn't even realize I was standing. "We've been over this; Kohen had no part in what happened that night."

"I'm not making it up!" I scream.

It doesn't matter how often I tell them what Kohen said; not a single person believes me. He's as guilty as they come, and doesn't have the decency to say it to my face.

"That motherfucker right there destroyed my childhood home, and you're asking me why I'm distracted in class? Are you kidding me? He took *everything* from me." All I had was the uniform I was wearing, my coat, and my backpack. Everything else perished in the flames because of *him*.

Nothing is waiting for me once I'm out of here. My mother hasn't checked on me once, and my father probably doesn't even know that

I'm alive. Grandpa will be glad that he doesn't need to try to keep me alive. I have no money for food, let alone college. Nowhere to sleep that isn't a shelter in the bad part of town. No job prospects. I have nothing going for me, and it's too late to do anything about it.

At least before, I felt comfortable knowing I had a house to sleep in. I could have gotten a dead-end job in town with St. Augustine written on my CV. It wasn't much, but it was *something*.

"Your inappropriate language will not be tolerated," Drishti snaps. "Sit down, Blaze."

I ignore her, my focus solely on the man in front of me—the man who had the *audacity* to dangle his money in my face just to mock how screwed up my life is.

"Why the fuck aren't you saying anything? I trashed your house. I destroyed your precious artwork and your entire room—your clothes, collections, trophies, everything that mattered to you." I want him to scream at me, accuse me of being a liar, say that he's above my lunacy, anything. Instead, his gaze drops to my neck, then to his ring around my thumb. "You ruined my life—you took *everything* from me, all my memories, any kind of cash I had, *all of it*—and now you want to fuck up even more by showing up here too?"

I can lie to myself all I want and say I won the battle by calling out Kiervan's name, but it's nothing in the grand scheme of things. I can win as many battles as I want; there will never be a war that I can win against Kohen.

He's the one with money. *He's* the one with power. He may be the family's black sheep, but people still look at him with respect. When he opens his mouth, people listen. When he does something, people watch with interest. They don't look at him because they're scared of him. They don't look at me because they don't want to.

"Miss Whitlock, that's enough—"

I move without realizing, shoving my face in front of his. "You haven't even denied it! Look me in the eyes and tell me you didn't do it. Tell me that I'm a piece of shit whore whose brain is so fried that I burned my own house down." My eyes burn with unshed tears. I haven't cried about that night, and I refuse to do it in front of him. "Look me in the eyes and tell me you were hoping you'd kill me that night."

Finally, he flinches. It's so small that I would have missed it if I hadn't been watching him for any reaction. He doesn't give me more than that.

"Say something!" A single tear rolls down my cheek, and he watches as it descends down the column of my throat.

Silence. That's all I get from him.

"*Blaze*, I'm going to tell you one more time—"

His head whips to the side from the force of my slap. I do it again. And again. And again. And he lets me. "Tell me, you fucking coward! Tell me!"

I'm ripped away from him before my palm collides with his face once more, and I scream. I cry out like I haven't had the chance to let it out since that day. I scream because I mourn for all the things I had, want, and never will have.

Before I get the chance to utter another word or throw the guards off me, a sharp pain radiates through my neck.

Everything goes black.

Hazy white light assaults my retina when I blink, causing me to squeeze my eyes closed. Somewhere around me, I hear murmurs. I can't tell if it's right beside me or in the distance. Then everything fades out again.

A jolt knocks me awake, but I don't open my eyes. One by one, different aspects register. A rhythmic rattling, the sway of my body, the hard surface beneath me, a tightening around my body, and hushed conversation.

I open my eyes. The room is still empty except for a man in a white coat standing with his back to me. My eyelids droop closed when they become too weighted to keep open, and the next time I wake up, the room is empty, and my skin feels too heavy and tight. I notice the machines this time as an overpowering sterile scent hits my system.

When I close my eyes, I don't wake up again until I hear beeping, and pressure builds around my arm to the point that it's almost painful.

Wincing, I peel my eyes open just in time to see a woman write something down on a clipboard. I try turning my head to see what's around my arm, but I can't.

The fog in my head makes it impossible to comprehend anything happening. I can make out shapes and people, but not what, who, or, most importantly, why I'm here. And where *here* is.

I groan, trying to move my head up or down or side to side, but it doesn't budge an inch. The same goes for my arms and legs. Try as I might, my shoulders and hips are also stuck in place. Panic sinks its teeth into my bones, and my attempts grow more frantic. What is happening to me?

"Oh. You're awake. That's poor timing."

I blink, trying to register who the old man in front of me is. I know him from somewhere... Dr. Van der Merwe?

Slowly, I take stock of the room. White walls; plastic, blue countertops; white cupboards; blinding white machines; a blacked-out, reflective window. My nose wrinkles from the medicinal scent of the room as I try to take in steadying breaths.

I swallow to clear away the sandpaper in my throat. "Where am I?" At least, that's what I try to say. The words come out too garbled to make sense of.

The panic kicks into hyperdrive as the fog clears away and the bindings seem to tighten, suffocating me. Anxiety hits me with full force, growing claws and wings, turning my stomach inside out as I thrash as hard as my body will allow. But God, I'm so tired. Every one of my muscles is fatigued to the point of failure. The adrenaline rushing through my system isn't enough to do more than jar the bed, but I keep going, fighting off the need to close my eyes and let darkness take hold.

Various wires connect to stickers all over my chest, ankles, wrists, and head. I manage to get the monitor on my pointer finger off, but the blood pressure monitor remains firmly around my bicep.

Oh God. Oh God. Oh God.

"What are you doing to me?" I cry out, pulling at the bindings around me.

I'm distantly aware of the beeping growing faster, but I can't figure out what it is except that I need to get out. I need to get these buckles off me.

"Undergoing a treatment plan," Dr. Van der Merwe says simply like it's the most obvious thing in the world. I'm in the medical wing, and it's clear they have every intention of restraining me for whatever fucked-up procedure they have planned. What isn't clear is the *why*?

"No, let me go." My attempts at sounding strong are out the window. I can barely breathe, and I'm pretty sure the tears stinging my eyes have something to do with whatever they injected me with.

He sighs and folds his hands in front of a clipboard, highlighting the scrubs he's wearing underneath his lab coat. "That decision is not up to me."

"You're a fucking doctor. I have the right to refuse medical treatment!"

This can't be happening. I didn't agree to any of this! They were meant to give me pills or get me to attend more therapy sessions, not *this*—whatever this is.

Despite knowing it's useless, I still pull at my restraints.

"Unfortunately, I cannot let you out, nor can I listen to your refusal of treatment." Dr. Van der Merwe says with an air of disinterest as if this is all a waste of his time. He places the file on my legs, a silent mockery of my inability to kick it off me.

"Yes, you fucking can," I growl, fighting back the tears that are so eager to spill. "I'm eighteen!"

"None of that matters, Miss Whitlock." My heart shatters hearing what I know. I yank at the ties as he pulls out a bundle of paperwork from the file, holding it right in front of me. "Tell me what you see."

I narrow my eyes to the scrawling swirls at the bottom of the paper. Bile rises up my throat as I choke out, "My signature."

The shrink pulls the paper away and gives it a quick glance like he's double-checking its contents. "That's correct. I'm assuming you did not read the contents of the documents before waiving your rights to make decisions during your stay at Seraphic Hills."

"Cut to the chase, old man." Neither he nor the nurse writing away in the clipboard react to the venom in my voice. Why be scared of the snake locked in a glass box?

He gives me a half smile like this is all friendly conversation and not at all like he's explaining my death sentence to me. "Your appointed power of attorney has the right to make all decisions on your behalf concerning your health, welfare, and finances. In other words—in case that was too complicated for you—your grandfather requested an alternative course of treatment, and he believes that it is worth trialing."

"Then I revoke my waiver. I'll sign it right now." Simple. We can end this right now.

My faux confidence doesn't even fool me.

"That's not how this works."

Famous last words. If it were that easy, I wouldn't be in this school. If I could dictate the terms of my life, I would have left a long time ago, not beg my grandfather for food and money just because he didn't let me get a job.

From the corner of my eye, the nurse starts playing with one of the machines, causing it to flicker and beep. "Stop it." I jerk against the restraints, slowly fighting off the pull of sleep. The line into my arm swings with the movement. "What are you doing?"

"Finally, Miss Whitlock," Dr. Van der Merwe says with sickening excitement, "you're asking the right questions. Do you know what ECT stands for? No? I didn't think so. Electroconvulsive therapy."

My heart claws up my throat, and I feel like I'm choking on it. I have no idea what that is, and I don't think I want to know.

"It's a delivery of a pulsed electric current to the brain to induce a seizure while you are under general anesthesia for therapeutic purposes. Despite the high levels of stigma, it's proven highly effective in assisting some abnormalities in brain functionality." He adds quietly, "Although it's been years since I've delivered this treatment regimen, and technology has advanced since."

I'm going to be sick. "You're not going to knock me out. You're not going to do any of that. I refuse." None of this can be legal, right? Even if it isn't, I can't afford a lawyer—especially not one that would go up against my grandfather.

"That's correct. We will not be administering anesthesia today even though it is an ethical requirement of the treatment." He gives me a sickening half smile, causing all the color to disappear from my skin. "It's an added expense that your grandfather does not want to finance, seeing as this is not covered under your insurance. However, your grandfather was kind enough to provide you with muscle relaxants."

"Let me go, or I'll report you to the medical board the second I'm out of here." There's no keeping the desperation out of my tone. It comes pouring out, fast and pathetic, as if my life depended on it.

"There's another issue you have that is not included in any psychology manual." He watches me hopelessly. "No one ever believes you—consider it a formal diagnosis, Miss Whitlock. Evidence is everything, and the evidence we have against you is... it's damning, to say the least."

"Get fucked, you disgusting piece of shit," I spit, using every bit of power to stop the tears that want to fall. It's the only minute shred of dignity I have left, and I'll do anything I can to hold on to that useless power.

Any semblance of warmth falls from his face, replaced with cold calculation. "Insulting me will not change the outcome of the next hour. In fact, I would go as far as to say that it is in your best interest

148

to convince me that you're an exemplary vision of what is expected of a woman your age." He takes the binder off my legs and pulls a stool from under the bed to sit on. "Do you know what ECT treats?"

"I don't give a shit. *Let me out of here!*" I scream the last part as loud as I can. Surely, someone can hear me. A guard, maybe. Or a teacher. Maybe another student. But what's the point? None of them will come to my rescue.

"Severe depression, severe psychosis, aggressive tendencies related to dementia, and catatonia," Dr. Van der Merwe explains.

"I have none of those."

"I'm aware."

My lips part. "Then why are you doing this?"

"Because Mr. Whitlock said so, and this is a relatively low-risk procedure." He shrugs. "This could have all been avoided. You see, ECT is a treatment for patients who have not found adequate success with talking therapy and medication. It's clear with your aggression, drug use, and compulsive tendencies, further treatment is required. Your grandfather and I agree that the risk of the treatment's side effects does not outweigh the risk of no treatment. Simply put, you threaten your safety and everyone else's."

He meticulously checks the stickers on my temples and forehead, then adds the attached cords. I try to track his movements as much as possible without moving my head, but he goes out of sight too quickly.

"You can't do this," I breathe, looking at the nurse, pleading for her to do something. But not once does she look my way. "You have to stop this."

The nurse stations herself and her clipboard beside the blood pressure and heart rate monitor. Dr. Van der Merwe rolls backward in his chair toward the machine she was playing around with earlier, and adjusts the dials according to the piece of paper beside him. "Consider this your first beneficial contribution to society. If this works on you, it's further proof that there is no limit to medical advancement."

My hands shake as I curl my fingers into a fist, thrashing around in a last-ditch effort. "No, no, no. I'll be good, I swear. Please! I—I'll stop. I won't steal anymore. I won't talk to Kohen anymore. I won't do anything! Please—I promise."

"It's too late for any of that, Blaze." He gives me an almost solemn look as his finger hovers over an orange button. "This should only hurt for a moment."

Bright white pain surges through me, and my mouth opens with a silent scream. My muscles contract as electricity rips through my veins.

Then, everything ceases to exist.

KOHEN

CHAPTER 10

I tuck the pen back behind my ear as I stick to the shadows, moving toward the other side of school. My backpack is only a fraction heavier than it was before my trip to the girls' dorms. Stealing isn't for me, yet I can't count how many times I've had to do it because of Blaze.

She wasn't at dinner, and Charlie claims the last time she saw Blaze was when she lost her shit at me. Am I really so bad that she'd rather be in solitary?

Word on the street is that solitary is Blaze's second home. She's the reigning champ for most stays in the shortest amount of time. Can't say she doesn't have any skills.

An access card gets me into the wing containing Dr. Van der Merwe's office; from there, it isn't hard to find the solitary rooms. They only have a skeleton crew of staff at this time of night, and the med wing never sees a soul except for the unfortunate ones locked in solitary.

The rooms are easy enough to find. They're aptly hidden behind a set of doors where no one would be able to hear them screaming. Their usual trick is to lock people in their bedrooms as punishment, but solitary is reserved for the extra-problematic students—the ones who get into fights, hit the teachers, or were caught with drugs on them.

The students are still sent to class, but from what I hear, the issue is with the stillness of the room—and the fact that their only form of entertainment is schoolwork and writing lines.

There are six doors on either side of the hallway, and one down at the very end. All the lights are off, so I have to peer into the small glass to figure out which slice of hell she has all to herself. Once I spot the klepto in the only occupied room in the building, I hover the card over the reader.

She looks so peaceful like this, curled up on the bed, oblivious to the fact that I'm fixated on everything that she is. My eyes follow the harsh curve of her hips, to her waist, then over the rise of her shoulders.

Sometimes this is my favorite version of her. When she's asleep like this, she can't look at me with so much hatred or tell me all the reasons why I will never be enough for her. I can just look at her without waiting for her to point fingers at me or tell me to fuck off.

The latch beeps as it unlocks, and I help myself into the room. Shutting the door behind me, I catalog the single bed pushed against the wall, the toilet and basin in the other corner, and the table and stool that are fastened to the floor. The only source of light comes from the moonlight on the other side of the frosted windows, and I take the moment to appreciate the sight of her up close.

Her back is to me, and her entire body is concealed beneath the thin sheet, but I would recognize her anywhere. The fact she isn't snoring like she's trying to wake the dead is enough of a sign that mini-Satan is awake. I'm more shocked than I care to admit that she hasn't started screaming at me to get out or continue with her demands from earlier today.

I drop the backpack full of food and water by the door. "A padded door? How fitting for you."

"Leave me alone," she croaks without turning to face me.

"So you do like the solitary aspect of confinement?" I bite my tongue to stop from saying something worse. Just once it would be nice to have her happy to see me—or at least *sound* it.

Something heavy settles in my gut. This isn't her usual reaction. She's more likely to throw things at me or attempt to rip my esophagus out. But to ask me to leave so… tiredly?

I shorten the distance and pull her onto her back by her shoulder, making her whimper in the process.

The sight that greets me is worse than any tone she's used on me and all the colorful ways she's told me to fuck off. What the fuck happened? Her eyes are sunken, and there's a pinch between her brows like she's staving off a headache. She wraps her arms around her middle with a curl of her lip.

"What's wrong?" I place my palm against her forehead and then her neck, checking for a fever she doesn't have. Her skin isn't clammy. She isn't tensing her jaw or gnawing it, has no shivers, no ticks, or nose twitching, and her breathing doesn't sound harsh.

But she's cold.

Too fucking cold.

155

It can't be drugs because she couldn't have gotten anything after they took her, and the haloperidol or benzodiazepine wouldn't have done this to her unless she's allergic—which, after almost three months in this place, I'm sure they would know which antipsychotic she's allergic to. "What happened to you?"

I swear her bottom lip quivers. "You did."

They're only two words, but they hit me like a sucker punch to the gut. "You're the one who was stupid enough to hit me in front of everyone."

She even cried today. Blaze has done many things, but in all my years of knowing her, she's *never* cried. Not when she broke her arm falling off the swing in second grade or when no one showed up to pick her up from her first day of middle school. And here she was today, in a room full of people, shedding a tear.

"No, *you* caused all of this," she hisses. Another whimper passes her lips as she pulls herself onto her elbows, raises her chin, and ignores her shaking arms. "The whole reason I was sent to this place was because of what *you* did."

Anger slices through me. I try to be nice to her, and this is what she does? "If it wasn't for me, you'd be dead."

She jolts, rolling onto her side to end up on her hands and knees, swaying as she does it. "Ding dong, your opinion is fucking wrong." Her words are slightly slurred.

I frown as I take in the hospital gown and gripped socks they've dressed her in. Seriously, what the fuck happened? It doesn't look right seeing her like this—and why is it so cold in here?

I cradle the back of her head, instinctively wrapping my arm around her waist, offering support as I silently hope that she might absorb even the slightest bit of warmth from me. As expected, she hits me weakly to get away. When will I do anything right in her eyes?

"I'm over listening to you talk about things you don't understand. You want to take away everything that's important to me, then fine. So be it. You have. The only two things I give a shit about are you and that ring you've been wearing on your finger."

She's irresistibly close, almost intoxicatingly so; a slight lean would be enough to taste those cherry lips again.

Blaze's eyes search mine like she's waiting for the punchline. I've seen her hungover more times than I can count, but I've never seen her as vulnerable as she is now, with her eyes glistening against the pale moonlight and the shadows circling her sockets. She looks like she's been hit by the fucking plague.

Everything she said earlier was wrong. I'd kill myself before I'd kill her. Ever since we were kids, she always thought I hated her when I was just trying to get her to like me. After a while, I hated her for hating me and being so fucking dense, not understanding my intentions. By the time I was old enough to realize the fault in my logic, the damage was done.

It's one of the many reasons why I hate Kiervan. Even as a kid, he understood how people work, but for the life of me, I couldn't understand why Blaze didn't like me. The harder I tried, the more she hated me.

Kiervan knew that girls don't like when you burn their hair because you want to show them how pretty they are. He understood that they don't like when you steal their things just because you want to bring a part of them home. Or break into their house to show her that you want to hang out and understand her better. Or give her a dead bird because you know how much she likes birds. Or *chase her through the fucking woods with a bat.*

So I got better, *careful.* Doing things that wouldn't hurt her, and I almost killed her because of it. Blaze could have burnt my house into a cinder and leveled it to the ground, and she still wouldn't have destroyed the one thing I actually care about.

Even now, I'm still pissed at her for not understanding. She's so caught up in her own mess that she still has no idea what I've gone through for her. And she doesn't even give a shit about me. In fact, she prefers everyone *but* me, when I was the one doing *everything* to keep her out of prison.

Does she think it was her grandfather's decision to send her to reform school?

No.

I got her here.

I've taken on more of Kiervan's coursework, and let our parents believe that I'm the reason some of their watches and jewelry were unaccounted for after Blaze's rampage—not that Kiervan's pawned it off. I agreed to *everything* he asked for, and in exchange, he'd convince our father not to press charges and exploit the Whitlock's investment bank instead. I'm still doing Kiervan's bidding because my father can think of a hundred ways to get her out of this school and into a federal prison.

Yet here Blaze is, actively trying to get herself kicked out.

Her lips thin into a straight line. "I stole the ring from you."

I lower my head to hers, forcing the irritation out of my voice to make the words flow as smoothly as possible. "Do you think I spent over ten years keeping it safe from your sticky fingers just to leave it on my desk when you and a school full of wannabe criminals were all around me?"

This is it.

This is the moment she realizes that her place has always been by my side and that everything that came before this moment was always for her. She'll finally open up to me and tear down the walls she's put up around herself.

She pales in the darkness, then scrambles out of my hold as if I've burned her. "Then you can take it back. I don't want anything from you when you've already done enough damage."

The disappointment that clutches my chest is gut-wrenching. My fingers curl into a fist as I look down my nose at her. "You have no idea what I've done because you're too blind to understand a fucking thing."

"Then tell me. Or don't tell me." She shakes her head and pulls the white sheet over her legs. "Either way, there's not a single fucking thing you've ever done that could make me hate you more than I hate you right now. You're a monster, a demon worse than the man who spawned me. Worse than the men you share your blood with."

I shake my head, breathing hard through my nose. "No, stop. Stop talking."

"Keep your head shoved up your ass, Osman. If you think I'm blind, you don't know a damn thing. So, I'm saying it again. This?" She waves at herself, and suddenly all I can see is the Band-Aid at the juncture of her elbow. "This is all your fault."

"*What did they do to you?*" I grab her arm and rip the tape off, ignoring her fight. Sure enough, a bloody, deep purple dot is right on top of her vein. "What the fuck did they inject you with?"

She snatches her arm back and rises to her knees on the bed in a pathetic attempt to equalize our height. "Your parents were right to pick your brother over you. I'd wake up every day and make the same decision."

My hand snaps out to wrap around her neck, and she's on her back against the bed before she can even blink. My body trembles as I remember all the times Kiervan wore a smug grin when he took his place above me. How my parents would ask me to stay in my room on Christmas mornings so I wouldn't see all the things he'd get. Or when people are told an Osman is coming, and the smile would fall from their face when I walk in.

Blaze's hate has no regard for status. She argued with Kiervan at school just as fiercely as with any other kid. She never chose him over me. Never asked for his presence instead of mine.

Then she goes and moans his fucking name.

And she says *that*.

I won't fight for someone who puts me in last place, just like everyone else does.

She wraps her fingers around my wrist, pushing it down against her throat.

I can't feel her pulse like this, only the movement of her Adam's apple and the vibrations of her vocal cords as she says, "Do it. Finish off what you started. *Kill me*."

Blaze's sterling-blue eyes watching me are colder than her old house during the winter months. The same fucking house I'd visit in the night just to make sure her parents hadn't taken another layer from her.

All that, and she still prefers Kiervan?

"There's no version of this where I won't spend my entire life making you feel even an ounce of what I feel, so you better kill me now, Kohen," she rasps against my hand, never once breaking eye contact. "Or are you too stupid to?"

I jump off her and run my fingers through my hair.

Fuck.

Fuck!

"I'm in this place because of you. *You!* Why don't you get that? Why don't you *ever* get that? I've told you over and over again that it's all been *you*. For you. Because of you. Always *you*. I failed all my classes last year just so I wouldn't get separated from you."

Her jaw drops dramatically with fake shock. It looks so wrong with the gauntness of her eyes. "Wow. So you'd fuck your own life up just to make mine hell?" Blaze scowls. "You're worse than I thought."

"Wrong again." I step forward to touch her again, but she jerks her head away before I can. "I did it because you're mine in every sense of the word, Blaze. You always were, and you always will be."

The sound of her scoffing sends my blood rushing through my body faster than I can handle. "Call Dr. Van der Merwe in again; the shit he did to me would be nothing in comparison." A sinister smile creeps across her lips that doesn't match her tired eyes. "Or maybe ask your brother to tell me the same thing, and I'll suck his dick so good he'll be addicted to me." She laughs to herself. "Or maybe I'll fuck your dad instead."

She doesn't get away fast enough to stop me from gripping the back of her neck. They aren't getting anywhere near her, and I've spent over half my life making sure of it. "They'd kill you."

Slowly, *so* slowly, she says with deadly quiet, "I'd rather be dead than be yours."

Everything stops.

My heart, my lungs, my blood. It all stops as I stare at her, the words repeating in my head over and over again.

My hand releases her before the rest of me does. I hold her stare

161

as I back out of the room, not breaking it until I slam the door behind me, then red bursts in front of my vision. She'd rather be dead than be with me. She'd rather fuck my own father than me.

Fuck her.

I'm slipping through the halls of the girls' dormitory and into Blaze's room without any plan or regard for what I'll do once I arrive. I want to burn this entire school to the ground just to see a decent fucking fire. I'm starved for the slightest flicker of a flame, but there's another soul-deep need that must be sated. Reaching into my backpack, I ignore all the snacks and drop the pair of school shoes I stole for her onto the ground next to the pile of boots and slippers.

I've done nothing for her? *Nothing*? Then what the fuck did I risk getting caught for? Why did I sort through Sarah's room looking for shoes Blaze can wear so she can stop wearing the tattered pair she's had for years.

Why did I raid the kitchen to bring her food in case they starved her?

But she wants my brother instead? *My father*?

The second my eyes fall onto the bed, I see her long legs tangled within the sheets and her perky nipples poking through the thin fabric. The thought has my cock hardening and pressing against my zipper.

My pants still feel soaked through from the way she rode my thigh; it's like the shape of her has been imprinted in my hand, and if I concentrate enough, I can still feel her warmth and hear the needy moans she made for me.

She can be sickened by me all she wants, hate every part of me that has turned me into who I am, but this isn't over. Whatever reality she's concocted where she ends up with anyone but me doesn't

162

matter.

Unbuckling my pants, I take my cock in my hand as I stand over her unmade bed. The first stroke has me grunting with primal need. I want to mark every inch of Blaze's space while imagining it's her on her knees and wrapping her slender fingers around my girth.

Her pussy would be dripping as she takes me in her hands, wishing I was abusing it and making her come like she knows only I can. I bet she'd love what I'd feel like down her throat.

Blaze can tell me she hates me and wants nothing to do with me; the reality is that her body knows what it wants, and it wants me.

How often do her pupils have to blow out every time I stand close before she realizes that she's been dreaming of getting my dick in her? The little minx was the one who pushed herself against my length when she was humping me. *She's* the one who bites her lip when she stares at my arms or looks at my hips for a beat too long.

My breathing comes out hard as I fist my cock, imagining her splayed out on the bed whimpering for me to fuck her. If she's been with Kiervan, I'll kill him then lock her up. I'll tie her to the damn bed if that's what it takes. I don't care. There's no hesitation about that. If she can't hate me more than she already does, I can't go any lower, right?

Does she think that I don't fucking hate her too? If I could get over this, I would have years ago. None of the shit I've gone through would have even happened if not for her.

She's lucky I've been as nice as I have after the stunt she pulled. Moaning my brother's name? Admitting that she'd happily give herself over to him? I could have gotten her on my lap or finally felt what she's so willing to give to anyone with drugs.

My grip tightens, and my movements become jerkier as I try to shove the image of her with someone else out of my head. The things I could do to that girl would make a nun have a heart attack. I'm not into exhibitionism, but maybe the next time Elijah thinks he can go near her, I'll fuck her brains out right in front of him. Or perhaps I'll keep her to myself, get her bent over a table and punish her for all the shit she's done.

I can picture it; the way she'd scream when I slide into her and how she'd claw at the table and arch her back to take more, even though she's at her limit. She'd scrape her long nails into the wood as her skirt bunches around her waist. I'd wind her long copper hair between my fingers and pull it back so I can feel her pulse hammer against my skin.

I pump my fist faster, delving into the fantasy as my balls tighten. Blaze would cry out her hatred for me at the same time she comes, and she'd do it all over again. Except she'd be up against a wall wishing I were dead as she kisses me with her legs around me.

Then she'd be curled on her side, taking every inch because she'll love how it hits her just right, and then she'd come all over again, and the name that comes out of her mouth will be mine. There won't be a single thought about any man in existence but me.

A feral, guttural sound slips from my throat as hot, white ropes of come shoot out, sending lightning zapping through my veins. The ribbons fall onto her sheets, drops spraying over her blankets and cheap cotton pillowcase.

I breathe heavily as I grab a pair of her panties from the top drawer. Using it to wipe my hands clean, I stare at the mess I've made over the place where she'll be sleeping in twenty-four hours.

What's that saying? She made her bed; she can lie in it.

BLAZE

CHAPTER 11

This is nothing like the times I've woken up hungover, like I've been out partying with Dionysus for three working days. For one, there's no nausea, and thank the *gods* there are no chills or muscle spasming.

I have a subtle, gnawing headache instead, and I feel like I ran fifty miles through the Arizona heat without pause. I think my heart might be missing a beat, but that may well be in my head. Apart from that, there's something even more off-kilter with my equilibrium than usual that I can't quite put my finger on.

Yesterday, I felt like death. Today, I feel like her counterpart: violence and loathing.

The soft drizzle of rain pebbles over my hair and the ugly orange umbrella I found in someone's open locker. I'm not sure how long the good doctor thinks it will take for me to miraculously be cured of my demons and become the picture-perfect image of an exemplary young woman who says her prayers, and considers what the bearded men upstairs will say about her actions when everything—every devilish impulse—is still alive and breathing.

Dr. Van der Merwe never gave me a ballpark figure. Placebo effect and all, I still don't think that shit is going to work. Well, at least today isn't the day for rebirth. Besides, I have a feeling there's a long road to recovery ahead of me, with no expressway to get there.

At least I'm guessing the treatment hasn't kicked in yet since I'm walking around school with a blowtorch in my backpack.

Mrs. Crichton from chemistry class writes down all the lock combinations in her diary. She's practically begging for someone to break into the room where the school keeps all its potions and elixirs.

It's truly marvelous that this school doesn't add more safety measures for cupboards containing items that would make a *stunning* insurance claim.

There's a little skip in my step as I move from class to class. Sure, the teachers look at me like I've gone crazy, and I keep feeling like someone is glaring laser beams into the side of my head, but this girl is on a deadline, and I am nothing if not an innocent princess going about her day.

And by deadline, I mean that on this rainy Thursday afternoon, right after track practice, my ass is going straight to my bedroom, where I'll hole up, leave for dinner, and nothing else. I won't even be leaving for any leisurely activities over the weekend.

Dr. Van der Merwe called it a probation period.

McGill gave the green light to the probationary period because, other than my meltdown, I was shaping up to be a reformed woman. Mainly, I simply didn't get caught until group therapy fucked me over once again.

For some reason—although, I'm sure it's a trap—the shrink thinks part of my treatment involves testing my ability to interact with my peers without acting out of line. I have a hunch there's been a memo that's gone around to encourage teachers to pit Sarah and Kohen against me.

Jokes on them; electrocuting me turned me into a brand-new person.

I even surprised myself when I took it in stride. My lips stayed sealed, and I rose above it. If I've got nothing nice to say, I will keep it to myself.

See, I'm now a woman of action. None of this "moaning another person's name" business. I'm playing the big game. If Kohen thinks the worst I've got is throwing things at his head, he has another thing coming.

The mud squelches beneath my new shoes as I head toward the groundskeeper's shed—not sure how these bad boys made it into my room, but they're mine now. They're a pinch too big, though nothing double-socking can't fix.

I also found some weird-ass stains on my bedsheets. I'm not sure what the hell that's about either. But that's a future me problem to clean.

I periodically survey my surroundings as subtly as possible to avoid seeming suspicious. Honestly, I'm going to need an Advil after this walk. My backpack has to be half my weight with all the stuff I've crammed in there, but the exhilaration makes me feel as light as a feather. I could get caught at any second, and it shouldn't thrill me as much as it does. What I'm about to do could also go very, very bad. And *shit*, if it doesn't turn me on a little.

What is life if I don't fuck around and find out? Dr. Fuck Face didn't agree to my promise and free me, so there's no agreement for me to reach.

First, I frame Kohen for a crime he didn't commit—preferably several of them.

Then, I borrow Charlie's phone, fuck Aaron, and snap a pic of him hitting it in doggy. The photo will somehow end up in Kohen's lap, and based on Aaron's build and skin color, the rumor mill will say that Kiervan came over on visitation day.

The second plan makes me sick to my stomach, but Kohen's face when he sees the picture will make every second worth it.

Once hidden behind a line of trees, I pull out a pair of men's sneakers I found lying around in the gym, then shove my feet inside. Walking with them on is a little awkward at first, and it's not exactly the most effective counterforensic measure, but it's enough to create the illusion that someone who doesn't have me-sized feet was here.

I do one more quick glance around at the rows of scattered trees and the gym in the distance, then book it to the old-people-green shed that's seen better days. Rust hems the edges of the tin structure, adding a pop of color to the eyesore tucked away at the corner of campus.

Slipping into the two feet of space between the boundary fence and the shack, I take stock of my surroundings once more. I don't usually care for wet weather, but boy, it is working for me today. All the groundskeepers are busy rewaterproofing the football stadium for tomorrow's semifinals, so this little slice of paradise is all mine.

My hot breaths plume in front of my face as I close the umbrella, balance my backpack against the wooden fence, and shove my hands into a pair of latex gloves. I peer into the backpack and internally wince. Mrs. Crichton's navy, knockoff designer purse is really shoved in there. It takes more energy than necessary to pull it out, and I accidentally rip the handle in the process.

Oops.

Shrugging to myself, I drop her bag onto the short grass, dig out the small blowtorch at the bottom, and then throw the shoulder strap back on.

I hear a sound in the distance and my muscles freeze. *Please don't be anyone. Please don't be anyone. Please don't be anyone.*

Holding my breath, I close my eyes to focus on the noise around my surroundings. No one can see me behind here, but I'll have a shit time trying to make a break back to school if a groundskeeper returns.

Slowly, I inch out from behind the shed to double-check that the coast is clear. When nothing but a couple birds flitter about, I launch back to my bag.

With my heart hammering in my chest, I reach into my pocket and throw Kohen's ring two feet away from the bag, so it's hidden beneath the grass in mud. But if someone were to look hard enough, they would be able to make out the reflection of the ominous sky against the silver.

I bite back a grin to stop myself from smiling like a lunatic. This is the perfect setup. Everyone knows Kohen has beef with Mrs. Crichton after he argued with her in chemistry about something she was apparently wrong about. She sent him to detention for it. Then he got a bad grade, and the argument they had was off the charts.

I tip Mrs. Crichton's bag upside down, watching her lipstick—and several other random items she has accumulated—fall and scatter onto the ground. Ripping up pages out of her diary, I tuck some in the zipper lining and stuff the main compartment full of scrunched-up pieces of paper.

The batteries I found in the science storage room are placed somewhere amongst the paper, as well as a spare phone I found in one of the drawers.

I let the smile spread across my face as I admire my handiwork. Polyester and PVC leather will already be a pretty mess. Add lithium batteries to the mix? A masterpiece.

I guess those science books were good for something after all.

My hatred for Kohen runs deeper than my fear of my grandfather and McGill's wrath. The seizures caused by the ECT might end up killing me, but I realize I don't fear death, only the idea that I might die without making a profoundly negative impact on someone's life.

Yes, Grandpa Jonathan, your little problematic princess is coming for you, guns blazing—emphasis on the *blaze*.

My racing heart roars in my ears as I light one of the ripped pages. Fire quickly climbs up the paper, consuming it in gold charcoal, undeterred by the misting rain that has made it into this alcove. I carefully drop the burning paper into the handbag and watch it catch on the next piece, then the next, then the next, spreading faster than I expected.

It's sad that I understand Kohen's fixation on the flames; they truly are beautiful in all their wildness and color. I'd stay longer if I didn't have an alibi I need to cement with Charlie. She agreed to say we were hanging out for the entirety of lunchtime in exchange for my silence about the other night when she knocked Liam out by throwing a loose brick at his head.

Loner Kohen will probably be finding his own corner of darkness to murder babies in or be mulling creepily around the school. Or, more accurately, he will not have a decent alibi for where he was when this particular fire happened.

The flames pick up their ferocity, crackling majestically. With one breath and an excited shiver, I throw the blowtorch into the bag and sprint back toward the school. I stumble as I take the sneakers off and chuck them into the trash can by the gym, then duck behind one of the pillars as the rain starts picking up.

I'll admit, I have no idea what's inside a blowtorch because the writing on the sticker has rubbed off, but the *bang* that echoes through the school is absolutely glorious. I don't think the shed will survive, and the fence will be an unfortunate tragedy.

I walk at a leisurely pace back to the dorm room where Charlie is eagerly waiting. No one bats an eye at my entrance, or seems phased by the sound of the explosion that happened a moment ago. I slide into the seat opposite Charlie and make a conscious effort to breathe slowly through my nose to calm my racing heart.

She glances up from her magazine, chewing on her bottom lip. "Is it done?"

I give her a tight nod in response. It's a mission not to laugh to myself and keep the displeased look I usually sport firmly on my face. "This school isn't big enough for two firebugs," I say.

"Phase one: complete."

I tap my leg. "It's time to commence phase two: fuck the other Osman."

A smile splits across her face, and she lifts her bottle up to me in cheers. "To the fall of Kohen."

Grabbing mine out the side of my backpack, I tap it against hers. "May he spend the rest of his life behind bars or in a grave."

"And that his dick game is as good as his smolder... and his cock is as big as the rest of him."

"*Charlie*," I scold.

She shrugs. "If you don't want to tap that, I will."

"Unbelievable," I mutter.

My lips curl into a smile. Play with fire, get burned.

KOHEN

CHAPTER 12

"The next time you pull a stunt like that, the consequences will be far more severe. You hear me?" McGill points a finger at my face.

I nod.

"You're lucky Mrs. Crichton agreed not to go to the police and thought four nights in solitary was enough for you to learn your lesson. You won't be so lucky next time."

He's said the same thing about eight different ways already. If he says it a ninth way, I'm going to test my luck.

This is all for appearance's sake, because he doesn't really believe I made that mini explosion four days ago. My file says I have aggressive tendencies toward men that result in my fists flying, not that I'm going to spend time in a lab cooking up a recipe to land me a one-way ticket to prison.

We both know who started the fire that burned down part of a fence and damaged the back of the shed. The only reason Blaze is not the one having this conversation with Headmaster Fifth-Divorce is because I admitted to it.

Four days ago, he dropped the signet ring on the table and everything fell into place from there. The lighter that was in my pocket was what made McGill doubt whether it really was her or not.

Brava, Blaze. Well played.

I didn't see it coming, and it's disturbing, yet unsurprising, how turned on I am by her form of retribution. If she had started the fire in front of me, I would have bent her over and taken her right then and there.

But no. I was stuck in a fucking room, going out of my mind for four goddamn nights. I was ready to put my head through the window. I don't know how she manages to survive that kind of life every few days.

I tap my fingers on my thigh, itching to feel Blaze's pulse thrum beneath my skin, to make sure she still *is* surviving. Unlike my grandfather all those years ago.

"Do you get what I'm saying?"

I nod, pretending I didn't just zone out to whatever rant McGill's gone on.

Apparently, I was lucky it was raining and the fire wasn't as destructive as it could have been. I'm also fortunate the torch didn't have much juice in it; if it did, the explosion would have been worse. Because of it, my parents have decided to cut my school spending allowance altogether—they don't know I've been cashing it out since I got here; buy food and clothes for other students using my allowance, and in return, they give me cash.

As long as they don't touch my trust fund, it's fine. That's my golden ticket. As soon as I get the pay out when I graduate, there's nothing left to tie me to the Osmans.

My grandfather used to tell me to take beatdowns like a man and know when to punch back. He was as ruthless as my father because he didn't care about respect or hierarchy. The only difference was my grandfather had a code of ethics on who to hit, when the strike comes, and how hard it'll strike.

I remember when he sat me down in his office after the school called him instead of my father about a fight I got into. A rusted shovel sat on the redwood table in his office, his curly salt and pepper hair cropped short against his scalp. Back then, I thought his impeccably fitted suit was like a uniform waiting to be handed down to me.

Creases lined his eyes like they held ancient wisdom ready to trickle down to me, and I hated every bit of it. Still, I was impatient for any slither of attention he was willing to grant. His dark eyes bored into me with neither disappointment nor affection; it was a warning that I now understand meant I should act more like my brother.

He told me I either acted like a dumbass or acted like an Osman, and to not get into fights with morons because they'll always find a way to dig their own grave. The secret to fighting an idiot isn't in the attack or the defense, but the foreplay of the fight, because only one of us has the means to lay out the scene.

I'm not the Osman fighter he wanted me to be, or the Osman man he tried grooming me into. But an Osman is one and the same as a moron. After all he said, he ended up dying in the grave he dug.

And above all, the beer-bellied man in front of me isn't intelligent or a fool: he's a pawn.

A pawn whose power comes from his mouth—which makes him

the worst pawn of all.

"See this as a life lesson not to take the blame for others when they wouldn't have done the same for you." An almost respectful— near prideful—look crosses McGill's face and it puts me on edge how much it reminds me of my grandfather. "Chasing tail might seem fun now, but three years later, you'll look back and regret all the hoops you threw yourself through just to please them. Trust me on this, son, it isn't worth it."

He can keep his trashy attempt at playing father figure. He's got enough kids of his own to let down. "Some people never learn from their mistakes," I say.

His eyes darken at the insult.

The warning bell rings, and I leave without being excused first. What's he going to do? Throw me back in solitary for going to class? I don't think so.

Blaze is already in her spot by the time I get to class. I instinctively reach into my pocket to feel the cold lighter, but it only makes me glare at her harder when I realize it isn't there. She throws me a fleeting glance before going back to her horrendous doodle. Does she expect me not to react to her blatant disregard of my existence after I took the fall for her ass? All signs point to her as the arsonist, and she has the audacity to look at me like I'm less than her?

There are two seats left in the room; one next to Sarah at the front and one directly behind Blaze. The former's eyes widen with hope, batting her lashes balefully as she sits up straighter. Sarah's brows scrunch in irritation when I choose to sit behind Blaze.

Taking my ring off, I drop it on Blaze's desk with a clatter and lean down to whisper in her ear, "Don't lose it this time." The murderous rage I feel coursing through my blood weaves its way into my voice, and it isn't nearly satisfying enough to watch her shiver beneath her uniform.

She's the lucky one here. If I had it my way, I'd take away her ability to walk—better yet, make her go nonverbal from how hard I'll fuck her after the stunt she pulled. The only two reasons Blaze is temporarily spared from either of those things is knowing that while I was sleeping on the rickety bed in solitary, she was getting all nice and cozy in her blankets—the same blankets that I painted with my come—and she doesn't even know it. Because even if she cleans her sheets, there's no getting rid of me from her mattress.

The other reason is something I haven't figured out yet. Something happened the day she lost her shit at me. It has something to do with McGill, but there's nothing that clearly indicates what it might have been beyond an antipsychotic. She was too chirpy the next day for it to have been a cold.

I slide into my seat behind Blaze and pull out my notebook, watching her slip the ring onto her finger as she leans back in her seat... until her hair is sprawled all over my desk. Swirls of copper and red cover my book, and I can't help it; I just... stop. I forget why I'm even angry.

I fight the urge for only a moment before I relent, weaving my fingers through her hair. *Spun silk*, that's what it feels like now. It used to be coarse and frizzy, dried at the ends from cheap shampoo, and flaky at the top from one too many benders in a row. Now, everything about her is coming to life. As much as I hate that we're both in here, reform school has done wonders for her.

Inch by inch, fiber by fiber, the tension in my back unwinds from the four days of wondering if she's still alive.

I spent all weekend itching to see the orange flicker of the flames and taste the ashen flavor of smoke on my tongue. But this is something else entirely.

Blaze stays there for over ten minutes, fidgeting with one thing or another, adjusting then readjusting herself in her seat, intentionally shaking her head so her hair moves across my desk. All the while, I stare at the dashes of red and threads of gold. If only I could see her piercing blue eyes, I'm positive they'd be wild and out of control as always.

The thrill seeker in her would have loved taking such a volatile element in her hands. *Fire.* It's fitting for her in every way.

She plays firebug, and I play thief.

Blaze forgets, two can play this game.

I tug out a pair of child-friendly scissors from my bag, grab a lock of her hair, and *snip.* Blaze whips around faster than I've ever seen her move. My lips quirk innocently as she gawks at me and the copper hair between my fingers. It's as if a switch flicks inside her, turning her cheeks violently red as she's brought to a boil.

Leisurely, I pull her hair tie off my wrist, holding her gaze while tying my new memento. "If you didn't want me to cut it, you shouldn't have waved your pretty red hair in my face."

Her hand flies up to cradle the back of her head. "You fucking psychopath!" she whisper-screams, her crimson blush accentuating the freckles along her cheeks.

I hold the lock of hair up. "*Thief,*" I correct. "*Klepto,* if you feel like misdiagnosing."

See, if the roles were reversed, I'd have reservations about Blaze having so much as a strand of my hair in her hands because I can picture her dabbling in dark magic. While I don't believe in its merits, I do believe in Blaze's ability to royally fuck something up so bad to the point that I might start worrying if there's going to be a clone of me out there.

She starts rifling through her hair, attempting to find the shortened lock. It's not as if she's going to miss it; she's got enough of it as it is. This is probably the first haircut she didn't give herself— really, she should be thanking me. Less weight on her head might make her think better.

"Miss Whitlock," the teacher calls, and I quickly tuck the souvenir into my blazer pocket.

Blaze snaps forward.

"A problem?" the teacher asks.

I cock a brow at the back of her head, watching the way her shoulder line goes rigid. If those gears in her head grind any harder, the whole class will hear them.

It's alright, you little shit. I know what you're thinking about.

Rat on me, don't rat on me.

Decisions, decisions.

Contrary to Blaze's usual *modus operandi*, she doesn't choose the path of most resistance. Much to my surprise, she crosses her arms and huffs a "No," then returns to whatever it was she was doing—probably her own version of anarchy. Except—and to no one's surprise—when the teacher switches her attention back to the whiteboard, Blaze twists around in her seat and growls under her breath, "Sleep with one eye open, Osman."

"Like you do?" I bite back a smug grin.

If it wasn't for all the shit she's pulled recently, I could almost die happy under those homicidal eyes. Her face is so beet-red, I'd almost feel inclined to call her cute—but the word is too mundane to describe what she is.

Alluring. Bewitching. Catastrophic. Certifiable.

Just to name a few.

A venomous little scorpion. Her eyes narrow into slits, and she tips her chin up in mock confidence. "I'm barricading my door so you can't get in."

"You have a window."

"It's a three-story building."

Pulling out the lock of hair from my blazer, I lean back in my chair and taunt her with it. My blazer lifts at the cuffs, uncovering the divot around my wrist from where her hair tie used to be.

Pity. I'll need to take another.

"Do you prefer I break down your door or your window? Don't say I never give you options, Thief."

"Maybe I'll break down *your* door. See how you feel about that, huh?"

I smirk. "I'll leave a blanket on the floor for you to sleep on. It'd still be a step up from what you're used to."

"*Marie,*" the teacher snaps.

Blaze glares at me one last time before fixing her gaze forward. "It's *Blaze,*" she grumbles under her breath.

One day, she's going to say "fuck it" with the world, and hell will have no fury. If she wasn't so fucking difficult all the time, I would've helped her out with that a long time ago. Alas, here we are, with her going in circles around her rusting cage, and me watching her go insane.

For the rest of the day, she makes a disturbingly conscious effort to avoid me, irritating me more than her shitty attempt to get back at me. McGill will be watching her from now on, waiting for the moment she slips up and puts her sticky fingers somewhere they shouldn't be... or inhales something that will get her suspended—both of which I have zero confidence she won't do.

I have no interest in being her babysitter or pulling her out of every mess she gets herself into, yet here I am, watching how her ass moves in her gym shorts as she climbs up the bleachers toward the huddle that includes Charlie, Liam, and dumb and dumber. Elijah and Aaron—the piece of shit who looks too similar to an Osman for my liking—glance over at my approaching redhead, eyes roving over her long legs. The hungry look they give her sets my teeth on edge.

Not only has she rolled her shorts up, she *had* to size them down. But if the rip and slight fading on the side is any indication, Jonathan either went secondhand with her uniform, or she went surfing through the lost property bucket for it.

The school knew the entire male student body would froth over the first sign of cleavage, because they'd made the girls' crew neck tight enough to choke. The moss-green gym shirt is unflattering at best. If Blaze had Sarah's budget, I'm sure she'd get the boxy sides taken in so her tits are pushed against the fabric.

"Hey, Kohen," Sarah says, lowering herself onto the seat.

I don't respond. The blonde is so persistent with her advances. It's annoying. Sarah seems to think that sitting two feet away from me when the rest of the gym is free will somehow convince me to take her to the mandatory ball.

Sneakers squeak against the wooden floors, and the pounding echo of a dribbling basketball and the grunts coming from the players are starting to do my head in, and I only just got here. LED lights illuminate the red bleachers surrounding the court, where various drills are being played out. The teachers haven't said as much, but my theory is that they make us do high-intensity workouts first thing in the morning and the occasional team sport in the afternoon to tire us out so we won't cause as much trouble.

Whether that theory is true or not is up for debate. I think Seraphic Hills ended up creating an army of uncontrollable athletes instead.

From my seat, I watch Blaze sidle up next to Aaron. I've never seen her exchange a single word with the guy, but then she places her hand on his arm. *Absolutely fucking not.*

I'm on my feet in a split second. Aaron can have his *arrangement* with Charlie all he wants, but if he goes near Blaze, he's a fucking dead man.

I'm not the only one who's taken offense to her choice of men, because Elijah rises from his seat in a heartbeat to pull her out of the group's makeshift circle. The other three groupies don't seem to give a shit about the iron grip around her arm or that Blaze is looking at him with a fury that's usually only reserved for me. *No one* gets to do that to her but me.

Rage seeps into my bloodstream. No one pays any mind to me—except Sarah, who flinches as I storm around the court toward them. Blaze slaps his hand off which only makes him step closer to her, but she doesn't back down. Her shoulders square and she stares him down as he says something to her.

The closer I get, the more words I can make out above the clamoring and squeaking. If Elijah touches her or hands her something, I'll paint my knuckles red with his blood.

She shouldn't have ridden my leg because it's awoken something primal inside that I'm beyond able to control.

My fingers ball into fists when he tugs on her shirt too erratically. "I've held up my end of the deal. Don't be a blue-balling bitch, Blaze." The words tumble out of Elijah's mouth, fast and slurred.

My eyes drop down to his jittery hands, then up to the slight gnawing of his jaw.

Wait. He's on something. Or withdrawing.

For fuck's sake.

"I'm onto bigger and better things now, *Elijah*." A surge of satisfaction rushes through me. That's right. I'm the only one she'll be seeing in her foreseeable future. *"You've got a lot of audacity for someone with a receding hairline."*

"I didn't ask for your bitchiness."

"It's on the house."

Red explodes around my vision, and I break into a run when he latches onto her arms. She stumbles into his chest with wide eyes when he yanks her toward him. "They said you'd be a fucking leech just like your mother," he spits out, walking her backward toward the stairs.

"Get your disgusting hands off me."

Liam and Aaron finally get involved, calling out for Elijah to stop, but the dumb fucker summons inhuman strength and knocks Liam back into Aaron.

Elijah grabs Blaze's face in a brutal grip. "You're going to suck my dick like you promised, and your mouth better feel like fucking gold after all the shit I've put up with."

The shrill sound of a whistle cuts through the air, and more yelling ensues from the rest of the gym.

"Bark at me, motherfucker. I bite." They grapple for dominance— she's mainly trying to get away, but he's desperately clinging onto

187

her.

I'm a foot away from them just as he starts saying, "You're going to fucking—"

Blaze yelps as they trip and tumble over the side of a bleacher row. I try to catch her flailing arm but she manages to stop herself two rows down from where they originally were, while Elijah keeps falling. One after the other, he goes over another row, unable to control his limbs. He manages to stop himself one row from the bottom, only to stand, then finish the job and make it to the bottom.

The blood dripping down Elijah's head and the ludicrousness of his fall would have been comical if it weren't for the fact that I'm three seconds away from finishing the fucking job.

The teacher rushes over to him—everyone does. They fawn over him like he's a goddamn child. Apparently, the perpetrator should get more attention than the girl everyone loves to hate. The only person who runs to check on Blaze is Charlie, but I get there before her.

There's an almost bleary look in her blue eyes as she scans the gathering crowd, and I mentally tally all the different injuries she could have gotten from the fall. But the lost look she's wearing only has a couple competitors.

It's either shock or a concussion.

Grabbing her chin gently, I lift her hair off her face to check for any obvious sign of head trauma, but she gut punches me the second my skin touches hers. "Stop touching me, creep," she barks and shoulders past me.

It's neither. Blaze is just a diagnosed bitch.

I narrow my eyes at her lopsided gait and unnaturally tensed shoulders, then to the white-knuckled fists at her sides. Each step is cautiously slow and tainted by a slight wobble. If Elijah wasn't considered a dead man before, he might as well get his death certificate signed now.

A blind man can tell how much pain she's in, yet she isn't looking to anyone for help. She's attempting to slip to the background, hoping no one pays her any attention so she can lick her wounds in peace. I get why she does it, and the look of understanding on Charlie's face tells me she does too.

But she's never needed to suffer through everything alone. I would have done anything for her if she just asked—if she stopped pushing me away for one damn minute, she'd know that. But no, she goes around touching other men and framing me for an explosion I'm embarrassed to have associated with my name.

Lithium batteries, a blowtorch, and paper? *Please.* I could have done that in second grade—points for trying and all, but I expected better fires from her.

Five steps are the only slice of freedom and self-indulgent stubbornness she gets to have before she's off her feet and in my arms. I'm practically vibrating with barely restrained rage as I fold her body against my chest and scowl at the injured foot. Her knee-high socks are in the way of me checking for any visible bruising around her ankles.

"Put me down, maniac," she grits out as I carry her down the bleachers.

If she weren't glued to me, I'd be storming to the piece of shit that's bleeding out, and I'd make it so there was nothing left of him for his family to mourn.

"Shut up, Thief. You're hurt. I'm taking you to the sick bay." *And you stupidly wrapped your arms around my neck. There's not a chance in hell I'm letting go now.*

The hardening lines around her eyes do the opposite of convincing me of her anger since her reddening cheeks are paired with a hitch in her breath. "I'm fine."

"And you weren't limping before?" I adjust my hold on her, curving my arm up to graze the underside of her tits. *See.* She wouldn't squeeze her legs together if my touch did nothing to her. If she wasn't attracted to me, she'd recoil in disgust like she does with Elijah. Why does Blaze keep fighting this when her body is clearly into me?

She clears her throat and raises her head in defiance. "Even if my leg were broken, I wouldn't need your help." Her eyes narrow on Elijah as we pass the congregating crowd—the same crowd who hasn't batted an eye at the woman in my arms. "I'm not a damsel in distress, so you can take your attention somewhere else."

I cock an eyebrow at her, noticing how, for the first time, she doesn't make my attention sound like a curse. "Are you in distress?"

"No," she says too sharply for it to sound like she's convincing anyone but herself. "Never."

"Great." I turn and push the doors open with my back. "Then you aren't a damsel in distress. Glad we have that cleared up."

She snorts and makes a half-assed attempt at fighting me off. "Save the hero complex for Kiervan. It's not the right look on you. If he were the one carrying me right now, maybe this would feel less like a trap."

My grip tightens around her, and I stop in my tracks. Everyone always likes my brother better. But I don't care about everyone; I only care if she likes me.

"Fine. Let's call him." I drop her onto her good leg and step far enough away that she can still reach for me for balance, but she opts for the wall instead, wincing as she does. "But don't come running to me when he sends you to the ER with a broken jaw."

If she wants Kiervan, then he can have her. I'm fucking sick of this. Enough people have been telling me I'm less than him, and I'm not going to sit around listening to her do the same after I spent a lifetime trying to prove my worth to her. There's only so much I'm willing to take, and after over ten years of this shit, I would say my patience is well and truly done for. Maybe.

Surprise turns into unease. "I don't believe you."

My jaw twitches. "Rich, coming from you. Especially when it's the same thing he told the three girls he paid off after he sent them to hospital."

Her chest heaves with her staggering breaths. "This isn't something to lie about, Kohen."

I shrug even though I want to check that her pulse is still thrumming, and there's still fire in her ready to burn. "If you don't want to believe me, then that's on you. I won't sit here and lay down the details of why Kiervan is the worst monster of them all. So I will say this one thing, and if you want to get down on your knees for another Osman, don't be surprised if I don't show up at your funeral. When dissecting animals stopped doing it for him, he thought beating women was the next best alternative."

Squeezing my fingers together, I fight the urge to pace or start a fire that will make what she did look like child's play. I don't add that I'd be in the grave next to her right after I murder my only brother. I'd never let him near her. I'd never let her near *anyone*. It's me or no one—*her* or nothing.

"Why are you telling me this?" Blaze asks, voice low.

I inch closer just so her scent can get into my head and fuel the beast that's been starving for her since the first day I met her on the playground, decking a kid two years older than her for calling her a carrot. I knew then that I was happy to burn if it was because of her.

"You want Duke. You want Elijah. You want Kiervan," I explain slowly. "You wanted a man who didn't confess to being your alibi. You wanted a man who pushed you down the bleachers. You want all the men who will kill you."

She eyes my curled fists warily. "And what are you?"

"The man you've never wanted, but the one who has, and will always take the fall for you."

BLAZE

CHAPTER 13

I don't know if there's a medical condition that could diagnose the gymnastics my brain is doing right now. Because firstly, what the fuck?

Secondly, *seriously*, what the fuck? I'm going to have to punch a wall or something to stop myself from blushing.

The man I framed for arson grazed my tit and carried me a whole fifteen minutes to the med bay because I have a sore foot, and here I am, avoiding eye contact because my heart is doing stupid little somersaults over the plainly chivalrous act.

Not to mention, when he went all serious and foreboding after our rather... unexpected conversation, his stoicness was almost pleasant.

Scratch that. My idiotic heart fluttered with the deluded prospect that he was being protective of me. Add that to the fact that he was holding me to his chest like I was special and not a piece of rotten meat to discard; my ovaries were having a party. The part about Kiervan is believable, the rest of the things he said to me *has* to be a blatant lie, but I'm just getting all giddy about it because I hit my head, and it felt scarily nice to be in his arms.

I'm not entertaining the touch starved theory to my reaction, because that issue can be bought and fulfilled by exchanging one thing for another.

Kohen carried me without expecting me to spread for him by the end of it. But I *refuse* to believe he did it out of the kindness of his heart. He's going to retaliate over the fire somehow, and I just have to be ready for it when it happens—which, right now, would be a very inconvenient time for it to happen. Not to sound dramatic or anything, but I think my ankle might be broken.

Dislocated, maybe.

Or a bad sprain—*twisted* sounds too mundane, but substantially more accurate than the other two. I think.

I'm no doctor, but if I can still move my foot around it's not broken, right? Who the fuck knows. Even if a bone is sticking out, the nurse will probably slap a Band-Aid on it and kick me out. I want to say this is the life of a woman going to the doctor, but I think this is more a me issue.

Seraphic Hills's selling point to parents is the school's one-stop-shop aspect. It might be situated hours away from a town with a population of over one thousand and in the middle of a fucking forest, but life still continues for the students because everything we could possibly need is right here. There's a semiretired doctor on retainer who lives close by and drives over if there are any cases beyond Dr. Van der Merwe's skills, as well as a helipad to fly people out for any significant issues.

I've never been to this part of the medical wing. I knew this place had an examination room; I just didn't think it was this nice. Clean white walls, gray floors, LED lights, random health and anatomy posters around the room, and various plastic organs and bones along the shelves. There seems to be everything in here, even a portable ultrasound, defibrillator, and a blood-test-checker-machine thingy. I'm honestly not sure what type of qualifications a psychiatrist and a retired general practitioner must have to operate all this machinery.

Oh, and I can't forget about the lovely ECT a couple rooms over.

The side of my face prickles; it has ever since the nurse directed Kohen to lower me onto the bed and left us both to wait while my good friend Dr. Van der Merwe finishes his meeting.

Earlier, as the nurse rummaged around the drawer for anti-inflammatories, Dr. Kohen Osman stepped in and R.I.C.E'd the fuck out of me. I was on my back with an ice pack on my elevated foot faster than I could figure out what every word in the acronym stands for.

Internally sighing, I swallow my pride and say the words usually only reserved for customer service. "Thank you." Then add, "For bringing me here."

Yuck. It even tastes gross. If I have to admit that I'm wrong about something or apologize, I'm going to throw up.

His lips part, eyes widening in shock.

Nope. That expression has to go. "But you can leave."

Good one, Blaze. Friendly, swift, to the point. Then I can go back to plotting how to ruin Kohen's psyche while simultaneously avoiding Elijah.

I'm going to need to get better at my uppercuts if that hopped-up fucker tries jumping me again. Or wait... guys love a damsel in distress—case in point, Kohen. Although, I thought he'd be inclined to add to my distress. There's still time for that to change.

Kohen takes this exact moment to decide that he does, in fact, want to add to my daily stresses. He gets all up in my business, placing his arms on either side of my body to cage me against the bed—not like I was planning to go anywhere with my broken foot and all.

And it's not like I can breathe with him this close. Or think. Or be any kind of functioning member of society.

Patchouli and mint smell even better in a sterile room. I should be a little more haunted by the fact that the place the doc tortured me in is nearby, but none of that seems to matter when I can feel his breath on my face... his lips are so close, and his hands are *right there*, so close to my—

No.

No.

I'm mad at him. I *hate* him. I am *not* thinking about those strong fingers brushing along my core. And I am most definitely not dreaming about mounting him for trying to stop the fight and then acting so attentively afterward.

God, I need to figure out how to get someone to smuggle a vibrator into this place. A Kohen-sized dildo would be a good alternative.

"Try to kick me out, and I'll tell the nurse about the..." His hand skates up the side of my thigh, and I'm ashamed to admit that my legs fall apart ever so slightly. Then, in a move that disappoints me more than it should, he reaches into my pocket and pulls out the strip of tablets I nicked when I thought no one was looking.

He blinks. Stares at the pills. "Laxatives? Really?"

Is that what those things were? I mean, you can't put a price on a functioning stomach.

I snatch the medication from him and tuck it back into my pocket. "I have IBS."

"No, you don't."

"Excuse me? How would you know?"

"That depends. Do you want to question how private your medical history is?"

Son of bitch.

The breath rushes back into me when he steps back, and his eyes follow the line of my body with more intensity than I can handle. He shifts his weight when he makes it down my leg. It's odd watching him blink hard when he gets to my foot, like there's some internal battle he's wrestling with.

Kohen clears his throat. "Take off your sock. I want to check your ankle."

I frown, both because that's a ridiculous request and because it makes me feel unreasonably special that he cares about me even when I'm trying to screw him up. "You're not a doctor. Plus, you aren't looking at my feet for free. This shit is a hot commodity."

Kohen cuts me a blank look. "Stop talking, Blaze."

Ugh, fuck it. Choose your battles and all that. Before I can play my independent-young-woman card, his hands curve behind my calf. The agonizingly slow speed in which they travel down my leg to remove my sock, is enough for me to start thinking about old people so I can stop imagining things involving the hard object tenting his pants.

Is it just me, or has he been getting hard a lot recently? I also think this room is getting unseasonably hot. And I'm wearing far too many layers. So is he. Maybe he could move his hand a little higher to—

Nope. Not thinking about that.

"Does this hurt?"

"What—ow!" I jolt up, slapping his hand away from my very red, very swollen ankle. "Yes, it fucking hurts. What did you think would happen when you go poking at a sprain?"

"It could be partially dislocated."

"Okay, Doctor," I mock.

When I bend my knee to get my foot away from him, I don't expect him to grab my other leg and bend it too, causing me to be too dumbstruck to do anything about it. The ibuprofen must be getting to my head; that's the only explanation as to why he's doing exactly what I was fantasizing before. One second his hand is around my leg, the next, both hands are at my hips pulling down my shorts—and, shit, the whiplash is sending a rush straight to my core.

Somehow, some way, I manage to stop thinking with my vagina for more than a millisecond to shove his hands away. "What the fuck do you think—"

"Shut the fuck up. I need this."

I'm not sure whether it's his words or how the gold in his eyes has turned into bronze embers against the poisonous green rings, but he manages to stun me into silence. He looks like he's about to explode. The pyromaniac takes my silence as an opening to yank my panties and shorts down my thighs in one single move, and I screech.

"You're—"

I'm bare from the waist down in the next heartbeat, barely able to breathe from the depleting oxygen in the room. I snap my legs closed, and the movement immediately sends a bolt of pain through my ankle. Still, I keep my thighs tightly shut so he doesn't see what his barbarian attitude is doing to my nether regions.

Kohen's eyes flare, and he sounds like he's skating the line of losing it. "I'm two seconds away from lighting a man on fire—if you don't spread your legs for me right now, I'm sending us both to prison."

It's a leg workout with how hard I'm squeezing my thighs together, and it makes the examination sheet crinkle beneath me. "I'm not doing shit for you."

"That's part of the problem, isn't it?" He pulls me down the bed, and I let out a pathetic little yelp when my shirt slides up with the friction. "You don't need to do a goddamn thing, and my dick is constantly hard as a brick for you."

My mouth falls. "*What*? Are you on drugs? What the fuck are you talking about?" By my count, I've seen this man hard twice. And if he hadn't been turned on by me riding his leg, I would have been offended.

"I'm talking about how you take center stage in all my wet dreams, and I can't go a single day without coming to the thought of you."

I blink twice. "Come again?"

There's no way I heard that right. Sure, I get that he recently developed some weird, deranged interest in me after deciding he doesn't like it when I'm around other guys. But his delusion can't be so bad that he's in his room every day, touching himself while thinking about me.

Now that I think about it, it's actually quite flattering.

My brain doesn't compute the blur of movement until one of his hands cradles the back of my neck, and the other wraps around the column of my throat, lifting me so our lips brush against each other. A shiver skates down my spine as I barely stop myself from sealing the deal.

You hate him, I remind myself. *He burned your house and got you medically tortured. You H-A-T-E him.*

"You've stolen my every waking thought since the day I met you, Thief. I've been wanting to feel your pretty pussy for as long as I can remember. I'm done waiting." I don't notice that his hand has left my neck until his fingers brush against my core.

It's like I jolt awake, fighting back the need to grind against his hand by clawing, hitting, and releasing the occasional kick with my good leg. His fingers stay precisely where they are, rubbing against my clit every time I move.

I growl, trying to fight him off—or maybe because it feels sublime whenever my hip buckles. Either way, I'm appeasing my mental and physical needs. The feelings are enough to make me forget all about the pain shooting through my foot.

Anyone could walk in right now and see me practically throwing myself at him—because no one will believe that he's jumping me. They'd slap a chastity belt on me, zap me with a lightning bolt, and tattoo *slut* on my forehead.

That should fill me with more motivation to throw him off, yet I don't, even though I could be risking it all just to get off. But isn't this just who I am? A junkie for the thrill of the danger.

Kohen grips my hair. "Fight me if you want, Thief. The only way you'll get me to stop is by mentioning another man."

I glare at him. Motherfucker gives me an out, and I can't bring myself to take it. Worse yet, this might seem like a win-win situation to some. But as I see it, I'm using him to get off. I'm his scapegoat in exchange, and his balls will be left blue. Ergo, the win goes to me and the loss goes to him.

Maybe it's a convoluted way of justifying why I'm pausing my crusade, but hey, orgasms feel better than drugs—one leaves me dying, and the other leaves me sated.

I scoff, putting up a half-assed fight as I sneer in his face. He thinks the act is from rage, but frustration might be more accurate.

There's a thick layer of desperation to how hotly he says, "Stay still and let me take care of you."

My brain short-circuits.

He can't say shit like that to me.

Take care of me? What the fuck? Those four words are all it takes to get me to fold for this lunatic? I'm meant to be a stronger woman than this. I don't need anyone to take care of me, but my body becomes jellylike and compliant as he guides my injured leg onto the stirrups that are built into the bed. Even though his eyes are viciously set on me, his shoulders soften as if caring for me relaxes him. The movement is so gentle; if I were more emotionally fraught about my altercation with Elijah, I'd get teary-eyed.

I didn't realize that a lifetime of aggression and fighting men would lead me to become broken by the concept of something other than pain. Kohen hates me just as much as I hate him. Why else would he go around choking me, cutting my hair, or doing what he did to my house? Hatred and loathing are the foundation of our entire relationship. How long do I need to wait until the punch line? Affection isn't possible without pain. Love doesn't exist without hurt. So when will this crumble?

I keep waiting for him to suddenly grip my ankle or say something that will make me regret letting my guard down, yet he doesn't.

Each of his minuscule movements goes against the years of bad blood between us. I can't reconcile the mutual animosity with how tenderly he's treating me, checking that my leg is sitting comfortably on the stirrup, tying the ice pack to my foot, making sure it's not too cold on my skin, and then moving to the other leg.

It's wild that he's doing this while I'm butt-ass naked—not that he's forgotten about it with how he keeps eyeing me with a sideways glance at the space between my spread legs. Any second now, the zipper on his pants is going to burst open, and I'd be a liar if I said I wasn't excited about the prospect.

Trepidation fills my lungs when he turns away from me to a table at the other side of the room, leaving me exposed and wanting. Dare I say it, I'm having to stop myself from panting. My muscles spasm in agitation and frustration from the position and need. I wonder if he's intentionally making me wait as a form of torture to see if I'll get any wetter from the tease.

Or if I'm just overthinking it.

I wish I could see what he's looking for in the various drawers. The sound of tape ripping and metal clinking causes anxiety to worm into my marrow. Is this the part where the hurt finally comes?

I've never caught him out on a lie before, and I guess realizing his words are all fake would be the thing that shatters the illusion of his niceties. It might also be exactly what I need to stop my traitorous heart and body from melting all over him.

I bite the inside of my cheek when he slams the drawer closed, and I glance up at the door like it might be wide open. He doesn't spare me a look as he rolls the heart rate monitor next to the bed, and places the trolley next to me.

While he's inspecting the items on it, my legs slowly fall closed. It's an odd combination of being frightened and turned on by my curiosity, but I flinch when he moves to lock the door.

Everything about him seems dangerous, like he's a second away from blowing up. But when he tugs off his tie, tosses his blazer onto the computer chair, and shoves his sleeves up to his elbows, I damn well almost come from how sophisticated he is in his distress—and those forearms.

Jesus Christ, those veiny forearms.

I try to fight him off for a little over five seconds when he tries taking my shirt off, then again when he unclasps my bra, folding both into a neat pile on the seat a few feet away from the examination table. The cool air kisses my skin, perking my nipples into points sharp enough to key a car. I've never been self-conscious about my looks or how much skin I show, but right now, I want to fold my arms across my chest because I know if he looks too long, he'll see what everyone else sees.

That I'm inadequate, a mess, a pariah. He'll remember that I'm better off dead in a ditch somewhere, and not someone he should spend his emotional energy getting jealous over.

Kohen falters when his heated gaze rakes over my body like a drag of a match, cataloging every inch of me with bated breath. The hardening in his pants makes me wet my dry lips, but at the same time, I realize that if his plan is to degrade me by leaving me naked on a slab, it's working. The vulnerability of it all is unnerving, just as it is alluring.

Another shiver rolls down my spine when he drags his finger along the side of my body until he reaches his station, hazel eyes transfixed on the trail of goosebumps pebbling my flesh from his touch.

"What are you doing?" I ask hesitantly when he puts the stethoscope on.

205

"A checkup," he says simply.

"You're not a doctor."

"Practice."

It makes even less sense than before, but the term *curiosity killed the cat* was made for me. I know I'm into foreplay, but am I into roleplay too? I guess I know the answer now.

"Breathe in."

Whatever, yeah. Okay, I'll let Kohen play his game, but if he pulls out a speculum or needles, I'm tapping out.

The cold surface of the bell makes me flinch. Come to think of it, this might be the first time I've had this done since I turned fourteen. Every time I've been sick, Grandpa labeled it a hangover and told me to suck it up.

"Hold."

I do as Kohen asks, stuttering when the chilled metal brushes over my nipples.

"Breathe out."

He's really taking this seriously, getting me to breathe several times, grazing my nipple each time he places the flat base on a different part of my chest. And much to my disappointment, not once does he touch me with his hands.

Surely, he's doing this longer than necessary. If I had to guess by his blown-out eyes, his focus is on my nipples and spread legs, not the sound of my lungs.

Kohen pulls away, placing the stethoscope back on the tray. The tendons in his forearms ripple; his veins move as he slips the pulse reader on my finger and the blood pressure cuff around my arm. Deep rivets form between his brows as he pushes random buttons on the heart rate monitor. He steps back once the first line jumps on the monitor, and the cuff tightens around my arm.

Keeping his stare firmly on me, my lips part as he grabs a pair of gloves off the wall. Do I have a latex kink, or does watching this male model snap on gloves do it for me? Also, what in God's name does he need with them?

His gaze drops down to the two gadgets reading me, then quickly to my tits, and back to the monitor. My heart rate must be astronomical right now—being anxious and horny and all. The machine beeps twice, and he nods approvingly as he reads the screen. Does he know what he's looking at, or is he a weirdly good actor when it comes to roleplaying? A hundred over sixty sounds high to me.

He takes the cuff off my arm and leaves the pulse monitor on, glancing at it smugly when it spikes as he reaches for something on the trolley. As if double-checking the data corresponds, he shifts his attention down to my wet pussy, and he nods to himself again. The Velcro sounds as he brings the cuff closer to my throat.

"No," I growl and he halts. "If you put that shit anywhere near my neck, my knuckles are going to be kissing your balls, lover boy."

Hands, I can fight off. Limbs, I can break. A machine? Something inhuman that won't listen to reason? No. No way. That type of shit can stay far the fuck away from me. It'll be like drowning without any water in sight.

When the tubing comes into view, my breath stutters.

"Yeah, no." I'm out. I don't like anything that might involve that.

"Hands," is all he says.

Ignoring my protests, he grabs both my wrists and ties them together using the plastic tubing.

I change my mind; maybe I do like things involving those. The evidence of exactly how much I like it is dripping between my legs. Kohen knows it too, evidenced by a single gloved finger catching another droplet before it lands on the medical-grade sheet, and I arch my back when he pushes it back inside me.

Who knows what else I'm agreeing to by doing this. Actually, I don't give a shit. As long as I get to come, I'm all game.

Kohen makes a sound at the back of his throat that makes the muscles in my core spasm. "You're so fucking soaked for me, Blaze."

Biting my tongue to stop myself from mewling, I squeeze my eyes shut to imagine literally anything else but what the latex-clad fingers feel like on and inside me. If Kohen's goal was to keep from dirtying the sheets, he's doing an excellent job of it. However, he's making an even bigger mess of me.

I grip the bedsheet with my bound hands when he slaps my pussy hard enough for me to feel the delicious pressure on my clit, but not enough to sting. He does it again, this time watching the monitor to see my pulse jump.

"Such an excited little whore," he muses in the same way a doctor does when analyzing results.

The term might be an insult when said by anyone else—anyone who isn't making my naked body flush and legs quake with need—but when Kohen says it, my hips roll into the pleasure he's giving me. I have a funny feeling that if he added *my* at the start of it, my eyes would roll to the back of my head.

I can go back to plotting his downfall once I leave this room. For now, I'm his whore as long as I get what I want at the end of this.

Kohen's eyes track the heavy rise and fall of my chest, and then he messes with something on the trolley that I can't see, pushing me back down with a solid yet soft push when I try to sit up.

"Don't touch me," I snap.

His jaw ticks, and his expression grows murderous again, but he doesn't look at me, continuing with whatever it is he's doing.

My eyes widen as my blood chills by ten degrees when he turns to me with a pair of forceps or tweezers—whatever the scissor-looking things are called. Cotton pads are taped down with gauze tape on each pointed end of the metal. Nothing betrays his expression as he lowers them down to my chest. Is he... Holy shit, he's going to use them as clamps.

He twists one of my nipples between his pointer finger and thumb. My body reacts on its own accord, pressing my head back against the table and pushing my tits against his hand to urge him on. Like the cruel asshole he is, Kohen doesn't work me harder, continuing with the leisurely, clinical pace he's set, rolling it around like it's a game.

I squeeze my eyes shut to focus on the sensations he's eliciting and keeping silent. A moan bubbles up my throat before I can stop it. Curses spill from my lips when his mouth wraps around my nipple. There's something almost... hesitant or uncertain about how he circles the aching points with the tip of his tongue before taking them between his teeth in a near-vicious pull. The way his mouth moves is wet and messy, but each flick still sends shockwaves through my body. I buck my hips upward, begging for the slightest bit of friction to alleviate the building ache.

Who would've thought this man would know what to do with his tongue? Actually, he doesn't deserve that high praise when he's such a prick. Still, it doesn't stop me from grabbing onto his shirt—which the stupid heart rate monitor makes awkward, but I'm barely aware of it beyond wanting his mouth to stay there so he can continue lavishing my breasts like he's been waiting a lifetime to do it.

"Greedy little thief," he murmurs against my skin after I yank him back when he tries to stop. "You get what you're given."

Legs? Spread.

Back? Arched.

I almost roll my eyes. If that were the case, Kohen would've pried my hands off and continued on his merry way. But here he is, doing half of what I want.

Kohen alternates between sucking the left and right tit, giving the other attention with his fingers when his mouth is preoccupied. My hips roll against the bed in search of relief. If he doesn't start touching me properly soon, I'm going to take matters into my own bound hands.

This time, when he pulls away, I let him—groaning as his teeth drag against my nipples. He almost looks proud of what he's done to my painful points. They're so sensitive it feels like they might rip off from a breeze.

I scowl at him as he holds my chin between his thumb and forefinger. "For the first time in your life, you're going to be a good girl for me and stay very, *very* still."

"Get fucked," I choke out as he lets go of my chin.

He ignores me, grabbing the forceps and bringing it to my chest. Out of instinct, I latch both hands onto his leg and dig my nails into the stiff muscles. This is going to hurt.

"Relax," he rasps.

All I can muster is a breathy, "I'm going to fucking kill you," followed by a hissed, "Asshole," when the forceps clamp around my nipple. The pain zaps to every corner of my psyche and sends a wave of desire straight to my core. The hiss becomes a whimper for more as I get used to the sensation.

"You can try." Cockiness laces his voice, but I couldn't care less about what he has to say as the second one pinches my nipple.

"Fuck." I jolt when he lets go, making both forceps swing, adding more pressure to my already hurting nipples. This time, the sound that leaves my lips is a starved moan. Every muscle in my stomach convulses, needing release more than I need air. Every breath moves the forceps, and trying to stop myself from mewling is hopeless.

I'm soaked beyond comprehension; worse than the frenzy I was in the night I fucked his leg. The sheet is entirely saturated, and I still feel myself dripping onto the bed. I've never denied that I'm attracted to Kohen's appearance; I just never thought he'd be the one to get me into a state where I'm swollen to the point of pain. I'm so raw, the still air feels like a gentle caress, sending pleasure up my spine.

If he isn't going to make me come, then I'll do it myself. I'm so worked up that it won't even take long.

My hands fall to my core, and the first draw of my fingers over my clit has me cursing. Kohen snatches my hands away before I can find out what sound I'll make on my second. The angle of my arms above my head makes the forceps drop lower and pull on my nipples.

"Don't you dare. You come when I let you."

I bare my teeth at him. I feel fucking feral. I could bring down a mountain, fight God, or become Him with how much pent-up frustration Kohen's injected into my bloodstream. I've hungered for things before—*itched* like it's the only thought that consumes my mind. There's never been a desire that my body, mind, and soul have ached for.

"Someone's going to get me off, and I doubt you'll be able to do it." *Lie.* Something tells me that he'll make up for what he might lack in skill with enthusiasm and size. I haven't tested it out, but he could cover my face with his hand. Having those monstrous-sized fingers inside me would send me to heaven and back before my untimely descent into hell.

The combined pain in my tits and the ache in my pussy is dizzying. He could barter with me, make me sell my soul, and give up everything I've ever wanted in life just so I orgasm hard enough to black out on this sterile bed.

Kohen straightens, letting go of my hands. His lips turn downward with a sneer. I didn't bring up another man, but questioning his abilities is just as bad, I suppose.

If there's something I know about Kohen, he'll rise to any challenge I throw his way.

He reaches for something off the trolley, keeping it out of sight as he throws another glance at the heart rate monitor. "Stick your tongue out," he orders. When I keep my mouth clamped tight in defiance, his nostrils flare. "Do it, and you get to come."

Now *that* is how you negotiate. I couldn't stick my tongue out quicker if I tried.

A brown stick comes into view, and I gasp, momentarily disarmed. That's not exactly what I thought he had in mind.

Kohen presses the compressor down on my tongue, looking down his nose at me in intrigue. Something wildly innate in me has an uncharacteristic urge to be the best possible patient I can be. It makes me push my tongue out and open my mouth as wide as I can.

What the fuck is this man doing to me?

The tongue compressor doesn't stay there for long before his fingers replace the wood. The rubbery scent fills my senses and settles over my taste buds as he rubs his fingers up and down my tongue. He goes all the way back when I don't expect it. My body reacts, closing my throat around him as I rear back and sputter a cough.

Kohen makes a sound of disapproval that makes me want to both lash out and cower. "You can do better than that, Thief."

The glare I give him doesn't go very far because his fingers are in my mouth before I can speak, going just as deep as before. Undeterred by my choking, he does it over and over again, going further back each time, almost as if he's training me. He tips his head to the side as if calculating whether my reflexes can handle him. The prospect of having his cock in my mouth does the opposite of sicken me and, for the first time in my life, I actually *want* this while being stone-cold sober.

His cock.

It'd be like a treat for being his good little patient.

"Suck them," he orders.

I try to do as I'm told, but I'm unable to because Kohen chooses that exact moment to finally—*finally*—push his other fingers into my aching core. And it feels like I just found God, Mary, and fucking Zeus. I visit every version of heaven there is just from the slide of his digits. It's divine ecstasy.

Bucking up into his hand, I quietly moan around him just so he doesn't get the satisfaction of hearing the full extent of my pleasure. Also, if I let myself make all the sounds I want to make, someone's going to call security, and I can't promise myself I won't be charged with homicide at the end of it.

Kohen pulls his fingers out of my cunt, and my eyes snap wide open.

How *dare* he stop? I'm going to fucking kill—

"Suck," he says, his voice low enough to vibrate in my veins.

There's no snarky comment I can make when my lips are wrapped around his glove-covered fingers in a game of tonsil hockey. If I buck my hips in search of his hand, he wins the round, but if I move my top half, pain will slice through my chest from the clamps. So we enter into a stare-off, with him still in my mouth and my core dripping and swollen.

I'm going to break first. He knows it. I know it. There's no point to the quarrel, but *boy* does it feel good to see his eyes turn to stone when I wrap my tongue around his digits and play with them languidly, just like he did with my nipples.

It's a sweet treat. A lollipop. It'd be a crime not to taste every inch of it.

The tip of my tongue runs along his latex fingers, pushing in the seam between them to give each the deserved attention. I pull back, kissing them, devouring them, acting out everything I would do to Kohen's cock. He's forgotten that he's not the only one who can be thorough.

His breaths come out heavy as he zeroes in on my tongue's ministrations. The same power I felt that night in my room flows through me as his hand closes the distance to my pussy.

That's right, Pyro. You're my bitch too.

He teases me just like I'm teasing him, skirting around my entrance and skating his latex-clad hand over my clit. The rubber adds an extra layer of pleasure I didn't think was possible. I mimic the move with my tongue, this time dropping my attention away from his hazel eyes down to the dent pushing against his pants. Just as I'm about to give in and behave like he wants, he pulls his fingers out of my mouth and uses them to breach my entrance at the same time he slams his lips to mine to swallow a silent scream.

The kiss is as bruising as it was the first night, except I'm needier and angrier, and his kiss feels desperate.

The same desperation tinges his voice when he slips out of me to discard his gloves on the table.

"I want to feel you when you come," he pants.

A low groan rumbles through his chest when he sinks his bare fingers back into me. My eyelids flutter at the warmth of his skin directly against mine. Something about the direct contact makes the touch more sensual and intimate as if this is not just a onetime thing, but rather the start of a bond. His rough, calloused hands waste no time pummeling me like we're about to get caught, and he wants to finish the job with flying colors. The metallic taste of blood blooms on my tongue from biting it to keep from making a sound. Anyone could come knocking on that door, and only one of us is naked right now.

If all doctor visits were like this and from men who look like Kohen, I'd be making weekly appointments.

He makes the act of fucking me with his fingers seem so medical, with his flattened brows and the hawklike focus in his eyes.

Actually, maybe *medical* isn't the right word. Methodical. Critical. An experiment to figure out what makes me tick and what makes me scream. Kohen's probably writing mental notes of his findings, and planning the next phase in his kinky clinical trials. It's the face of a man with a goal in mind, and every intention to succeed beyond measure.

The lewd sounds of his fingers vigorously pumping into me fills the air. It makes me preen knowing he wants to study me and become familiar with every facet of my body so he knows how best to treat it.

A different kind of pressure builds in the base of my stomach—a feeling I'm not familiar with.

"You think Kiervan or Elijah could make you feel this good?" Kohen flicks my nipple, and I bite down a scream, making the heart rate monitor go berserk. "I asked you a question."

"Better," I snap, even though the thought of going near either of them makes me sick to my stomach. They both deserve to rot for all the shit they've done.

Kohen curves his fingers just right, hitting the spot that makes white light dance behind my vision. The buildup of pressure doesn't just ease, it falls over the edge and crashes into the water below. I cry out, throwing my head back as warmth gushes out from between my legs and soaks the sheet. The sudden motion causes the clamps to create delightful pain.

"Shh, not so loud. We wouldn't want someone to come in and see you like this." He covers my mouth with his hand, his sinister, teasing voice wrapping around me to make my toes curl. His attempt at silencing me doesn't do much other than muffle the sounds. "Figures my klepto would be a squirter."

The first thought that goes through my mind is to bite him. And that's exactly what I do; I open my mouth and sink my teeth into the tender flesh of his fingers, using them to stifle my moans.

"Fuck," he growls, keeping his hand exactly where it is, and his fingers curled to make the pressure in my core soar higher.

Now I understand why women want vocal men. I hurt him—on purpose—and he sounds like he's going to reach a violent ecstasy. The same ecstasy I'm chasing to new heights. It hits faster than I realize because my teeth come down harder as I choke on a scream. Scrambling for his chest or the sheets of the bed with my bound hands, anything to keep me grounded as fireworks explode through

216

every cell in my body so savagely I think I might pass out.

Kohen frees his hand from my bite the second I go lax, his other sliding out of me with a loud, wet noise. The next thing I know, his belt is off, along with his shirt, pants, and underwear, until he's standing before me in all his naked glory.

Adonis. The word perfectly describes him, and his perfectly chiseled abs, to the sprawling line of his chest and torso. There isn't a single inch of him that hasn't been molded into a masterpiece. His bronze skin looks artful under the fluorescent light as he grabs something else from the trolley.

The tattoos on his chest are perfectly symmetrical: two coiling snakes that wrap around his back.

The real showstopper is the *thing* saluting me from his hips. I had no intention of letting this go beyond my own orgasm, but now that I see his cock outside of his pants... I guess it's one hell of a way to die. Charlie better get her eulogy ready; there aren't many hills I'm willing to die on, but as of today, there is a mountain I'm willing to conquer—and I'm no hiker.

Fuck it. Today, I'm all about trying everything at least once.

For my sanity's sake though, I put on a show of fighting him as he positions himself between my legs, condom rolled on already—Jesus, it really is one size fits all. The heart rate monitor goes flying off my finger in the scuffle.

He wrestles my wrists above my head with a single hand, stationing himself right against my entrance. For some reason, the fury in his eyes hasn't dissipated. He looks like he despises himself for wanting to do this. If that's the case, then even if he comes, I'm still a winner because he would have hated every second of it.

My lips fall on a silent gasp as he pushes himself in. He's only put the fucking tip in, and I think I'm about to see Mother Mary. I continue thrashing against his hold, moving my hips in the process to feel the sheer girth of him stretching me to the point it stings.

Cursing under his breath, he moves and places the full weight of his trembling upper body on the hand beside my head. He lets go of my wrists and withstands the onslaught of my fruitless fighting while trying to adjust our hips.

My breath stutters as he releases the forceps from my nipples, never once slowing in his descent. *Sensitive* isn't an apt enough description of the state my nipples are in. It's so bad I have to bite the inside of my cheek to stop myself from groaning when his chest brushes against mine.

Increment by agonizing increment, he pushes himself into me. The heat of his stained gaze never once leaves my face. It's like he's trying to remember every part of this—every part of me—while loathing me all the same.

Kohen traps my arms between us as he sinks the entirety of himself inside me, reaching so far back that I swear I can taste him in my throat.

"*Fuck*," he says, voice hoarse. The arms beside my head shake as if this is the most difficult thing he's ever done. "You feel unreal—so goddamn good."

My cheeks heat at the compliment. He had been imagining what I felt like. The ache that radiates through my center has me tensing up, ready to push him back out. But instead, he flattens his hips with mine, giving me more when I thought there was nothing more to give. I squeeze my eyes shut to focus on something other than the pain.

This is it. This is when the hurt starts, where the final betrayal will happen, and Kohen becomes irredeemable.

He'll hold me down despite how many different names I call out. He'll grab onto my injured foot and pummel me into the exam table until my insides become unrecognizable. He'd do it all with a smile on his face, laughing because he finally broke my body.

Only he doesn't do any of that. He stays right where he is, giving me time to adjust, rubbing circles over my clit to loosen my muscles.

Stay still and let me take care of you.

That's what he said to me. He took the clamps off because they'd hurt when he thrusts. He took steps to keep my ankle free from added discomfort—*demanded* that the nurse give me ice and painkillers. He made me see God with his fingers before he gave me his cock.

Let me take care of you.

If this is all a game, it's going to hurt when I lose. The betrayal won't just impact him; it'll be irreparable for the rest of my life. What other ending is there if I'm letting the man I hate in? If I sat still just because he asked?

I will realize I don't hate him nearly as much as I thought. It isn't soul-deep or life-altering. I'm angry—pissed—but here I am, letting him tie my wrists together and strip me bare when anyone could barge in.

Even though I know he's holding on by a thread, he hesitantly pulls out of me just as slowly as he went in. His ragged breaths brush my skin as he moves his fingers from beside my head to press his thumb against the pulse point in my neck.

Maybe some innate part of me trusts him enough to do all this because I know his rage is as vast as mine. I pulled the trigger; it was only a matter of time before he retaliated. Yet here he is with vehemence in his eyes, the same look he's harbored since the first day he met me.

He's fucking me with so much tenderness it almost feels like he cares about me. His hips thrust into me, the type of rolling motion that doesn't shake the bed or jolt through my body. Nothing about it is forceful or harsh.

It's gentle.

I don't deserve gentle.

I don't deserve the care he's expressing, even if it is all fake.

Someone like me doesn't get love or the dashing young prince who will save her from the big bad dragon. I was born alone, and it's already been written in the books of life that I'm meant to die alone, never knowing anything but carnage and emptiness.

In drugs, I could find that solace. I'm less alone in the company of blankness or colorful sounds.

Right now, I hate him not for what has happened in the past, but because this is the cruelest thing he's ever done to me. Giving me a taste of what I will never have. I'll spend the rest of my life yearning for an idea that was never real.

I squeeze my eyes shut when they start to sting.

Then Kohen kisses me.

Oh, he kisses me.

His lips move like they have finally found their counterpart. They taste like lost dreams. I savor it because if all of this is a sham, at least when I die, I'll know what it feels like to be important to someone.

So I kiss him back because I want to know what it feels like to have someone genuinely matter to me. While we kiss, I'm struck with the agonizing realization that I could get used to this; the feel of it all, consuming me completely until I tip over the edge and into a hangover I'll never recover from.

Hazel greets me when I open my eyes, staring back into my empty abyss. He always watches me even when I don't want him to. It's another thing I could overfill myself on; having someone's eyes on me and only me.

Kohen drives his hips into me faster, pushing me out of the spell of my own mind to swallow down each moan he forces out of me. Gently, he takes my legs off the stirrups to deepen each thrust. There's something almost... uncertain about the way he moves, as if he's trying to figure out whether he's on the right track.

The painful ache in my core is gone. All that's left is the fierce desire to find the high I had felt before he treated me like I was something to be cherished. He keeps circling my clit, drawing the pleasure through me.

"What happened to rest, ice, compression, and elevation?" I pant out the acronym for R.I.C.E, not sure he can understand the words I'm saying.

"That's why your legs are on my shoulders and not shaking against the bed." His next thrust comes exceptionally hard, paired with a frown of concentration.

I reach for the wall above my head to stop the bed from hitting the wall and alerting everyone to our tryst. He doesn't falter in his brutal pace, driving into me with desperate vigor.

The orgasm is forced from me without warning, shooting stars all around us as I tighten around him and cling to the top of the table. In an ungodly feat, he moves faster, hitting me harder with each thrust until he drops his head against mine, releasing a groan that fills the room.

"Fuck," I whisper as my body convulses with the aftermath of my second orgasm, and I unintentionally lurch forward when he pulls out after a few heated seconds of heavy breathing.

A sheen of lust covers my vision as he pulls off the condom. My brows pinch momentarily as I try to make sense of the fact that he isn't getting off the bed or throwing it away.

"What the fuck do you think you're doing?" I screech. My hand flies out to swat him away, but it's too late.

"You fucked up." The warm liquid of the emptied condom slowly drips from my pussy. A grin works its way across his face as he pushes his come back into me with two fingers. "You fucked up bad, little thief. You're mine now."

"You fucking asshole."

He nods toward the trolley where a packet of birth control awaits me.

How romantic.

BLAZE

CHAPTER 14

I'm going to kill him.

I'm going to tie him up to a pole and beat the shit out of him.

Yes, there are many *hims* on my shit list, but this particular culprit's name starts with *E* and is the reason I'm hobbling around on crutches with a sprained ankle—the bruised cervix is courtesy of a different *him*.

Don't get me wrong, I want to do the exact same thing to that six-foot-something wall of drop-dead gorgeousness, but he redeemed himself too many times within a couple hours to really kick my gears into place.

After he made me come twice, I was ready for round three when he demanded to get Dr. Van der Merwe to reexamine my foot. Then, I limped after the doctor tried sending me away, and Kohen got me crutches and an ankle brace. Maybe it's overkill, but now I also have a daily dose of anti-inflammatories. My heart couldn't take how gooey it made me feel.

Figures the only time a doctor has taken me seriously was when a man was there. It's a good thing Kohen threw hands on my behalf too, because when I looked at my ankle this morning, it was a beautiful shade of cerulean.

What I want right now goes beyond an ibuprofen. It hurts, yeah, but I need my brain to shut the fuck up for two solid seconds, and the only person who can get me what I need is the prick who caused all this to begin with.

If Elijah hadn't gotten all hopped-up and came at me, neither of us would have tumbled down the bleachers and I wouldn't have gotten a taste of something I'll never have.

Screw Kohen for doing those things and saying those things to me. How dare he fill me with that kind of false hope—and his fucking come? I need to purge the memory out of my brain, so cue the bender that I'm going to make Elijah finance as an apology for *pushing me down the bleachers.*

A petite, box-dyed black head of hair walks past the library, and I crutch faster to catch up. *Fucking hell, this is an arm workout.*

"Charlie," I whisper-yell when I catch her sneaking by.

"Huh?" She whips around. There's a dazed fog in her bloodshot eyes and a lock of drenched hair in her mouth.

Looks like I'm late to the party. Charlie's half-cast eyes stare somewhere in my general direction as she mindlessly chews on her hair, waiting patiently for me to reach her.

"How's the leg?" she throws over her shoulder.

A good friend would stay put, maybe walk at half speed, or suggest we sit down so I can catch my breath after spending the past hour searching campus for the little fucker, Elijah. But Charlie simply resumes walking at the same speed as before, like a woman on a mission.

"Great," I grind out. "Have you seen Elijah?" No point beating around the bush. Whenever she's in this kind of state, she finds a place to zonk out or someone to fuck her.

She shakes her head, quickly pulling her hair out of her mouth and behind her ear like she just realized she's doing it. "No one's seen him all day."

"How convenient." If he's hiding, I'll sniff him out. "Let me guess, a concussion or something?" Maybe solitary as well?

She shrugs as she rounds the corner and heads down the hallway leading to the dorm rooms. We've already had dinner, so it's only a couple hours until we're forced to be holed away in our rooms.

"Apparently, he's in the hospital."

My eyes widen. "For a concussion?" I'm trying really hard not to breathe heavily right now, but could this girl walk any faster?

"No."

I stare at her profile, waiting for her to elaborate, but she doesn't. Jesus Christ, woman. "Then for what?"

She sneers, waving her hand like it isn't important. "Something about broken bones and shit. I think there was mention of a coma or surgery or something."

My brow line flattens. "Elijah was standing upright when I left him. For the love of God, Charlie, what the hell do you mean he's in a coma?"

"Ugh." She rolls her eyes. I get it. I'd be mad too, if someone was killing my buzz. "Aaron said they found him by the cemetery, passed out, beaten up, and badly burned. That's all I know. Happy?"

Weird, but also this is extremely inconvenient. Serves him right for being a jackass, I guess. It also explains why he wasn't in class today.

No wonder McGill was grilling me about my relationship with Elijah this morning. He asked me to explain what happened at the gym five times in ten different ways.

"Where's Aaron now?" Follow-up questions: is he carrying anything, and is he willing to share?

"Church."

I groan, loud and obnoxious. That's quite literally the one place I don't want to look because it's so damn far. Crutches and mud sound like a disaster to me.

"Thanks," I mutter.

"Oh, by the way, he replied."

A cold film washes over my body, and I swallow the lump in my throat. "What did Kiervan say?"

"Yes."

I didn't think he'd respond. It was a long shot that he'd see my message request from yesterday morning, let alone reply to a text asking if he wanted to meet up. Now that I know what type of person he is, I want absolutely nothing to do with him.

"Okay," I whisper. "Thanks."

She nods as she takes the exit toward the dorms, and I take the one leading toward the church.

I want to choke on the guilt. It felt wrong contacting Kiervan to begin with, but I still pressed send because it didn't feel like I was doing enough damage to Kohen's psyche.

What happened in the medical wing was an accident. It's never going to happen again—it shouldn't have happened to begin with.

What are my options now? Mess around and hope I'll forget about the full-body high Kohen gave me, or trudge through the outdoors for the possibility of a hit?

The latter. Definitely the latter.

I'm not moving anywhere near as fast as I'd like to while trying to avoid detection—especially since I'm like a damn beacon with these crutches. Anyone can hear me from a mile away, and there's no way I could pass off as anyone other than a student.

It's not as cold anymore, but we haven't been getting much more in the way of daylight, and the weather is still miserable half the time. I avoid looking to the left at all costs. The lake always appears more daunting at night, just a black hole that could swallow things up.

I manage to make it to the tree line without getting caught. If any security guards around don't hear the crutches, they'll hear how heavy I'm breathing. Here I was, thinking I was substantially fitter from the morning drills.

"Where do you think you're going?"

I swallow a yelp and spin around, tangling my feet in my crutches only to land on my hurt foot. I rear back from the pain that thunders up my leg and throw my hand out for support on the nearest tree.

Kohen reaches for me, but I attempt to multitask by avoiding him and gaining my balance at the same time. Fortunately, I do the second one successfully. Unfortunately, Kohen's arms are around my waist, and then patchouli and mint hit me, bringing back the memory of how gentle he was yesterday. Just like he is right now—the prick.

I elbow him in the gut and manage to hobble out of his arms, biting back a wince. He narrows his hazel eyes at me, silently chastising me for a long list of things, I imagine.

"What the fuck are you doing out here?" I glance around for

Liam, but he's nowhere to be seen. The only time Kohen heads out to the church is if Liam is in tow.

"He won't be there."

I'm too busy stabilizing myself with the crutches to process his response. When I do, I pause. "Excuse me?" Why wouldn't Liam be there?

"Your boy," he explains. "He won't be there."

Elijah? "Why do you say that?" *I* know that. But how does *he* know that? Last I checked, Elijah and Kohen aren't exactly buddies.

Kohen shrugs, giving me a blank look. "I told you. Bad things happen to people who touch what isn't theirs."

Oh.

Oh.

So I'm an object now, is that it? Some piece of meat to be handed between the guys? I want to be somebody's, but I sure as hell am not a possession—prized or otherwise.

Although... it does feel a little nice that he's figuratively marked me as his territory.

But more importantly—and I cannot stress this one enough— "You put him in the hospital!"

He has the audacity to look disappointed. "I was aiming for the morgue."

I gape at him. He *what?*

Which part of his response should a rational person be surprised and disturbed by? That he was wanting to kill someone, or that he was willing to kill someone *for me?* Because I'm definitely nowhere near as disturbed as I should be that he wanted to do the latter.

He grabs me before I can react, tipping the world upside down. "Whoa, what are you—put me down right now, Kohen Osman," I snarl, beating his back as he balances me on his shoulder.

Of course, he doesn't put me down. Instead, he tucks the crutches beneath his arm, raises his hand higher up my legs so they sit on the sensitive skin of my thighs, a couple inches beneath the part of me he got overly familiar with yesterday.

The touch of his hands makes my body start priming itself, producing slick as if we're going to have a rerun of yesterday. And there's absolutely zero way that's going to happen. My poor nipples still haven't recovered. I even considered not wearing a bra today to let them breathe.

"You're acting like a caveman!" He needs some serious lessons in social skills if he thinks it's okay to grab a woman's crutches and then throw her over his shoulder. "You're not even going to say anything?" I screech, attempting to kick my legs out, but his burly arms hold me down easily. When I tug on his hair, I swear he shivers.

The lunatic responds by shifting his hands higher to slip a finger beneath my panties. I have to bite my tongue to keep from making a noise. Seriously? I thought I was raw and recovering. Now, I feel ready to take another pounding? Jesus Christ. If I keep this up, I'm going to add nymphomaniac to my file myself.

"Where are you taking me?" If I wasn't worried about being caught out here, I'd scream the question.

Nothing.

Silence.

I hit the back of his head. *Asshole.*

After several minutes of walking, I get bored of attacking the plane of muscles of his back, and I most definitely stop yanking on his short hair because it only encourages those teasing fingers to move.

I have enough control over my mental faculties right now to

know not to succumb to him a second time around. In a month's time we'll have finals, then graduation, and I'll never see him again. He'll go off to do whatever rich nepo babies do after sucking at school, and I'll end up in a ditch somewhere after wandering aimlessly for miles.

Survival isn't an instinct I hold. Living isn't a thing I understand how to do. I don't go through the motions or learn as I go. Life goes on, and I stay exactly the same.

There was a time when I tried so hard to be better, to be the person my grandfather would want, and to be the type of daughter who would bring her mother home. I wanted to be good so badly that I became bad. I didn't forgive, and I didn't forget. I didn't get over it either.

I'm tired of it. So fucking tired.

Life hasn't gotten more accessible; I've just stopped pretending I give a damn that it's killing me.

Even if I wanted to get out of this shithole in one piece, what would I do? Hell, how long would I even last? Whatever, I'll figure it out.

I'll be here, and Kohen will be over there. I'd rather not keep seeing what I'm missing out on because I'll be hooked and on a mission to find the same feeling in random men.

"Put me down, Kohen," I say, losing the energy for any of this. Anger is exhausting.

"Wait." The word comes out gruff as he shoulders open the door into the English and Language Wing using a key fob. Where do I get myself one of those? "Be quiet."

I roll my eyes. "Or what?"

He slips two fingers into me, causing me to get a full-body spasm. I sink my teeth into my bottom lip to stop my cry from echoing down

232

the empty corridors. There's no point reaching around to slap his hand away as he effectively turns me to putty by curling his fingers and hitting the spot that makes me claw at his neck until I draw blood.

I gasp for breath when he pulls his thick fingers out abruptly, opening the door to one of the classrooms. He navigates between the groups of tables, then lowers me onto one of the desks, and I clamber to stand.

"Stay," he orders. "I'll be back."

"I'm not a dog," I snap.

"You're wearing a collar."

I whip my hand up to my throat, feeling the black ribbon I took from the home economics room. "It's called fashion. I don't expect you to underst— Wait. Where the fuck do you think you're going?" I call out to his retreating form.

He ignores me and keeps walking toward the door with my crutches tucked beneath his arm. I slide off the table to follow him out the door, but my attempts last a single step.

Oh, you little...

"Get your ass back here!" I yell, leaning against the desk to take pressure off my foot.

He just chuckles quietly as he closes the door behind him.

"Kohen! I swear to God I'm going to sell your kidney on the black market if you don't give me back my crutches!"

I wait for a beat. Then two.

Nope. Nothing. Not a sound.

He's gone.

I hop on my good foot to the door and swing it open, looking left and right. Where did the—soon to be dead—motherfucker go? Christ, I'm out of breath already.

He left me here. He seriously left me here? Literally, what the fuck? Who takes someone's crutches like this?

Fuck it. You know what? I'll give him five minutes. If he's not back by then, I'm tracking Charlie down, putting my morals aside, and somehow taking both Osman men down. Kohen, by his jealousy. Kiervan, by... I don't know. Maybe I could frame Kohen for the murder of his brother? Does "trying anything once" extend to murder?

Hopping back to the table Kohen deposited me on, I stare out the window to the Science Wing. It's not close, but the modern construction sticks out like a sore thumb against the rest of the gothic structures around here.

It's... almost peaceful sitting in the dark, being somewhere no one but Kohen knows. At least it's peaceful from the outside looking in. On the inside, I'm itching all over. It feels like any second now, I'm going to suffocate under the weight of my impending failure. When have I ever done anything successfully?

My eyes snag on the desk at the front of the class and my fingers start to tap on the corner of the table. The need to steal something tickles the back of my brain, an incessant buzzing that doesn't stop. No one's around. I have pockets.

I gnaw on my bottom lip. If I get caught, the punishment would be so much worse. I wish that fear made the urge disappear, but it only pushes me forward tenfold.

Fuck it. I grit my teeth and jump back off the desk, bearing the pain that slices up my foot and up my leg.

Screw Kohen for leaving me here.

Screw Jonathan Whitlock Sr. for being such a dick.

And screw Elijah for putting me in damn crutches.

I limp over to the teacher's desk and try all the drawers. I'm not about to sit around and wait for Kohen to come get me without an award. I deserve compensation for my patience, and I'll take that in any way I can.

There's no joy in stealing when there's no pressure. If this is a trap, I'm fucked whether I go through the desk or not. If it isn't, then the thrill of it isn't there anyway, so this is a mindless grab to fill the time rather than a compulsive tendency that would have Dr. Van der Merwe scribbling away on his pad. Or is this an impulsive decision?

You know what? It doesn't matter.

None of this matters. Everything is temporary, and I'm going to die eventually anyway.

"Bingo," I say when a drawer finally gives.

My shoulders deflate when I see what's inside. Books? Where's the fun in this? I pull out the books, piling them on the table, flipping through each one as I go. *The History of Literature. The Modern Day Shakespeare. The Art of War. The Aeneid. Pride & Prejudice.*

I drop the books back into the drawer and slam it shut. Well, that was disappointing.

All the other drawers are locked, but it doesn't stop me from trying to wiggle them open. With a little bit more light and the gods' good graces, I might have been able to pick the locks.

The sound of footsteps makes me still, limbs locking just as I'm about to try the cupboard. It grows louder a little too quickly for comfort.

I make a dash for the spot Kohen dropped me in, ignoring the pain as I drop down onto my haunches behind the desk.

There's the thrill I was after. The heart-racing, blood-chilling exhilaration that comes with the suspense of waiting to see who is coming this way. I'm a full-time pessimist until it comes to times like this. Part of the joy of situations like this is being anxious enough to know I might get caught and cocky enough that I'll probably get away with it.

My anxiety-induced racing mind quiets so the sound of the approaching footsteps is all I can hear; I can't even hear my blood pumping or my quickened breath.

Purpose and intent: the two things I can get for free without scrounging around for cash. It's always too short-lived, but there's something to be said about being able to feel every second of it. The sound of my pulse roars in my ears. The way the hairs on the back of my neck stand on end. How a chill settles over my skin. It's almost as good as getting high or having sex with Kohen.

I hold my breath when the lock to the door clicks open, ducking further down and narrowing my eyes to try to make out the person from between the table legs. I grasp the closest thing behind me as the person approaches. Slowly, *quietly*, I pull a thick book off the shelf.

I grip both sides of the book, ready to beat the shit out of the person with *English Grammar For Dummies* when they step out of the shadows and into the moonlight.

Boots. Black jeans. Leather jacket. A row of rings.

I leap up and throw my arms up, waving the book around and roaring childishly. Then I drop my arms and look at Kohen blankly.

"You could at least have the decency to look surprised or even *slightly* shocked."

He says nothing, but the barest hint of a smile curls his lips. This can't be good.

I scream just as he wraps his arms around me, catching me as the entire building shudders and a loud *bang* detonates and lurches my heart into my throat. I whip my head toward the noise just as a giant plume of fire explodes through the broken windows and shattered roof.

Sirens blare across campus as I stare at the violent dance of copper and gold.

The science building just fucking exploded.

BLAZE

CHAPTER 15

"*That's* how you make a bomb." Kohen's voice comes from behind as he releases me. "Next time you try to start a fire, make it as destructive as you are."

Inch by inch, I turn my head toward him. "You built a bomb?"

He sits on the table's edge and tugs me onto his lap. "The instructions are on Google. They had everything I needed in the lab."

"*You built a bomb?*" I repeat.

I'm crazy. I must be crazy. There's no way he's saying what I think he's saying.

Ludicrous. He's absolutely batshit insane. It's the only explanation.

The golden light from the fire outside flickers across his face, reflecting off the greens in his irises, kissing the arrogant pull of his lips. "Happy belated birthday, Thief."

The reality of what's happening hits me all at once. The heat emanating through the window, the sirens, the dark room, Kohen's hardness pushing against my ass. "What"—and I cannot stress this one enough—"the *fuck?*"

Any hint of smugness or pride falls from his face. "Don't you like it?"

My lips part, opening and closing, entirely at a loss for words. "Am I meant to be *impressed?*"

Kohen's brows draw together, and *he* has the audacity to look offended by my question. "I think I deserve a kiss as a thank you," he says with complete seriousness.

Wait. Holy shit. He's serious? He... did he really do that for me?

This is the sweetest, most fucked-up shit anyone has ever done for me. My cheeks are burning hotter from the grand gesture than the fire.

I snap my mouth shut. This would be cute and all if it weren't for this one *teeny weeny* fact. "You burned my house down—a little on the nose, don't you think?"

The muscle in his jaw flickers. "I didn't burn your house down, Blaze."

I throw my hands in the air, then point at my chest. "It sure as shit wasn't me." I point at him. "So it's gotta be you."

The pyromaniac's nostrils flare with a sharp inhale. "It was an accident. None—" He runs his hand down his face, looking more distressed than I've ever seen him. "None of that was meant to happen. I didn't mean to set your house on fire."

I gape at him. I've heard some bad excuses in my time, but I have never heard something this messed up. "How did you accidentally drive several blocks to my property, walk down a long-ass driveway, then *accidentally* light my house on fire?" I'm bad at math, but this isn't adding up.

"I was—fuck, this sounds so stupid." Kohen hangs his head back to stare at the ceiling, massaging his temples like he might be able to avoid the consequences of his actions.

"Stupider than accidentally burning someone's house down and letting them take the fall for it?" I narrow my eyes, pushing off his lap to lean against the window behind me to ease the pressure off my throbbing ankle. "Try me, buddy. I'm all ears."

He takes a deep breath and looks at his hands lying in his lap. "I was there."

"No shit."

His eyes meet mine. "That night of the fire, I was waiting for you," he explains, desperation lacing each syllable. "I was sick of you hating me so much and wanted you to just shut up and listen for once. So I came over and started a fire just below your window, expecting you to come out."

I frown, shifting my weight.

"I waited and waited, feeding the fire so it wouldn't be dead by the time you came out. So you'd be warm." He sucks in a staggered breath and runs his hand over his mouth like he's recounting one of the worst moments of his life. " I was going to go inside, but I was trying not to piss you off even more than usual because I... I wanted to impress you. I wanted you to see how serious I was and that I could be the type of man you want. Instead, I got pissed off waiting around for you to come down, so I went inside to find the place empty. The first thing I saw when I pulled out my phone was a picture of you sitting on Duke's lap, and I just..." He rolls his neck side to side, trying to ease the tension in his muscles as his lips pull into a thin line. "I went back outside and kicked the firepit," he continues. "I thought

I put it out. There was just… the leaves were so dry, and the breeze was…"

Nothing but the flames outside and the fire alarm can be heard as the air sizzles between us. "Let me make this clear," I say slowly, pushing off the window to force Kohen to look dead into my eyes. "You burned my house down because you were jealous? *Fucking jealous?*" I shriek.

Kohen explodes too, lurching up to grab my throat, jaw ticking and shoulders tight beneath his leather jacket. "I'm here because of you!"

I roll my eyes and hit his chest. "Not this shit again—"

"Who do you think I sent into a coma just to get here—to *you?*" The question hangs between us as he stares at me so intently it feels like he's unpacking every inch of who I am so he can figure out how to make me understand him.

A stone lodges in the center of my chest. "You mean Elijah?"

"Duke."

My lips part.

He touched something that didn't belong to him. That's what he told me the first day he was here.

I stare at him for a moment, waiting for the punchline. My eyes drop to the fist curled at his side, and for the first time tonight, I notice the red outlining the fresh black ink etched into crooked dashes that goes in a semicircle on the side of his pointer finger.

Teeth marks.

My teeth marks from yesterday.

I'd stagger back if he weren't holding me. This… none of the emotions he's been showing me is new to him—this *lust* or infatuation or whatever it is he's had for me and never communicated before.

242

Did it start right before I was sent here, or around when I went out with other guys? He's never said anything nice to me, flirted, or did anything an average person would do if they were interested in someone. Why is he suddenly showing his interest in me?

Kohen permanently ingrained *my teeth marks* into his skin before telling me the truth about the biggest sin I hold against him. More than that, he did it knowing I could spend the rest of my life hating him even after discovering the truth.

"I'm sorry."

My gaze cuts to his hazel eyes. "What?"

I know what those two words mean—I've heard them plenty of times, read them, spelled them, but not once have they ever been directed to me.

"I'm sorry for hurting you." He lowers his forehead to mine, speaking just loud enough for me to hear. "Let me make it up to you."

My heart pinches. Kohen can't say that either. He isn't allowed to. But I didn't realize how badly I wanted to hear it.

Softly, he says, "Let me show you how important you are."

I swallow. "You let them believe it was me."

Even if he didn't mean to do it, he still committed the crime I was sentenced for. Because of him, I lost the place I called home. I lost the useless things that brought shape to my meaningless life. And I... I can't find it in me to hate him for it.

His forehead wrinkles as he tries to make me understand just by the look on his face. "I can get to you if you're here. I can't risk losing you forever if I go to prison."

I want to scream at him. I want to riot. I want him to explain why he never said anything before. I want to hurt him for hurting me. I want all of it because there's one thing I know with absolute

243

certainty: he's telling the truth.

He says it was an accident, and I believe him.

He says he wants to take care of me, and I believe him. I just don't think he knows how to—I don't know either. Nobody has ever taken care of me. Hell, I've barely taken care of myself. My stomach turns as I watch the way the blacks of his pupils consume the golden hues of his irises when our gazes collide. Don't they say your pupils dilate when you see someone you care about? Whatever it is he thinks he feels, it's wrong. I'll never get the prince because I don't deserve it.

"I wanted you before I even knew your name." Kohen runs his thumb along my cheek, and the one simple touch feels unlike anything I could imagine. "It's always been you."

His voice comes out low, like he's found the words somewhere beneath all the darkness in his heart. It's louder than the sirens and the pulse racing in my ears as he kisses a path up my neck.

I shake my head.

"It will always be you," he whispers against my skin and brushes a kiss over my lips. "You're a necessity to me."

My tongue flicks out, tasting mint. Kohen is the only constant I've had my entire life. Whether he was sick or injured, he'd always be waiting for me by the tree on my route home. Kohen walked inside my bare house, met my mother, saw me high, saw me hungover, saw me over every other man but him. I've hit him, screamed at him, framed him, did things I know would hurt him, and he's still here.

Two endless pools of gold stare back at me, molten and hypnotizing as his warm hand slips up my skirt and toys with the line of my panties before pushing two fingers into me.

I curse and grab onto his leather jacket. When he pushes his hips against me, I don't move away. When he unbuttons my shirt, baring my plain black bra to him, my hand falls to the hard dent in his pants, making him hiss against my skin.

I'm not going to ruin him; he's going to destroy me. It was foolish to think there was any version of this story where I'd emerge the victor. I think if I were to die right now, I might be lowered to the ground with a smile on my face.

Knowing all this, like the pain that will follow once it ends and the hole that will grow bigger in my heart, I still unbuckle his pants.

Any control I've ever thought I had was an illusion; at least right now, I'm not trying to fool myself. With the fire warming my back and the sirens a distant tune, I give in to what my body wants so badly.

His dick is just as big as the first time I saw him without his pants, and it seems even more daunting when it's in my hands. My name comes out of him like the embodiment of yearning at the first stroke. I only manage three more before he throws off his jacket, picks me up, and wraps my legs around his waist, using the window behind me for support.

Pushing my panties aside, he slowly brings me down on him, stretching me out to the point of pain. We both curse as he breaches my entrance, and my muscles tighten to try and keep him out. A whimper comes out instead of a moan, and he kisses me in a way I hate. With just the press of his lips, every single wall I've built comes crashing down, sending shockwaves all through me.

"It hurts," I whisper, not sure whether I'm talking about the gnawing ache in my core from taking him, or the soul-deep torture of admission.

"I know. I've got you." His harsh breaths fan my heated skin. "Just a little more. I'm right here."

I squeeze my eyes shut, hating the way his words tear through my defenses. He's seen me when no one else has.

Kohen's lips meet mine in a searing kiss. He moves, and I move with him, screaming at myself to stop but knowing I never will. It's not like I know what's good for me.

Inch by inch, I take a little more of him until I'm so full, it's dizzying. Just as he lowers me to the hilt, he breaks the kiss, piercing me with his gaze as he whispers against my lips, "At the beginning, middle, and end, you're the only one I'll ever want. You're mine, Blaze."

"Don't." My voice cracks.

If he keeps saying that, I'll never find it in me to hate him the way I used to. In the end, even that was a lie because did I ever really hate him? He annoyed me with his incessantness, and sometimes I hated the words that came out of his mouth, and all the shit he pulled when we were kids. But none of those things ever caused me the type of pain that my own family caused. Maybe it wasn't hatred for Kohen that I felt, but hatred at life in general.

There are so many reasons why none of this can happen. I'm going down, and I don't think I want to take Kohen down with me. Not when he's looking at me the same way he looks at fire whenever he plays with his lighter. Not when he's holding on to me like he will never let go.

I'm bad news—the worst kind there is. My grandfather knows it, everyone around here knows it, so why can't he see it too? Why is he torturing me by giving me the thing I always wanted when I've already accepted I'll never have it?

A tear falls, and he wipes it away before I can pretend it never happened, pulling his hips away just a fraction, only to push back into me. "I'm yours, Thief. I'm never going to stop wanting you."

"Stop talking," I beg, digging my nails into the back of his neck like a desperate prayer that he might listen.

Kohen keeps grinding his hips into me, going incrementally faster. "I've seen every single part of you. All the broken parts—even the parts you hate, and I'm still going to stay."

"Shut up." The roles have reversed. Now, I'm the one pleading for him to stop saying words that will hurt.

"I don't want to be your enemy. I don't want to be your friend. There's only one way this ends." Sex is intimate and raw, but it doesn't strip me bare like the feeling of being understood.

He doesn't let me drop my head against the crook of his shoulder or hide from every intensified part of him. So I have no choice but to look back at him and know this is it for me. Nothing will ever compare to this moment. Every thrust, every heartbeat, every word that comes out of his mouth, and mostly, *him*.

"For you? I'll burn it all."

How he's looking at me is enough to push my head against the window to get away.

There's a fire blazing at my back, but his stare is on me. I hold the eyes of a pyromaniac. How dangerous is it to be chosen over flames?

This isn't power; it's a one-way path to destruction. Kohen looks at me like he's taking the first hit of his favorite drug. He's heavy-lidded with eager eyes that've been swallowed by an abyss of black, knowing he would have crawled over glass for a taste of the thing he's been hungry for his whole life.

"You're so fucking beautiful."

I choke on a sob. "Please," I beg again. I can't handle it. "Stop talking, Kohen."

"Say it again," he gasps.

"Stop—"

"No, my name. Say it again. You don't sound like you hate it." Desperation laces his voice, even though his eyes are laden with despair.

"I hate you, Kohen." He's right. I don't sound like I hate him. Not a single part of what I said sounds convincing.

"Yeah, you do. But you love the way my cock feels." His lips tip up in a slight smile as he tallies up another win.

"In your dreams, firebug." He slams into me as I speak, turning my speech into a cry.

"What was that, Thief?" A grin stretches across his lips, full of hope and all the good things he'll never find in me.

"I'll never be with you," I say on a gasp as he drives me into the window.

"You make it sound like I was giving you an option." He might have been gentle with me before, but it's like he somehow knows it isn't what I need, because his hand moves around my throat, pressing me back as he pummels his hips into me.

Each thrust pushes away the storm clouds in my way until all there is are the sensations spreading through my body and the pressure building in my core. He captures me in a kiss and pulls my bottom lip between his teeth, making me moan.

"You don't have any idea what you do to me," he rasps.

"Oh, I think I do. And I could make you so much worse."

The grip around my throat tightens, cutting off the oxygen to my brain as I gasp for breath. "You're my special little whore, aren't you?"

My.

Special.

Little whore?

He's really pulling out all the stops today.

I like it more than I should.

The force of his thrusts makes me slide up the window. "All pathetic and wet. I barely fingered that tight pussy of yours, and now look at you."

I gasp for air as my eyelids shudder, threatening to close. Kohen presses his lips against my ear, holding my ass as he fucks me like it's his last chance at finding heaven.

"You're taking my cock like you were made to be fucked by me." His voice is dripping with sin, promising me an orgasm that will shake the foundation of my being and shatter my brick walls.

For the sake of my sanity, I need rage. The tenderness of his words, of his looks, is too much. The vicious animosity that makes Kohen lose the fight with temptation and let himself fall from his nonexistent grace.

My lungs burn and scream for air; every inch of my body does. A cold sheen prickles over my skin, and white spots dot my vision. My hands find his arm—the one holding a tight grip on my throat—to grab onto. It doesn't matter how hard I try to draw air into my lungs, his hold on me cuts off all the oxygen.

"Do you want to breathe?" The look on his face is nothing short of maniacal as he takes in my paling skin and the plea watering my eyes. "You do?"

I nod—or at least I try to when he's holding me hostage like this. My brain doesn't want it to stop though, because all that is on my mind is the way he feels inside me and how close I am to reaching ecstasy.

"I can't hear you," he mocks.

"Yes." I form the word with my mouth rather than say it.

His eyes darken. "Louder."

"Please," I croak, even though my orgasm is catching up faster than I can handle.

"You're such a good little slut when you listen," he muses, studying the way I swallow hungry gulps of air when he lets go of my throat. "Only I can give you what you need, isn't that right?"

I moan louder, clawing at his back as I roll on his cock without his help. That only makes him pull out. I growl, hitting his chest when he yanks the impending release from me.

"Ah, ah." He grins. "You don't get to come until I let you, brat."

I'm going to kill him.

I glare at him, chasing his cock with my hips. "Stop being a bitch and *fuck me.*"

The fucker is enjoying this way too much. Being consumed by frustration is still better than crying in front of him.

"Beg like the desperate, needy girl you are." He slips his tip inside of me only to pull out straightaway.

"Fuck you," I hiss.

"Beg me to fuck you," he repeats.

"Hard pass."

I scream out when he plunges me down on his cock, making me take him to the hilt. "Fuck. You feel so good, baby." His voice comes out hoarse and anguished, but it doesn't stop him from pulling me right off him with a strained smirk. "Too bad you aren't going to come."

I bare my teeth and yank his head back by his hair. "I hate you, Kohen Osman."

"You've brought this on yourself." He does the exact same thing to me, grabbing a fistful of my hair and holding me back, seething beneath his lust-filled stare. "Say my name, Blaze. Tell me how sorry you are for keeping that pretty pussy away from me for so long. Tell me you're going to learn and make decent fucking fires."

My lip curls into a smile that's all teeth. "Maybe I'll just ask—"

My eyes widen when he drops my legs and spins me around to face the window. Both my hands fly forward so I don't fall. "You're going to watch what I did for you while you come on the cock of the man you hate."

A cry rips out of my throat when he slams into me with a single thrust. The fire still rages, and I watch as people mill about observing the fire while others rush to the evacuation area.

Someone could have seen me get fucked against the window—someone still could. In this moment, I couldn't care less about either when this angle hits each and every part of me that amplifies the feel of him. A single drive of his hips and I know that it won't matter how hard I try to fight it, I'm going to come on his cock.

"If you want me to be your enemy, I'm going to fuck you like I hate you." *Thrust.* "You're not going to be able to walk after this." *Thrust.* "You're not going to be able to move with how thoroughly destroyed you are." *Thrust.* "Every time you fuck yourself with your fingers, you're going to wish I never ruined you." *Thrust.* "So hate me, Thief. Tell me you want me dead because you're the only reason I'd end up in a grave."

One second, he's slamming into me with his hands on my hips; the next, he's rutting me like he's lost all his inhibitions, and all he knows is the heat searing through us. Pleasure thunders through every corner of my body, turning my nerve endings into live wire as my muscles spasm around his cock, milking him for whatever he has when he comes at the same time. It spills into me and drips down my thighs even as his dick is still twitching inside me.

His fingers wrap around the front of me, grasping me in a tight hug. Kohen's soft lips graze the shell of my ear as he whispers, "Hate me all you want, Blaze. But I could never hate you."

BLAZE

CHAPTER 16

"And where were you?"

I roll my eyes. "Getting rawdogged in the English Department."

McGill's eyes twitch as he narrows them at me. He's gripping his fountain pen a little too tight for comfort, and I wouldn't put it past him—or Boris and the other guard standing two feet away from me—to stake me with the pen, then label it self-defense.

Dr. Jackass watches me closely from his spot on the couch beneath the window that overlooks the long, dooming driveway into this hellscape. I've sat on this green velvet chaise more times than I would like, but this is the first time I'm not lounging on it as I talk about my feelings to the resident shrink.

Dr. Van der Merwe's and the headmaster's offices are the only two decent-looking rooms in the school—both gloomy and stinking of entitled rich men's testosterone. It looks like it too. Mahogany walls and floors, an oversized antique red rug, rows upon rows of science books and weird little skulls, and—wait, is that a real brain?

Christ. I'm not sure how I missed that the ten-plus times I've been in here.

Contrary to the guards' usual tactic of taking me to the headmaster's office, they dragged me to this room to recount the events of last night because I was one of the last people to reach the evacuation point—being carried bridal style by Kohen, no less.

Word on the street is the preliminary investigation shows that the Science building blew up because of a gas leak. But they can't be certain yet without doing a full investigation. Bitch Face One and Bitch Face Two here haven't said as much, but I suspect they think it's foul play by yours truly.

It's flattering they'd think I could pull something like that off. I could only dream of causing an explosion of that magnitude.

I cross my legs and immediately uncross them again because of the ache at the apex of my thighs. *Kohen is a fucking monster.* Sighing, I slump down in my seat. "I told you already." Three times, to be exact. "I was walking around looking for Elijah when I heard a loud bang. I fell over from shock and screwed my foot"—*cervix*—"up even more, so I was struggling to walk. That's when I ran into Kohen, and he carried me the rest of the way."

I'm sure they're all collectively thinking, *we don't believe you.*

I can practically hear those four words playing on a loop in their heads. What's the point of this little get-together if they aren't going to believe a word that comes out of my mouth?

"Why were you looking for Elijah?" McGill asks.

The only silver lining to this unfortunate turn of events is that no one thinks I started the fight with Elijah or pushed him down the bleachers. There were enough witnesses to say that he came at me. As for the part where he's in hospital, apparently my puny arms couldn't manage something of that magnitude, so I'm off the hook for that.

"Because I wanted to clear the air about what happened and ensure nothing like that happens again." Okay, yeah, that doesn't even sound believable to me. I huff out a breath when McGill gives me a look. "I wanted him to apologize to me for screwing up my foot."

"You wanted drugs," Dr. Van der Merwe speaks for the first time since I sat down ten minutes ago.

"*Ding, ding, ding.* They didn't make you a doctor for nothing." I mock-clap. If I deny it, they won't believe me. If I stay quiet, I'll feel like a cornered animal.

I flinch when McGill suddenly slams his notebook shut. "Let's cut to the chase, shall we?"

Shifting uncomfortably in my seat, I shoot a wary glance at the two guards. If McGill is being this short with me, something terrible is probably about to happen.

"Your grandfather is interested in confirming what he already suspects so he can plan how your future looks. Elijah gave you drugs in exchange for your *services.*" McGill motions to my body with his last word, and I cringe at the implication. He's wrong. I'm not like my mother—not entirely. "You stopped providing your end, and he lashed out. Now, your supplier is indisposed, and you're looking for another troubled soul to make your life feel dismally better."

I hold my breath as I watch him reach for the bag on the side of the couch. He rummages around, and my heart stops beating when he pulls out a small ziplock bag holding white powder.

"You see this?" McGill waves the bag, and my eyes follow it like

I'm a starved dog and he's pulled out a fresh slice of meat. How long has it been since I had any blow? "We confiscated it from a student last month." He sounds pleased with himself—probably because he has me exactly where he wants me. "Cocaine is your drug of choice, correct? An expensive vice you have, especially with such a nonexistent wallet."

I wet my lips and grip the seat. "What do you want?" My attempt at cool indifference falls short.

"Isn't it obvious?" he asks, a condescending grin on his lips. At my blank look, he sighs. "Dr. Van der Merwe and I believe in exploring different avenues before resorting to more extreme measures. Bribery is one of the most well-known forms of acquiring information or goods—you of all people would know that."

My lips flatten into a thin line. "I'm not a prostitute."

Even if I were, who gives a shit? I'm not hurting anyone—Kohen is though.

McGill drops the bag on the wooden coffee table between us, and every cell in my body becomes hyper-aware of its existence. "Admit to causing the fire or tell us who did it, and it's all yours."

I quickly do the calculation in my head. It's a big bag. That has to be at least an eight ball of cocaine. If I ration it out well, it could last me long enough until I get out of this place. If I'm strapped for cash, I could sell off a gram to another student. Maybe offer bumps.

I can think about doing the last two all I want, but every time Tony swung me some extra cash, it went straight toward the thing in front of me.

Isn't this the perfect outcome? I get back at Kohen and end up with the bag. Only my mouth stays shut, and my eyes remain firmly on the bag. When will it end? I'll accept this one bag in exchange for information, and then what's next? Dance on the table for a joint? Bend over, or I'll tell your grandfather all about what you've done?

Not just that, how far will I go in my crusade against Kohen? He already put himself in here because of me—risked imprisonment *for me*, not just once, but three times already—four if I include the accidental arson that I haven't forgiven or forgotten about.

And he's… he's been kind. *Nice.* Those aren't the right words, but admitting that he's being anything more will send me into a spiral.

I could never hate you.

My gut churns at the memory. But it dissolves when my eyes crash with McGill's as his voice breaks me out of my stupor.

"It's unfortunate that it's too soon to do another ECT. No matter." He smiles apathetically. "There are always alternatives."

Three things happen at once: Boris lunges for my legs while the other guard traps me in a headlock, forcing me to lie on the chaise. I suck in a futile breath and scream as loud as I can, thrashing as I do. Lastly, the part that has me most worried is when McGill crosses over the room and squats down at the foot of the lounger with a diabolical look lurking beneath his calm facade.

"We tried playing nice with you, Miss Whitlock." Boris clamps my legs down as McGill slowly places his hand over my sore foot.

My heart rattles against my rib cage as I try clawing at the sleeved arms around my head. My ankle hurts more today than it did twenty-four hours ago because of how much I was using it. I whip my head side to side, but all it does is chafe my skin.

I can feel bruises forming beneath their hands, yet the pain of their hold doesn't make me falter. It doesn't bring me any less comfort that they won't zap me again, but they can torture me in other ways.

"Get your disgusting hands off me!" It's all in vain, the fighting, the screaming, the thought that I'll get out of this. But I don't stop. I can't. I didn't survive this long to be deterred by hurt.

McGill presses the balls of his fingers into my swollen ankle, and white-hot pain scorches my veins. I cry out, using the adrenaline to throw any of the three men off, but they have countless pounds of muscle on me.

A shuddered breath bubbles out of me as the headmaster loosens his hold just enough to lessen the pressure.

"Let's try this again, shall we?" McGill cocks his head to the side as he gives me a pitiful look at my thrashing. "Admit to the explosion, and I'll stop."

I hesitate, only for a second, but my mouth opens, and I say the three words I can't take back. "Kohen did it."

I took the fall for his crimes once, and I'm not doing that again.

The guilt feels acidic in my stomach, but I swallow it down and keep looking straight. How many times do I need to be in this type of situation? With someone else's hands on me, held down, debased to something that's so expendable, the word *dignity* doesn't need to be attached.

"This again?"

My heart sinks to my stomach.

Stupid. Stupid. Stupid.

For a second there, I was delusional enough to believe that my words meant anything to anyone.

They can grab my foot as many times as they want, strap me to the chair and electrocute me, or wave that bag in front of my face; nothing will sting as badly as this.

"The shed," is all I manage to say.

Hopeless.

That's the word I'm looking for.

That's what I am.

I stop thrashing around. I stop fighting. What's the point? It won't change anything.

"Do not take us for fools. We know it was you."

"It wasn't," I lie through my teeth. I might as well confess to it. That would probably be the first time in my life any kind of authority figure believes me.

"Mr. Osman may have willingly taken the blame for you once; there won't be a second time."

My lips part. "Willingly?"

Does he mean Kohen never tried to argue his way out of it? Never tried placing the blame on someone else or even claimed he had no knowledge of it? He just... he confessed to the crime I committed.

McGill doesn't give me the courtesy of an answer. "Last chance," he says, subtly squeezing my ankle. "No?"

I grit my teeth and let out a silent cry. They don't deserve to feel satisfaction over my pain. No one around here can hear me, and no one except Kohen would do a damn thing about it even if they could.

"That's enough." Dr. Van der Merwe steps forward. I slice my gaze over to his flattened brows while his eyes capture the scene.

"Confess." A single word is all McGill gives me.

"Does my grandfather know you're doing this?" I blurt out, trying to buy some time as I process this new information. After everything Kohen said about trying to get to me, he told them it was him? Even knowing they could have pressed charges—slim as that risk may be?

"No, but I doubt he would be opposed. As I'm sure Dr. Van der Merwe has said, your grandfather takes your rehabilitation very seriously."

"Bullshit." I spit, trying to summon the dwindling fight in me. "You're torturing me for information I've already given you, and to get your sick fucking kicks out of it." McGill made his hatred toward me clear the second I started stirring shit. "Kohen said he started the last fire; why aren't you questioning him about what he might know?"

"There's no point wasting anyone's time when you could tell the truth." McGill bares his fingers down, squeezing so tightly that tendons and joints give way beneath his grip. Even if I tried, I couldn't stop the feral screech that tears out of me. "*Confess*, Blaze."

"*That's enough.*" Dr. Van der Merwe claps a hand on McGill's shoulder and tugs him back.

I slump back onto the chaise, desperately trying to catch my bearings, which is hard when I'm in a headlock. Both men wear rugged looks as they stare each other down. I study the nuances of their interaction, the posturing, and the subtle hints written on their faces. Where the shrink's lips tip down with disapproval and the headmaster's curl with irritation. I can smell their bad blood from here.

"We agreed *not* to harm a student like this," the shrink chides.

The good doctor is fine with scientific torture, but this is where he draws the line? What the fuck even is this place where they've already had that type of discussion?

McGill straightens to his feet, readjusting his suit and righting his tie as he looks down his nose at his colleague. "Fine. Have it your way." He pivots slowly on his heel as he grabs his satchel and walks toward the door. "Don't complain to me when she doesn't talk."

The doctor's lips press into a tight line as if he has more to add, and he's been saving them in a folder beneath his desk. His attention stays on the slammed door for a beat longer before it turns on me.

My moment of reprieve is short-lived, and my impending doom makes itself known when he says, "Take her to isolation."

This time, when the guards each grab an arm, I don't bother fighting, not when Boris digs his fingers into the soft skin of my arms, or when they throw me into the room with nothing but a water bottle and a granola bar, and the eight ball of coke taped to the other side of the safety window.

The silence slowly becomes deafening as seconds tick by into minutes, and minutes tick by into hours. With only a sliver of light coming from the window, it's hard to tell what time it is until dusk falls, filtering soft, orange streams into the desolate room. Then everything turns bleak and gray.

I've learned about another privilege today: electricity. I've gotten by without it before. McGill has deprived me of light before while I'm stuck in this room. But unlike all the times I lost power at my house, the front door was still open for me to leave. I wasn't confined to four empty walls and nothing but my mind to pass the time. This punishment is worse than holding me down and inflicting pain because they've left me with two worse things: my own thoughts and the packet of faux freedom taped to the door, just out of reach.

Teasing me.

Goading me.

Mocking me.

One line and this entire night could blur away in a whirlwind of random thoughts. Or maybe I'd have a panic attack. Either way, at least *something* would happen.

It doesn't matter how many times I pace, night still doesn't turn into day, prison into freedom. I can stare at the white powder, count how many specs there are, study the lines in my fingerprint, and tell myself it's a labyrinth to my liberation, but I'm still in here with an empty bottle of water and the ripped-up granola bar wrapper.

I don't know why I think that at any second, I'll find Kohen at the door, ready to be my knight in shining armor, about to whisk me away from this hellhole. I told him I'm not a damsel in distress when I'm a walking cry for help.

But I was right at the beginning; I'm in here because of him in every sense of the word. He gave me the gun, loaded it with bullets, cocked it, and told me where to aim. So I pulled the trigger. Take the gun away, and what's left?

Night turns to a stormy day, and the same words are said. "Confess or tell me who did it." When it comes out of the doctor's mouth, it's kinder. Sympathetic almost. Like maybe he doesn't want me in here just as much as I don't want to be in here.

Either way, I say the same thing. "Kohen did it."

I say the three words not because of any feelings I harbor toward Kohen. I say it for myself.

I have never needed him to save me or get me out of my mess. I managed to keep myself alive—barely—for the better part of eighteen years. A man isn't going to swoop in to change that, regardless of the trajectory I'm on.

Dr. Van der Merwe leaves me the same thing he did the day before: a small bottle of water and a granola bar.

This time, I ration it, taking a bite and a couple sips every hour. The patheticness of it makes me smile to myself. I guess I am capable of new things.

The sun sets behind clouds of gray, and the sky breaks into darkness, battering the roof with bits of ice.

The same happens on the third day. A proposition, three words, then food and water.

On the fourth, the same. But this time, the door stays open, and four different words are uttered instead.

"You didn't do it."

To that, I respond with another four. "I told you so."

And it feels good to say.

KOHEN

CHAPTER 17

A gas leak? The internet really does have everything on there.

I'd be gloating if it weren't for the fact they've kept Blaze holed up for the past three nights. The motherfuckers even changed the keys to keep me out.

I stalk through the hallway, following the head of copper hair weaving between people while on two crutches. I can't count how many books and sheets of paper have turned to ash in the days Blaze was gone. She bolted out of class as quickly as she could, thinking she could blend into the lunch crowd and evade me entirely.

The thief has another thing coming.

I haven't gone to McGill's office every day since they took her, demanding to know where she is, just for her to try to run from me.

The distance quickly closes between us. Even though Blaze protests when I lift her up, no one intervenes as I whisk her into the closest room, bearing the brunt of her attacks via crutches.

Reminder for next time: make sure she's free of weapons before kidnapping her.

"What is wrong with you? You can't just do that!" She shoves me away as I sit her on top of the kitchenette.

Hello to you too, Blaze.

The break room is ten by five feet, if that. Nothing but a long bench hugging the right-side wall, a single stool, a bar fridge, and a mini sink.

"Didn't anyone ever teach you not to pick someone up—*or deprive them of their walkers, Osman?*" Her arms flare around, enunciating her words.

There are several things I notice while she pretends to be angry about my tactics rather than something else on her mind.

One, she still hasn't jumped down or told me off for locking the door.

Two, she isn't slapping my hands away as I pull her backpack off, lowering it on the floor next to mine.

Three, she went in reverse. In a span of three nights, she's returned to the gaunt girl whose shineless hair fell flat against her scalp and whose skin was devoid of any warmth. Sunken cheekbones, hollow eye sockets, colorless lips. Broken blood vessels line her throat, puckering the skin with a pinkish hue that didn't come from me.

Wrong.

This is all wrong.

"What happened?" The words rumble through my chest.

My hand reaches for her throat before I can think it through. Her pulse almost feels as weak as the night I visited her in isolation.

She rams the palm of her hand into my shoulder, and I let her.

Mostly because if I push for an answer, she'll never tell me. And I'm already two seconds away from losing my shit. Arguing won't improve those odds.

"Why do you care?" Blaze's icy glare drops the temperature by thirty degrees.

"Why do I care? *Why do I care?* Are you out of your mind? If you're still asking me that question, maybe my methods of showing you should be more extreme."

How much more obvious can I be? I accept the possibility that I was too subtle about it before. But since I've come here, the only other thing I can do is tear my heart out of my chest and wrap it in a bow.

She'd probably miss that hint too.

I told her that it was always her, and she will *always* be the one for me. If that were a lie, my first time being intimate with a woman wouldn't have been on an examination bed.

"No, I'm definitely *not* out of my mind." The lines around her eyes crinkle as the klepto narrows them at me. "I have done nothing but think for the past four days, and I salute you, Osman." Blaze leans in closer, jaw tensed, looking like she's ready to start an explosion with me as the single casualty. "Well fucking played. You really had me there. *Let me take care of you. I'll be gentle. I could never hate you.*" Shaking her head, Blaze curls her lips into disgust. "Fuck. You. Kohen."

I rock back on my heels. What the fuck is she talking about?

"The Science building? *Genius.* It's better than anything I could have thought up—which isn't surprising. No one thought you caused the explosion with Mrs. Crichton's things, so what better way to get back at me than by burning the department she works in? You took the fall in the shed, evened the score, so no one looks further than me. *Genius.*"

My chest tightens. It's hard to even look at her. After *everything* I did, the thief thinks this is a game? A sick, perverted scheme to get back at her for tearing up my room and four days in the can?

"Maybe you didn't understand me before, *Whitlock.*" She flinches, but I keep going. "I don't say anything I don't mean. If you want a liar, go run to Kiervan. If I wanted to get back at you, I could have ten times over—you steal, you drink, you fight, you use. You're the perfect crime already, and I wouldn't have to lift a finger."

She doesn't want me as much as I want her. She won't turn the world upside down for me like I would for her. I would turn this earth into cinders—strike a single match and set this horrible world ablaze—if she asked me to. I've accepted all this because everything would be worth it as long as she feels something other than hatred toward me.

She didn't love me last week or right now. She may not even love me a decade from now. But I will be wherever she is, even if she doesn't want me. Man will always follow the light where there is darkness, and she is fire. The world is cold and empty without her.

"I caused the explosion—risked *everything*—to show you how serious I am." Blaze thinks so little of herself that she thinks I see her the same way. When will she realize that I will do anything for her? She doesn't ask for anything, and I already do it anyway. "I went to McGill's office three times in three days to tell him it was me."

With every word, her expression falls more and more until her eyes drop to the tattoo on my finger, and mine go to the ring around hers. "You confessed?"

I nod. "Get your shit together, Blaze."

Blaze jerks back. "Excuse me?"

"No one else is going to do it for you. If you think you are getting away with your shit now, there will come a day when everything catches up to you, and you're going to regret every step you didn't take."

"Oh, and you're so high and mighty and Mr. Perfect, huh?" She rolls her eyes. "Don't give me shit when you got held back."

"Don't," I warn.

She tips her head to the side. "What? Don't like people calling you out on your own shit?"

"I didn't pass because of you," I blurt. "You didn't hear me the first time I said it, so maybe you'll hear it now. The plan for it was in the works for three years. I couldn't have passed all the previous years and failed the last. I had to be disciplined about each exam I failed and when I failed it. If not, they would have made me take a couple make-up exams or slide in a couple extracurriculars."

"You're so fucking delusional. None of that has—"

"Shut the fuck up and listen to me." I grab hold of her head in both hands. Maybe then she'll hear every word I say. "I failed all my classes *because of you.*"

"Like I said, your head is shoved so far up—"

I let go of her and run my hand down my face as I pace the small room. Why is it so hard for her to understand? "*Everything* I did, I did it *for you.* Staying back a year. Leaving my food on the desk for you to take, or buying your groceries because your grandfather/ Whitlock Senior forgot to. Letting you pawn the watch I borrowed from my dad to buy a new bed because you slept on the floor after your mom took yours. Asking my brother for money three years ago just to buy the coat you always wear. Writing all of Kiervan's college assignments. Doing his bidding for the past ten years. Changing your locks. Fixing your window when the latch wouldn't close. Your house. *Being here.* I did all of it for you. And you know what, Blaze?"

Her sterling-blue eyes drop to my chest, unable to look me in the eyes as her throat bobs.

Tilting her chin up, her gaze collides with mine, and I'm struck with awe at how breathtaking she always is. "I would do it all again for you." My fingers skate over the side of her face, admiring the red flush that's returned to her cheeks.

The silence stretches between us as she searches my eyes for more until she speaks. "What did you do for Kiervan?"

The corner of my lips almost ticks up. It wouldn't be Blaze if she didn't pick my story apart. "Whatever he wanted."

A wrinkle forms between her brows. "Why?"

"If my father found out about you, he'd set your house on fire. Only this time, you'd be in it. So I've been doing everything he asks just to keep you safe from him."

She pulls back from my touch, and my hands fall to her thighs. "But you think I'm less than you because of my parents and the drugs." Her lips pull into a tight line.

"That's not true."

"Bullshit." She shakes her head. "All you've ever done is give me shit over it."

"I don't care who your parents are or what they do. You're the one who came to that conclusion all on your own."

She squints at me like she's trying to read me. "Do you even hear yourself? How many times have you compared me to my mother?"

"Convenience." Her lips part like she can't believe what I just said. "Whether it was your mother, your nephew, or a stranger on the street, I'll make that comparison because that's the path you're on." Grabbing the back of her thighs, I tow her to the edge of the bench so I can station myself between her legs. "All those people can do whatever they want and get their shit anyway they like, but they aren't *you*. You aren't going to be like them. You aren't going to end up like my grandfather."

"And where do you even get the confidence to think that you'd be the one to *fix* me? You—" She swats my hand when I press it against her pulse. It's faster than before but no less weak. "Jesus Christ! Why the hell do you keep choking me? Burning my house down wasn't enough; now you want to kill me too?"

"I want to make sure you're still alive."

My answer makes her stop in her barrage of trying to get out of my hold. "Of course, I am."

"You might not be."

"Clearly, I am." Her forehead pinches as she studies me.

"I sat next to my grandfather for six hours before I realized he was dead."

She gapes at me. "What?"

"I chose to stay with him over the summer when I was eight while Kiervan and my parents went to the Hamptons—Kiervan and my father are both textbook psychopaths, and I try to avoid them at all costs," I explain. "My grandma was already dead, and I didn't like my grandparents on Mom's side—and didn't want to fly to see them either."

I can still picture the estate clearly: perfectly mowed lawns, gardens to the nines that my grandma planted before she died, giant white colonial pillars, and a door twice my height. It was just outside the city, where the air is cleaner and, at night, I could see the stars.

Dropping my hand from Blaze's throat, I reach for the pulse point at her wrist. "He always worked late into the night, holed up in his office for hours on end. Once or twice, I found him asleep at his desk or napping on the couch. When I was five, I woke him up, and he was so upset with me, I could barely sit for two days from the bruises he gave me. I never did it again." I never would have done it to begin with if Kiervan hadn't convinced me to do it under the pretense that Grandpa wanted us to wake him. "When everyone else was away in Vermont, I woke up from a bad dream and went to his office because sometimes he'd tell me a story or a life lesson that was so boring I'd fall asleep. If I was lucky, he'd let me have a sip of his scotch, then send me away."

I pause, looking down to see her slender hand covering mine, but mainly looking at Grandpa's ring on the thumb running over my knuckles.

He would have hated her because of how wild she is, but there's another life lesson he wasn't around to tell me. If the intention is to control them, then it isn't true love, it's loving the idea of them.

"He had bad lungs from contracting pneumonia as a kid. The whole house could hear him snore every time he slept—but it was quiet that night. He was in a maroon dressing gown that Grandma made him before she died. I remember finding the silence weird, but I didn't dare try to wake him."

Blaze's copper hair falls in loose waves around her face, and I almost reach out to touch it. I remember when I entered his office, a soft fire crackled in the hearth, slowly dwindling from embers to ash. When I found him asleep, I sat on the floor, barely an inch away from the couch, to watch the fire glow from gold to bronze to red. I remember thinking how calming it was to watch chaos dwindle into nothing.

"At some point, as the sun was breaking into dawn, I saw his blue lips and touched his hand, thinking he must be freezing. I started worrying when he didn't warm under the blanket I got for him. Or the second. Or when I moved heaters into the room." I smooth my finger over the ring Blaze is wearing. "There was a trash bin by his desk that I moved right next to the couch. I piled it with paper and kindling and struck a match. But it grew too big too soon, and I tried to put it out myself so I wouldn't hurt Grandpa." I look down at the scar on my thumb from the first time I tried to control fire. "I cried out when I accidentally burned myself, and the cook came running up."

"Kohen," Blaze whispers.

My gaze snaps up to hers when her cold fingers touch my cheek. "They think he might have died around the time I got there." She sucks in a sharp breath. "Overdose," I explain. "Opioids."

She drops her hands from my face, and I hold them in mine to warm them.

"I'm sorry, Kohen."

I've always heard her voice in my sleep. Imagining her talking nonstop or huffing and puffing with how much she wishes I'd leave her alone. I pretended I could feel her heart beating, and there was a pink blush between her freckles. I'd tell myself she was lying in her bed. Warm.

But I knew she wasn't.

I helped myself into her room more times than I could count just to check if I could still feel her breath against my skin.

It was always worse when she'd go on benders, because sometimes I'd find her room empty, and I wouldn't be sure if I'd find her name on the obituary list instead.

"It's not your fault," I say. I finished grieving my grandpa a long time ago, but the wounds will always remain.

"I know," she says softly, searching my eyes for something I can't see. "I'm not your grandfather."

"It doesn't matter if you are. Dead is dead, and I'm not losing the only other person I've ever cared about to something I can prevent." My hold on her tightens. I can't go through something like that again. "I can lock you up, keep it all away from you, but none of that will mean shit if you don't want to."

"I'm not your responsibility," she says breathily, peering up at me with blue eyes.

"And yet, there is nothing in this world that will keep me from being by your side. Dead, alive, or somewhere in between. I was there for you before. Then once everything is said and done, and you're looking for someone to hold your hand or be your gun, I'll still be there."

Crimson deepens her complexion as her lips part. I want to kiss her right now and know what it's like to mean something to her. But the way she's looking at me seems too fragile for what I want from her.

She takes a deep breath and shakes her head like she doesn't want me to notice the teardrops gathering in her eyelashes. "I don't understand where any of this is coming from. Why haven't you told me how you felt after all the time we've known each other?"

My brows twitch together. "Just because the words aren't said, doesn't mean I don't wake up and feel it every day—regardless of how much you piss me off."

Blaze squeezes her eyes closed. "How am I meant to know about it if you never tell me?"

"I thought my sacrifices were enough to make you see me." I brush my lips over hers, feeling her breath stutter against my skin. "I won't stop until you do."

BLAZE

CHAPTER 18

The stress is going to give me a heart attack. After going to the bathroom three times in the past hour, I wring my hands together once I resume my spot by the car park. Nervous peeing is a real issue.

It's visitation weekend, and I'm just about ready to go to the bathroom for the fourth time.

This is a bad idea.

A really, *really* bad idea.

I tracked Charlie down straight after Kohen dragged me into the kitchenette yesterday, and typed up a message to Kiervan saying I had worries about Kohen I wanted to discuss. The response came back in a matter of seconds, and there was no going back from there.

He's traveling five hours to see me even though I insisted we communicate by phone. It would have been a one-minute call where I tell him to fuck off and leave Kohen alone. He's been there for me since day one, and I want to have his back too. Lord knows I've screwed Kohen over enough times, and I have every intention of evening the scales.

There's no going back after this, and no way of seeing the sunlight if things take a turn for the worst. There's another thing on my mind—a niggly little feeling that's wormed its way down to my chest and hasn't left since yesterday afternoon. It spreads warmth to my fingertips and the very ends of my toes. It's as if I finally know what sunlight feels on my skin after watching from the shade my whole life.

Knowing that I'm truly wanted is a heady feeling that makes me want to laugh and cry at the same time. The pieces were falling into place as I lay in bed last night. Kohen did everything he said he would, and I didn't need to ask.

And maybe, just *maybe*, when I die, I'll still remember what being cared for feels like. I push my back against the brick building, hoping it will swallow me whole. It's getting incrementally harder to breathe with the weight of regret on my chest. Seconds feel like hours as I mentally gnaw on the bars of my cage until I *finally* see him. It was impulsive and stupid, and I wish I could take it back, but now he's here. I stayed up all night practicing what I would say to him. Now that he's in front of me, I can't remember why I invited him to begin with.

The other Osman.

Kiervan.

He's impeccably dressed in a T-shirt and blazer combination. The soft black curls at the top of his head bounce with his stride up the steps from the car park. His stature is slightly smaller than Kohen's, but he puffs his chest out like he's double the size. When his sights land on me, he draws his wide smile like it's a weapon, and I finally see the inky darkness beneath the mask.

How did I not notice it before? I've seen what it looks like when someone gets close to the grave. He's got the look of someone drugged up on a cocktail of everything they could get their hands on; I can tell by the rot hiding beneath his smile.

There's the slightest swagger in his step as he advances towards me. The smile he gives me is meant to be friendly and disarm me like it does to everyone else, but there's nothing natural about it. I may not have the best survival responses, but I know for a fact he is a threat.

And I just invited the demon into my home.

Kohen may never forgive me for approaching his brother without telling him. He may not fully understand why I'm doing it, but at least one person will be in my corner if things go south. It makes my chest warm knowing that I have someone watching my back.

Yesterday, I started probing for details about everything he's had to do for Kiervan: taking the fall for Kiervan's drugs, always sitting a grade below Kiervan in each class they both took, doing his share of the chores, being his alibi, acting as his punching bag, and so much more. And Kohen withstood all of it just to protect me from his family.

Kiervan's canines peek through as his smile broadens, waving at me like we're old friends catching up after years. "Hey, Blaze," he says once he's at the corner of the brick building I've chosen for our meeting spot. It's hidden enough that someone will only see us if they come from the car park. "How've you been? It's been, what, like, three years?"

"Cut the shit. I know you're faking it, you goddamn psychopath." I cross my arms so my fidgeting hands don't give me away. His eyes catch the movement, and the smile the psychopath wears morphs into a beast's with a mouth full of razor-sharp teeth ready to rip my throat out. But his eyes change to something eerily familiar; it's the same analytical stare Kohen has every time he's cataloging a new piece of information.

Kiervan stops for a second. Just long enough to make my heart pound against my ribs, screaming it's time for me to take flight. His lips twist to the side as if he's decided this is a game he can't wait to play.

"Didn't anyone ever teach you not to poke a bear?" There's truth to the way his eyes morph into maliciousness as he cocks his head like he's a hunter who's just found his prey. He stalks forward, and it takes every ounce of my being not to bolt or tell him I was wrong and there was no reason for him to come all the way out here.

I swallow the lump in my throat and jerk my chin up. "I was willing to do it over the phone; you're the one who decided to drive out to see me."

He shrugs innocently. "Your text made it sound so urgent. I'm just trying to be a good brother and watch out for the little guy."

"Really? You mean it? You want what's best for him?" Of course, he doesn't. That doesn't mean I don't want him to say it.

"Of course." His brows dip down, and he holds a hand over his heart in fake earnest. "He's family. I always want what's right for them."

"Then get your slimy claws out of him and fuck right off," I hiss.

The laughter that ripples through the air sends goosebumps raining over my skin.

Oh, I fucked up. Bad.

"No wonder he likes you." I swat Kiervan's hand away when he pinches my cheek. "You're so cute when you act so dumb. It's like a match made in heaven," he muses. "Darling, pray tell, where exactly did my brother claim my claws are? And don't skimp out on the details. I like to be thorough." The piece of shit backs me up against the wall, and I suck in a sharp breath when he leans his hand against the brick above my head.

He's a bully. An abuser. Plain and simple.

I square my shoulders even though I want to knee him in the family jewels, then crutch away as fast as I can. "Well, I heard that you haven't got all that much going on up here." I tap my temple. "And you need your little baby brother to do all your dirty work for you."

His eyes harden. "Is that so?"

I nod. Kiervan and Kohen may hate each other's guts, but there is no denying their similarities in the rage boiling beneath their skin. The fundamental difference I am woefully unprepared for is how each brother strikes.

Kohen's attacks can be seen a mile away. It always ends up with him inches from my face and his hand around my throat. The extent of the damage will only be on the surface, while my sanity will remain within arm's reach.

Kiervan is the type who will strike at night when his opponents are most oblivious. He'll swoon and charm, then rip their heart out the second their defenses drop. He's a mastermind in it for the long game.

What am I? Fuck around and find out doesn't mean much if my strongest attack involves my knees.

"What precisely does Kohen think he will achieve by sending his girlfriend to yap in my face?"

"It doesn't matter what he thinks. What does matter is that you need to leave him the fuck alone. He isn't your bitch. And I'm not his girlfriend."

He cocks a brow. "Or what?"

I open my mouth but nothing comes out. *Or what?* Or nothing. I don't know what the hell I was thinking. "I'll tell your college you're getting someone else to do your work for you. You'll be done for cheating, then you'll never get your degree."

Kiervan chuckles as if I'm a child. "You know what I think?" He curls a loose strand of my copper hair around his finger. "The only reason he's taken any interest in someone like you is pity. He gets a sense of comradery in knowing that you're just as pathetic as he is. You'll be abandoned as soon as he finds someone else to coddle, to make him feel like he's important. Left alone to rot in your house—oh wait. My bad. You don't have one." He smiles casually.

A lump forms in my throat as his words become parasites that wiggle into my brain. He's probably right, and I've made a fool of myself by trying to play the hero. I just... Kohen did all those things for nothing. I don't want him to keep doing things for me in vain when I'm going to disappear the second the gates open. He can't follow me down or try to save me as we both fall.

After everything he's done for me, I'm returning the favor.

"You're going to die alone, hated by every person you've ever encountered." It's a weak response. Only I don't know who I'm directing the words to, me or the monster in front of me.

"Wow. Being stupid with a poor memory is an unfortunate combination. Have you forgotten already, love? Nothing you can say or do will hurt me. I'm untouchable, and you're..." He scoffs, slowly closing in on my personal space until there's barely an inch between us. "You, on the other hand?" Kiervan trails a finger down my cheek, and I stop myself from cringing away. "There are so many ways I could make you scream."

"Doesn't change the fact you're too stupid to do any of your bidding yourself. I guess your mom gave your brother the only functioning brain."

He grabs me by my throat, except it isn't tactful like the way Kohen does it, where I can still breathe. Kiervan's only intent is to harm. Pain ruptures across my throat, cutting off my oxygen in an instant. Clawing at his arms, I bring my knee up, only for him to step forward to block my attack. White spots splatter over my vision as my hands flick out toward his face. I sink my thumbs into his eye sockets without a second thought.

A vicious growl breaks through the air a split second before I soar into the ground, crutches and all.

"Fucking bitch!"

I splutter for breath as he pulls me up on my feet, taking away any chance I have of an upper hand. Crying out, I reach for my hair, feeling strands snap away from the roots. It still doesn't stop me from curling my first and aiming for the general vicinity of his dick, missing it narrowly. "Get the fuck off me."

He buckles forward, clutching his stomach while unrelenting with his grip. Murderous eyes crash to mine, and he says with flaring nostrils, "You're going to regret—"

"What the fuck are you doing here?"

We both snap our attention toward the voice, my stomach sinking to the deepest depths of hell. I had hoped to have at least a couple hours to regroup before Kohen found out about this.

Kiervan straightens, beaming from ear to ear. "Oh, what's up, baby bro? Me? Blaze invited me over. We go *way* back." Letting go of my hair, he grabs a handful of my ass. I jolt out of his hold, and my fist goes flying, knocking him square in the jaw. Pain blasts through my fist, radiating up my arm to my shoulder.

His head whips to the side, and his body follows. There's no chance to bask in my victory because he recovers almost instantly, lunging for me. This time, I'm ready. There's space to move and no second thoughts. I pivot on my bruised foot, grab the collars of his blazer, and drive my knee forward.

The howl that follows is the most beautiful thing I've ever heard. The cry that comes out of me is less so. My bad foot gives out, crumbling my balance. But a pair of arms catches me before I can finish my descent.

Kohen protectively tugs me to his side. His breaths come out short and sharp while his wild eyes remain on his brother. "You may be a psychopath, but touch her again and I'll make sure you feel me break every single bone in your hand."

A smug grin blooms across my face as a crimson bead drips down Kiervan's chin from the corner of his lips. Any sliver of self-satisfaction vanishes when his mouth pulls as if he's just concocted a plan that will make a drop of blood look like child's play.

"You should really learn how to leash your pet." The maniacal lilt to his voice has me edging closer to Kohen. His brother slowly backs away toward the steps down to the car park, cutting his lethal eyes to me when he says, "Dogs who act out get put down."

Not for the first time today, I realize I've bitten off substantially more than I can chew. I'm not sure what exactly went through my brain when I typed up the message to Kiervan—or better yet, *why I kept fucking responding.* But something tells me I'm about to lay in the bed I just made. And boy, is it a shit bed.

If the crow that's eying me from one of the trees isn't an omen, then the fact that I can hear each one of Kohen's heavy breaths definitely is. Neither of us moves a muscle or speaks as we watch Kiervan stroll back to his car, whistling as he spins his keys around his finger. It isn't until his Mercedes revs off down the long driveway that Kohen slices through the tension.

Any semblance of gentleness or patience has abandoned our fraught relationship. The grip he has on my shirt makes him look just like his brother with his hair-trigger temper and savage ferocity. He pushes me up against the cold brick wall, disregarding my whimper of pain.

"Why was he here? Was he telling the truth? Did you call him over just to fuck him?"

With each word, my heart sinks lower and lower until it feels like I don't have one anymore.

I've seen this man pissed off before, but never like this. There's no opening for reason in the way he looks at me. He's made his mind up.

I'm a whore just like my mother, and I'm picking his brother just like everyone else. He believes both those things to be true, even when he saw how I was being treated by his brother.

I contacted Kiervan *for him.* I put my ass on the line and risked my grandfather's wrath on the off chance that Kohen might have more freedom. And this is how he reacts?

Something switches inside me, and I can't find it in me to hang on to the hurt. If Kohen thinks so little of me, then fuck him. I'm not going to stand here and get shit on by the Osmans. If he listens to what I have to say, good for him. If he doesn't, then good riddance. I am *really* fucking sick of everyone throwing me around.

I had a taste of blood, and I want more. With every ounce of adrenaline coursing through my veins, I shove him off me. His hands loosen from my shirt, and I slip out from under him. He's taken so off guard he blinks, and there's almost a moment of clarity in his eyes before it vanishes again.

I widen my stance despite my ankle's protest. "Pushing women around seems to be an Osman trait."

"Fuck you," he bites.

I rear back like I've been hit.

Throwing his head back, Kohen laughs humorlessly as he looks up at the cloudless sky. "I was so *blind*." His stare cuts down to me, coated in disbelief and laced with hatred. It's the type of look that makes me want to recede into a shell and wish the world would disappear by the time I reopen my eyes, because this? It hurts.

"Everyone said you were a mess, and I'd screw myself over by trusting you. I've met one—maybe two people who tolerate you, and both of them wouldn't give a shit if you ended up dead. Then, after everything I told you—" Shaking his head, Kohen drags his hand through his hair. "I thought you were over wanting him. I thought—it doesn't matter what I thought. Because there you were with my brother. *My brother.*"

My lips part. He is *not* seriously trying to slut shame me right now. "You goddamn delusional fucking dumbass," I yell. "What part of *any* of that looked consensual? The part where he tossed me around or when I decked him? Wait, let me guess, kneeing him in the balls was the giveaway, wasn't it?"

"Maybe he was too rough for your tastes, and it was too late for you to back out." He sounds more like he's trying to convince himself.

This is why it's better to be lost at the bottom of a bottle or safe in my tower. No one can touch me there, even once I lay my heart out it'll still be safe because I'll forget it exists.

"You think I'm in my head all the time? Look at you! You think I want that man when he threatened to torture me?" Screw it. I'm not going to try to convince him anymore. "I called him over to tell him to leave you the fuck alone. You can call me a liar all you want; the truth is that I was trying to help you by getting him off your back."

He pauses, staring at me with his hazel eyes as if I just spoke another language. Kohen is so still, I could be convinced the world has frozen. But finally he says, "I don't need your help."

"So you're above my help, huh?" I scoff, face heating. I thought he fucking understood me. God, I hate being wrong. "You can help me, but as soon as I do something for you, it's suddenly not good enough, right?" Tears prick my eyes, but I blink them away before he can see.

His eyes widen a fraction as he steps forward. "No, that's not what I meant. Help yourself first."

Rocking back on my heels as he reaches for me, I say, "You're right. I will. Like you said, no one else will. You're obviously so full of shit with your claims about supporting me."

Kohen's lips part. "Blaze—" His voice cracks on the single syllable.

"No, I'm talking, Kohen." I hold my hand up then yank my arm out of his hold. "Helping someone means having their back even when people try to pit you against them. *Caring* about someone means believing them when they say they got hurt." I raise my chin to look down my nose at him, praying to whatever god that's listening that no tears will fall. "So truly, from the bottom of my heart, fuck you for being like everyone else. I'm sorry for trying to help. This is the last time I'll ever do anything for you."

Dejection spears through his face, and I feel its sharp sting down to my core; it's cold and unrelenting in the misery it brings. His plea is evident in his eyes alone, but I never thought that hurting him might end up hurting me.

"Wait, no, Blaze—fuck." With each step forward, I step back. "Stay. Please stay."

Irritation runs down my spine. "You think I'm daft for not seeing everything you did for me. Well, right back at you."

He halts, holding his arms out in surrender even though tension lines his silhouette. "You're right. I'm sorry. I was wrong, but you shouldn't have contacted my brother."

"How many times are you going to apologize before it loses meaning?" I squeeze my eyes shut and take a deep breath. "Look, I was wrong to use your brother against you before, but I'm over that shit. Knowing everything Kiervan has done, and what you continue to do for him, I still put myself on the line *for you*. Your life is shit, but it doesn't have to be."

"What about you, Blaze?" Exasperation bleeds into his voice. "When are you going to start taking responsibility for your life?"

I gawk at him. "I didn't choose this life! I became a villain just for being conceived by the wrong people."

"And you stayed the villain because, at the end of the day, chaos is the only time you get to spread your wings and pretend you're in control."

Shaking my head, I swallow the boulder that's lodged itself in my throat. "Don't make this about me, Kohen. You've got your own shit to sort out. Acting like I'm the only one who needs saving isn't going to change that." My chest aches as I try to steady my breathing. "You and the rest of the universe might think it's you versus Kiervan, and it is. But someone will pick you, and you're going to ruin it because you've picked him."

Silence hangs in the air between us as his chest rises and falls. Slowly, *carefully*, as if I might spook if he speaks too loudly, he says, "You aren't unlovable. You're just so desperate for it you've stopped understanding how to accept it."

A staggered breath rushes out of me as I study the green rings around his eyes. Despite everything he said, I'm prepared for whatever punishment comes my way. Kohen has put himself out there for me every single day when I never asked for it. For years he's sacrificed his sanity and dignity for me. I just hope he knows that there's someone on this earth that sees him, and is willing to bleed for him too.

"Right back at you, Pyro." I give him a sad smile.

We're at a stalemate.

We've both still got issues, and we both still hate ourselves.

He turns to retrieve my fallen crutches for me, and there's an almost conceited glint in his eye when he hands them back.

"Next time, Klepto, if you need to make a bomb, come to me. I've got the parts, and if you're good, I'll even let you pull the trigger. I call it a kill switch."

BLAZE

CHAPTER 19

Everyone hates Mondays.

Well, as I've gotten older, and therefore wiser, I've come to realize that I hate every day of the week. I don't actually have anything personal against that particular day.

I do, however, have beef with the man standing at the classroom door. It's like Boris brought a plague with him. My insides turn, and I'm sure my skin bubbles from his proximity. That man is the harbinger of death, I swear to God.

When he turns his beady brown eyes on me, it's like the fiery gates have opened, and it's time to step right up to my eternal damnation.

"Miss Whitlock, Headmaster McGill would like a word with you," the English teacher says after speaking to the security guard for all of three seconds.

"A word? Just one?" I slap my hand on the desk and drag all the loose paper to my chest, dumping it into my bag. "Must be Christmas."

Both of their eyes darken, but at least Charlie snorts beside me. "Little shit," she snickers.

I give her a condescending smile. "Try not to miss me too much."

Slipping my backpack through my arms, I take my time leaving. The crutches squeak as I move between the aisle, though I'm putting a little more pressure on my ankle today than yesterday. I'm pretty sure Dr. Kohen Osman is correct, and it might not be a sprain. He said he's going to *look into it*—whatever that means.

"Hurry up," Boris grunts.

I halt and nod toward my foot. "Don't rush me." Then, I move slower. They go low, I go lower.

He tries rushing me along through the hallways, and it gets to the point that it takes more effort to rebel than be complacent. And I'm in the mood to preserve my energy if I have to listen to people squealing about prom tomorrow. It seems like hundreds of posters clutter the walls of the halls, advertising the event; it's starting to hurt my eyes.

It's hard to keep my head held high when we walk past McGill's office and continue towards the medical wing. The physical torment of my last *session* in that area was just bearable. But I'm not sure how I'll cope if I'm thrown in there for another three days with zero enrichment in my enclosure.

Boris walks ahead to push open the door to Dr. Van der Merwe's office. The air seems to chill by thirty degrees as soon as I walk in. The cold bites deep into my marrow and renders me frozen in my spot.

The door clicks shut behind me, and every instinct hardwired into my being is telling me to run. Bang on the door and break bones if it means getting out of here. Except I can't move a muscle. No matter how hard I try to get my body to comply, the entire world has crashed onto my shoulders, and the only option is to sink.

Cold blue eyes bore into me, the same upturned shape as my mother's and just as empty. With a single look, he pierces the bubble of delusion I've lived in for the past three days. Just by existing, he's a reminder that I'm not the type of person who's meant to be loved. *Happy*.

The men in front of me don't rise to their feet. They don't smile. They don't react. Only a single word comes out of my grandfather's mouth.

"Sit."

"I'll stand." I'll do anything but get closer to him.

His salt-and-pepper hair is impeccably styled, just like his three-piece suit and the long coat hanging at the back of the leather couch. I've never seen him with a single strand of hair out of place. His pocket square is never crooked. The designer tie always sits precisely where it should. His Rolex is shined, never so much as a minute off. The man defines opulence as if he was born to be a magnate.

"*Sit*." The single syllable rolls through his diaphragm, coming out no louder than a whisper.

The room is so silent the monster in front of me can probably hear my heartbeat. Even McGill steals a glance at Jonathan Whitlock Sr., and I swear his lips part on a silent gasp. On the other hand, Dr. Van der Merwe has his eyes firmly set on me as if he's trying to anticipate my next move: obey or rebel?

Swallowing the lump in my throat, I lower myself onto the only remaining chair right in the center of the room. Two security guards stand at my back, McGill on one side of my front and the doctor on the other. Then, front and center is the man who took responsibility for his kin by throwing them aside. The structure of the setup is imposing, like they're trapping a bird to kill it rather than harmlessly interrogate it.

"Stop slouching."

My back snaps ramrod straight.

"And fix your tie." My grandfather's lips turn in disgust. "I warned you not to cause any more trouble."

He can't control you anymore, I tell myself. Soon I'll be graduating and ditching the curse of the Whitlock name.

Still, that doesn't stop me from sitting up straighter than I usually would. There's something empowering about knowing that beyond those doors, there's someone in my corner. Well, I hope he still is. The knowledge seeps strength into my skin.

"When has your warning been able to change my entire personality—"

"You speak when I tell you to speak." My grandfather cuts me off. "Exercising your own sensibilities is a waste of this earth's resources." I grind my teeth together as red dots my vision. "Stay away from *both* the Osman boys. You were lucky the good one of the two brothers decided to come to me first. Had it been their father, you would be in a *very* different position."

I blink. Wait. What? "If the—"

"What did I just say, Marie?"

"I'm going to speak if I want to," I growl. I did the math before talking to Kiervan, and I decided whatever their father wanted to do to me was worth the risk. "If the point of this was to make me stay away from him, why the hell did you make me his buddy the first day he was here?"

With slow, deadly calmness, my grandfather turns his head towards McGill. "You paired my granddaughter with that *boy*?"

He hesitates, moving his lips like he's running through all the excuses he can make. "It was a—a request made by Mr. Osman to..." McGill clears his throat. "On the first day, he wanted me to reintroduce the two in the hopes of discovering what kind of relationship they have, and..." He shifts in his seat.

"And?" my grandfather prods.

McGill's beard twitches. Mr. Fifth-Divorce never stood a chance against my grandfather—the owner of the most prominent investment banking company on the East Coast. "He hoped her reaction would be extreme enough to garner proper institutionalization."

"What you're saying is you have conflicting interests."

"No. *No*," McGill rushes to say. "I assure you, Mr. Whitlock, it was a onetime occurrence that will never happen again."

"I assume I don't need to explain the consequences of it *happening again*." Grandpa cocks a brow and grabs the crystal tumbler from the side table.

McGill flattens his hand over his cheap tie. "No, no need."

Prickles go down my spine when my grandfather's attention settles back on me.

"It appears that threats do not work in convincing you to behave. Perhaps a bribe will instead." He pauses to take a sip of bronze liquid. The crystal glass clinks as he places it back on the side table. "You have no money to your name. No home waiting for you at the end of this. Keep your filthy hands away from that family, and in six months' time, I will give you $100,000 dollars." When I do nothing but stare at him blankly, he continues. "If your behavior costs me a contract with them, I will ensure you never know a moment of peace in your life."

A contract? What contract? When did the Osmans and the Whitlocks start doing business together?

"So, *Marie*, you will do what you must—break that boy's heart if you have to. All I know is that you *stay away from them*. I took care of you when your own mother didn't want to. It's the least you can do."

I take one breath.

Two.

The third one is the deepest, stretching my lungs to maximum capacity. Then, my lips stretch into a smile. "Are you"—I push onto my feet—"*fucking kidding me*? Who the *fuck* do you think you are? You, your money, and not a single fucking word out of your mouth means *shit* to me. I'll be stuck in this place for another month, and after that, there's nothing you can do to me. I'm out. I'm free. Your threats are empty, old man."

"Are they?" The raise of his brows unsettles me enough to make me sway.

"You don't own me."

"Don't I?" he says cooly. "It appears there was some miscommunication at some point. This *freedom* you speak of was never made for you."

"Spit it out." I breathe hard through my gritted teeth.

The look he gives me is almost pitiful. "You are sorely mistaken if you think you can just traipse around wearing the Whitlock name."

The blood drains from my face as he explains. This is worse than anything I could have imagined. I'd rather end up dead and broke than live under his thumb for the rest of my life. I haven't spent my entire life fighting this hard just to stay in the same place. Then I'll truly be another version of my mother, chained to a man who cares more about status than if I died.

"Your uncle and I have worked hard for our reputation, and a bastard grandchild is not ruining that."

I launch myself at the man I call *grandfather*. My nails find purchase with loose skin, and I don't hesitate. I rip. I claw. I throw my hands out over and over again until my shoulder collides with the hard surface of the floor, and pain pangs down my spine.

I'm yanked back onto my feet in the next breath, and my mouth opens with a silent scream. Agony radiates out from the throbbing point in my ribs. The searing pain reaches every inch of my body, feeling like I'm being struck by a thousand bolts of lightning as all my muscles spasm at once. The crackling sound of static can barely be heard above the silent scream lodged in my throat.

The tension releases from my muscles as soon as the sound stops. Throwing my arms out, I try to push the guards away, but the room seems to spin as I do. I fucking hate getting tased. My legs give out beneath me, and I struggle to get back up. The world moves as I try to make sense of my shifting surroundings. My eyes refuse to move into focus as I'm dragged down a set of stairs that I've never seen before.

"Where are we going?" My voice comes out garbled and distorted, but there's a slight echo to it. "Stop. Let go of me."

I jerk at the hold around my arms and try to hold my own weight as the temperature drops the further down the stairs we go. A whimper breaks through my chest when my back crashes against a rough stone wall.

The sudden impact clears away the bleary haze enough for me to notice the three fluorescent lights hanging from the high concrete ceiling. The musty smell of the windowless room makes me scrunch my nose. Benches and shelving push against the walls surrounding the tub in the middle.

I gasp when my blazer is torn off me. My shoes follow the pile on the floor, and I kick out, narrowly missing Boris. They tug me forward, and everything seems to pause and focus on the tall metal tub.

They're going to put me in there.

They're going to put me in the water.

Images of falling into a frozen lake flash in my mind. I'd kick my feet and move my arms, and it won't matter how hard I try to make it back to the surface; the darkness drags me under. I'd scream for help. Beg to a god I don't believe in to save me. My lungs would burn in search of oxygen, and then I'd make the mistake of opening my mouth. Water then pools into each crevasse of my organs until, eventually, there's nothing.

"This is not right." Dr. Van der Merwe's voice echoes through the stone room. "I do not approve of this treatment—science has proven that this does nothing to help a patient. This—this is *torture*. I will not stand for it." I throw a futile glance at the doctor, silently pleading that he'll demand they release me.

"You know where the door is," McGill says simply.

Dr. Van der Merwe gives me one long, tortured look. "ECTs are board approved, based on fact, science, and *reason*. It can *help* patients. If you put her in there, you will do more harm to her than good. What you are doing is barbaric, unethical, and beyond any realm of acceptability." He backs away, shaking his head.

My pulse ricochets against my skin as panic rises up my throat. "Stop it." My voice commands no authority with how much it cracks.

The pebbled surface of the water comes into view, and energy floods back into my veins. "I'm not going in there!" I scream, gnashing my teeth and thrashing my limbs about.

The two guards are too strong for me to fight off. My feet hit the outside of the frozen tub, and I use it as leverage to kick back. I manage to swing my elbow back and knock one of the guards, but he recovers quickly. The two guards change tact. Boris grabs both my legs and throws them into the tub.

"Settle down, Marie," I think I hear my grandfather say.

A shrill cry bursts out of me as the cold bites into my bones. I try to catch my footing, but I slip further into the water each time I do. The near-frozen liquid absorbs into my uniform, clinging to me like a second skin. My hands meet the guard's flesh over and over, slapping him. Scratching him. Punching him. I have to get out of here. They can't—they can't put me in here.

My burning eyes turn to my grandfather's. "No. No. No. No. Please don't! I'm sorry! I'll stop! I'll stay away from them! I promise! You don't need to do this!"

The ice bobs against my skin and clatters against the metal, growing louder and more violent each time I move.

"Did you know they called this the 'water cure' during the eighteen hundreds?" Grandfather says coolly.

My eyes dart to McGill, praying he'll see that even this is too far—that even the doctor thinks this is so far beyond the line of what is acceptable. But all I find is a man on a leash, hanging on to my grandfather's every whim. Fucking *coward*.

Boris places a canvas sheet over the bottom half of the tub, stopping my legs from trying to escape. "No. No. Please. I'm sorry, okay? I'll be good. I won't go near them. Please, Grandpa."

Another guard runs down the steps as the two men wrestle my arms into the tub. Boris's gaze catches mine and the satisfaction strewn across his features makes my stomach churn. My eyes burn with unshed tears as I look between my grandfather and McGill, hoping to find even a glimmer of compassion.

I don't want to die in here. I want to breathe. I want to feel the wind and taste the fresh air. I want to move my arms and not feel trapped.

"I'll leave them alone. It won't happen again. *Please.*" I sob.

The third guard slides the second half of the sheet in place, keeping everything but my head beneath the tub. My fists collide with the cold metal as I feel around for a latch of some sort.

The ice skates along my skin with every move, making it feel like I'm trapped with a thousand living things all fighting to keep me prisoner.

"I did some research on the way here," my grandfather says, patting his bloody cheek with a handkerchief.

I keep hitting and kicking with all my might. The cold has numbed any of the pain that would otherwise be there.

"Psychologists used to think submerging a patient in freezing water could 'kill' the mad thoughts. Sometimes, they'd place the patient into near-boiling water before moving them into ice water to 'shock' the patient into submission or sanity."

I kick my knees up, banging against the sheet as hard as possible when the cold has rendered my muscles stiff. "Grandpa," I wheeze. "Please stop this." The tears slide down my cheeks, dripping off my chin.

The two guards exit the room, leaving only me, my grandfather, McGill, and Boris.

He raises his shoulders in boredom. "See this however you wish—punishment, therapy, or simply wasted entertainment. Your views have no sway in any of this."

My grandfather condoned the electrocution and the violence. He spent my entire life abusing me with his power, using his money as a means to starve me or keep me leashed to him like a desperate puppy.

I was always aware he was pushing the buttons and calling the shots. We didn't speak on the phone where I could hear his voice; I only saw him once every few years. Jonathan Whitlock Sr. was a series of letters and numbers that dictated how much misery would be let into my life.

Jonathan isn't a man behind a screen anymore. He isn't a myth or a story on the news. He's flesh and bone with sinister eyes. He's *there*. Right in front of me. Calling the shots, with orders of my execution waiting on the tip of his tongue. It's real. A living, breathing human being whom all darkness stems from.

He is the maker of my own personal hell. A conduit for all the bad that's happened so far.

My grandfather tucks his bloody handkerchief back into his inside pocket. "You were given the opportunity to make a dignified choice; however, you chose not to do so. This is the consequence of your actions, Marie. This"—he nods at the tub—"can be a common occurrence."

I will not die like this.

I will not die letting men like him survive on my wilted corpse.

"Why can't you just care about me? Why do you have to do all of this?" My teeth chatter as I say the words.

My grandfather slides his arms into the sleeves of his coat. "Some people weren't born to be wanted. Existing is the most they will ever receive."

My gaze cuts to the three remaining men. "If you don't let me out of here, I swear on my life that you will all die because of me. I will hunt you down and make you regret treating me the way you do." My grandfather. McGill. Boris. They will all die by my hand.

Jonathan huffs an empty chuckle. "I'll see you at graduation, Marie." He toes my blazer that's lying on the floor. "Don't forget your jacket. It's cold outside."

BLAZE

CHAPTER 20

I pull the hood further down my head as I huddle closer to my bedroom door so none of the squealing girls pay any attention to me.

The perpetual chill from the ice-cold water I was forced into rakes another shudder down my spine, and I can't hold back the hiss that comes out when I grab onto my keys. My knuckles and knees are a canvas of violet and indigo blotches, with smears of red on the highest points.

Silver lining: I iced my injuries.

Another silver lining: I don't need crutches anymore.

It's been over twenty-four hours since I've been out of the tub. Almost twenty-four hours with Dr. Van der Merwe in the med wing with a constant IV drip and heat pads. Still, I feel like I'm in the damn ice bath.

The good doctor told me everything from here on out is in my head. My core temperature is back to normal, the melted ice has been flushed down the drain, and the tub is sitting in the basement, empty. There were two words he used that made me flinch. *Trauma response.*

Forty-five minutes. That's two-thousand and seven-hundred seconds they left me in the frozen water. I can still picture the clock directly across from the tub, the way the long hand ticked, ticked, ticked.

The pain stopped after a while. Everything seemed to stop after feeling like I was burning alive. At some point after everyone left the room, I couldn't move my limbs anymore. Then the shivers stopped, and I thought I saw my mother walk in with a dirty ribbon to braid my hair.

The sound of my bedroom door unlocking beneath the keycard makes me wince as if the lid is trapping me in place all over again. The ache in my jaw has traveled to my neck from gritting my teeth against the phantom shivers.

Dr. Van der Merwe gave me today off and a pass from attending prom tonight. I don't think I could tolerate the loud music and all the bodies if I went sober. All of it feels so insignificant. None of it matters.

Taking a deep breath, I shoulder the door open and stumble into the room. My feet don't make it much further than that. The weight of everything that happened makes me crumble to the floor. The carpet drags against my sensitive cheek, both grounding me and unleashing me with the pain it brings.

When I close my eyes, I'm back in that tub, back in the room that smells like death. My grandfather's disinterested blue gaze is on me, reminding me I will always be more insignificant than a speck of dust on his designer coat. I'm a shadow of my ghost of a mother, but even a wraith would have more importance.

A wail builds in my chest, bubbling and clawing; it feels like sandpaper beneath my skin. Each grain is another meaningless indiscretion. Everything I've gone through and survived, every time I've fought like my life depended on it, was all for my grandfather's benefit. My wings aren't clipped; they don't exist.

And I'm fucking sick and tired of it.

I'm done.

"Come here," a voice whispers. Sudden pressure around my waist makes me jolt up to get away. Instead, I'm pulled forward against a hard chest that smells of patchouli and mint.

Then everything breaks.

Years of bottled tears spill over, trailing a path of fire down my skin.

"It's just me. It's okay," Kohen says, just loud enough for me to hear.

My knuckles protest when I grab onto his shirt. "Don't—Let go of me. No." Everything hurts. Pushing against him feels like an impossible mission that takes me back to yesterday when my body wasn't my own any more than my life was.

"I'm not going anywhere." Gentle hands run down the back of my head. The tender touch fills my aching heart with the warmth the frozen waters took from me. He arranges our bodies so my knees are up against my chest, and he holds on to my curls like they're a life-saving treatment. In here, it's warm and miles away from the tub.

Stay away from the Osmans.

You will never know a moment of peace in your life.

Break that boy's heart if you have to.

This can be a common occurrence.

I shake my head against Kohen's chest. My tears soak into the material of his shirt. I've had enough.

I need another hit.

I need the baggie they were bribing me with.

I need the sweet release that comes in powder form and makes me forget about all of this shit. There won't be any more pain. Any heartache. It'll make everything feel right for just a moment.

I fucking *need* it.

"I've got you." He holds me like someone is trying to take me away from him, but he'll never let go. Ever since I was a child, I wondered what it would feel like to be held like this. He's taking my firsts in the ways that truly matter.

He was the first man to kiss me like I'm a one-of-a-kind masterpiece that's too precious to be displayed on a wall. He was the first person to touch my skin and not make me wonder if I'd find bruises where his fingers were. Mostly, he's the first person who saw my dying heart and wanted to bring it to life.

I'm not breaking his heart, even if he's inadvertently hurt me more than once. He has enough demons to drown in, and I have mine. I don't want to see him as an enemy anymore—lord knows I have enough of those.

His breath is feather-soft against my hair, and I squeeze my eyes shut, basking in the feel of it. "Everything is going to be alright."

Alright. That's not a word in my dictionary. Things are never *alright* unless my nose is twitching from the powder I snorted. *Alright* is a state of delusion.

This can't be the last time I feel those firsts. I want something more than momentary euphoria. I've always had a house to go back to. It was a structure with many walls and a single roof that leaked

310

in certain places. It had rotting floorboards and gaps between the windows that let the draft through.

What I want isn't just a house; it's a home. Somewhere I can rest my head and not worry about someone creeping through the windows or breaking into my room when I'm not there. I want to be able to call it mine and know that even if it is temporary, it stays strong whenever I'm not.

"I was looking for you." Kohen's hands find mine, and he stiffens beneath me. One by one, he unfurls my fingers, revealing the cacophony of mangled flesh. "What happened?"

"It doesn't matter," I say through a hiccup and snatch my hands from him, stuffing them in my hoodie pocket. "Everything is fucking pointless anyway."

"*What happened, Blaze?*" he repeats, pulling my hands out from the pockets of my hoodie.

Blaze.

I've always been Blaze to him. Despite wanting to get under my skin, I was never Marie or Miss Whitlock. I've always been me.

"When?" I choke.

His brows lower in question.

I wipe my tears and sit straighter on his lap. "How far back do you want me to go? Do you mean way back when my grandfather decided I'd never be free from him? Or a few weeks ago when they strapped me to a chair and fried my brains after I blew up at you in group therapy?" Rage bubbles up my throat. "When they tortured and starved me to find out who blew up the Science building? Or yesterday when my granddad locked me in a tub of frozen water for almost an hour because your fucking brother is a snitch?"

The blacks of Kohen's eyes eat up the golden hues. "I'm going to

311

fucking kill him—*both of them.* Who gave you the bruises?"

I squeeze my eyes shut, picturing the silver tub and the way it would reflect the hanging light. "Me. When I was trying to get out."

"I thought something might have happened to you. There was no sign of you in McGill's office, or the doctor's. I snuck into solitary and couldn't find you there either. I—" He sucks in a sharp breath as if the thought is agonizing. "Where were you?"

Curling my trembling fingers around his shirt, my lips almost refuse to let the words come out for fear I'd be dragged back there. "The dungeon," I whisper. "There's a single tub there. It looked—" I clear my throat as a shudder runs down my spine. "It looked like I was the first person to use it in a while."

"They left you in there the whole night?"

I flinch away from the fury rolling off him in tangible waves. "They kept me overnight at the infirmary for..."

"Hypothermia," Kohen finishes for me, his hold tightening around my body.

All I can do is nod.

"Who let you out?"

"Boris." I frown. "I think." I could barely make out the face of the man who unlatched the lid. It was a blur of colors and dots as my eyes refused to stay open. "It's all a haze... I just woke up in the infirmary and it felt like my body was on fire."

The muscles in his jaw twitch and he clutches me tighter. One of his hands drop down to my wrist where he presses two fingers to my pulse point. His eyes drift shut as if he's focusing on each beat of my heart to make sure I'm not as dead as I feel.

"What do you want?" The question rumbles out ominously from his throat.

My lungs contract as I look into his darkening hazel irises. "I—what do you mean, *what do I want?* Neither of us can change the past or anything that happened to us. What I do or don't want won't change any of it."

"No." He shakes his head and closes the distance between us, feeling his breath shudder against my lips. "*What do you want?*" He tips my chin up and gives me a look that says all he needs is a word, and he'll go to war. "Anything. Ask me anything, and I will prove to you that I will *always* be there for you."

Each exhale comes out heavy to match the rise and fall of his chest. "I—It—there's..." So many things, but none I can find the words for.

Caressing his thumb over the burst blood vessels along my throat, he says, "They hurt you, didn't they?"

I hesitate for a second, then nod, pursing my lips. Hurting implies they have power over me. Denying it won't change that fact.

"I told you bad things happen to people who touch what isn't theirs. Let's make it to the morgue this time, shall we, Thief?"

I've never nodded so quickly. It makes the corners of his lips twitch up. Every corner of my heart fills and expands. He's picking me. He's choosing to be in my corner and be the support I've never had.

"But for now," Kohen motions behind him, and I finally notice the two garment bags lying atop my unmade bed. "Will you be my prom date?"

It's such a mundane question. It almost makes me feel like I'm an average teenager who will jump into bed squealing and kicking my feet because a cute boy asked me out. Isn't normalcy a medication for a sick mind?

"From murder to corsages." My lips twist into a coy smile that

313

hurts to wear, but it's enough to push back the darkness clouding my thoughts. "Are you giving me a choice?"

He shrugs, tucking a strand of hair behind my ear. "You either walk in alone or with me by your side. Either way, we're leaving together. I told you once, your death is mine, Thief. If anyone makes you cry, then their death is yours. I just need to know if you want it served on a silver platter or gold."

I glance down at the dried blood crusting over my knuckles. "Silver. It looks better against red."

"Knife or fists?"

"Baseball bat." A slow grin spreads across my face. Damn him for knowing how to pull me out of my head. "Can we play classical music in the background?"

My breath catches when he kisses my forehead. "As my batshit crazy woman wishes."

My cheeks heat. *His. Kohen's.* I shrug noncommittally. "I'll think about your offer."

Kohen's eyes darken. "It's a yes or no question."

I hum. "What do I get out of it?"

"I'll wear a silver and black sapphire ring. If you manage to steal it, I'll let you keep it."

Narrowing my eyes, I say, "You always let me keep it."

He holds up his left hand where there's a signet ring on his index finger. *My* signet ring that *I* took from him. "Do I?"

My jaw drops. "Give it back."

"You know my conditions."

"Fine."

"Fine."

"Bribery doesn't look good on you, Pyro," I grumble, crossing my arms.

"Everything looks good on me, Klepto."

I poke him in the chest while he helps me to my feet. "Just so the record shows, I'm agreeing under duress."

He lets out a chuckle. "Shut up and get ready."

Muttering profanities under my breath, I flip him the bird as I back away into the bathroom. I try to keep the air around me light even though every inch of my body and soul feels as if it's been hit by a boulder.

The door clicks behind me, and my muscles protest before I even start getting undressed after turning on the shower. My fingers tremble and ache as I grip the edges of my hoodie, and my shoulder screams as I pull it off. I drop all my clothing onto the floor as condensation climbs up the walls from the steam billowing out of the shower.

But I can't bear the thought of water touching my skin. What if I step in and the water goes cold and ice rains down over my bruised flesh? What if I shut the glass shower door and it doesn't open again? The water could fill up, and what if, this time, the water doesn't stop at my collarbones?

Stepping away from the shower, I'm struck by my reflection in the mirror. Only a day ago, my skin was a textured canvas that had already been dragged across the dirt. Now, I'm a brushstroke of indigo and violets, splattered with forest green and lime and topped with blotches of scarlet. It's everywhere: my hands, shoulders, elbows, legs, ribs, and even the corner of my chin. If I was meant to be art before, is the destruction of art still considered art?

It's as though cracks are running through the plastic mirror, breaking it into a thousand shards that make up the various facets of my being. None of the fragments fit together. Still, they make a whole. Just a pile of splinters put together to create sharp edges in my armor that's filled with cavities.

In a way, I look exactly the same, but I don't recognize myself anymore. Everything was always there, prickled and fragile, but it was hidden under layers of tape. I don't feel human. I'm not sure I ever really did. I'm a byproduct of my grandfather's wrath and my mother's shortcomings. Born into a crumbling, gold-plated cage with nothing but darkness to guide the way. I survived in a place where monsters are made.

I could have been beautiful without the curse of my family. But Medusa was beautiful before they called her a monstrous creature for turning men who wronged her into stone. It wasn't a curse; it was a gift.

I don't want to feel human. I want to feel unstoppable.

The door swings open, and I jump back, realizing I never responded to whatever it was he asked.

"Ever heard of knocking, perv?" A quiver runs through my voice, depriving it of any malice.

Kohen's eyes flick to the running shower, then to the hands trembling against my naked body. His shoulders fall as he steps forward.

"Blaze..." The deep tenor of his voice acts as a blanket over my aching shoulders. A whisper that chases away the nightmares. If I could wrap myself in it, maybe everything would cease to exist, and I'd finally be able to take a breath and taste the air.

"I—" A stone catches in my throat as I avert my attention toward the shower.

He says nothing. Shutting the door behind him, he reaches for a towel from the rack on the wall. With a single gesture from him, I lower myself onto the toilet lid and watch him turn off the shower then run the tap. His corded muscles in his back ripple against his straining white button-up, and I catch a glimpse of his fingers tracking up his arms to fold his sleeves.

I bring my knees up to my chest as I watch him work. The pressure of the tap flickers as he tests the temperature of the water. He brings the towel into the sink and grabs some soap from the shower.

When he turns to look at me, it's as if all the oxygen has evaporated from the room. My attempts at decrypting the emotions hidden behind his eyes are forgotten when he kneels on the floor in front of me, and I choke as an onslaught of feelings threaten to come out on a sob.

The saturated cloth sits in his right hand, and he holds his left out to me. "Let me take care of you, Blaze."

Throughout my life, I've faced so many things I didn't deserve—things that shouldn't happen to anyone. If there's one thing I know for certain, it's that I do not deserve this man.

I don't deserve the way he makes the pain go away. I don't deserve how he looks at me like he might actually love me. I don't deserve the life he could give me.

Woe is me and all that, but I can't help wanting it. I'm so tired of being alone with Kohen on the sidelines.

Hesitating for only a moment, I take his hand, and something settles between us that I can't quite name. It's too shallow to be called love. Too deep to be called infatuation. But something in between that tastes like acceptance.

The cloth seeps warmth into my skin, soothing my aching muscles. It's just wet enough to dampen my skin without feeling like

I'm about to be submerged underwater. Kohen is meticulous with his movements, gently going over blemished skin to massage my tender flesh. His eyes always stay on his task, never straying to my chest or between my legs or staying too long on bruised areas.

The lack of judgment or pity in his attention isn't something I thought I'd come to appreciate. He knows as well as I do that the decision I made that landed me in that tub is all on me. Yet, he isn't pointing fingers; he's helping me pick up the pieces of the fallout.

Watching him bathe me is enrapturing, just as it's frightening. It's like I'm laying my heart out for him to do with as he pleases. And what he wants to do is take care of it.

I'm not letting my grandfather take this away from me. I've already lost too many things I've never had, and there's only so much one person can lose before nothing is left to be taken away.

"I know what I want." I swallow, touching his hand to make him pause. "I want it all to burn. I want it so the only thing they have left is the clothes on their back."

I don't want to rise above. I don't want to find peace in the ruin. I want enough blood to fill a bath so I can wash away the sins of my mother and father.

When the hate is gone, there will only be pain. But that pain means nothing when it's all I've ever known. My grandfather has built his life on top of my starving body. He let my bones whittle, and infections fester within the rotting walls of the structure he built.

Before Seraphic Hills, the drugs kept me going. I itched for them because there was nothing else for me to reach for. Now, when I close my eyes, I can see my grandfather's cold indifference and McGill's cowardly stance. I can still recall how Boris's eyes gleamed as he shoved me in the tub, and the men's faces as they locked me in there.

"I am done paying for the crime of my birth."

It's time those men reap the consequences of their actions. No matter the cost.

Something akin to pride blooms in the golden irises of Kohen's eyes, and sparks of admiration curve across his lips.

"I told you, Thief. If you want a fire, you just need to ask."

CHAPTER 21

If Blaze doesn't walk out of that bathroom in the next fifty seconds, several possible things could happen.

One option is to kick the door down. She pushed me out over two hours ago, and I don't like how silent she is in there. It doesn't help that she was groaning on and off earlier. When I tried opening the door, she almost took my hand out when she slammed it in my face. I nearly lost my eye during my second attempt—it turns out she just needs to be injured to have impeccable aim with her shoe-throwing.

The second option is to track McGill down and flatten his frontal lobe against his spinal cord—which, in all honesty, is going to happen either way.

The third is the same as option two, plus a trip to Jonathan Whitlock Sr.'s house, where I do the exact same thing to him.

There's a dip in the carpet from where I've been pacing, and the room smells of smoke from how many times I've lit my lighter. Sweat has started to gather between my shoulder blades because half an hour ago, the little shit said she'd be ready in ten minutes. But she's still in there. And she won't let me see her to make sure she's okay. If I had known she'd take forever, I would have waited to get dressed instead of suffocating in this suit.

Huffing, I discard the jacket of my tux onto her bed and resume pacing, rolling the wheel of my newly acquired lighter as I do.

I pull out my phone and check the news for the latest updates on Oskadine. Every single headline is about how Osman Pharmaceuticals is ready to start mass-producing the medication that my grandfather started working on before he died. Seeing my family succeed turns my sour mood from bad to worse.

My parents should enjoy their success while they can. They won't have it for much longer.

Stomping up to the bathroom, I angle my head to the door. "How much more time do you need?" I bite out.

There's a yelp followed by a clatter against the bathroom sink. "For fuck's sake, Kohen," she growls. More clattering ensues. "If you ask me one more time, I'm never coming out."

I take a deep breath at the sound of her voice. "Don't make threats you can't back up, Thief. You're cute when you're thrown over my shoulders."

A cupboard slams. A scuffle. Cursing. "I am not *cute*." I stumble back when the door whips open. "Do I look fucking *cute* to you?"

"Certifia—" The word hangs as I take in her appearance.

My eyes travel up her body, devouring each and every inch of her like it's my last meal, and she's the most mouthwatering thing I've ever seen.

Jesus.

Fucking.

Christ.

There's not a word in the English language that could encapsulate just how stunning she is.

The lace hemline of the silk skirt teases up the side of her thighs, exposing creamy white skin beneath fishnet tights. Black gloves hug her arms and stop around her bicep. The leather corset has pushed her tits up to the point where her nipples are almost peaking over. My fingers twitch with the need to unlace her so her tits can go where they rightfully belong: in my hands and mouth. I'm going to have a hard-on the entire night if she walks around looking like this.

A black ribbon is tied around her neck, and even though neither of us has a religious bone in our body, two rosary beads drape over her collarbones and hang between her cleavage. My lips tug into a smile because her accessories are just things she's stolen from the school. Her copper strands are styled into messy, blown-out waves, making the thick smudge of kohl around her eyes seem more unhinged.

My allowance has never been better spent.

Her scarlet-painted lips turn up into a saccharine smirk. "You stole my look."

It causes physical pain to look away from her and down at my suit. The lace pattern on her dress is identical to the fabric off my lapels. Instead of a tie, like her, I've opted for rosary beads and a chain. The best part? The little blunt cut of hair.

We're a match made in hell.

Blaze nods at the cross hanging over my chest. "Won't you accidentally get exorcised wearing that, or are your demons built in?"

"I plug into mine," I drawl, feeling my dick harden as I get lost in the way she looks.

I want to put her in thirty different positions and fuck her in each one. I've never been a man of God, but I would get down on my knees and worship her until the day hell takes me. She's radiating feral energy, and I want to consume every last drop.

The best part? She's all mine.

The closer I look, the more I notice the flaws in how she's put herself together, and it turns my stomach into tight knots. No amount of makeup can hide her sunken eyes or the purple hues beneath them. Blaze can spend hours in the bathroom; it won't make the blues of her eyes any less drained. The dress is ever so slightly crooked, dots of mascara are scattered over her eyelids, and there's a barely noticeable uneven line on her black eyeliner. The patch of blue and purple along her chin and shoulder has seemingly vanished beneath the makeup.

Then my eyes drop to the gloves hiding the bloody bruises along her hands, and realization turns my knuckles white. That's why Blaze was taking so long.

One day, she'll figure out how to ask for help.

This woman, who's all hard edges and burning rage, is covered in scars inside and out. Some of the wounds are still gaping, bleeding a sea of red as she holds her head up as if the world isn't out to get her. She's the strongest person I know, and I want to spend every day making sure she sees it too.

My brows knit together as I eye the reflection glinting off her gloved fingers. Three silver rings decorate them. A chunky bracelet that's too big for her sits on her wrist, threatening to fall off with the slightest movement. When the fuck did she steal that from me? I know for a fact I was wearing those when I walked into her bedroom three hours ago.

Blaze raises her middle finger, where a black sapphire ring sits proudly against her black gloves. "What do you think of my new ring? The previous owner didn't take care of it very well."

"Give it back."

She looks good wearing me.

Blaze drops her arms to her sides after wincing partway through crossing them. "You said I could keep it if I steal it."

"Only if you're my date," I point out.

"Yeah. That's going to be a hard *no* from me." Her lips twist into a coy smirk as she attempts to saunter toward me, but it comes across as an awkward limp instead. Still, ten out of ten. It worked. I'm hard.

"A girl like me is in hot demand."

My dick deflates.

"If you walk in there with anyone but me, their family won't have a say on whether they get cremated or buried."

She moves around the pile of shoes in the corner with the balls of her injured foot. "Dead is most people's best color anyway."

Dr. Van der Merwe's sessions clearly aren't working for her.

I grab a pair of boots from my duffle bag and drop them on the floor.

"Where'd you get those from?" Blaze asks, eying the combat boots suspiciously.

I shrug.

She cocks her hip to the side. "I'm the klepto here. You know that, right?"

"And yet you look so pretty against flames."

She needs to be comfortable, and comfort won't come from heels

325

or someone else's shoes. Plus, she deserves to own something she didn't get secondhand.

Blaze snorts and slowly lowers herself onto the bed. I grab the boots before she can, ignoring her incessant protests as I slip her feet into them, lacing them carefully to not add too much pressure on her ankle.

She wiggles her feet as I tie the last knot, then help her up. "I'm like a fucked-up Cinderella."

"Are you going to turn into a pumpkin at midnight?"

"Really? An ginger hair joke? What are we, in middle school?"

I stare at her blankly. This is the girl I fell for. Not the fiery hair or the blue eyes, but the explosive personality. Filling a whole place with her presence. Throwing jokes even when exhaustion lines every inch of her silhouette. As long as she has room, my girl will always burn. But no fire lasts without someone giving her the things she needs, and she's been slowly dwindling out for years.

Holding the door open for her, she limps ahead and tries to stay two feet ahead of me as we make our way to the hall. The corridors are practically deserted with everyone already at prom—which means she's out of luck if she thinks anyone can save her from me.

The closer we get to the venue, the harsher her breathing becomes and the slower she moves. Music pulses through the air from the hall in the distance, and people filter in and out of the gothic structure, mingling on the lawns before heading back in.

Blaze gravitates towards me, just enough to brush her arm against mine as if double-checking I'll catch her if she falls. I pull her gloved hand into mine just before we reach the first lot of students on the lawn, and I'm careful to avoid knuckles as I tug her tightly to my side.

"Hey!" she protests, but half-asses her attempt to get away. "That's for dates only."

"Do you ever want to come again, Blaze?"

She narrows her eyes at me. "I don't need your assistance or permission to come."

"You will if your hands are tied. Hold my goddamn hand, Thief. Say you aren't my date one more time, and you're walking into the hall with your panties ripped, and my come dripping down your leg."

Blaze curses my name fifty different ways beneath her breath, but agrees with an air of reluctance that doesn't match the smile beaming across her lips. The moment makes me pause.

She's smiling.

She's smiling *at me.*

It's intoxicating. A euphoria I never thought I'd understand. I see how addiction starts now. *That* was the missing piece—the slice that perfectly fixed every wrong. Maybe this isn't the start of an addiction; it was always there. I've just found the correct dose.

"Don't look at me like that." Blaze whispers, staring up at me with her eyes the color of the hottest fire.

"Like what?"

"Like you want to eat me alive." Her gaze goes down to my lips, then back up.

"I've been dying for a taste of you since the moment I was born."

Her sharp inhale rings in my ears. Everything about her commands me. "Don't say things like that."

"Then shut me up."

Blaze hesitates for only a second before her scarlet lips ascend on me, stamping her mark in red on my cheek. I've waited a lifetime for her to touch me with something other than the tips of her claws and the points of her sharpened teeth. But the soft press of her lips is too fleeting.

"I'm wearing you; it's only fair that you wear me too," she explains, grinning at her handiwork.

I glance down at the bite mark permanently etched into my skin. "Cover me in it then, Thief. Make me yours."

This time, there's no waiting. Blaze launches straight for my neck like she's a fucking vampire. The kiss is aggressive like she's trying to conquer instead of just claim. The lunatic doesn't stop at my neck. She leaves a trail of lipstick marks down to the collar of my shirt. When that doesn't sate her, she whips my blazer aside and stamps another mark in the center of my pec—I'm not sure if she realizes that the heart is in the center of the chest, but I'll take it.

I pry her head back to slam my lips to hers and assault my senses with cherry and smoke. By *God*, she's fucking perfect.

The klepto grabs a fistful of my shirt and burns her stare into me as she says, "If anyone touches you, I'll rip their ear off with my teeth."

Satisfaction ripples down my spine as my brows lift. I always knew she'd be the jealous type. "Why the ear?"

Blaze gently tugs me down to her lips. "They don't get to touch and hear you speak too. I don't like knowing you talk shit to someone other than me."

Oxygen punches out of my lungs as she shoves me back. Copper hair whips in my face as she saunter-limps to the front door, where a teacher checks off attendance. Her long legs peek through the slit of the dress with every step she takes, and it's hard to think of anything but what she'd look like wearing nothing but those tights.

"Hurry up, date," Blaze throws over her shoulder, the silk skirt molding around her ass as she moves. "Before my acceptance expires."

I'm going to have gray hairs by the time I'm twenty.

We get into the hall without a hitch. Blaze acts like there aren't Halloween decorations everywhere and beelines straight for Charlie. The place is cast in blue and red hues. Purple light seeps through clouds of smoke, blanketing the dance floor and surrounding tables. Fake cobwebs hang from chandeliers and between the branches of artificial trees. Headstones sit on the center of round tables decked out in crystal glasses and wilted flowers, and skeletons hang on the walls.

How this theme got approved by the school board is beyond me.

I spend the majority of the time watching my date beeline everywhere while downing five glasses of spiked punch—courtesy of Liam. I've never seen her so elated without the involvement of drugs, dancing and hobbling around with Charlie, arguing with Charlie, then throwing utensils at Aaron... with Charlie.

At one point, Blaze gets up in the quarterback's face when he accidentally bumps into her. He opened his mouth and promptly closed it when he saw me behind her. The entire night is filled with her starting fights and stuffing my pockets with all the items she's stolen while simultaneously complaining that I should have gotten her a dress with pockets.

McGill silently scrutinizes us in between schmoozing with the other staff. But even drunk, Blaze's sticky fingers prove exceptional. After over an hour of watching her narrowly avoid getting murdered by the other students on numerous occasions, I call it quits. Blaze has had enough time to herself. It's my turn now.

She squeals when I loop my arm around her waist and carry her at my side to the center of the dancefloor. "Use your words, fucking Neanderthal."

"Stay still. You're going to hurt yourself."

The eyeful of tits I, and the entire student body, get when I look down makes me question whether I want to let her stand on her own.

Then I hear Aaron laugh close by, and I couldn't put her down faster if I tried.

I hold her close to me to take the weight off her feet. The way she immediately wraps her arms around my neck makes me forget about everyone else in the room. She pulls me from side to side as we dance to the music. There's nothing graceful or sensual about the way she moves. Everything about it is carnal and unfiltered, completely thoughtless, as her body becomes a vessel for the music. I could watch her dance all night.

The charcoal around her eyes makes the glacial blue of her iris sharper against her sweat-stained skin. Strands of orange hair stick to her face, and her ruby-tinted lips have lost their rich color. She's still just as beautiful as she always is.

Blaze takes my hand to twirl herself, and I catch her before she stumbles into the jock she's been beefing with all night. "Before Seraphic Hills was turned into a school, the nuns treated this place like an asylum for people who they believed were possessed by the devil."

She narrows her eyes at me in a way that says she won't hesitate to slap the shit out of me should the occasion require it. "Are you saying this because I have red hair?"

I cut her with a scathing glare. "I'm saying it because you're the craziest person here."

Self-satisfaction colors her cheeks as she pats my chest. "Flattery will get you nowhere, Mr. Osman."

"Is that why you're blushing?"

"It's called makeup. Don't get too cocky." She pushes my shoulder playfully.

My dick—that's been at half-mast all night—perks up at the mention of the word *cock*. "Say that last word again, and we're going to have a problem."

"What? Cock—"

I press my thumb against her lips, and her eyes flare as she takes it between her teeth. *Jesus fuck.* "There are five exits. The one on the left beside the stage leads to a trap door. Who do you think will be louder, you or the music?"

"Ohh, is that what that thumping sound is?" she asks, releasing my thumb and missing the insinuation entirely while she bobs her head to the beat.

Her jokes are fucking horrendous.

So is her dancing.

Her singing? Next-level terrible.

And I still wouldn't change a single thing about her.

She stops suddenly and pokes her finger in the juncture of my jaw and neck. "Where'd you get that scar?"

My heart warps. I've had it for over seven years, and this is the first time Blaze has noticed it. I clear my throat and sway stiffly with her. "I shoved a boy you were having a screaming match with. A minute later, you told me you hated me, then threw a book at me."

She squints like I might pull out a video of the day. "I have no memory of this."

I chuckle. "Probably because you did shit like that weekly." There's no such thing as a dull moment as long as she's involved. "We're scars to each other, Blaze. You can like or hate it; we've stuck together longer than anyone else."

Blaze scrunches her nose. "Because you wouldn't leave me alone."

"Then your lonely world would have gotten smaller."

Her finger grazes over the small scar. "Just confirming, is the scar from me or the boy?"

Of course, that's what she got out of the conversation. "The book."

Her eyes brighten. "Was it *English Grammar for Dummies*?"

I blink. "What?"

"Inside joke," she sighs.

"With who?" Fucking Duke? *Elijah*?

"You had to be there, I guess."

Anger zaps through me at her words as McGill comes into view at the corner of my eyes. "Miss Whitlock, may I—"

"Fuck off, old man." Blaze and I say the first part in unison. The second is all her.

His eyes drop to the red lipstick stains on my collar, then to the evidence of the same crimson still on her lips. I don't like the callous gleam in his eye, the threat-tipped words he pairs with it. "Excuse me?"

I start to pull her behind me, but the klepto shifts her body instead, standing a foot away from McGill as if she's shielding me from him. Blaze lowers her voice and says, "I'm doing as my grandfather asked." The notes come out ominous and dramatic, as if she's trading state secrets.

McGill watches her curiously for a second before swinging his gaze to me as if trying to see if I have any inkling of what she's talking about—I do. But he doesn't need to know that.

"Very well." He nods. "We will discuss this tomorrow."

She nods stiffly, but as soon as he turns away, she flips him the bird. We both watch as he slinks away back to the side of the stage, where a group of teachers is doing an even worse job watching over us than the security guards.

"He needs to go," I mutter.

She leans against me, lifting her ankle off the ground as if it hurts to stand on. "You took the words right out of my mouth, lover boy."

"Tonight," I clarify. Blaze is sorely mistaken if she thinks there's any chance they're having their discussion tomorrow. For now, I want to watch my little thief move in that black dress and look at me like I'm someone she can trust.

"Should I head out first, then you join me later?" she asks.

"I told you, we're coming and leaving here together. That's never going to change."

CHAPTER 22

This is insane.

Certifiable.

Batshit fucking crazy—even for me.

Everything about this is ludicrous—from both the outside looking in *and* the inside looking out.

I didn't think we'd actually pay McGill a visit tonight. I thought I'd have to spend weeks planning and making contingency plans in case Kohen bails. But he's here. And he planned it all while I was playing makeup in the bathroom. I'm not sure whether that surprises me more, or the fact that I agreed to spider-monkey this shit by hopping onto his back so he can carry me all the way to McGill's place so I don't have to use my injured foot.

Kohen said I'd slow us down and I'd breathe too loud. Either the vodka has well and truly gone to my head, or I'm a woman full of agreement, because I then lift my arms up and let him bundle me up in his hoodie and beanie.

I'm not sure how Kohen knows, but apparently, McGill lives at a house just outside campus. He started renting the place earlier this year after his wife left him, and he still hasn't finished unpacking.

Shock. That's the only thing that can explain why we're about to do Lord knows what, and I have my head shoved against his neck to breathe in patchouli and mint from the source. I'm not sure at which point the shock started. When I was thrown into frozen waters yesterday. When he confessed to a crime he wasn't being questioned for, and told me about everything he did for me I had never realized days before. Or when he *offered to kill McGill for hurting me?*

I'd be a liar if I said it didn't make me a tad bit aroused. Who knew he just had to murder a man to get me compliant. A giggle bubbles out of me just as he jogs down the concrete steps into the courtyard, rattling me against his back. The alcohol and anti-inflammatories have numbed most of the pain, but even without those two, the adrenaline would be enough to keep the hurt at bay. The only thing that would make this moment seem perfect is a bump. I'm trying not to think about it, but it's hard not to.

Just one line and I'll feel like a million bucks. Undefeatable and able to conquer the world. But I won't get my revenge if I'm too high or strung out to function. I need my focus.

"Be quiet," he scolds as I play with the neckline of the sweater he's wearing to focus on anything other than the fact my body is itching for a hit. I pinch the cotton collar between my fingers. Pity there's no lipstick stain on this shirt. Seeing the smile drop from Sarah's face when I walked into prom with him on my arm was amazing. But if she saw us right now? I almost wish I could take a video of us like this. We're the parody version of the *James Bond* movies.

Scratch that. We're more like a cartoon TV series with two incompetent fools pretending to be spies. Or assassins.

We haven't even started causing mayhem yet, and I can't contain the smile that keeps breaking out across my face.

Out of all of Kohen's admissions, seeing his dedication in action makes me want to kiss him the same way he always kisses me, so he knows that somewhere deep down, I appreciate him for being there on the good days and the bad days. It's making me all mushy inside.

What made me swoon even harder was when he returned to my room in the middle of the night after he dropped me off from the dance. He had a big duffle bag full of snacks and a heat pack, pestering me as he complained I needed to start keeping myself warm. I fought for a solid two seconds, then almost started twirling and fluttering my eyelashes from all the attention. When Kohen started dressing me in his clothes, I felt like a goddamn princess. He looked like he was borderline concerned for his safety.

I drag my fingers over the chain around his neck as he keeps us to the sides of the buildings, dashing into the tree line in the opposite direction of the church.

The night is still except for the sounds of our heavy breaths and the crunch of spring beneath Kohen's boots. The moon is hidden behind sheets of clouds, obscuring light from reaching our path beneath the trees. I keep thinking he's going to trip over a hidden root or slide through the mud, but he keeps carrying me like I'm a backpack. I barely have to use any muscle to hold on because he's gripping me with frightening ease.

This is like a fucked-up bonding session. A couples therapy exercise even though we aren't a couple. What's the next thing we'll do? Summon a demon? I might be down for that too, if he keeps spoiling me like this. I feel like I'm on a power trip and never want to come down.

"This is so much fun," I whisper-yell, loving the exhilaration coursing through my veins. "Do you do this often?"

Kohen halts and angles his head to give me a perplexed look. "Shut up, Blaze."

I make the motion of zipping my lips shut, and he starts walking again. "But seriously, do you?"

He sighs.

"Okay, Mr. Drama." I roll my eyes. "Chill out. It's a genuine question. I'm just trying to figure out whether I'm murdering someone with an amateur or a pro."

"No, Blaze. I do not commit homicide often," he says, exasperated.

I push my bottom lip out and wiggle my feet in the air. "That's disappointing." I pat his chest, feeling the ache spread across my knuckles at the movement. "Still time to change that, bud."

"I'm not your *bud*." I can practically hear his molars grind as his gloved hands tighten around my thighs. Glancing down, I notice him wearing a pair of shoes I've never seen before. Antiforensics? Nice.

I rub the top of his head, which is covered by a hat. "You're right. We're acquaintances at best."

"I know how your pussy tastes. What you feel like when you come on my cock. That you prefer fast over hard. How you look when you squirt, and the way your legs shake after I fuck you. I'd say we're beyond friends."

"Frenemies—"

Kohen pinches my thigh.

"Ow! What was that for?" I flick his ear. "Plus, I already couldn't walk properly. So it doesn't count."

"Stop talking, Blaze." He sounds like he's regretting this adventure.

Too bad I want to see this through.

I groan quietly. "*Boring.*"

"I can use the tape on you, if you prefer."

Grinning, I nip at his jawline, making him tighten his hold. "Don't threaten me with a good time, lover boy." My voice is saccharine, promising a night of fulfilling his deepest, darkest desires. Bloodlust really is a thing.

"If you don't stop talking, I'm going to fuck you against this tree over here." He points to the left. "Then you're going on your hands and knees on that boulder over there." He nods toward the right. "After that, we're going to the med bay so I can stretch your pussy out with a speculum while I fuck your ass."

My face burns with the image, and I subconsciously roll my hips. Maybe I might be interested in a speculum after all. "Where does murder fit into this schedule?"

"One or the other, Klepto," he says with an air of finality. "Behave or be punished."

I consider my options for a moment.

"Both." I nod. "I pick both."

Kohen shakes his head and lowers me onto my feet as we reach a steel barred fence with spikes decorating the top. It has to be at least eight feet tall. I don't think I could scale it on a good day, let alone when my foot is screwed, and I'm still feeling run-down from the past three days.

"Not to be a buzzkill or anything, but how the fuck do you expect me to get over that?"

He takes a deep breath and squeezes his eyes shut. They reopen on an exhale, and he gestures behind me. "The gate, Blaze. The gate."

"Alright, alright." I hold my hands up. "Drop the attitude, smart-ass."

Leaning against the gate, Kohen unzips the front pocket of the duffle bag to retrieve an old-fashioned primary key that looks like the ones the groundskeepers always have on hand. He stands back to let me hobble through after unlocking it, then stuffs the key back in his bag and shuts the gate behind him.

The princess treatment has well and truly gone to my head, because I place my hands on my hips and wait for him to carry me again.

Independent young woman, my ass.

I doubt my mode of transport is practical, but I let him pick me up and carry me against his chest like I'm a little kid. It's kind of sad to admit that my inner child is preening at the way I'm being held.

"It's easier," he explains as he cups my ass in both hands and gives it a solid squeeze.

"Yeah," I agree breathily, dropping my head against his shoulder when he uses his hold on my ass to grind me against his length. "Not hard at all."

His steps don't falter and neither does his breathing when I squeeze my legs around his middle, and all but choke him with my elbow against his esophagus. Moving probably hurts me more than it hurts him, but the black and blue marks covering my body are keeping me grounded. They're the reason why we're trekking through the forest in the middle of the night. As the bruises fade on me, I will bring them upon those who have made me suffer.

The rise and fall of his chest slowly steadies as we hike through the forest. Watching him grow calmer the closer we get to McGill's house is fascinating. This is his element—not murder or home invasions. He looks like he has the thing I've been lacking: purpose. *Vengeance.* It looks glorious on him.

I was wrong to think that I didn't deserve a prince. They simply were never made for me. I don't want the prince. I want a villain.

Holding on to Kohen tighter, we approach the property. It's not the type of home I expected McGill to live in. For some reason, I thought he'd live in a shack or a mansion that's barely holding together. I'm not too far off on the latter, but this place looks... homey, I guess. Fresh cream weatherboards, two stories, a brick chimney, coral roofs and awning, a flag swaying in the wind at the side of the house. A few bushes line the deck's front, and several enormous pine trees circle the structure. It's everything you'd expect from a country house.

All the curtains are closed, so it's impossible to see what might greet us once we're inside. A single light is on in one of the rooms upstairs, and Kohen lifts his pointer finger to his lips in the universal sign of *shut the fuck up*, as if the situation isn't obvious enough. I pull the finger in return, and the bruises on my hands immediately make me regret my decision.

Kohen quietly settles me down on the first step of the back porch, then creeps in front of me to try the handle. When it doesn't budge, he raises his fist toward the door like he wants to smash the window in.

I roll my eyes and push him aside. Sure, let's alert McGill to our break-in. If you want a job done right, send a woman and all that.

Huffing, I drop down to my busted knees and pull out gloves and the two paper clips I brought for this exact reason, but the latex gloves make the thin material harder to grip and mold. Only a slither of moonlight shines on the brass door handle, making it trickier to see what I'm doing. Kohen crouches beside me to monitor our surroundings as I shape the paper clips and slip them into the keyhole. I hold my breath to listen for any sounds from inside, and all that comes is the classical music playing from another part of the house.

Tsk, tsk, McGill. You shouldn't be up this late on a school night.

My lungs fill with cool air as I try to calm the roaring in my ears and focus on the task at hand. It's been a while since I've picked locks, and if Kohen's impatient glances are any indication, I'm taking far too long. He glares at me whenever the door rattles as I try to depress the pins, but I shrug him off. There's enough wind to make the noises unsuspicious, and frankly, I'd like to see him try to do a better job. At least I wasn't the one who was about to break a window.

"Score," I whisper when the telltale *click* sounds through the night.

Kohen helps me to my feet and then reaches into the large duffle bag. I survey our surroundings and keep an ear out for any movement inside when he pulls out a bat with nails hammered into it. Without a word, he pushes it into my hand, then whispers, "I recommend the knees, but the face works too."

When the *fuck* did he have time to organize this? I gape at him as he ushers me behind him and takes the lead. He sent two guys to the hospital for me? Blew up a building as a birthday present? Now he's helping me murder a man and making me my very own weapon to do it?

And here I was, thinking that chivalry was dead.

Hugging the baseball bat to my chest, I can't help but smile to myself as butterflies let loose in my stomach. It makes this whole situation all the more perfect—aside from the pain that explodes through my knuckles when I grip the cold wood. Biting the inside of my cheek, I push aside all thoughts of the bruises and scrapes to concentrate on the next few minutes. I wonder what McGill will look like when he sees me with the bat. What will it look like when his bones cave beneath my new present?

The anticipation tastes so sweet, and the impending bloodshed so bitter—it's an intoxicating combination I never thought I'd experience.

Either from arrogance or delusion, dread hasn't wormed its way into my veins. Kohen's presence is a safety net I never thought I'd be able to latch on to, and I'm greedy for it. If worse comes to worst, I won't be alone in this. No one can say I forced him to do this. No one can accuse me of doing this alone. If I go down, he goes down with me.

I, however, hate that he's pretty much like a bodyguard or hired gun. While having a partner is nice and all, I don't love the reminder that my flesh limits my physical strength. It's unnerving that I'm relying on him for my safety. What if red and blue lights start flashing, and the police raid the house? He might bolt and leave me behind. Or if McGill pulls out a gun? It'd be every man for himself.

The door creaks open, and we collectively wince, pausing to wait for a reaction. When nothing but music sounds through the house, Kohen creeps forward, holding a hand out to keep me behind him.

Jesus Christ, I need even more psychological help if that alone makes me blush.

The back door opens into the hallway shared with the main entrance. There's a bathroom directly to our right, and boxes marked with illegible handwriting scattered everywhere. I focus on steadying my breathing and keeping my footsteps light on the old wooden floor that groans beneath our feet as we head toward the stairs that hug the wall shared with the living room. It smells vaguely of smoke. There's nothing special about the space that screams "headmaster of a pompous school." It's the type of farmhouse I'd expect from a late-nineties movie—minus the excessive photos hanging off the floral wallpaper. So far, the nicest thing about this place is the fully stocked liquor cabinet in the hallway.

A haggard cough rumbles through the walls, followed by lip-smacking, and we still. But Kohen doesn't move forward even though the coast is clear.

I tap my fingers against the bat. Can Kohen move any faster up these steps? It's going to be Christmas by the time we get to McGill.

Poking Kohen in the back to urge him forward does nothing but make him give me the "Are you fucking kidding me?" look. So I drop the bat and let it swing around as I shuffle up the steps behind him. He keeps stopping every time the staircase makes a sound, but Old Man McGill doesn't seem to notice.

We break onto the second floor, where yellow light floods the hall from an open door. More boxes and Bubble Wrap are littered around the place, and my fingers itch to take a thing or two... Okay, just one.

With all Kohen's attention forward, I reach into the next box we pass and grab the first thing I wrap my fingers around. A... Oh, that's stupid. I'll still take it though.

He whips around, looks at me like I'm insane, and then shakes his head when I shove the used candle into my pocket, then continues on his slow, creeping pace.

Sighing, I push past him to the door into what looks like McGill's office and throw up a little in my mouth. The ripped, moss-green wingback office chair is reclined all the way back while his ankles are crossed on the desk. His blue, checkered shirt is unbuttoned to reveal his hairy beer gut that's partially covered by a pale hand and an unlit cigar. A crystal tumbler is in his other hand, with only a couple sips of the amber liquid left.

Drinking on a school night too? We're really setting good examples here.

A fireplace crackles against the wall I'm leaning against. Directly opposite it is a ratty couch with an equally ratty blanket. The empty cigar case on the desk is balancing on a piece of paper. Paperwork and bills are strewn across the room, a pile of wood lies haphazardly next to the fireplace, and more boxes are stacked in the corner labeled *Court Docs*. A blue leaflet is open on the desk, and the familiar red logo staring back at me makes my mouth go dry.

Whitlock Investment Banking & Partners.

He... My jaw hardens. McGill isn't *old friends* with my grandfather. McGill is his fucking client. It makes so much more sense. The shitty house, the bills all around the room, the court files. How much trouble is this man in? Has he sold his soul to my grandfather just to fix it?

The headmaster has a noose around his neck that's controlled by Jonathan Whitlock Sr. Without my grandfather, how deep would McGill's grave be with all the overdue bills he has lying around? My grandfather owns him.

The man who held me down and tortured me looks pathetic like this, with his guard down and completely vulnerable. Something twisted inside me curls with pleasure, knowing that no one will miss him when he's gone. He has no more wives. There's not a single photo of any of his children anywhere. None of his kids want anything to do with him. How many different child supports must he be paying his ex-wives? Four? *Six?*

He's the image of a man who's lost everything. So I'll be doing him a favor by finishing the job.

The smooth brass vibrates through the floors as the flute patters against my eardrum. "Is this Beethoven or Mozart?" I muse.

McGill's eyes snap open. He scrambles in his seat, dropping the cigar and tumbler.

"Prokofiev," Kohen grunts, shouldering past me through the doorway and sending me a death glare.

"Who?" I ask as McGill leaps onto his feet, sending the chair careening into the wall.

"What are you doing here?" he stutters, using the desk as a makeshift barrier between us. He clamors to button up his shirt. I assume it's to preserve the little dignity he has left.

I swing the bat onto my shoulder and push off the wall to stalk toward him as Kohen attempts to corner him. "I was so excited to have our discussion that I decided, *why wait?*"

McGill's eyes flick back and forth between me and Kohen as if trying to gauge who's the bigger threat. *Me*, he decides. I guess I'm just that intimidating. I tip my head to the side and watch as he fumbles, straightening his shirt. He draws his stiff shoulders, putting on a mask of faux confidence.

God, the smell of his anxiety is enough to get drunk on. Is this what he felt when he ordered men to hold me down? Or when he summons me, knowing the level of pain he will inflict? My grip tightens at the memory of all the bruises that have formed on me because of him and my grandfather.

AVINA ST. GRAVES

"Neither of you are allowed here." The words come out wavered as I hum, swinging the bat around the air as if it were a toy. "I'm calling security to have you both escorted back—" His fingers tremble as he reaches for his phone.

Kohen cuts him off without an ounce of emotion on his face. "That isn't happening." McGill halts in his procession. He eyes Kohen as if realizing his mistake in thinking I'm the bigger threat when the pyromaniac is only a couple feet away from him.

"Whatever prank you two are pulling, it ends now." He looks at me as he says it. I assume it seems like I'm the mastermind of all of this, what with Kohen standing there stoically, arms crossed. *Weaponless.* I'm sure that makes him all the more frightening.

"Kohen doesn't do *pranks*," I sigh with disappointment as I block McGill between us. "But I assure you, this is *very* serious." My hands tremble in anticipation when I turn to Kohen. "Hey, Pyro. You said knees, right?"

He nods, sneering at McGill. "Face works too."

The headmaster raises his arms with a cry when I use every fiber of my muscles to smash the bat against his shoulder. My body screams from the movement, but I don't let it stop me. My rage takes hold of the swing, pouring months of bottled-up torment into my veins.

Kohen narrows his eyes at me as if he can tell I'm just going to do the opposite of whatever he wants. McGill's howls rip through the room as blood splatters onto my face. Elation fills my marrow and makes my body feel as light as a summer breeze. The pounding in my ears is still there, but I'm convinced that invincibility exists.

McGill crashes into the wall and crumbles onto the floor, clutching his weeping shoulder, refashioning his blue shirt into scarlet. Another sob cracks out of him when he looks at the red

347

covering his hands. "Stop," he pleads.

I can barely look at the morbid sight. It's a scene from a horror movie where the victim's skin is dotted with holes, and the arm doesn't look like an arm anymore. *You did that*, I tell myself. *You're making him suffer.*

"What was that?" My eyes flash. "Stop? Stop? Come on, McGill. You didn't think your words held any meaning, did you? I always knew you wouldn't be a fighter. You get other people to do the hard work for you while you sit on your lazy fucking ass." He flinches as I wave the bat in his direction. "You're a lazy, useless coward." I glance around and continue goading him. "Where's your family, by the way?"

McGill shakes his head as the music starts to reach a crescendo. "You don't want to do this, Blaze. You won't get away with it."

I throw my head back and let a maniacal laugh rumble through me. "Oh, *now* I'm Blaze? How convenient that this is the first time you got my name right." I follow the bat's momentum, driving it into his shoulder again. The scream that follows pierces my eardrum and rushes down my spine. Flesh splits beneath the force of the nails, lodging deep enough for a *crunch* to vibrate up my arms. My dinner lurches up my stomach when the blood makes a suctioning sound as I pull the bat out.

"Please!" he sobs, rolling onto his side against the wall.

"*Please*," I mock. "How many times did I beg? I cried, and I screamed, and I prayed." I kick him after each word. "I pleaded for you to let me out until my throat burned with the words. I told you that you would all die if you left me there. I made you a *fucking* vow." My voice comes out guttural, as if on the precipice of losing all sense of reality. "And you left."

"I'm sorry," he grits out between cries.

I drop the bat on the floor and feel my muscles rage as I rip the blood-spattered hoodie off. Layer after layer, I strip down until I'm in my bra and the sweats, baring all my battle scars to him. McGill's eyes fall to the floor by my feet as the heat from the fire warms my pebbled skin. "Look at me." I snarl as he huddles closer to the wall. "I said, *look at me!*" I point my gloved hand at the bruises on my ribs and along my shoulder. "You both did this."

He shakes his head. "I was just doing as your grandfather—"

I yank the bat back off the floor, and his eyes slam into mine, then fall to the evidence of my pain written on my skin. I *swear* I almost see guilt on his face.

"Do you fucking hear yourself? You don't believe those lies."

How fucking dare he deny it when I have the marks to prove it? He could have refused. He could have lied to my grandfather. He could have done *everything* in his power to keep his students safe.

"Tell me, what is it Jonathan offered you in exchange for torturing me?"

McGill's skin grows paler with each passing second as his blood soaks into the wooden floor. "N-nothing, he's my friend, and I was looking out for—"

"*Liar!* All you do is fucking *lie.*" I hit his cheek with the top of the bat and shove the Whitlock Investments folder in his face. "Jonathan doesn't have *friends.* If he did, he wouldn't call some lowlife piece of shit like you his friend. No property, no money, no family. You're a fraud with nothing left. So I'm going to ask you. *One. Last. Time.* What is my grandfather offering you? *Confess*, McGill." I raise the bat, ready to strike.

"A loan!" he sputters out through his chattering teeth as Kohen rummages around behind me. "He's wiping my credit card debt clean and helping me get back on my feet. No bank wants to lend money to me. If I go bankrupt, I'll lose my job! Jonathan offered to fix everything as long as I petitioned the court to have you sentenced to Seraphic Hills and let him choose your treatment."

I drop the bat to my side and take in a deep breath. So that was the price of my sanity? It's not even a clean slate or a fresh start. It doesn't even help him stay above water, and he still took it, knowing it could cause me, a fucking child who he doesn't know, irreversible damage. He's left out the second part of the truth; I was his scapegoat. With no kids, no friends, no wife, who else would be his free punching bag?

"Say you're pathetic."

McGill glances at Kohen and then back to me, taking shallow breaths. "W-what?"

"Tell me how every relationship you've ever had has failed. Tell me how your kids won't shed a tear for you. Look at me and say that you're a pathetic, spineless old man." He screams when I push the end of the bat into his wound. His screams hit the high notes at the exact same time as the music.

"He's going to go into shock," Kohen says from beside me.

My nostrils flare as I release pressure and let the bat fall back to my side.

"Blaze," McGill whimpers. "*Blaze, please.* I-I had no choice." His chest quakes with each breath he takes. "Jessica took everything!"

"Why?" I force the syllable out, feeling the moisture from my hands build within the gloves.

"I mean, we—we separated, and she took me to court and got the kids—"

"*Why*, McGill? Why are you living alone, in your own filth, surrounded by empty bottles? Why did she leave? Why did she get it all?"

He stutters, unable to string together a coherent sentence.

Kohen shows me a stack of papers, turning each and every sheet for me to read. "Gambling?" I say, looking at page after page of transactions, overdrafts, and payment claims from casinos, bookmakers, and banks. Then the final page: an advance of $400,000 from Whitlock Investments. "You wrecked my soul to pay off your *gambling debts?*"

I've never felt so cheap in my fucking life. Adrenaline has my grip shaking around the bat. I want to hit him again. I want to do it over and over until he's a mangled pile of bone.

Fuck him.

Fuck my grandfather.

Fuck *all* of them.

McGill raises his one good arm as the bottled-up rage comes bubbling out to fuel each swing of the bat. I do it over and over until his entire shirt turns a haunting shade of crimson, and even then, I keep hitting his shoulder, screaming my frustrations as I do. Cursing him. Cursing my grandfather. Cursing my parents. It all comes out. I don't let up until his arm is barely attached to his shoulder and the rug beneath him is soaked in his blood.

"I was thinking about how I saw this all play out. Whether I'd break your bones one by one, or find some loose wiring so you know what it feels like to have your brains fucking fried. Whether I'd let Kohen finish you off or if I'd do it myself." My voice wavers as I speak. "*No one* gets to take my revenge for me. I thought about torturing you, drawing it out for hours—*days*— just like you did to

351

me. But if I thought my life was sad?" I scoff, clutching the bat in both hands. "Look at you. You're pathetic. Tell me." I tip my head to the side. "When you take your last breath tonight, will you die knowing what love feels like? Or will you die knowing that your own children don't want you?"

Tears gather along his lashes. *"Please."*

"You're crying? How sad." I step on him, pressing my weight to his side and watch him squirm beneath me. "You tortured me, McGill. You made me suffer for your own twisted pleasure because it's the only time you get to feel powerful during your own pitiful existence. Now, my face will be the last one you ever see. My voice is the last you ever hear."

I raise my shaking arms and he squeezes his eyes shut like a coward.

"One more thing." Kohen stops me mid swing with a hand on my arm, then drops down onto his haunches in front of McGill. "I *did* burn down her house, almost killed Elijah for touching her, then blew up the Science building because I wanted to impress her. And you see those nails in that bat? I put them there for her. You once asked what Blaze is to me. She's my vice. My fire." McGill's lips part as Kohen rises to his feet.

"Don't worry, McGill. I take your treatment plan *very* seriously, and I've already decided you need to be put down."

This time, when I aim, the nails bury into McGill's face. One pierces his eyeball as another caves into his skull, splattering blood up the walls and around the room. The *crunch* that resonates through the air melts with the fading music.

I keep hitting and hitting and hitting. His head. Shoulder. Hands. Stomach. Legs. Chest. The rage rolls through me with the force of a hurricane as I scream, letting the weapon loose on every inch of him. Blood splatters all over my skin, and each shattering bone feels more sickening than the last.

Warm liquid falls from my cheek to my chest that's aching from my haggard breaths, and drips down my bare stomach. I choke on a sob as I bury the bat into him one last time, bile rushing up my throat.

Power floods through my veins as I sway back and watch the bat slowly dislodge itself from his head and clunk onto the floor, McGill spurting blood from all of his orifices.

He's dead. *I did that.* I killed him.

I fucking killed him.

He can't hurt me anymore. He can't run and tell my grandfather about all my crimes. He can't hold me down or lock me in ice water.

For the next few weeks, I have no warden watching my cage. No one to coat my skin in black and blue for the sake of fucking *gambling debts*. All that's left is Boris and Dr. Van der Merwe. The former will have his time. The latter? He will suffer, but death will not be his ending.

For the first time in my life, I feel like I've finally won a battle.

I stumble back and crash onto the floor, grabbing the trash can to empty out the contents of my stomach. The acid burns up my throat and chokes me as my eyes water and the tears fall into the plastic bin. My stomach muscles contract with each heave, and ache with each breath of the putrid air. I jolt when something soft touches my lower back, but I keep going, dry heaving like I might be able to rid myself of my sins. All the while my eyes stay glued on the first domino, ingraining the sight into my memory; every wound and broken bone, mangled and distorted against the rising tempo of the music.

The bruises on my body are still there, and in time, they'll heal. McGill is forever immortalized to be an unrecognizable creature, turned by the very monster he helped create.

I'm not sure which part is making me sick, the fact that I murdered someone, or that one of the locks on my cage is gone. It feels like freedom is finally within reach, and I don't know how to cope with that knowledge. The only time I've felt free was at the bottom of a bottle or a couple grams deep. Now that I'm sober, it feels surreal, as if at any second McGill will wake or my grandfather will walk through the door.

But I'm not free yet. Not until they're all dead.

I don't care how many times I have to throw up, or lose a part of myself each time I spill blood, my grandfather doesn't get to live after what he's done.

Kohen's hazel eyes greet mine when I turn to face him with tears streaming down my cheeks. "Blaze, you know what you did to my place? Do it again. Without the bat this time. Destroy it all." Kohen drops the six letters of demand for payment from casinos and gambling companies nationwide. "We're here to collect your debt. So collect, Thief."

CHAPTER 23

Turning up the volume dial on the stereo, the music fills the background of the chaos and I go back to watching Blaze.

Wiping traces of us clean from this house is going to be a nightmare. The murder weapon will need to go, the nails disassembled, the bat disposed of, and the paperwork from Jonathan will need to be strategically placed. Anything and everything to stop the police from linking this back to Blaze.

It needs to be clean, but not so clean that it looks like it was done by a professional. It must be done messily, just enough to make it seem like the intruder didn't spend long here.

Blaze, on the other hand? She's doing her job *spectacularly*. Kicking boxes, emptying them upside down, flicking lamps across the room, ripping pillows in half, turning the bed over, and checking every conceivable hiding place known to man. She skirted the line of *crime of passion*; now, she's a woman on a mission. I'm not sure what exactly she's looking for as she checks for hidden drawers and coat pockets, but she's in her element, coated in blood, half naked, and seething with rage.

She's a whirlwind of complete and utter chaos. Watching her come undone is the most mesmerizing thing I have ever seen. My heart aches seeing her as unbidden as she is now, with her eyes glazed over with unshed tears. The thread she was holding on to earlier has turned to ash, and all that's left is for her to fall.

Leaning against the balcony, I flick the wheel on my lighter and watch her rampage through the house, tipping over everything in sight. The music from the speakers vibrates along the wooden floors, barely loud enough to be heard above Blaze's frenzy. It's odd that she hasn't once pocketed anything or put something aside to take later.

Minutes roll by as she rapidly turns the house into an abandoned bomb site rather than a home. She pants and grunts as she runs around with zero methodology to how she zigzags through the house.

A stack of paper falls over as my lighter digs into my palm, feeling like a lead weight. It would be so easy for me to bend over and put the flame next to it—

I stamp down the thought. This is her moment, not mine.

Blaze huffs out a breath and marches to the only untouched furniture in the house: the antique redwood liquor cabinet. For the first time since the floodgates opened, she pauses. Standing before the cabinet, she eyes the selection of wines and near-empty bottles of whiskey and bourbon. It's the only part of the house that might indicate McGill works amongst high society.

Blaze lunges to the side of the cabinet and lets out a feral cry, sending the glass hurtling onto the floor. She jumps back against my chest as the glass flies across the room in an explosion of browns and white. The last shard settles on the floor, and everything becomes still except for the heavy rise and fall of her chest.

The music is a distant melody as the air grows thicker with each breath we take. The more she eases her weight onto me, the more she trembles, tearing at a part of my soul. A sob racks through her whole body and I squeeze my eyes shut. I never thought a sound could make my heart splinter in two. The pain of her sorrow winds its way around every organ, every cell, every fiber.

I tuck her head against my chest and carry her into the living room, where there's the sharp smell of smoke lingering in the air from the dying embers of the downstairs fireplace. The lights are on, revealing the wreckage of broken furniture, emptied boxes of clothes and ornaments, and the empty space before the fireplace. I lower her shaking form onto a spot on the rug, then stuff a piece of newspaper into the coals and add another log to the pile. Grabbing the lighter, I hold it to the corner of the paper. Turning the spark wheel, I watch it catch fire and quickly eat up the words written on it.

My lungs feel like ash as I watch her rock herself in her spot, muffling her sobs with a hand over her mouth. Her brows are etched together in a vicious frown as if the tears burning down her cheek are from a place of rage.

I had never heard her cry until we were sent to Seraphic Hills. If I can barely handle the sight of her hungover, nothing will undo me like seeing her tears. It hurts far more than any words she's shot my way because it means it's gone too far. *She's* gone too far. I should have done the final blow or made her stay behind as I took him out.

She deserves the whole fucking world, not scraps. My girl is a fighter; always has been, and always will be. She's been through more battles than I have, and I will never be half as resilient as she is.

But the fighting will have to stop. One day, she won't have any more punches to throw.

I don't want to be her grief. I don't want to be any part of the reason she feels the need to curl her fingers into fists or keep her walls up around herself. I don't even want to be her everything.

I want her heart to beat easily the second she wakes up in the morning. I want her to smile for the sake of smiling. Laugh, cry tears of joy, skip around until she's shitting fucking rainbows. I want her to be happy. And if everyone has to die for that to happen, then I better get good at digging graves.

"I'm sorry, Blaze. It's my fault." I drop onto my knees in front of her. "I shouldn't—"

"Don't," Blaze grits out, yanking me down to her by my shirt. My arms flick out to stabilize myself on either side of her. "Don't you dare finish your sentence. He was my tormenter, so he was mine to kill."

The muscle in my jaw twitches. "But—"

She slams her mouth against mine, crushing me in a bruising kiss. Her arms snake around my neck as she climbs on top of me, trapping me down with her thighs. I'm too stunned to do much more than let her. The cold wetness on her cheeks smears across my skin as our lips move together as if I'm the cure she's been searching for all her life.

"Blaze," I say between her fevered touches. She pushes me back to straddle my hips, and I curse when she grinds on me. "Blaze." It comes out more sternly this time, and she reacts by gripping my short hair to deepen the kiss. The warm air from the fire caresses my skin when she tugs my shirt up, and I wrap my hand around her throat to push her back. Her pulse rampages beneath my thumb as her breathing comes out in short bursts. "*Blaze*," I warn, voice hoarse.

"*Please*." She claws at my shirt as the fire starts to roar, making my dick grow even harder. "I want to feel human again."

My heartbeat catches from the sheer desperation in her voice. "Anything for you, Thief." *Anything.*

Our lips collide, and it's as if I can hear her walls crumble around her. Salty tears mix into her taste of cherries and ferocity, and my lungs expand to get my fill of her. Each kiss sends another heady thought straight through me, and I kiss her back with the same reverent intensity. The movement of our lips is saying more than words ever could: *I'm sorry for everything. I trust you. I need you. Stay.*

When she reaches for the bottom of my sweatshirt, I let her pull it off my head. It isn't lost on me that this is the first time she's reached for me. Ever since we've met, I've been the one who crawls to her, wanting whatever scraps she drops along the way. I laid awake at night dreaming about her, wondering what it would feel like to have her smile directed to me. I dreamed that I would be the one she called for, the one she could rely and lean on. And lately, I've been imagining what it would be like if she's the first one who leans in to kiss me. If she's the one who hugs me and touches me just because she wants to.

Blaze rips off both our gloves and never once falters in grinding her hips against my cock. The dried blood on her skin flakes away with each pass of our bodies.

She whimpers when I break the kiss to flip us around so she's lying on the vintage rug. "I need to taste you," I pant against her lips as I undo her bra then tug her pants and panties down.

361

Moving back, I take a moment to admire my very own fiery little thing: completely bare from the neck down, legs spread, and impatient for me. Every inch of Blaze is—and always has been—stunning: the freckles dotting her chest, the mole on her hips, the red tint of her pebbled skin, the pucker of her swollen lips.

Violent. Deranged. Disastrous.

Perfect.

"You're so fucking beautiful, Blaze." I've barely touched her, and she's already swollen and raw. I'll never get over how fucking delicious her pussy looks when she's dripping wet. A moan tumbles past her lips when I drag my tongue along her wet core. Sweetness explodes on my taste buds as I dive in for more. I knew she'd be my favorite addiction from the moment I met her. Even once I'm six feet deep, I'll still be craving every part of her. I want to consume her, taste every inch of her until I get sick on it, and then do it all over again.

I circle her nub before kissing her bloodstained skin, living for the way it makes her shudder. The friction of the carpet against my chest stings, but it doesn't stop me from slipping my tongue into her pussy. Her moans engulf every one of my senses as I bask in the taste of her. I have no idea what I'm doing, but there isn't a thing about her that I'm not willing to learn. Everything I have to give is hers.

Her hands fly into my hair with a whimper, painfully twisting the short strands through her fingers. She keeps my head steady as she grinds her hips against my waiting tongue. This woman can do whatever she wants to me as long as it makes her feel good.

Curses spill from her mouth as she bucks in an erratic rhythm. She cries out and mutters a string of pleas I can't make out, and I decide that she's had enough. I shift from my stomach to my knees, and clamp her hips down with my arm, holding her still. She gnashes her teeth in protest, then her eyes roll to the back of her head when I push my fingers into her warm cunt.

I keep glancing between her and the fire, experimenting as I pummel into her pussy; hooking my fingers, swirling my tongue on her clit, licking up and down, side to side, until she cries when I suck on her nub.

Her claws descend on me, kicking and scratching as I continue my incessant ministrations. The bottom of her cherry tattoo peeks out as she lifts her legs, and I have to stop myself from placing my hand there. The lewd sounds from her pussy, the taste of her, her moans, the heat from the fire, it's all too much. My cock strains against my jeans, but I can't reach down to alleviate the tension without letting go.

Her breathing shudders as it quietens, her muscles roiling and tightening around my fingers. "Come for me, baby." My voice rumbles against her clit, and she sucks in a sharp breath before spasming around me.

Blaze barely gives herself a second to recover before she's wiggling out from under me. Something about the wild spark in her eyes drops my defenses and allows her to push me onto my back so my head is a foot away from the fireplace.

She yanks my pants down my hips far enough for my cock to spring out. In the span of a single breath, her lips are around my cock, and all of the air punches out of my lungs.

Jesus fuck.

There's no easing into it. No experimenting. Blaze takes me as far down as she can go as if she's been starved her entire life and I'm her saving grace.

"That's my good whore." I groan, gripping her hair as she moves. She gags but doesn't let up, gagging and moaning as she twirls her tongue around my beading precum before closing her mouth around me.

"Look at you, choking on my cock," I muse and push up onto my elbows to get a better view. My legs quiver as she pushes her head down until I touch the back of her throat. She does it over and over, relentlessly, using her bruised hand to pump what she can't fit. "Pathetic. You can barely handle it."

Her eyes harden as they tear, taking me further until the muscles in her throat convulse around me. It's hypnotic watching my cock disappear into her swollen lips. She gags and moans and shudders, but her determination never falters. The orange glow brings out the threads of gold within her hair as if she has a halo of fire. Blue eyes pierce mine, as saliva webs around my cock and drips down her chin like she's feasting.

"That's it," I croon as tears keep streaming down her face. *Fuck*, the only time this girl is ever allowed to cry is when she's choking on my cock. Her glassy eyes catch the gleam from the fire behind me. "You can take it." I wind my fingers in her hand and hold her down as I fuck her mouth, loving the ensuing sounds and her small act of revenge as she digs her nails into my thigh hard enough to break layers of skin. My head tips back with a groan. "If you keep going like this, I'm going to coat your pretty mouth with my come."

The second I let go of her head, Blaze is on top of me, sliding her soaking pussy along my cock. I latch onto her nipples when her tits close in on my face, and she reaches for the fireplace behind me.

"What are you doing?" I ask, eying the charcoal in her shaking hand.

"Are you mine?" Her breathless words make me still. The corners of her eyes crinkle as tears continue to fall; I only wish I knew why she's crying. "Kohen, tell me you're mine." Desperation bleeds into her voice as she grips the charcoal tighter.

"Every part of me is yours to take, Thief." I reach up to wipe away her tears and sit upright on the floor to wind my arm around her waist, almost making us eye level. "You haven't just marked my brain, Blaze. You're forever engraved into my skin."

"What if you make me come undone and find nothing there that you want?"

Brushing my lips over hers, I say, "I've seen all of you, and you wedge yourself deeper into my soul every time I see more."

I frown when she pushes me away. Then, my heart feels like it will implode on itself when she takes the stick of charcoal to her bloodstained skin. Each line is messy and uneven beneath her trembling hands, some letters smudged by a wet streak. I stop breathing entirely when she stops writing the letters across her chest.

There, written in the remnants of my vice on her skin, is one name.

KOHEN'S

Wiping away the tears with the back of her hand, she says, "I want to be yours, Kohen." There's so much surety in Blaze's voice that I feel like I've been hit a thousand times over.

She's saying my name and she's saying it like she loves it. Wants it. *Needs it.*

I cup her jaw in my hand, swinging my gaze between her and the letters on her chest. "You always have been. It's not something you've ever had a say in. *Blaze and Kohen.*" At her furrowing brows, I explain, "That's what I carved into the bat I wanted to give you when we were kids."

The fiery beauty in front of me sniffles and wipes away the remainder of her tears. "You were trying to kill me with it," she protests, all hard lines and brimming with fire. *There's my girl.*

"No, Klepto. Your arms were weak, and you were shit at throwing punches."

Her jaw drops.

"I got it for you so you wouldn't hurt yourself and you'd finally do some real damage."

Blaze's face twists into a mix of irritation and shock until it settles on a barely restrained smile that lights up the blues of her eyes before her pupils dilate. She lowers her forehead to mine. "Kiss me, Pyro."

"Say please."

She hits my chest. "*Now*, asshole."

I shrug. "You know what you need to say."

"Fine."

A grunt escapes me as she shoves me onto my elbows, then raises her hips, positioning me at her entrance to lower herself onto the tip. The muscles in my abs quake as her cunt swallows my cock, milking me without even moving.

"My little slut is doing so good," I say when she whimpers and halts her descent. Balancing on one arm, I circle my thumb around her clit and capture one of her nipples between my teeth.

She unleashes a strangled moan that has her easing herself further onto my cock. White dots flash behind my eyes, and I have to concentrate on the sound of the dying fire so I don't finish before she gets to come again. The tension in my balls tightens as she starts bouncing on my dick, taking me a little deeper each time she goes.

Leaning back, I watch her eyes flutter closed and her lips part as she cries out every curse known to man.

I flip us over and pummel her into the floor. I tower over her as I imprint each letter of my name on her chest into memory. *Blaze is mine. She finally wants to be mine.*

I kiss her because if I don't, I might say something that will make her take the words back. My eyes dart up to the fire above us as I nuzzle into the crook of her neck, feeling the blood bead along my back from her nails digging there.

She clamps her teeth down on my shoulder, and I grip her thigh, slamming into her to make her scream and release my flesh from between her teeth.

"How many fucking bite marks am I going to need to tattoo, Thief?" I growl.

She shrugs, panting as a coy grin spreads across her face. "Until you're covered in them."

I could get used to this.

"I'm burning for you." My voice comes out like gravel as I fight the urge to come.

She snorts. "That's the most embarrassing shit I've ever heard."

Fucking hell.

My fingers move from her clit to her neck. "Enough talking, Blaze."

She manages to wink before I start rutting into her, slamming all the way into her each time I do. My kleptomaniac slaps my back uselessly as my vision swims. I grab onto her throat, keeping her right beneath the fireplace that's coating us in a fresh layer of smoke.

"Who's my dirty whore?" I grunt, breathing in the smell of cherries and ash.

"Get fucked," Blaze moans, struggling to keep her heavy eyelids from falling.

Displeasure cuts down my spine. "I said *who's my dirty little whore?* You want to come, Blaze? Then you better fucking say it, or else you're walking out of here with my come dripping down your thighs."

"You're pulling out," she threatens.

A smirk splits across my face. "Or what? You're so helpless like this," I tease, slamming into her with brutal, unrelenting strokes. "How do you think you're going to stop me?"

I cut off her oxygen before she can respond, but still, I manage to hear her whisper the words I want to hear. *I'm yours, Kohen.*

Once I start rubbing her clit, it doesn't take long for her to hit me aimlessly as her core tightens around me and she's gasping my name, choking my cock for everything that it's worth. Her hips buckle against mine as white heat blinds me, sending pleasure to each corner of my body as I coat the inside of her with my come. She tries to kick me away, but I hold firm, emptying myself out and marking her in more ways than one.

"You prick!" Blaze yells as soon as I release her throat and ease out of her.

Using my fingers to push my come back into her pussy, I rumble against her ear, "If you let any of it fall out, I'm taping your pussy shut once I'm done filling you next time."

Blaze hasn't said a word since we left the house in a state ready for the cops. Her arms are limp around my shoulders and her soft snores brush the side of my neck, and I have to carefully adjust her legs around my waist so as not to wake her when she only stopped shaking ten minutes ago.

The sky slowly lightens with the coming dawn. My arms are dead, my back is killing me, and it feels like my legs are going to give out as I continue walking aimlessly through the forest just to let Blaze sleep a little longer.

I've always wanted this too.

For her to trust me enough to let her guard down. To let me bear her burdens.

She'd freeze up every time she saw McGill's body while we were cleaning. Sex was a temporary distraction, but reality always comes back, and hers is bleaker than most. She thought I didn't notice how her hands shook or that I heard her throw up again. But I noticed it all.

She may have chinks in her armor, but it's still ironclad. There's no doubting her resilience. When she wakes up, the events of the past forty-eight hours will hit like a ton of bricks. It will probably still hurt tomorrow, the day after, and maybe even months from now. But she'll get through it, and I'll be there every second of the way. Nothing will separate us.

Just before the sun tips over the horizon, I head back into school. Somehow, she must know our night is coming to an end because she stirs in my arms and I hold her tighter, not wanting to let her go.

"Not yet," Blaze's warm breath fans over my heated skin.

"I'd do this all night if my arms weren't about to fall off."

"You lack the dedication," she murmurs sleepily.

I smirk and gently kiss the top of her hooded head. "Dedication is all I've had for years because *someone* kept being a bitch."

"Your fault." She snorts softly as she nuzzles closer to my neck.

"We can sit. You're comfy."

A soft smile spreads across my lips. "Do you think you can just order me around?"

"Yes."

God, she's fucking right.

I station us on a log hidden away from any of the main buildings. Blaze doesn't move from her spot, keeping her arms and legs around me as if she's fusing herself to me—I like it too much to fathom. I want this girl tattooed onto my skin and engraved into my heart, so even when I die, I'll still have a part of her with me.

"How do you feel?" The words feel different on my tongue. I've never asked anyone that before. Blaze has always worn her emotions on her sleeve, so it's never been very hard to work her out. But she needs to talk about what happened.

"Fantastic," she says sarcastically.

"How do you feel?" I repeat, my voice lower.

She sighs, running her fingers up and down my back. "I just killed a man."

I silently wait for her to continue.

"I killed a man, and I don't feel bad that he's dead. I killed a man, and I would do it again. I killed a man, and... and it won't change anything." There's an air of hopelessness around her that I don't like one fucking bit.

Slipping my hands beneath her clothes, I start rubbing the soft skin of her back in slow, steady circles. "McGill has paid for what he's done. That alone is priceless. Now, for the next month you won't have him breathing down your neck or going anywhere near you."

Blaze shakes her head. "But my grandfather is still alive."

"For now."

"And he's going to lock me up the second I get out of here."

"Not happening." And that's the truth.

"How do you know that?"

I grasp her cheek to stare into the sterling-blue eyes I've been getting lost in since I was a child. "Because *you* won't let that happen. You'll fight until your nails bleed and everybody has fallen. Not because you have to, but because that's who you are. You're a fighter. But you don't need to fight the world alone. You never did."

She leans her forehead against mine, letting me take her weight. "What if..." Her eyes search the space between us. "What if my grandfather wins?"

"Then we'll both go down together." Her eyes flash at my declaration. "Maybe I haven't made it clear to you; I will hunt you down to the end of the earth just so you don't feel alone for a second. I will find you, even in another lifetime. If you're in hell, then I'll burn willingly. My soul is yours, Thief."

A sad smile touches her lips as her cheeks beam red. "That's the cheesiest shit I've ever heard."

"Shut up, Blaze." I scoff.

"What about you?"

I frown. "What about me?"

"I'm not the only one with a horrendous family."

The muscle in my jaw twitches. "As much as I hate them, I don't want them dead. That's too easy an escape for them. Their downfall has been on my agenda since the day they chose my brother." I tuck a strand of hair behind her ear. "The Osmans are idiots. We're destined to fall on our own swords eventually."

"And what's your sword?"

I press a kiss to her forehead. "You."

"But I'm more of a baseball bat kinda girl." She grins half-heartedly.

"Then we have a month to turn you into a blade."

"Sounds like *Blaze*," she whispers under her breath.

Fucking hell. This girl.

"You get my point," I grumble.

She holds her pinky finger out to me. "We both get our revenge."

Something in my heart expands and grows five times its size. With or without a pinky promise, I'll help her burn each and every motherfucker who has ever wronged her. It's hard enough to see her bruises without breaking out of here to make her grandfather my first kill. But she's always been the fire. She's the one who strikes the match. I'm here to watch it burn.

I interlock our pinkies and nod. "We both win."

KOHEN

CHAPTER 24

"Show me," I order Blaze. *One last time.*

"Get fucked." She crosses her arms and plonks herself down next to my luggage. My dorm room is even more cramped than usual since all of our things are packed into the bags on the floor. It's graduation and move-out day, and the little shit is violating the uniform code one last time by wearing bright red lipstick. "You can't tell me what to do."

I lift an eyebrow. "Is that a challenge?"

"It still fucking hurts, you dipshit," she growls, pushing her bottom lip out in a pout. "Fussing over it won't make it heal any faster."

"Trust me, Thief. This is purely for my self-interest." I reach over only to snatch my hand back when she snaps her teeth at me. The last time I tried calling her bluff, she bit down hard enough to bleed. I'm not in the mood for stitches again. "Let me see—"

"No."

"*Blaze*," I warn.

"You've seen it enough times." She tilts her chin up like a petulant child.

"I'm going to spank the shit out of you if—"

"Ditto, *bud*. Your ass slaps back when I smack it."

The muscle in my jaw twitches as I narrow my eyes at her. Why did I think she'd magically become less difficult when she decided she wanted to be with me? It's been a month since McGill died, and she still insists on fighting me at every fucking turn.

The headlines called McGill's death a home invasion. The suspect? A tall male who is approximately three hundred pounds. Tracks led to and from the school, which was an unfortunate piece of evidence I had no way of getting rid of. Blaze got off scot-free, while the entire male student body became suspects—though the police couldn't interview them. Rich kids with even richer parents? The big guns came out straightaway. No questioning unless being charged, and Mommy and Daddy's top-shot lawyer has to be in the room.

Lots of students openly hated McGill. As for me? So far as everyone is aware, the old man and I have interacted twice. So, in other words, the suspect is at large, not a single eye is looking either of our ways, and my girl is graduating in our horrific uniform while I wear her lipstick stain on my wrist.

This past month has been the highlight of my entire life. Our days have more or less gone the same; we bicker in class then glare at each other and Sarah during lunch. In the afternoon, I'd attempt to tutor her—the key word there is *attempt*. I love her, but fuck if she isn't the most insufferable student to have ever existed. Then, once the lights were out, I'd sneak into her room and choke her half to death so she wouldn't wake up the whole dorm with her screaming.

A couple times, she's told me to fuck off to hang out with Charlie, and I somehow end up around Liam if I'm not busy at practice or doing Kiervan's work. Either way, it always ends with me in her bed and another bite mark on my skin to carry me through to the next day.

I raise the silver chain ring I stole back from her an hour ago. "If you want to wear it, you'll show me." A psychiatrist would have a field day hearing that our push-and-pull relationship comes in the form of stealing from each other on a daily basis.

Blaze sneers, glaring me down for a solid five seconds before huffing her reluctance. "Fine."

Smiling internally, I drop down onto my haunches in front of her and pull down her bottom lip where the word *KOHEN'S* is inked in black onto the soft skin. The part of my soul only she can reach comes alive, pulsing and vibrating as I read it again. Red lips. Copper hair. Blue eyes. She's my fiery little thing.

I yank my hand back just in time to avoid losing a finger, and she bares her teeth at me. If she wants to bite me, she's biting me with my name on her lips. And that's worth bleeding over.

"You're a psychotic animal," I mumble, then drop onto the floor across from her, plucking her off the ground and onto my lap. Her warmth seeps through our clothing the second her body touches mine, dispelling any thought that this could be the last time we see each other.

It'll work, I assure myself. *The plan will work.* "Do you want to go over it one more time?"

Blaze rolls her eyes. "If we have to go over it one more time, I'm going to forget it out of spite," she groans. "We split up. Steer the fuck clear of Jonathan. I shut up, behave, and haul ass out of here. You come back with stacks of green sticking out of your underwear. Then we sail off into the sunset."

Less eloquently put, but pretty much spot-on.

I nod stiffly. I don't like letting her out of my sight for more than a couple minutes. The fact that I might need to for hours is going to be torture in and of itself. If her grandfather catches her, then I lose everything. Any life plans we both decided on over the past month would go up in flames. Any thought of a future would be gone. My life starts and ends with her. If anything happens to her...

My fingers reach up to curl around her throat and feel her pulse thrum against my skin. *She's alive.* I have to keep reminding myself that, but it's difficult not to think about how easy it would be for her to be ripped away from me.

If she's gone, then what? My brother's shadow is long, my father's is even longer. They both think I'm a failure who's unworthy to have my last name. They've always been wrong about it because they're blinded by their own narcissism. But if I lose Blaze, they'll be right in every sense of the word.

I didn't deserve her before. I don't deserve her now. Even once I'm dead, I'll still fight to be worthy of her. I've captured and locked away everything she's ever offered me so I can be buried with it; every time she places her trust in me, or smiles in a way that lights her eyes and softens her shoulders. I'll keep it all with me. Always.

"Kiss me," I say. Whether she hears the desperation in my voice or smells the fear emitting from me, the tension unwinds from her muscles as she slumps into my arms.

"Say please," she chides softly.

"I need you."

The touch of her lips to mine is nothing short of tender, moving as if we've been lovers over lifetimes. She's telling me all the things I've told her, without putting them into words. *I'm yours. It'll always be you. I'll take care of you.*

And I kiss her back saying the three words I haven't said out loud: *I love you.*

But the moment crashes around us when one of the teachers yells to get our bags and start heading down. Blaze and I slowly break apart, leaning our foreheads together as the heavy air settles around us. This *won't* be the last time we do this. I refuse to let it be.

Tonight, she'll be in my arms as I fall asleep, and we'll both be free.

Blaze holds her hand out, palm upward. "You owe me a ring."

"Marie Whitlock."

Blaze stomps up the steps and snatches her diploma from Dr. Van der Merwe's hands while glaring at the deputy headmaster.

A shrill scream echoes through the hall, followed by a "Go Blaze!" from a fist-pumping Charlie. Blaze beams at her and subtly pulls the middle finger at me before trotting off the stage, taking the stairs two at a time.

My eyes instantly snag on Kiervan when I glance back toward the audience up on the bleachers. He gives me a crooked grin that increases my internal temperature by four degrees. Dad is beside him, tapping away at his phone; Mom is doing the same, except she's simultaneously silently judging any person who walks by her.

I run my thumb over the spark wheel of my lighter and tighten my grip around my diploma, fighting the urge to light the fucking thing. There's still no sign of Jonathan. He'll have to show up at some point to collect Blaze, and like hell will I let that happen.

Everyone returns to their seats as the deputy headmaster drones on about the school year, fundraisers, and everything of zero interest to me. Applause fills the air one last time when she gives her final congratulations to the graduates, and I watch a head of copper hair zip out of the side of the hall as soon as we're dismissed.

The entire student body and every single visitor starts to pool out of the main door and into the blinding sunlight. I clutch the lighter in my pocket, silently counting to ten as I weave through the crowd, keeping an eye out for Jonathan and my girl.

Sweat beads along my back, sticking the white material of my uniform to my skin. The weather has grown increasingly unbearable as we head into summer, and I have to squint just to see over the heads of all the excited students. Some people rush to the lake to take pictures, others hug their parents like surviving the academy is their greatest accomplishment. There's happy faces and laughter everywhere I look.

A hand clamps on my shoulder, and I whirl around with a scowl.

"Congratulations, baby bro."

The three words combined with the sound of his voice is enough for fire to start in my stomach, and spread over my skin in a rage of fury and hatred.

My fists tremble around the lighter as I let Kiervan shove me toward our parents. It's been months since I've seen him, and I wish I could have put it off for longer. It's harder than it should be to keep the glower off my face as I quickly scan the area for any of the Whitlocks.

Blaze better have stuck to the plan.

"Mother," I grate out when I meet the dead eyes of the woman who gave birth to me. The warmth from her umber skin somehow looks cold, and her lively coiled hair is straight and lifeless.

"Kohen." She briefly touches my arm unaffectionately with her manicured hand, giving me a smile that does nothing to hide the fact she doesn't want to be here. I'm thankful the brush of her hand over my blazer is the most affection I'll receive from her.

The man who sired me hasn't looked up from his phone once, while the woman who gave birth to me darts her hazel eyes to every student that comes within five feet of her, and she clutches the bright red designer handbag beneath the arm of her white dress suit.

When Kiervan throws his arm over my shoulder and says, "The Osmans are back, baby," I flick the wheel and release the gas while sliding my thumb over the chamber to stop the flame from catching the pocket of my polyester uniform pants. "What do you say we all go get some ice cream to—"

"No." If he keeps talking, I might burn him alive.

"Do *not* cut your brother off," Mother scolds.

Kiervan gives me a sideways grin as the muscles along my fists vibrate with the need to make my brother one with the concrete. I've been in my family's presence for all of ten seconds and it's already like I've never left. Mother takes Kiervan's side, Father doesn't react, and my brother does everything humanly possible to get a rise out of me.

My father stuffs his phone in his breast pocket, inspects me from head to toe, then starts walking to the car park with a dismissive "Let's go."

Mom spins on her heels, casting a disapproving glance at one of the giggling girls nearby.

I hold firm in my position despite the shove Kiervan gives me. "No."

Both of my parents stop, turning back to me. My father cocks a patronizing brow. "No?"

"We need to talk."

"This oughta be good," Kiervan snickers from beside me, then takes a big step back to avoid any association with me.

"Go on." The vein in my father's forehead pulses, and my mother closes our circle like she doesn't want anyone to hear.

"My trust fund." I don't need to say more than those three words because they know exactly what I'm talking about. "I got accepted into college." With a full scholarship—they don't know that though.

"A community one," my mother scoffs.

"Still a college," I argue. "There are two conditions to those funds: I'm over eighteen, and I go to college."

The tendons in my father's neck twitches as he stares me down. From the corner of my eye, I see Kiervan's shit-eating grin, and I have to fight the urge to pull out the lighter to catch a glimpse of the fire.

Not yet, I tell myself. *Get the money. Get the kill switch. Then watch it blow up.*

"That's not what was agreed," my father says.

I twist the lighter between my fingers, stamping back images of what my family would look like as flames engulf them. It's making me question my decision to let them live.

Pictures of copper hair and sterling-blue eyes come to mind as I try to reign in control over my emotions, but it feels like concrete has been poured into my lungs and sucked the oxygen out of the air. The people in my family are like sharks, ready to strike at the first sign of an opening. To them, emotion is a weakness, and I'm the weakest of the lot.

"That's not what the terms of the trust fund say. Kiervan received his the day he graduated," I argue. My voice comes out clearly without giving away any of my desperation or homicidal thoughts.

We need those funds.

Blaze and I will need a roof over our heads, food on the table, and cash to make our families bleed for what they've done. I won't have time to work enough hours while studying, and Blaze isn't exactly going to be the most outstanding employee. Disowning my family while I'm penniless isn't an option.

"You have done nothing to earn it. Your brother, on the other hand, has. For example, *he* hasn't been associating with the *wrong* Whitlock." My blood runs cold as my sperm donor continues. "You think I didn't know about your relationship with her? I know everything, *boy*. And you have me fooled if you think you will get any of *my* money to finance her *habits*." He draws his phone out of his pocket and resumes walking to the car park. "We are not speaking about this out here any further." Lifting the device to his ear, he effectively dismisses me.

Mom picks that exact moment to pull out her phone and type furiously as she follows my father, leaving me behind with the spawn of Satan.

I grab Kiervan's wrist before he has the chance to lay a hand on my shoulder, and throw it off to the side.

Kiervan raises both hands in surrender as picture-perfect innocence gleams in his unfeeling eyes. "Careful, Koko. My claws are bigger than your little kitty's." He makes a show of looking around. "Where is she, by the way? Maybe we should introduce her to dear ol' Dad." A malicious smile splits across his face. "Or maybe she and I could head into one of the janitors' closets, and I can give her the *Kiervan special.*"

Anger lashes through me, red and hot. He stays put when I take a step toward him. My hands stay glued to my side because I'll kill him if I don't restrain myself. "If you say her name—or even talk about her—I will gut you. If you're on the same street as her, I will rip your eyes out and make you choke on them. If you so much as think of her, every inch of you will be covered in sixth-degree burns."

He chuckles, closing the distance so we're chest to chest. "You don't have it in you."

"For her, I'll do whatever it takes."

My brother smiles, showing off his gleaming white teeth. "Then it's a good thing you're finished with my assignment, right? If not, Jonathan might want to hear that she's been trying to contact me."

"She hasn't," I say with so much conviction, the Devil himself would believe it. Blaze wouldn't hurt me like that. Not anymore.

"He doesn't know that." Kiervan's eyes dart to a spot behind me. "Should we tell him? I'm sure he'd like to know all about her constant harassment."

I whip around. Sure enough, Jonathan Whitlock Sr. is sitting inside a black SUV with his windows rolled down, searching the crowd as I spot at least five suited men moving with purpose between the throngs of people. Still, Blaze isn't in sight, but it doesn't stop the knots tying in my stomach.

If she doesn't stick to the plan, I'll kill her myself.

Flicking the lighter again, I glare at Kiervan and follow him to the car. Swallowing my pride, I say through gritted teeth, "The conclusion and references need to be written. Then it's done."

BLAZE

CHAPTER 25

"Fuck, fuck, fuck, fuck," I whisper as I slam the access card against the door.

I scan my surroundings for any security guards or Grandpa's *Men in Black*–looking goons, then dive into one of the classrooms to grab my go-bag that Kohen and I stuck here earlier this morning. I duck behind the screen and strip out of the formal uniform for graduation and quickly change into a hoodie, a pair of jeans, and boots. I slide the hood over my head even though it's too hot for any of what I'm wearing, but my red hair makes me stand out far too much.

We should have gotten a wig. Or a hat. Or shaved my fucking head.

Sneaking out of here to smoke a joint and getting arrested after fucking up the Osmans' place didn't make me break out in hives. But trying to leave Seraphic Hills without anyone associated with the Whitlocks is proving to be one of the most stressful experiences I've ever had. Fourth to being locked in a tub, being medically electrocuted, and getting so high one time I thought I was being abducted by giants.

My eye is twitching, my fingers are trembling, I'm lightheaded, and I can barely fucking breathe. Somehow, this isn't the same high that comes with stealing or doing shit I'm not supposed to.

If I don't make it out of here, I'm going to die. That's not me being dramatic or presumptuous; if my grandfather catches me, a part of me will die, and I will never get it back.

I didn't hold on for this long to end up worse than where I started. But also, how fucking embarrassing would it be to die as soon as I graduate high school?

My hand slips into the front pocket of my duffel bag and wraps around a solid plastic gadget, which I stuff into my pocket. The cold sweat breaking over my skin makes my hands shake as I throw my duffle bag over my shoulder and peek out the door before gapping it. This is a shit plan. A really, really shit plan. But it's the best one Kohen and I could come up with in such a short period of time. And my plan relies on one person who could very well let us down.

I slam to a stop and glance around another turn. My breath hitches when I spot the other son of a bitch on my hit list. Motherfucking Boris, the security guard that crawled out of Lucifer's ass. The coast is clear behind me, so I could leave this wing if I wanted. It'd just mean being outside and exposed for longer.

Or I could go with the original escape plan and take the eastern exit. And fuck up my initial plan at the same time.

His back is to me, hunched over what I assume is his phone. The man sways in the middle of the hallway, shifting his weight from side to side as a video sounds through the otherwise silent hallway.

Kohen would be pissed off to no end if I didn't make a run for it when I had the chance. He'd be extra pissed off if Boris and I had an entirely avoidable altercation without my guard dog present.

I breathe in deeply through my nose as I pull the taser out, nice and slow, clutching it tighter to stop my fingers from shaking.

Kohen will be mad. Furious.

I should run. Gap it before Boris sees me or Tony decides our friendship is limited to drugs and partying, so he doesn't pick me up.

But I don't move away.

My shoes pad softly against the wooden floors, careful not to make too much noise as I creep through the wide corridor of the old gothic structure. My heart hammers harder against my chest as I get closer.

The day I was locked in the tub, I made a promise to three men that they would die by my hand, and they laughed in my face. One of them is in the ground, the other is searching for me, and the last? He's right in front of me, just within reach.

I don't need to close my eyes to remember all the times Boris has laid his hand on me to hurt me and make me feel less than human just because McGill let him. Or how many bruises he's given me in the few months I've been here.

But mostly, it's the *click* of the latch that haunts me at night, then the sound of retreating footsteps as ice sloshes and clangs against the metal tub.

McGill died surrounded by the evidence of his broken soul.

Boris will die on academy grounds so he can spend the rest of eternity wandering these halls being a slave to this school. He tried to kill a part of me, so I'm going to kill him.

I leap forward and ram the taser against the back of his neck. Static fills the air and vibrates down my spine, filling my veins with electricity. Boris's mouth falls open with a silent cry as his muscles seize and his entire body quakes. I don't release the button when he drops to the floor or when tremors shake through his body, picturing how the silver of the tub reflected off his face that day.

I count to three and release, dropping my trembling hand to my side and breathing hard as I take in his body. A lump forms in my throat and liquid hatred runs through my veins as I spit out, "Sorry, I forgot to say you'll feel a slight tickle." He twitches when I kick him in the side for good measure.

Fucking cunt.

I gaze up and down the hall, and then with a strained huff, I drag Boris' partially conscious form to the closest room. But Jesus fucking Christ, this man must weigh like two hundred pounds. My muscles in my weak leg are already quivering, and I've only made it five steps.

Once I'm out of here, I'm going to need to get my back cracked like a glow stick.

Silently muttering a string of curses, I put my entire weight into pulling him backward by his wrists. Barely hearing anything beyond the roaring in my ears as I slap the access card against the reader into the room. The lock beeps, and I shoulder the door open, panting as I yank the fuckwit the rest of the way.

I discard him at the front of the room, then lean over and place my hands on my knees to catch my breath. I think the asshole made me tweak my back. It only makes me burn hotter that he can still hurt me even though he isn't conscious.

Well, if I need a room to commit murder in, I guess this place is as good as any. Conveniently, I had history class here, so my fingerprints will already be everywhere. What's less convenient is that Mr. Blake is at school, and his satchel is leaning against his desk.

There's no telling when he'll come back.

Pulse thundering in my chest, I get straight to business and drop onto my haunches next to Boris and bitch-slap him across the face. He jolts, blinking groggily at the room. Did I look this stupid every time I woke up from a tasing?

"Wakey wakey, eggs and bakey," I sing, roughly tapping his cheek, my voice echoing against the walls of the hundred-year-old room.

He bats my hand away, mumbling something incomprehensible, and I retaliate by slamming the butt of the taser against his nose, knocking his head back with a cringeworthy thud. Blood spurts from his now crooked nose causing a wave of nausea to swim through me. It takes a second too long for him to reach up and clutch his broken nose. I must admit, it's a satisfying sight, but the victory short-lived. The timer in my head ticks, second by second, as a constant reminder that I need to haul ass before I get caught or miss my ride.

I yank one of the seats from off the table, and bracket the legs around Boris's body. Sitting backward in the chair, I quickly zap the taser in the air for dramatic effect. The guard groans, moving his head from side to side.

"I get it, dude," I say. "It usually takes me a few minutes to figure my shit out after getting tasered. Sometimes it even gives me a headache for a couple hours."

I should be at the tree line now, the little voice in my head reminds me as I glance up at the clock.

"What are you doing, you bitch? I—"

I cut him off. He didn't actually say the last part. I don't think he said the first part either. But I'm guessing that's the translation of whatever language he just spoke.

"Right, let's speed this along." I clap my hands together. "We've never had a proper conversation before, and I don't plan on starting now. So here's how this is going to go." I swing my leg over the back of the chair as he says something in the same garbled language as before, gaining enough consciousness to push himself up on his elbows. "I'm going to break your ribs, then bludgeon your head in with this chair. Once I'm done, I'm going to leave you here to die." I push myself onto my feet and instantly miss my three seconds of rest. "How does that sound?"

"No," he coughs out, fruitlessly attempting to get the chair off him.

"That was a rhetorical question." With every ounce of energy in my buzzing veins, I flip the wooden seat over and bring the back down onto his diaphragm.

Still too disoriented to fight back, he folds like a lawn chair. I can practically hear all the air punch out of his lungs in time with the *crack* that follows the impact. But the seat tumbles onto the floor when I lose my grip, and I buckle over.

Boris groans and hugs his center as he rolls around the floor like a worm. I yelp when his large hand wraps around my ankle and yanks me off my feet. Crashing onto the ground next to him with an unceremonious thud, my instincts take over. Kicking my free foot at his face, he cries out, loosening his hold around my other foot. I keep kicking for the hell of it; his face, stomach, ribs, everything I can.

Strands of hair stick to my sweaty skin, and my knees click in the process of rising to my feet. I glance up at the clock and curse. If Tony doesn't stay and wait for me, I'm killing him too.

Pulling my leg back, I add as much power as I possibly can into burying my boot into his side. Pain thunders up my foot as soon as it collides with flesh. His wails bounce off the cold walls, and I do the first thing I can think of: I throat punch the motherfucker. Sound and air instantly cut off with a gasp, and he sputters and chokes while he futilely tries to stand.

I move to the chair, stumbling from the ache that tears through my foot. For fuck's sake. Twist—or partially dislocate—your ankle once, and that shit will never heal.

"No hard feelings," I pant, voice hoarse with exhaustion as I raise the seat over his head. Hundreds of images flash behind my eyes of all the times he's thrown me around, kicked me, yanked my hair, spit on me, and fucking *groped* me. Boris deserves to die. "You're just a fucking dick."

His eyes widen as I bring the chair down with the rest of my meager energy. Boris doesn't get the chance to fight back or move out of the way. The black metal leg of the chair pierces straight into his eye socket, creating a *shlurp* sound that has bile lurching up my throat. I slap my hand over my mouth and stagger back to stop myself from emptying out the contents of my stomach. Men like Boris don't deserve my suffering anymore.

But *Jesus fuck*. That is vile.

He twitches once. Twice. Six times. Then stops. All that's left of him is the blood oozing from his broken nose and punctured eye, spilling onto the floor in pools of brown and maroon.

This is mercy compared to what I had planned for him. I planned on breaking each and every one of his bones until he begged me to stop, praying that I'd let him go—the same way I did when he locked me in the tub. But this form of vengeance is far more poetic after all he's done to me, because Boris died while the sun shone and the grounds were packed with people.

He could have screamed. He could have shouted his pleas to the rooftop. But his voice was taken away. So no one heard him. No one came to his rescue.

Just like the day in the tub.

I pat myself on the back, ignoring the shiver that runs down my spine as I commit the sight to memory.

I'm no expert, but I'd call it a clean kill. Whatever a man can do, a woman can do better.

Suck my dick, Kohen. I didn't need you on guard dog duty.

Maybe if I thought this entire interaction out first, I wouldn't be murdering a man when there are over a thousand people on campus and I'm meant to be making a getaway. And I most fucking definitely wouldn't be killing this man with a fucking *school chair*. Either way, dead is dead, and Boris is on his way to hell.

See you there, asshole.

Two murders in one month. Other than my timely disappearance, I doubt they'd lead this back to me when everyone hates Boris because of all his manhandling. Plus, little ol' me couldn't possibly do this. *Or* be the reason behind McGill's closed-casket funeral. I'm rainbows, butterflies, and a goddamn fuckin delight. I shit innocence and exhale purity.

With one last glance at the clock and the corpse, I wipe down the chair with my sleeve, pocket the taser, kick him with my good foot, then haul ass out of the room. The added weight of the duffle bag makes it harder to move quickly when there's pain slicing through my ankle every time I put pressure on it.

The heat of the outdoors hits me as soon as I break out the back door of the cold gothic structure. I pant heavily, darting my eyes around the terrain to ensure no one is around. I still when movement from my left side catches my attention, and I push myself back against the brick wall. A couple of students trip over each other as they laugh, moving between the main block toward the boys' dorms.

There's a good hundred-and-fifty yards between where I am to the first tree line, and there's nothing but wide open space between here and there. I don't have a choice but to make it work. If someone catches me, I'll have to drop my bag and make a run for it.

Taking a stabilizing breath, I double-check that all of my hair is hidden beneath my hood, and I slip a pair of shades on to conceal my features—honestly, I think I only look more suspicious. Pushing Mrs. Crichton's sunglasses up my face, I try to hobble toward the trees inconspicuously, side-eying my surroundings as I go. But my attempt at moving toward the tree line in a calm, orderly fashion is thrown out the window when I catch a glimpse of one of the Whitlock's FBI-looking guys.

All logic and reason disappear from my brain, and I book it the rest of the way, then zip behind the first tree I reach. Gripping the bag strap with clammy hands, I inch around the thick trunk and immediately snap back into place.

I really wish I had just kept running right about now. At least three security guards and two of my grandfather's men can be seen from this angle. None of them are looking my way, but there's one guy uncomfortably close to the tree line a few hundred yards from here.

Taking deep breaths through my nose, my eyes dart over the forest in front of me. Sunlight filters through the canopy of bright green leaves and blossoming flowers. Birds chirp, hopping from tree to tree while the insects sing their song, oblivious to my existence.

There's half a mile between me and the fence I need to get to, then nearly double that to get to the spot where Tony is meeting me.

And Grandpa's guard is only a few paces away from entering the forest with me.

Fuck it.

Fuck it.

I either get out of here, or I die trying. Pushing off the tree, I run as fast as I can through the forest, hugging the duffle bag to my chest with one arm and clutching the taser in the other. I don't dare look back, too scared to see someone run toward me or lose my footing over the exposed tree roots. My lungs scream as I jump over bushes and run between trees, trying to keep as quiet as possible, but my jaw is aching from biting back a whimper every time my feet hit the ground. It hurts more than the first time I injured my ankle. My hand flies out against the closest tree when my ankle gives out and I tumble forward, skinning my knee against the ground as I go. The joints in my ankle feel like they're grinding against shards of ice as I crawl back onto my feet, kicking up dirt behind me as I go.

"Stop!" someone calls from somewhere behind me.

Clutching the bag to my chest, I limp ahead as fast as my body will allow, muttering a string of curses as my eyes sting from the pain. I can't let them take me. I *won't.*

I don't make it more than a couple steps before something collides into me and I'm thrown to the dirt, all the air punched out of my lungs. My fall is cushioned by the bag and the meager shrubbery. The taser flies out of my grip, and I cry out at the loss as panic claws at my throat.

The heavy weight on top of me moves, his hot breath burning the side of my face. "I'm taking you back—"

I whip my head back as hard as I can, clocking him in the face. A curse flies out of his mouth just as white spots dance behind my vision from the adrenaline rush. My hand snaps over my shoulder to latch on to his collar, and I use the gap between my body and the ground to wedge my knees beneath me, swapping our position. His arm automatically latches around my waist as he crashes onto the ground, while the other goes out to steady himself. I use the opening to bury my elbow beneath his floating ribs, and he grunts.

I've been in catfights since I was six, and I've been throwing hands against guys older than me the second I came out of the womb. This motherfucker has another thing coming if he thinks I'm a princess who's just going to hold my wrists out and let him shackle me up.

"Stay still," he grounds out. Both of his arms wrap around me, locking me in place against him. The single move is telling more than he realizes.

If he were Boris, he could punch me in my side to subdue me. But he isn't. Whether it's because he has a moral code against harming women, or because he's under orders to capture me without harm, this man is on the defensive.

I curl forward, then swing my upper body back, knocking his head again and forcing the wind out of his lungs. His arms loosen just enough for me to shift onto my side and bite down on his arm without restraint. The layers of clothing between my teeth and his skin do very little when the human bite can register over 120 PSI—thank God for biology books.

"Fuck," he snarls, letting go to shove me off him while he scrambles to his feet.

Just as I wanted.

I skitter along the ground to reach for the taser and bring the butt of it against the soft spot above the side of his knee. As the limb buckles, I shove my elbow right up into his balls. He howls as he crumbles to the ground, and I knee the asshole right in the gut to wind him.

I didn't listen to most of Kohen's teachings, but I sure as shit gave him my undivided attention when he was telling me about pressure points.

My legs protest with every one of my movements, but I force myself to straddle the security guard despite his attempts to throw me off. My knuckles bleach from the grip on the taser as I hook my fist toward his temple. The moment skin collides with skin, I bite back a shrill cry from the agony that rips through my hand, all the way up my arm. A high-pitched ringing sound screams through my ears as I tip to the side, clenching my trembling hand as I roll in the dirt to push back the pain. Metallic blooms on my tongue as I bite down on my lip to distract from the pain.

A chill seeps into my bones, because I swear I can hear footsteps approaching.

The man beside me is out cold, and I have no idea if he told anyone that he's found me. I have to keep moving.

A sob rips from my throat as I stumble back onto my feet. Everything hurts. Everything is fucking horrendous. I want to catch my breath or check out my middle finger that's turning purple. But I keep going. I keep moving, feeling the tears burn my cheeks as I fumble for a pair of gloves from the bag and put them on to unlock the gate and limp to the other side. I keep tasting blood as I lock it behind me and blink away the dots scattered over my vision.

Cold sweat drips down my spine as my body pushes forward with nothing but adrenaline to keep me going. I can't help but wish

Kohen were with me so I could feel less alone in my pain as I skirt around McGill's house and down the driveway.

The only hope I have is that I'm almost there. I'm late and I'm filthy, but at least Tony's car will be waiting for me at the end of the driveway. Then this will all be over and I'll be free. I'll make it to the motel, where Kohen anxiously awaits me. And it'll be over. I just need to get to the car.

Except once I get to the end of the driveway and look around, there isn't a car in sight. I spin and turn, feeling the panic clog my throat as I look for him.

No Tony. No shitty Corolla. No nothing. Just miles of road and forestry.

"Fuck," I cry, pushing my broken knuckle against my lips as the first tear trails over my dirt-stained skin.

My drug dealer let me down after all.

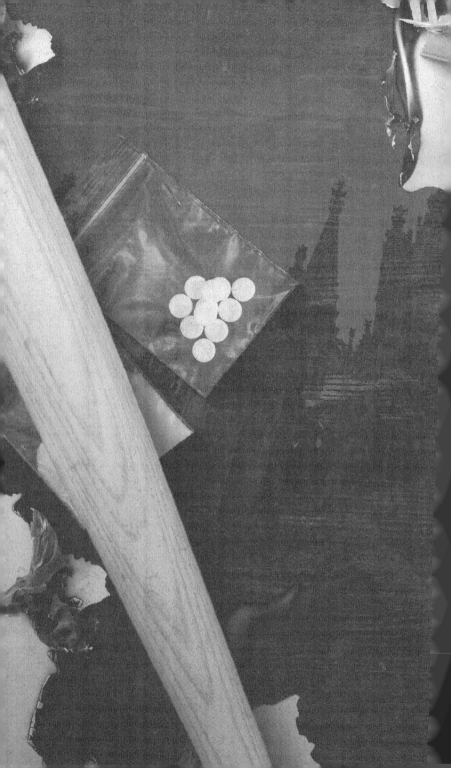

BLAZE

CHAPTER 26

The bag wrinkles as I hug it tighter to stave off the nighttime chill that rakes down my spine. My teeth continue chattering loud enough for everyone in a five-mile radius to hear. But I'm grateful for the cold. It means that my limbs are too numb to feel the pain. It means I'm no longer sweating out every drop of water in my body.

I can't feel my broken finger. Or my toes.

I'm too tired to even limp anymore.

The harsh glow of the full moon casts ominous shadows over the woods. I glance up at the clear sky above the canopy of fluttering leaves, praying that this fever dream never happened. Each star is a perfect little white dot sprinkled against obsidian, unobstructed by plumes of clouds. A couple times I've heard an owl hoot in the distance and a rabbit dart across the path. I've even heard twigs snap and bushes rustle. I've heard the purr of engines and seen the golden orbs of forest creatures. I can't bring myself to tense up anymore. The fight has drained from me.

I left Seraphic Hills at two o'clock. It has to be at least nine by now, if not midnight.

My foot catches on an exposed tree root, and I let gravity take hold. My muscles don't have the energy to break my fall or make any attempt to stay upright, barely registering the pain from the distorted surface against my back. All I do is lie there, feeling the cold breeze bite my skin as I get lost in the blanket of stars above.

It looks so peaceful up there. Calm. I wonder what would happen if I became one with the stars. Would it be serene, or would life be like it is down here? Would I still be an inferno of rage condensed into one body, moving through space because there's no other choice? Will people call me pretty from a distance, but turn their eyes away the closer they get?

Hot to the touch. Able to destroy. More terrifying with each piece of knowledge acquired.

But still, *pretty*. Just from over there. Like a star.

Hidden away to only come out at night, when the sky is clear and the clouds pushed away. And only if the smoke from the city doesn't choke the heavens, turning the stars into a dwindling speck of dust, barely visible to the naked eye.

Kohen calls me a fighter. But if this is what fighting means, I don't know how much more fight I have in me.

He calls me fiery and beautiful and wild. I don't feel like any of those things. I want to line up white powder and forget the world exists after a couple inhales. I want to close my eyes and hope that I don't wake up so I won't have to live with pain anymore. I want to curl up and wither away to become one with the earth; maybe then

I'll do something good for once in my life.

But I don't want to be good. I don't want to feel weak anymore.

Staying here means that my grandfather wins. It means that every person who ever saw me as lesser becomes right.

I'm compulsive. Unhinged. The epitome of self-destruction.

I've killed. Maimed. Drank until I choked on my vomit. Got so high I tore skin from scratching so hard.

I've been starved. Left for dead. Tortured. Locked up. Beaten.

My mother neglected me. My father didn't care what his fucked-up friends did around me. My grandfather keeps a noose around my neck like a collar.

They don't get to fucking win.

They don't get to dance on my grave or spill cheap wine over my fallen corpse.

Another shiver runs down my spine from the biting cold. A whimper falls from my lips as I drag myself back onto my feet and limp in the direction of the road. I can barely peel my eyelids back open every time I blink. It doesn't help that my mouth is dry, and my stomach turns in need of food.

Only a couple more miles. I try to hype myself up, even though I know it's a lie. After over six hours of walking, I'm no longer confident I'm heading in the right direction. Left and right, north and south, blur together into one direction.

Even though there are a few roads leading to and from Seraphic Hills, I've been avoiding the main streets to stay hidden within the safety of the forest in case my grandfather drives past. Kohen chose *Tornne Motor Inn* as our backup rendezvous point if Tony let me down, because it's just off one of the main roads and looks like the least likely spot where... where I might feel tempted to consume

403

things I shouldn't. And I've been really fucking tempted lately.

Kohen never said as much, but I think part of the reason he's kept me entertained at night was so I wouldn't succumb to the urge to sneak out to the church. Each time I'd start walking in its direction, he'd be there to steer me back on my path with three words: *Jonathan will win.*

So I've stayed sober. Four weeks now. No alcohol. No drugs. Nothing stronger than the recommended dose of Panadol and ibuprofen.

But there's still a voice in my head saying that one bump won't hurt. Just a single one, and everything will get better.

It won't. I know it won't. None of this shit will fix itself unless I do something about it. I just wish it were easier.

I shiver again as I double-check that I can still see the road. Kohen made me memorize the route in case Tony bailed. Had there been a car waiting for me in front of McGill's house, I'd be heading a hundred miles from Seraphic Hills with no chance of being found. Instead, I'm limping through the forest with a broken knuckle.

Another hour passes before I spot an old building up ahead, a neon sign blinking on and off. Even if it isn't the right motel, I will crash there for the night. There's no way my feet will take me any further than they already have. My heart pumps faster the closer I get to the building, and soon the words *Tornne Motor Inn* clears, and I find myself running the last leg.

It's a sleepy-looking building, with flowerpots and rose bushes all around the single-story blocks. None of the motel rooms look like they hold any sign of life. There's a single bug-shaped car and a truck at the back of the property, right in front of the house with the gnomes, flowerbeds, vegetable garden, and a sign that reads

Reception.

I rub the soot off my face and hands with the inside of my hoodie in the hopes I'll appear semi-presentable. I can't imagine what I must look like, covered in dirt and dried blood. If they turn me away, then... No, they can't turn me away.

I'll sleep outside if I have to. I'll drink from the fucking garden hose. I just need something. Anything.

The house seems still; there's no sound or light except for the buzzing lamp above the porch. My legs wobble as I climb up the two steps and press the buzzer on the door. It must be late. They might not even wake up. I'm tempted to push it again, but the fear of rejection stops me. What if they do wake up and kick me out? What if they call the police or tell the school that someone escaped? What if my grandfather had warned them I was coming and told them to contact him the second I arrived? What if—

I hold my breath when the door opens to reveal a woman with deep cobwebs indented into her skin, wearing a floral nightgown wrapped tightly around her middle. She pushes her glasses up her nose then looks down at me with a scrutinizing stare.

"Evening," I croak and force a smile on my face because if I don't, I might collapse. *Please, let me stay the night. Just one.* "S-sorry to wake you. Is there a room booked for Bethany Milroy? I'm meeting my boyfriend here." At the woman's skeptical look, I add, "My car broke down, and my phone is dead."

That lie doesn't make any fucking sense.

Her weathered eyes drop down to the dirt and dried blood coating my jeans and my raised foot, softening when they land on my bruised knuckles. The look she gives me isn't pitiful or frightened or filled with the disgust I'm so used to. The door creaks as she backs

405

away to let me inside the small reception area, and I almost burst into tears. She's a complete stranger, letting me inside in the middle of the night, whispering unspoken words to me that say *I understand*.

"Have you had anything to eat, love?" Her voice is so... gentle, in the way only a mother knows how to be. Or at least it's how I imagine it would be.

I chew on the inside of my cheeks to stop the teardrops gathering along my eyelashes from falling. Shaking my head, my attempts fail miserably as I wipe my cheeks using the back of my sleeve.

"Okay." She says the single word with more compassion than I've ever encountered, then grabs a key off the hook without asking me for any details. Cautiously, she adds, "Your boyfriend isn't here."

My heart sinks.

No, Blaze. Don't think about it. He'll come tomorrow. He said that could happen. He didn't leave you.

The woman tips her head up. "We have a room available for as long as you need—we can accept cash if need be. It has a working heater, shower, and fresh drinking water from the tap. There's no mini fridge or vending machine, but just give me a call and we can see what we might be able to do about meals."

"Thank you," I whisper between shuddering breaths.

She nods once and takes the cash I hand her without counting it. I wait in silence when she slips behind the counter and through the door. A few minutes pass before she returns with a packet of porridge and a couple instant soup sachets. Neither of us speaks again as she leads me to one of the bedrooms, walking slowly to account for my limp. The innkeeper checks that all the amenities are working, and subtly wipes dust off the counters with the palm of her bare hand. She hesitates momentarily by the door, then drops her eyes to my bruised hand.

"I will leave some painkillers and a bandage in front of your door in the morning."

My lips part in disbelief. "Thank you," I say again, meaning it from the bottom of my black soul. "I appreciate your help."

"Sleep well."

The door clicks behind her, but I don't eat the food she left behind or take a bath in the shower she made sure worked. I've slept in filth and gone to bed hungry more times than I can count; I want the temporary feeling of death that comes from sleep. So once my head hits the pillow, I welcome the darkness with open arms.

My back slips down the bathroom door as I slump onto the floor. I drop my head against the wood and stare at the entrance directly across from me.

Is this what my freedom means? Loneliness? Placing trust in people I shouldn't have?

My grandfather would laugh at me if he knew that for the past four days I've been sitting around at a rundown motel in the middle of nowhere, waiting for Kohen to show up.

Kohen, the man my grandfather told me to stay away from.

And where the fuck is he? Out of everything I've endured this year, placing my trust in Kohen may prove to be my biggest mistake. I thought I might have... I bite the inside of my cheek. It doesn't matter what I thought.

I've become too codependent on him. Like a useless child, I was dumbstruck when I stood before the shower. For the past month, Kohen has been the one who wiped my skin clean and lathered shampoo into my hair. It was part of our nightly ritual. It isn't like I can't do it myself. I just... Knowing he's right beside me makes it easier to forget about the tub.

Now he isn't here.

He's three days late.

When he doesn't come on the fourth day, it's as if he's shoved a knife in my gut. On the fifth, the knife twists. By the sixth, it starts to feel like I'm waiting for my mother again. I'm five years old, nestled in blankets at the bottom of the stairs, waiting for my mother to return on a Friday night because she promised she'd be home to make me dinner. I slept there that night. Then, the night after that. She never came.

A week later, she came back and made the same promise. But this time, she said she'd do better. Like a dutiful young daughter wanting to make her mom proud, I sat on the bottom step and waited. She never came.

I was a child, so the fool was her. But here I am, sitting on the floor across from the motel door, waiting for Kohen.

Other than my parents, Kohen is the only person I've trusted to keep their promise. Maybe I'm just a fucking idiot for hoping—*trusting*—in anyone.

I pull myself onto my feet and limp over to the bed, crashing onto it face-up and staring at the water-stained ceiling. As I let myself ruminate over my situation, I conclude that I'll wait for Kohen for only seven. After the seven days are up, our love story is as good as shit, and I'll be on my own. Just thinking about it has the metaphorical dagger in my heart twisting, leaving the skin permanently disfigured.

If Kohen isn't here by tomorrow afternoon, I'll take up Sue—the innkeeper's—offer for a ride into one of the towns to get a one-way ticket out of here. I'll leave a note for him with Sue, then carry out the rest of my plan without him if he doesn't reach out to me, and he can do whatever the fuck he wants by himself. Because we'll be over. Done for.

Tears bead along my lashes just thinking about it. For fuck's sake. I thought I was above abandonment issues. Figures the one dude who ever treated me like a human decided to throw me aside just like everyone else does. *One more day*, I remind myself.

I grit my teeth and turn and shove my head into the pillow to dispel the negative thoughts. My stomach growls like a natural alarm clock that goes off whenever dinnertime hits. But I still lie there, unmoving. Sue has been feeding me for the past six days, and I can't keep being her charity case because I fight back tears every time she doesn't treat me like shit.

This woman has been more of a mother to me than my mom and grandmother combined. Hell, she even knitted me a really ugly beanie under the guise that "sometimes the heater drops off at night." She's actually a crazy old bat—and her husband's a dick—but I've already decided I'd die for her.

A knock at the door stirs me to my feet. It's the same gentle knock I've heard every day around this time since I've arrived. I glance at the clock hanging on the wall, showing both arms pointing to six. *Right on time.*

Sighing, I open the door, ready to reject any insistence that I eat dinner with her. Except the concerned look on her face stops me short. Her fluffy, short white hair is lacking its usual bounce, and there's a stain on the linen blouse she always seems to wear.

"Do you know a man named Emir?" Sue cuts right to the chase.

A tidal wave of emotions hits me all at once. My head moves up and down almost as fast as my accelerating pulse. "Yes. Why?" It's Kohen's alias, and I never once mentioned his name to her. "Is he here? Did he stop by? Where is he?"

I push out of the room and onto the gravel driveway. The motel is as deserted as it always is, with the only sign of life being the woman beside me.

The deep lines on her forehead crease with worry. "He left a message to say he'll be here soon, and there's been an issue on his end."

My brows pull together. He... he called? After six days? Another line of thought has my lips parting; Kohen hasn't left me. A little voice pipes up at the back of my mind, saying *I told you so.*

"Anything else?" Specifically, what issue did he encounter? What the hell is taking six days? He said the trust was clear-cut so long as he got his high school diploma and accepted a college offer. Kohen made it sound like the transfer would be immediate.

She shakes her head. "Is this the boyfriend you mentioned?" she asks cautiously.

I nod uneasily, unsure of where this conversation is going.

She shifts her weight. "It isn't my place to pry, so forgive me if I'm out of line. I once gave a man my whole world, and he left with it. I did it all over again with the next man. If it weren't for my husband, I wouldn't have survived it—life for a young woman such as yourself isn't the same as it was for me back then. What I'm saying is that there are good ones out there. But just because one person isn't as bad as the other doesn't make them any good."

I swallow, my heart sinking deeper. She would have been a great mom. It's sad to think this is the type of life I could have had if I had family like her.

"He's one of the good ones." Despite my anger, I've never been more certain of anything.

Sue's lips twist to the side. "Are you sure?"

I shrug, a ghost of a smile on my lips as I recall the past month with him and all the years before. "When he was seven, he tried gifting me a bat to fight off the other boys at school. To this day, he's still handing me bats."

She chuckles, shaking her head. "That's a true man; the one who sits back and watches their woman raise hell." She points at my face. "You make sure you keep him."

I laugh softly. I don't want to lose him; I know that to be truer than anything. I'll survive without him, but he's been helping me feel alive. Even though worry churns my gut, to put her at ease, I say, "Were you a hell-raiser, Sue?"

She winks. "Bats are child's play, love. I've got a shotgun if you want to see what real power looks like. Dinner's ready—say no again, and I might consider taking payment in the form of cleaning my bathroom."

Biting the inside of my cheek, I try to ignore the way my skin warms.

"It's shepherd's pie," she adds.

I suck in a sharp breath. I've never had anything homemade until this woman. "I'll take a slice—only because you're forcing me."

I pace up and down the length of the room. Nine *fucking* days, and I've been going out of my mind. I haven't heard a single peep from him since he contacted Sue, and the motherfucker turned his caller ID off, so I have no way of calling him back.

411

I squeeze my fingers around my bandaged hand, focusing on the feel of the coarse fabric beneath my skin instead of the throbbing in my knuckles. Sue keeps telling me I need an X-ray and a doctor. I keep telling her no because I can't afford either. So her husband prescribed me what he claims is the best medicine: a concrete pill.

With a frustrated sigh, I throw myself onto the bed, ignoring how the contact makes my body ache. I swing my legs for the sake of swinging them and avert my eyes back to the TV where the only working channel is one that only plays infomercials. After nine goddamn days in this place, I'm buying a goddamn *ShamWow* as soon as I'm out of here and have the money.

The front door whips open, yanking me from my boredom. I jump to my feet and snatch the lamp off the nightstand even though my poor hand screams at the action. It takes a second for my brain to register the person standing at the door in a leather bomber jacket and black jeans, but as soon as I do, every cell in my body comes alive.

The second his eyes land on me, his shoulders relax. I almost don't recognize Kohen with the scruff growing along his jaw, his skin ashen, and his hazel eyes seeming to have sunk deeper into their sockets. He looks like he's been through Hell, Tartarus, the river Styx, and then whatever shit he had to face out here.

Seems like he's about to have an even worse time. I drop the lamp back onto the table and round the bed like a fire is lighting my heels. "Where the *fuck* have you been?" I growl, tears stinging my eyes. Whether in relief or frustration, I'm not sure.

"Hello to you too." Exhaustion weighs heavy on his voice, and it turns to steel when his eyes land on the bandages wrapped around my fingers and palm. "What happened to your hand?"

"No, you don't get to ask the fucking questions," I snap, hiding my arm behind me. Out of sight, out of mind—and I have a shitload to say. "I busted my ass trying to get here. My ankle is fucked. My feet are covered in blisters. I have a bruise on my ribs. *I broke my fucking hand.* Killed someone—"

"You *what?*" His eyes widen with each revelation. With the last confession, they almost pop out of his head, and his skin turns bright crimson.

Guess he's fucking awake now.

"*No questions*," I hiss, poking him in the center of his chest. "I almost died trying to get here. I saw a fucking coyote—"

The look on his face is somewhere between amused and mortified. "There are no coyotes around here. But—"

"Fine. I saw a bear—I don't fucking know." I can feel myself start to hyperventilate. "I was out of my mind. Covered in blood. In *agony*. But I was like, 'You know what? It's fine, because Kohen will be waiting for me.' And, *God*, I missed you so fucking much."

Kohen steps closer, grasping my throat. "I'm sorry. I'm here now," he says, voice low and soothing.

I grip onto his shirt, not wanting to let him go. "I've been worried sick—I've never worried this much before." Tears bead along my eyelashes. "I wasn't sure if you were okay or needed help. But then you called me *once* after six days. I thought you could have died, Kohen. I thought my grandfather got to you, or your brother went crazy. I thought if you weren't dead, you were washing your hands clean of me."

"*Blaze*," he says sternly. "I'm back."

"Nine fucking days," I whisper. A single tear burns a path down my cheek. "I thought you were gone, Kohen. I thought you left. I don't want to lose you."

"Blaze."

"I thought your promises were as empty as my mother's and that you were just as cruel as my grandfather. There wasn't a single word from you, and I hated you for it, and I hated myself for trusting you. Everyone realizes I'm a piece of shit eventually, and I kept thinking it was only logical that you came to the same conclusion." I can't stop myself from talking or calm by breathing. "And I feel so selfish because I never stopped to think that you might be suffering more than me. What happened? Are you okay? I need to know you're alright, Kohen."

When he cups my face in both his hands, I let him. "Blaze. I'd leave everything behind just to be with you. I have, and I'd do it again. I loved you when we were kids. I loved you when you framed me. I loved you nine days ago. And I love you now. Nothing is going to change that. As long as you're there, I will always be alright."

I love you.

The three words choke me. Kohen's made me feel cared for and cherished, like I'm the only girl in his world. In reality, it all translates to one simple thing and I never understood what it was: he made me feel loved. It's on the tip of my tongue to say it back because I want to make him feel the exact same way I do, like he's loved. But the words won't come out.

It feels undeserving coming out of my mouth, as if I haven't earned the honor of loving him when I still haven't earned any of his attention. Like there's so much more than me that he deserves, and... I can't say it to him when I can't say it to myself. How could he love me when I'm me?

I know he means the words with every fiber of his being; he's proven it more times than I can count. But I don't feel worthy of receiving it.

Instead of saying it back, I clear my throat and wipe away the tears as I wrap my fingers around his wrist. "What do you mean you left everything behind? I want to know everything that happened."

The disappointment in his eyes guts me deep, and I look away so I don't have to relive the moment I let him down. "Let me take a look at your hand first."

I shake my head. "Later. Tell me first."

Kohen drops his head with a defeated sigh, running his fingers through his hair. "I couldn't get the money. The funds could be given to me after high school, only at my father's discretion. He said he'd only give it to me if I continued living under his wing, work at his company, study what he wants me to study, and move back in with him every summer. I spent the past nine days trying to figure out a way to get my trust fund—or any funds. My father still refused."

I frown, reaching up to hold his face with my good hand. He leans into my touch and closes his eyes as if he can finally rest. "It's okay. We can do without it."

Kohen's trust fund was part of his grand plan, the thing that's meant to set him—*us*—up for the future. Thanks to all the scholarships he's received, the full ride through college will help, but the money would be the buffer that would set us up in the meantime. It's one of his many *fuck yous* to his father.

I dip forward, curling my body around him in the type of hug Hallmark wouldn't be able to replicate. His arms wrap around my waist, and he hauls me up against him as his lips meet mine in the type of kiss that makes me forget everything that happened over the past few days. Every single worry I had disappears with the touch of his lips, and it's as if here, in our little bubble, nothing could ever go wrong.

My legs curve around him, kissing him harder like my life depends on it, because I want him to know that even though I couldn't say the words, I wouldn't trade him for the world. "I missed you," I say as he moves into the room, kicking the door shut behind him.

"That doesn't begin to describe how I've been feeling this past week." His chest rumbles against mine, and I hug him tighter, breathing in his scent.

"If you had left me, I would have hunted you down and killed you with my bare hands," I whisper against his neck.

His sharp exhale ruffles through my hair as he lowers us down onto the bed, never once breaking us apart. "That's a good way to go in my books."

Minutes roll by in silence with nothing but our heavy breaths and the fucking infomercial to fill the small space between our bodies. Patchouli and mint shroud me in its warm embrace, and I run my fingers through his hair—it's longer than he's ever had it before. My eyes drift shut as the hollowness in my heart fills with each breath I take. I'm not alone, and I never will be again. No trust fund can put a price on that. I want Kohen whatever way he comes.

Reluctantly, I pull away and break the silence first. Hazel eyes meet mine, creased with concern and heavy-lidded with fatigue. They don't soften nearly as much as I'd like when I press a kiss to his nose.

"What about the plan with Kiervan?" I ask carefully, running my fingers up and down his back so he knows that with or without the money, I'll still be here for him.

The tension around his eyes bleeds away, replaced by a gleam in his iris and a smile full of teeth, which sends a shiver down my spine.

"Eighty grand in my bank account. It cleared yesterday morning."

I blink.

Eighty?

My jaw drops. "It worked?"

It's not the $5 million Kohen was hoping to have full access to when he graduates, but $80K is more than most people earn in a year. If we play it smart, that will be enough money to keep us afloat for a couple of years.

I whistle. "Had I known blackmailing Kiervan would work, I would have suggested you do it sooner." If Kohen can't have a slice of his own trust fund, what better justice than taking a slice of his piece of shit brother's. Shoving it to Kiervan is so much more satisfying. "What did you say to him?"

"That you're in the wind, the money is out of my reach, I have evidence that I've been writing his assignments for him, and that my silence can be bought for a hundred thousand dollars," he explains.

My brows knit together. "Did your brother seriously try to barter when you're hanging his livelihood over his head?"

"He's my father's son. It just means phase two comes earlier rather than later." The smirk that paints his lips has me on edge. Kohen's revenge plan hedges on the long game, and I couldn't fathom waiting years to make my grandfather pay.

"One hundred grand buys him three years of freedom. Eighty buys him two. My father's decision to withhold my trust fund means his glory days end this week." Letting go of my waist, he pulls out a flash drive from his pocket. "His password is the year he won his first golf tournament and the name of his second yacht." Kohen places the USB in the palm of my hand. "In ten weeks, Osman Pharmaceuticals will issue corporate bonds to Jonathan in his personal capacity, and Whitlock Investments. Seventeen weeks from now, Osman Pharmaceuticals will be a fifth of the way through manufacturing their miracle drug, and that kill switch in your hand will end up in my father's competitors' laps." The smile he's wearing is beaming with light. "The hard drive holds all of the company's latest research, data, processes, and every single piece of information I've downloaded since I was fourteen years old. But most importantly: how to make their miracle drug."

My lips part. The motherfucker didn't tell me about any of this. Kohen told me that there are worse ways to make a person suffer, and he really is the master of it all.

He covers my hand with his own. "We're going to burn the Whitlocks and turn you into the queen of the ashes. And together, we're going to make the house of the Osmans fall." Raising my knuckles to his lips, he plants a gentle kiss on the unblemished skin. "You're going to need a bigger bat." My very own pyromaniac tucks a loose strand of hair behind my ear as his eyes go hard. "Now who the fuck did you kill?"

BLAZE

CHAPTER 27

Six Months Later

Blood rushes through my ears in a roaring rhythm as I tap my foot against the car floor. My swollen bottom lip aches from how much I've been gnawing on it these past few days. Kohen squeezes my thigh and continues rubbing soothing circles while keeping his other hand on the wheel. He's been shooting me worried glances since we left our apartment this morning—even more, now that we both have ski masks on and my vengeance is within reach.

"Breathe, Klepto."

"Don't tell me what to do," I snap, gritting my teeth.

The radio can barely be heard above the roar of the struggling Honda Civic I stole in another state last week. The engine is screwed up, but the model is new enough to pass through any neighborhood without raising alarm bells. We changed the plates to a new set, and there's a fresh—badly done—coat of silver paint on it, so no camera can link the car back.

The quiet streets we drive down are filled with mansions, sprawling farmland, and forestry, all deserted under the obstructed moonlight. My grandfather's manor is out in the countryside, where the government hasn't bothered using tax dollars to buy streetlights to illuminate the barren roads. Which means there's no telling how many cameras are witnessing our arrival.

I haven't seen or heard from Jonathan since I ran from Seraphic Hills six months ago. Kohen has heard from his family plenty of times—less now that they're experiencing financial difficulties. But my grandfather? Dead silence. Part of me thinks we're about to walk into a trap. The other part—the *hopeful* part—suspects he doesn't want to waste resources trying to find me. When I was younger, every time my mother fell off the wagon, and I went running to him to find her, his response was always a cold "She'll show up eventually. People like her always do." Maybe that's what he thinks of me.

Picking at my nail bed, I try to figure out what I will say to my grandfather. I've had months to work it out, but nothing feels right. I have so many questions, but I also want to make him beg for my forgiveness even though I know he'll never lower himself. Men like him will never kneel for anything unless I cut off his feet.

But what if my grandmother canceled her trip to my uncle's and stayed home. She's a grade A bitch, but I don't want to kill the woman. Tonight, only one person dies.

Six months of planning, learning how to carjack, deciding how I want him to go, figuring out my grandfather's schedule and his security—or lack thereof nowadays. I've been busy, to say the least. All the while, Kohen has lived a seminormal life in college and has been taking weekly extracurriculars to keep the scholarship grants coming. He even got me taking a martial arts class, and I learned how to use a gun. Kohen's becoming an upstanding citizen while I'm shaping up to become the perfect criminal.

Kohen gives my thigh another squeeze as he pulls onto the curb and parks the car a couple yards away from the border of my grandfather's property.

"You ready?" Kohen's voice usually soothes the violent thrumming in my veins, but tonight, no amount of smooth-talking will settle my nerves.

Any snarky comment or joke I want to say to lift the somber atmosphere dies before it makes it to my tongue. Once we step out of the car, two things could happen.

One, we succeed. My grandfather dies, and then Kohen and I go back to our normal lives.

Or two, we fail miserably.

I give him a tight nod in response to his question, then step out of the car, double-checking that my gun is safe in my pocket before righting the oversized black coat that's been lined with weights and stuffed to make me look larger than I am. We didn't see any cameras in this particular area all the times we've staked the place out, but there's no telling if we might have missed one. Not to mention that even though it's almost midnight and the temperature is toeing the line of freezing, there could be someone out here to witness our crimes.

Glancing back at Kohen, he tosses me one of the duffle bags stuffed with more empty bags. Then he swings his own duffle onto his back and readjusts his ski mask before grabbing the three gas canisters.

My oversized boots slap the ground as I follow behind him toward the brick wall that stands two feet taller than me. Kohen kneels on the wet grass in front of the fence, cupping his gloved hands atop his knee. I shakily place my foot into his waiting hands and mentally prepare myself for the ache that will follow. He bears the brunt of my weight and gives me a boost up the wall, but it doesn't stop me from swallowing a whimper as I grip the edge of the brick. Just as I expected, pain slices through my middle knuckle as I force my fingers to latch on to the fence. No amount of exercising will change the fact that the knuckle didn't set right—and we don't exactly have the finances to afford surgically correcting it.

So I'm left grinding my teeth as I swing my leg over when Kohen hoists me up the wall, hissing under my breath when my hand slips out from under me.

Kohen catches my waist before I tumble down. "I've got you," he whispers.

Both of my hands tremble in my attempts to pull the rest of my body onto the ledge. Adrenaline won't change the state of my knuckle, but it's doing a good job of numbing the ache that cuts through the inside of my thigh when it scrapes against the edge of the fence.

Panting, I take the three gas canisters from Kohen and balance them on the wall. I offer Kohen my good arm to help him up. He rightfully ignores it, hauling himself up the side of the fences with more grace than a feline. He drops to the other side without so much as a thud. One by one, he lowers the canisters onto the ground, then holds his arm out to help me down to limit the pressure of the fall, because my ankle still gives me grief intermittently. And tonight, of all nights, is not a time for grieving.

I pull my leg over and jump into his arms. Neither of us hesitate from the second I hit the ground, weaving between the trees planted on the outskirts of the manor, careful not to make a sound. My harsh breaths come out in a cloud in front of me as my heart pounds in my ears. Every snap of a twig and rustling of leaves seem as if they've been amplified through a microphone, and it might as well be a siren to alert everyone to our presence.

None of my grandfather's help will be on the property since everyone has been sent home for Thanksgiving—at least that was the excuse he made. The truth is that he's cutting down costs where he can. Meaning he's all alone in the redbrick mansion to drown under the mountain of paperwork and debt caused by the man beside me. Once the first glimpse of sunlight blooms across the sky, staff will trickle in to start working so the neighbors think it's business as usual.

The Whitlock Investment and Osman Pharmaceutical transaction has blown up in their faces, leaving good ol' Grandpa short of $120 million. Whitlock Investment has lost almost triple that.

No interest on his investments. No return. Half a billion dollars just... gone.

All the while his big-dog lawyers make him bleed more money. It brings me more joy than anyone will ever realize to know that my grandfather has spent the last few months of his life swimming in stress.

We stick to the outskirts, hidden within the safety of the trees, as we sneak deeper into the property. Kohen and I have staked out this area a couple times before. I thought the familiarity would dispel my worry and replace it with misguided arrogance, but it doesn't. My gut twists as we break past the line of trees and head into open space. It's as if I've never been here before from the rush of uncertainty that floods my veins.

My grandfather is right behind those walls. What will he say once he sees me? Will he be surprised, or scared, or will he not give a shit? Will he beg me to spare his life or run like a coward?

Cameras are stationed around the redbrick house, flashing a green light that makes me falter as we move through the courtyard. I have to reassure myself that the cameras mean nothing when the mainframe gets torched. His security team won't arrive for a few more hours. And either way, we're dressed well enough to conceal our identity.

A shiver runs down my spine when I spot the indoor swimming pool. We avoid all windows and sprint to the kitchen door. Some lights are on inside, but not a soul is in sight.

I would give anything for a hit of coke or weed or fucking anything I can get my hands on, just to ease the pain beneath my chest. I thought fighting the cravings would be easier after seven months, but still, every morning, I wake up itching for the euphoria that comes from delirium. I'd be fucking unstoppable if I just had the slightest bump.

But I can't. Not anymore. I've come too far to fall back into the same habits. I have a mission—a goal—and that's what matters now. I can get my kicks from making those who wronged me suffer.

It felt satisfying killing Boris. It was empowering to hear that Dr. Van der Merwe lost his practicing license following an "anonymous" tip. And I can only imagine what it will feel like to get rid of the man who caused it all—my grandfather.

My ankle tweaks from running, but I push forward, breathing hard through my nose as cold sweat builds beneath the mask. It gets harder to breathe with each passing second, and my vision blurs with the rush of energy that zaps through me when I kneel in front of the back door. I blink the haze back, attempting to push all thoughts out of my mind to focus on the task at hand.

Emotions are a weakness that leave room for error. I'll never forgive myself if I fuck this up because I couldn't keep my feelings in check. The counselor back at school always said a little anxiety is a good thing; having a lot is where the problem lies. I'm trying so hard to find the balance, but steadying my racing heart doesn't come any easier.

The thin lockpick sits awkwardly in my right hand as I grip it, my gloved fingers making my hold lighter than I would have liked. My middle finger sticks out above the rest, and the little muscles in my hand strain to compensate for the lack of support. I've had to practice picking locks every single goddamn day for this very reason. Kohen could've been the one to do this, but instead he's spent the past six months whispering words of encouragement every time frustration took hold because of another failed attempt. But he never once offered to learn because he knows I need to prove to myself that I'm not limited by the confines of my flesh, and that I'm not defined by my wounds. Each time I improve my skills, I'm reminded that I don't need to be perfect to be powerful.

The lock clicks open in under ten seconds—it would be faster if I had a better hold on the tools.

In the name of practice, we've broken into a few people's homes over the past six months, so it's easy enough to fall into our roles without needing to say a word. I push the door open and Kohen slips in first, gun in hand, leaving the canisters where they are. I stay on my haunches for a moment to take one more solidifying breath before slipping in behind him.

The kitchen is shrouded in darkness; even so I can tell it's spotless. *Lifeless.* The only light in the room comes from the dim hallway. I only vaguely remember the layout of the interior from when I was a child. We navigate through the halls, following the light leading from the foyer. Our feet pad softly along the wooden floor as we keep our heads on a swivel for any sign of movement.

There's not a single sound coming from inside the house other than my thundering pulse, but I know my grandfather is here. I can feel it in my bones.

My breathing shudders as I look left and right, drinking in every inch of the place. The manor hasn't changed much as far as I can remember. The walls are still pristinely white, the staircase is still grand, and the crystal chandelier is still bright. Great, big antique vases and flowers line the corners of the otherwise barren entrance hall. Baroque- and Impressionism-style paintings decorate the walls instead of portraits or family photos.

I think it's smarter for us to split up—it's an argument Kohen and I have had before, but each time he wins because I can't curl my hand into a fist if something goes wrong, my ankle ends up bruised and swollen every time I use it wrong, and frankly, I'd rather have Kohen by my side. So we stick together and move through the foyer toward the east wing.

The sight of the poster beds, goose down pillows, and tables that aren't being balanced on folded food boxes makes my anger push through the anxiety that's clogging my throat, turning the room into various shades of red.

This is how he's fucking lived while I questioned when my next meal would be. In the middle of fucking winter, I had a goddamn T-shirt in place of glass for my window. I didn't have a lock on my front door, and only a broken latch in the bathroom. My mattress was as old as I was, and a couple planks on my bed frame were being held together by duct tape and a miracle. My grandfather sent me fifty dollars a week to live off. He'd hold food hostage. He waited two years before fixing the leak in my bedroom. At one point, I didn't have a working fridge for seven months.

All while my grandparents have been here with heated floors and thousands of dollars' worth of art on *every single wall*. He has a crystal fucking chandelier, an indoor swimming pool, a golf course, and a ten-car garage. The assholes have three water fountains for Christ's sake.

My grip tightens around my gun, and I relish in the ache that pierces through my knuckle.

Fuck the Whitlocks.

Fuck. Them.

If my grandma is here too, may she rest in peace.

As we slip further into the house, the pounding in my chest morphs into something twisted and fueled with bloodlust. A smile almost tugs at my lips as we check all the rooms downstairs to ensure they're empty. With each room that comes up empty, the exhilaration becomes more intoxicating, as if I've caught a scent and I can already feel the flesh rip beneath my teeth. The thrill of the hunt, a predator chasing down its prey—it has to be the best part.

Jonathan Whitlock Sr. is going to die tonight. This time, the thought comes with a jagged edge of sadistic glee.

Kohen nods to himself when we find the control room that holds the security footage from around the manor, likely making a mental note to come back to it later. When all the rooms downstairs come up empty, we slip back into the main hall and inch up the stairs without a single creak of the wood beneath our feet.

A Fabergé egg greets us as soon as we reach the top step. Kohen slips it into my duffle bag, no questions asked, then points toward the open door further along. A couple lamps are lit in the corridor, but light streams from only one of the rooms. If memory serves correctly, it's my grandfather's office. And if the silence that envelops us is any indication, he's alone.

I hand my duffle bag to Kohen so he can stockpile it with sellable tokens to make up for my lack of place in my grandfather's will. Kohen's strong hand wraps around the top of my elbow before I make it further, and he drops his forehead to mine, enveloping me with his warmth. It's a silent reminder that I'm not alone. He'll be right there on the other side, waiting for me.

Kohen brings his face down next to my ear, rubbing our masks together as he whispers, "I love you."

I love you too.

It's on the tip of my tongue, but I still can't bring myself to say it after all these months. I love him, and there's nothing else that could be truer in this godforsaken universe. He deserves to know that at least one person in the world will always be in his corner. Even if he never heard the words spoken to him as a child, he's still capable of being loved.

He needs to hear it just as much as I do. Still, the words don't come out. I will always be a failure in some ways.

Kohen pulls away, leaving me in the middle of the corridor with the lingering remnants of his comfort to head toward my grandparents' bedroom, where he'll stockpile, then empty the gasoline canisters all over the house.

I don't know how long I stand there, frozen as I look around the place I could have called home, if only my grandparents loved me in the way grandparents should. Maybe I would have smelled my grandmother's baking and learned my cousin's first name. Maybe I'd have discovered whether my uncle looks like my mother in real life or just in photos. I could have played dolls on the stairs or done a twirl as I descended toward my prom date who I'd have two-and-a-half kids with. I might have even bought a house in this area and stayed home to raise children while my husband has one too many "late nights" at work.

But none of those things has or will ever happen.

My mother may have started her life in this hell, but she ended up on the streets. On the other hand, this kind of life with private chefs and maids isn't a life I'll ever be familiar with. Now I have a roof over my head, food in the cupboard, a human heater to keep me warm through the night. Safe. Consistent. It's more than I could've ever asked for. I've even been talking to Sue on the phone every week since I left the motel—last month we went down to have dinner with her too.

Money doesn't equate to happiness. No amount of land will keep a smile on my face. Kohen fell off the social ladder the day he picked me, and I've never seen him so at ease... and happy—even if he's had to learn how to live without a maid and a cook.

This type of life with glitz and green would have turned me complacent. My claws would always be retracted, and there wouldn't be any fight in my veins. I think that's what differentiates me from my mother, because all I've ever known is darkness. One day, I hope she figures out how to break free from my grandfather's chains and know what freedom feels like. I just won't be the one to help her.

Taking a deep breath, I pull the mask off and tuck it into my pocket, then stuff my gun into the other. I stretch my neck from side to side, biting the inside of my cheek at the rising wave of anxiety. It's now or never.

The floorboards don't make a sound as I pad along the rug, slipping into his office before I get the chance to hesitate or tip him off. Neutral-toned cushions line the window seat, and various awards and sporting memorabilia decorate the white walls of his office. The place has a modern touch with the white leather couch against the wall, and the big glass table that faces the middle of the room, contrasted against the soft Persian rug beneath my boots. Paperwork, ledgers, and various journals are scattered around his desk and on the floor. There's no color here, just a series of whites and grays. It's as bleak as he is.

My grandfather doesn't notice me at first. He looks so human like this; sitting at his desk in his vintage brown dressing gown, with his face shoved into both hands as if exhaustion has made a home in his bones. It's surreal seeing him in the flesh with his guard down. Growing up, I'd usually see pictures of him online, and he always looked as foreboding as he does in person. But right now, he looks like he's just a man.

An empty man. Cold, ruthless, and undeniably human.

This is the moment I've been looking forward to for the past six months. Not only six months, for all my life. Now that I'm here, I don't know how I should feel. There's a glimmer of anticipation for my impending liberation, but beyond that and the anxiety... I'm not sure. My hatred for my family has driven me for the past few months, and it'll drive me for years to come.

Once my grandfather is gone, there will no longer be a physical manifestation to direct my anger; rather it will evolve. I'll tear him down out of anger, and prosper out of spite. I'll make sure he'll turn in his grave and carry his regrets on his shoulders as he descends into the fiery pits.

Most of all, I want to move on. Get this shit over with because I've already spent a lifetime suffering under my grandfather's thumb, and he doesn't deserve another second of it. For months now, I've been looking over my shoulder, waiting for the moment he turns up and drags me into his version of purgatory.

I've never felt powerful in front of him, but right now, for the first time in my life, I do. I have things that make me happy. I have consistency, emotional connection, and all the physical necessities. He can't control me anymore.

My heart pounds as I breathe in the scent of sandalwood, feeling cold sweat bead between my shoulder blades. The grandfather clock ticks in the corridor, counting down the seconds until the man before me meets his maker.

He controlled me. Tormented me. Manipulated me. Abused me. When he reaches death's door tonight, he can tell them that he created the weapon that caused his own death. After all, I'm the demon he made me to be.

Jonathan Whitlock Sr. pulls his hand down his face with a muffled groan. Before he can spot me, I say, "This isn't how you should spend Thanksgiving."

His blue eyes snap up to mine. "I was waiting for you to show up," he says as if he was expecting the trash to drift in on a breeze. "To what do I owe the pleasure?"

"You—"

"Let me guess," he interjects, and I curl my hands into weak fists. My nose twitches as the smell of gasoline hits my nostrils. "You want a couple thousand dollars to get you on your feet, and this will be the last time you ask for money. Then you'll come crawling back in a few months because it all disappeared up your nose. Just like your mother."

My mouth dries, lighting a fire within me. "How is she?"

Jonathan straightens. "Your Houdini of a mother escaped rehab again."

Ah. So that's where she was. Was the plan to send me there too? To make me a prisoner? Part of me doesn't want to know the answer. "Why do you do it?"

"Are you incapable of asking a complete question?" he asks flatly.

"Why the fuck did you send us away to that house?" I growl, stepping forward as a wave of anger crashes through me. "If you wanted to protect your reputation, you would have sent Mom to rehab to begin with and took me in—or even sent me into the foster system."

"So you can continue tainting my bloodline?" He scoffs, arching a patronizing brow.

"My mother—"

"Is too old to have any more children—not that she could after the complications she had because of you. I thought letting her pretend to be a mother would give her some fake sense of purpose. I suppose I was wrong."

What kind of fucking support did he give her? Did he expect her to suffer through a pregnancy, have birthing complications, then miraculously get rid of the urge to hit up her veins?

I press my gloved thumbs into my temples in an attempt to comprehend how ridiculous his thought process is. "Let me get this straight. You made my life hell, and you plan on locking me up, all so I don't spawn another Whitlock?" Rage crawls up my throat, shredding the skin into fiery ribbons with each word that passes my lips.

"Not just another Whitlock. Another *you*." The head of the Whitlock empire sneers down at me as if I just shit on his expensive fucking rug, and I'm tempted to rip it up just to wipe the look from his face. "You're so daft, Marie. Perhaps delusional is a better word. It perfectly describes all the outbursts you've had since you were a child. It landed you at Seraphic Hills, after all."

I jump forward, whipping the butt of the gun across his face. He hisses as blood gushes from his busted nose. The sight of it soothes the sadistic beast clawing at my skin. His eyes widen as spots the weapon, then they squeeze shut when I punch him in the gut.

"My name is fucking *Blaze*." Venom drips from my tongue, raw and agonizing. "You think I need fixing. You think I'm crazy. You think I'm fucked in the head. Maybe *you're* the problem."

Even though he's wheezing for breath, he rolls his eyes as if I'm just being dramatic. "You were always this way."

"Those words would mean something if you were ever around." He flinches when I wave the gun at him. "But if you want crazy, Grandpa?" I chuckle humorlessly to myself. "I can be crazy, as long as you remember you made me this way."

I have no intention of putting a bullet between his eyes. No. Back in the day, doctors would shove patients into near-boiling water, then straight into ice. Some believed the first would suffice.

Tonight, I'm going to drop him in his precious indoor swimming pool and pull the cover over him so he knows how I felt.

Tonight, he'll drown in the water while the manor goes up in flames.

"Put the gun down, Marie." His voice comes out sharp and stern as he grips the arms of his ornate wooden chair, ignoring the blood dripping from his nose.

"My name is *Blaze*!"

My fist descends on him again, but he doesn't block it in time, and he continues as if didn't almost topple over the seat from the force of the blow. "Don't blame your lack of drive on me. I gave you every opportunity you needed to succeed, and you squandered it. Private school education. Additional tutoring. Extracurricular activities. Your failures are no fault of mine."

Red spots dance in my vision, growing darker with each word he says. The butt of the weapon slams against his cheek, and he falls onto the floor. I kick him in the gut and relish in the sound of his groans as the sight of crimson pooling on his cheek.

The gun clatters on the table, sending paperwork flying onto the ground and freeing my hands. I yank him forward by his collar. "You made me this way. You left me, kicked me aside like I was nothing more than a problem you were trying to get rid of. I never had the chance to be anything but the way I am."

He laughs. *Laughs.* I have him by his collar, and he *laughs.* "Had you shown any level of success throughout your life, I would have deemed you worthy of this family and took you in. But all you've managed to do is successfully prove that you are just as incompetent as your mother."

"Have you considered that you're the reason she's using?" I spit out, shaking him before punching his jaw. The fact he isn't fighting back is only pissing me off more.

"Yes. I spoiled her." Jonathan's lips curl in disdain as he recalls the memory. "I gave her all the money she ever asked for. Made it so

436

she didn't have to lift a finger or work a day in her life. Look what happened. Purposeless. Worthless. *Useless.*" He leans into my hold and stares up at me in plain mockery. "You have your mother's eyes, Marie."

My fists shake with the white-knuckled grip I have on him, and every muscle in my body strains with the need to make him more disfigured than McGill was when he died.

Deep breaths, I imagine Kohen saying to me.

Emotions leave room for error, I remind myself. Jonathan is baiting me, and he's winning. He knows how to push each and every single one of my buttons. But I know one of his.

Fire burns through my veins, refusing to be doused by any reminder of the cards in my hand. Still, I pry my fingers from him and take a step back, away from him and the desk. *I'm winning,* I tell myself. *Jonathan Whitlock Sr. will die tonight, and I will be the one who kills him.*

I fold my hands behind my back to keep from wringing his neck. "It's a pity what happened to Osman Pharmaceuticals, losing their technology and research." I whistle and cock my head to the side as he climbs back onto the chair. "That must have cost their investors a pretty penny. I do hope you weren't helping them out."

Jonathan's mouth parts as realization dawns on his paling face. "You?" He scoffs. "You couldn't have possibly done it."

"You're right. I'm too stupid. I couldn't possibly have made several copies of a certain hard drive, then mailed it out to each major pharmaceutical company and news outlet in the world. No, no." I shake my head and pout. "I'm too much of a nothing to do anything like that." I tap my temple. "Like you said, the drugs turned my brain to rot."

437

In a move that sends dark ripples through my bones, he gives me a disbelieving huff and raises his chin. "Don't flatter yourself, *Marie*. There is no universe where you could have achieved something like that. You lack intelligence."

My fingers tremble behind my back. He's fucking right, but I've made my peace with it. Still, I hate that my own grandfather doesn't think I could be capable of anything. "I'm not. But Kohen is. You know Kohen Osman, right?"

"How *dare you*, you ungrateful little brat." He slaps the arm of his chair as he rises to his feet. "After everything I've done for you, this is how you repay me?"

"You've done *nothing* for me." I sneer.

"Nothing?" He raises a brow, stormy eyes burning into mine. "What do you think would have happened if I left you with nothing but your mother and waste-of-space father?"

"I'd end up exactly like my mother if I was raised by the likes of you. But nobody fucking raised me, and now you're in the center of the public eye for your failed investments. And let's not forget about the tax the IRS found that you forgot to pay."

I want to see him riled up. I want to see him angry beyond measure. I want him to choke on the rage I've been bottling since I was old enough to walk. I want all these things, but mainly, I want him wiped from this earth.

"But I'm not done," I say, low and unbidden. Our happy little reunion is over. The corner of his eye twitches as they narrow on me. "You're going to die tonight."

Five words. That's all it takes for the bloodlust to rewind its way around my heart and braid into my veins. It pushes aside the blurry-eyed fury and hones my emotion into a single-minded weapon. For

438

the first time tonight, actual fear twists his features, and he becomes the prey that he is.

Until he doesn't. Until it comes crashing down, and all my fears come alive.

We glance at the table simultaneously, and I realize my first mistake. I didn't keep my emotions in check.

The second…?

My grandfather leaps for the gun faster than I can. The weapon makes it into his hand just as Kohen steps into the room.

The third mistake comes from a bloodcurdling *bang* following one word.

One cry as Kohen lunges across the room.

"Blaze!"

Then he drops onto the floor, and his head rolls to the side.

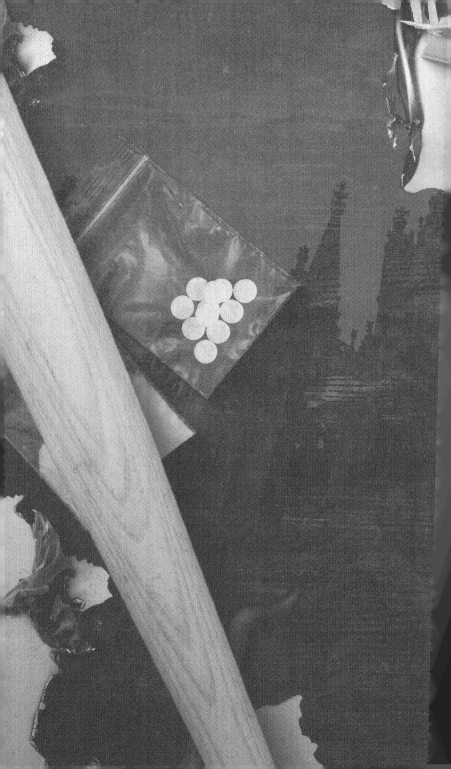

BLAZE

CHAPTER 28

"Kohen," I whisper, frozen to my spot as I watch his black hoodie soak up the blood pooling on his lower abdomen.

I can't fucking breathe.

He isn't moving.

I can't see his chest—

No.

No.

No, no, no, no.

Fuck.

He—he can't. He fucking can't be—

"Kohen!" I scream as my grandfather points the gun in my direction.

"Don't move." My grandfather's voice is a distant sound.

I rush toward Kohen who's lying by the entrance to the room, crashing onto my knees beside his fallen form. Tears spring to my eyes as I rip his mask off and touch his clammy skin. "Kohen. Open your eyes. Kohen, baby. Wake up. *Open your fucking eyes, Kohen.*"

He doesn't. The only movement comes from the blood soaking through multiple layers of clothes, turning the rug crimson. A soft groan escapes his lips.

"Kohen," I repeat, voice cracking as I press my lips against his and gingerly press on his wound. "Come on. I'm right here. I'm not going anywhere."

The space between his brows wrinkles, and his head lolls. The walls around us seem to close in, and nothing matters but him.

"Kohen," I plead, shaking him by the collar. The tears burn down my cheeks, making it harder to see. "Come back to me. You promised you'd never leave me." I keep tapping his cheek, getting harder with each second that passes. Panic grips my lungs in a vise, squeezing hard enough to make acid climb up my throat.

"Step away from him, Marie."

My head whips toward the voice. My grandfather is barely more than a blur from the tears that cast a haze over my vision.

That *motherfucker.*

Thunder and fury flood my veins, coursing venom straight into my heart. The sound that comes out of my mouth barely sounds human. "*You did this.*"

He's a fucking dead man.

Jonathan steps back as I prowl forward, keeping the gun fixed in my direction. Just before I lunge for him, a *click* sounds through the room and I freeze, dropping my gaze to the weapon.

The asshole tried to kill me.

And he didn't hold down the safety.

The fury explodes through my marrow, and everything ceases to exist. The gun flies out of his grasp when our bodies crash together. I don't feel the pain in my muscles or the cramp in my hand. He hits me. Kicks me. Does everything a desperate man would. All I'm aware of is the feeling of my hands around my grandfather's throat, the way he tries to throw me off when I pin him to the floor, and the man who owns every inch of me who's bleeding out on my demon grandfather's rug.

I can't make out my grandfather's face through the tears. The sound of his cries and useless pleas are lost to me as my fists descend on his face. I hit him for the years of trauma he could have prevented. I hit him for the years of abuse at his hand. I hit him because of the pain he caused, even during his dying moments.

He's the one who's meant to die. Not Kohen.

I choke on a sob. "You think you can just kill me?" *Punch.* "I'm the monster you created." *Punch.* "I'm the reason for your ruin." *Punch.* "I'm the fucking victor." *Punch.* "I can't. Fucking. *Lose him.*" A strike accompanies each word, even though my grandfather stopped fighting long ago. My fists keep descending onto his face even as my punches slide into the dip in his skull. I cry out when the last hit collides with his broken features, jarring me back to the present.

Kohen.

I grab the gun from the floor and tuck it into my pocket. "Kohen!" I scream, clamoring up next to him. I rip my glove off to feel his clammy skin in my hands and cup his face just like he does to me. "Kohen, wake up. Come on, baby." My tears fall onto his face as I pepper kisses all over his face. "Please wake up. Kohen, I swear to fucking God, if you don't wake up, I'm going to bring you back to life just to kill you again."

He doesn't get to fucking die. There's still so much we haven't done. So much he said we will do. He promised me a trip to Bora Bora because he wants to see me lounging around in a bikini all day. He swore we'll get a house of our own, and I can get a cat with an absurd name who I'll train to do random tricks. We're meant to go to the woods three days from now and start a bonfire. We have tickets to some stupid sci-fi movie that's had him geeking out for the past month.

Kohen's meant to get his degree and get into medicine. He'll keep saving people because that's what he does. He's meant to go old and gray, and we'll be the couple everyone hates at the retirement home. He needs to know that I love him more than anything else in this world. That I would give it all up for him too.

He deserves to live. Not me. Not the screwup who left the gun unattended.

"Please. Get up. You have to get up. I... I love you. Okay? You can't fucking die without hearing it. I love you, you pyromaniac. *I love you.* You can't—" I choke on the words while trying to press on the wound. "You can't leave me. I won't let you."

"Say it again." The three words drift out in a whisper. My chest squeezes as he peels his eyelids open, revealing a hint of hazel. They start to close again, and I slap him across the face. Hard.

"Don't you close your eyes on me, you fucking cunt!"

His eyes snap open when I slap him a second time.

"Say it," he croaks, his eyes glazed over as if he's fighting tooth and nail just to keep them open. Still, they're right on me. They're always on me. *Seeing* me.

"I love you, Kohen. Get out of this alive, and I promise to tell you any time you want," I sob.

"I'd like that." He sputters on a cough, a sad little smile playing on his lips that tears at my heartstrings.

I peel back the layers of fabric to look at the wound. Kohen prepared me for this exact scenario. He sat me down one night while we were still at school and walked me through everything I needed to do if either of us were ever shot. I refused to listen to it at the time or comprehend why he insisted we carry a first aid kit on us. Now I realize it's because he was always willing to die for me.

It's why he made me learn how to fight. How to point a gun, shoot, and throw my fists to cause a knockout blow. After all this time, it's because he thought he might not be here to see it through. He wanted me to be prepared in case he had to leave.

But he doesn't get to just die on me. I still need to kick his ass for all the shit he pulled on me when we were kids.

"Yeah?" I say, trying to keep him talking. "Maybe we get those words tattooed too, huh? We don't have any matching ones." I yank his top up and gag at the sight of the blood pooling on top of his abdomen.

"You keep copying my style." The words are barely audible, referencing our outfits from prom.

"I need to seal your wound. Okay?" I say, trying to keep my voice calmer than I feel. I bite down another surge of acid as I squeeze my hand between his back and the floor to feel for a second wound. Unzipping my coat to grab the first aid kit on the inside pocket, I rip straight into the gauze. "I'm so sorry. This is going to hurt."

Bile lurches up my throat at the sound of his groans, and I narrowly stop myself from retching at the squelching noise his body makes when I push the gauze as deep into the wound as I can without doing more damage and tape more of it over the gunshot.

"You've always been the one to save me," he whispers.

It sounds like the confession of a dying man. I choke as my tears slip past my lips, spreading their salty taste over my tongue. Fuck, I can't lose him.

"You saved me too, Pyro." Blood smears over my cheeks as I try to wipe away my blurry vision. I put my gloves and both of our masks on and move into a crouch to grab one of his arms. "I need you to walk for me. Can you do that?"

"Anything for you," he slurs, then winces as I try to pull him onto his feet.

Kohen stumbles. My body protests but I manage to haul him back upright and tuck his arm securely around my shoulder. He sways like deadweight against me as I try to get us to the stairs and out the door.

My own legs threaten to give out, and it only becomes harder to walk when we step onto the slippery gasoline.

"Just a couple more steps, and you can have a break," I lie, pausing to lean against the wall to catch our breaths.

I pull him forward again, each step a more monumental struggle than the last. My heart sinks as soon as we reach the top step. Pushing him down seems like a viable option, but something tells me I'd cause more harm than good.

"Baby, I'm going to need you to hold on to the banister while we go down, okay?"

A grunt is his only response.

I manage to catch him before he falls headfirst, but he does exactly as I say, even though I'm sure it only worsens his wound. Nausea rips through me from the exertion of carrying half his weight, and my head swims from inhaling the gasoline.

He crumbles onto the floor at the bottom step and makes no

attempt to sit up. I help him lie back and put another fresh layer of gauze over the wound with my shaking hands. "You can hang on for me, right? I'll be right back."

He mumbles something that sounds like yes, and I take it as my cue to sprint down the driveway to the front gates, passing piles of duffle bags as I go. The sharp winter air burns my wet cheeks as my boots pound against the concrete. An ache forms in my ankle and doesn't go away even as I reach the gates.

Nothing matters but getting Kohen to a hospital. I don't give a shit what happens to me; whether I get sent to prison or killed, Kohen lives. This is all my fault. This was my quest for vengeance, and I dragged him into it. I left the fucking gun on the table, now he's hurt.

It should be me lying on the bottom step, bleeding out. It should be me making peace with my demons before meeting them all in hell.

"Fuck," I scream as I slam the Open button on the gate.

I push myself harder as I sprint down the street toward the car. I need to be faster. I need to be at the hospital right fucking now. If he doesn't see a doctor soon, he's going to fucking—

No.

He's going to be fine. He's a fighter. He's all fury and fire. This isn't how he dies. This can't be how our story ends.

My fingers shake as I grip the key and unlock the car. Every second feels like hours as I rip past the gates and tear down the driveway at breakneck speed. My entire body trembles from the combination of adrenaline and fear. The car screeches to halt as close to the front step as humanly possible.

"I'm here," I call, opening the back door before I bound up the steps.

Kohen hasn't moved from his stoop on the stairs, and the battle with sleep is clear in his eyes as they drift open and shut. "I'm bleeding everywhere," he mutters.

"Exactly why I need to get you to the hospital," I pant, wrapping my arms around his torso without warning. My back strains in my attempts to get him up, but Kohen tries to push himself up after a couple seconds of delay.

A whimper breaks past my lips as he slumps against me, but I try to hold firm and shuffle us closer to the car.

"If you don't clean up, we'll get caught." Kohen's voice sounds distant. Even on his deathbed, his brain is still turning, analyzing and plotting.

I huff out a breath as I walk us backward toward the car, careful not to slip on the gasoline. "I—*No.* You're bleeding out. Just—just shut up. I'm getting you out of here."

He says something I don't understand as we struggle down the steps, and my arms give out as soon as we're next to the Honda. He drops onto his back, then attempts to push himself up onto his elbows like he wants to get out of the car.

"What are you doing?" I ask, stuffing him into the back seat. "I need to get you to a hospital—"

His bloodshot eyes meet mine. "If they find my blood, they'll *win*," he mumbles, swaying with the effort to lift his head.

"If you die, they'll win!"

"Please. I want to see a fire one last time."

I bite back a sob. "You aren't going to die," I insist.

"Please."

One word. That's all it takes. *Please.*

I slap my hand over my mouth to swallow down the sob that

wants to come out. Somewhere in the back of my mind a voice tells me that it's his dying wish, and if the roles were reversed, he'd burn the heavens and save me at the same time.

Tears stream in a constant pour down my cheeks as I make sure his legs are in the car before slamming the door shut. Quickly, I throw the bags Kohen filled into the trunk and round to the front of the house to take one last look at the place where my family prospered while I starved. I fish out the box of matches from my pocket, and picture the girl I could have been if life hadn't fucked me the way it did. But I can't grieve someone who never existed.

"You won't need a jacket," I say beneath my breath as I light the match, recalling my grandfather's words when he left me inside the frozen tub. "It's warm in hell."

The match falls into one of the puddles of gasoline that's decorating the house, and the entire hallway lights up in golden flames in the blink of an eye. I sprint back to the car without appreciating the sight of my past turning into cinders, feeling my soul scream in terror for the man in my car.

I fire up the engine and turn back to look at Kohen, only to find that his eyes are on me, not the destruction painting the manor in gold. "You've always burned prettier, Blaze," he whispers. "You've always been my fire."

It smells of death in here.

The beeping, the coughing, the soft murmurings, the squeak of rubber soles against the lino. The man in the bed behind the curtain divider is snoring away softly. I curl up and try to soak up the morning sun that trickles through the hazy curtains along the back wall of the shared hospital room.

A nurse comes in to check on Kohen and scribbles away notes in her chart like she does every half hour. I gave up trying to ask how he is an hour ago when I kept receiving the same response.

He lost a lot of blood.

He needs to sleep off the anesthesia.

We just need to wait and see.

I'm trying to follow the motto of "Do not bite the hand that feeds," but it's fucking hard not to pickpocket every person or take the random things that I pass by. The urge to steal is stronger than it's been in months. But it isn't the only battle going on in my mind. The need to sneak out of the hospital doors to find the closest dealer has sunk its teeth into my marrow. Only three things play on a loop in my mind, so loudly it blocks out every other thought and sound.

I need to steal something.

I need to get a hit of something—*anything.*

I need to save Kohen.

But I can't do any of those things because I'm stuck watching him waste away right in front of me.

It should be me lying in that bed, not him. I thought I knew what being a failure felt like, but this is something else entirely.

Blood streams around my nail bed as I continue picking at the skin with my teeth. His heart rate monitor looks steady, but what the fuck do I know? The doctors said his surgery was a success and he should make a steady recovery. They also mentioned some more medical shit to me and showed me pictures that I'll leave for Kohen to translate for me if he wakes up.

When. Not *if.*

The police stopped by at nine this morning, asking questions about the bullet the doctors found in his gut. I'm not sure which part shocked me more: the fact that they didn't accuse me of being the one who shot Kohen, or that they believed me when I said it was a drive-by. Maybe the jeans and the knitted jersey Sue made me sold the story. Picture-perfect innocence and all. Or maybe it's the fact that I couldn't stop myself from sputtering and crying like a little bitch.

I peel the skin on the side of my nail, lost in thought from imagining a life without Kohen. I don't know how I would cope without him when he's helped me get this far without falling back on my urge to get lost in white powder. I'm barely on the wagon as it is. Losing him might tip me over the edge, and I don't know if I'd return. But the more I picture it, the more I realize that even if he didn't make it out of this hospital, I'd make him proud. For him, I'd stay clean just to burn the Osmans to the ground, because if he dies for my vengeance, then I'll die for his.

Squeezing Kohen's hand, I stare at the bite mark tattooed on his finger and freeze mid skin-peel when he squeezes back. I launch to my feet and crowd his space, placing my hands on either side of his head as his eyelid twitches.

"Wake up, dickhead," I whisper urgently, tapping the side of his face. "Nap time is over."

He mumbles something that sounds eerily like "Fuck off."

I huff and slump back in my chair. "I'll give you another hour," I grumble.

Time ticks on far too slow for my liking. I have no phone to keep me entertained, so the only option I have is the TV which only has the news—which is depressing as shit—and more goddamn infomercials. Only this time, they have subtitles and no weirdly catchy music. Neither of those two options are appealing to me, so

I liberated a coloring book and crayons from the kids' area earlier, and I've almost finished coloring every page despite how much my knuckles protest. My postkindergarten-level art is mortifying, but it'll be Kohen's *Get Better Soon* present.

"You suck at drawing."

My attention whips to the voice. "I'm coloring, not drawing, idiot," I snap, then send the book careening onto the floor as I assault him with desperate kisses along his cheeks, forehead, nose, eyelids, lips, throat. Anywhere and everywhere.

He's alive.

He's a-fucking-live.

The words replay in my head, turning into gleeful shouts as his fingers wrap around my wrist. I don't notice the sobs tumbling out of my throat until liquid salt seeps through the seam of my lips. Wiping the snot and tears on my sleeve, I slap him lightly on the cheek. "Don't you ever fucking do that again."

"I'll keep that in mind for next time." Kohen's voice is a low grumble that takes me back to just a few hours ago, when he could barely speak while I had his blood on my hands.

I swallow the lump in my throat. "I'll kill you if you do."

"That's my preferred method to go." His eyelids droop and reopen slower than normal. Every medical professional here would say he needs to rest, but I'm a selfish person. I need to hear him speak to know that taking my grandfather out didn't take Kohen from me.

Against my better judgment, I flick his ear. "Don't you joke with me, Kohen. I thought you were going to die."

"You can't get rid of me that easily, Thief." He winces as he brings his hand up to my face to wipe away my tears.

"I don't want to get rid of you," I whisper, grasping his hand to

452

kiss the inside of his wrist. "I love you, Kohen."

His mouth breaks into a soft smile. I wish I could capture this moment so I'll never forget how his eyes light up like he's finally reached the pearly gates. All because of thirteen letters.

"About getting those words tattooed…"

I roll my eyes and chuckle as he traces my lips with his thumb. "I have no idea what you're talking about."

KOHEN

EPILOGUE

A Year and a Half Later

"Did you bring popcorn?"

I glare at Blaze as I drop down onto the empty space beside her. The scratchy material of the picnic blanket wrinkles as I try to get comfortable on the hard ground. "I didn't exactly have time to fit *making popcorn* into my schedule." Anticipation pumps through my veins as I recheck my watch.

She shakes her head and kisses me while savagely plucking the innocent grass. "Misplaced priorities." The thief sighs, reaching over me to get to the picnic basket—wait. Since when do we own a picnic basket? Secondly, how did she manage to steal it? Blaze waves the bag of popcorn in my face. "It's a good thing you have me to make sure you don't forget anything."

I snort and snatch the bag away from her to grab a handful before she can. We settle into silence as we stare out at the twinkling lights of the city and listen to the sirens blaring in the distance. The sounds started the second we got to our spot, right on cue.

She leans against me, and I wrap my arm around her shoulder to pull her to my side, running my fingers over the small strip of skin between her crop top and skirt. We found this slice of abandoned property last year while scouting the area in preparation for this day. It's situated on a hill that overlooks the industrial part of the city, and has the perfect view of the big, white and silver building that has people filing out of big glass doors and onto the footpath. *OP* is printed in big red, cursive lettering on the side of the building, bright enough to be seen from a mile away. *Osman Pharmaceuticals.*

The place where the magic happens.

It's my family's headquarters. Their main lab is based in that hideous building, and so is their primary manufacturing facility— since they lost all of their overseas FDA approved factories, that is.

Everything inside the building is covered in white to hide the rot that comes from inside. I've been in there more times than I can count for the various events my parents have hosted. The night would always start with pictures of me, Kiervan, and our parents smiling for the camera. There'd be a speech or two, some food, then I'd be sent to my dad's office while everyone carried on without me.

Despite all the disappointment my father has in me, he wanted me to work at Osman Pharmaceuticals. I assume it was so he had an employee he could push around until the day he retired.

During the day, the silver building is bustling with people, and it's slowly been getting busier now that the buzz from the information release has died down and some of the labs have closed to preserve their business. Osman Pharmaceuticals is all the hype again now that it's in the lead with a different medication that its competitors haven't been able to replicate yet.

Medication that's being manufactured behind those doors.

"We should have brought s'mores," Blaze says to herself as she pulls a blanket over our lap. I press my lips to the top of her head as she fusses about getting comfortable while we wait for the timer to go off.

Emergency services are supposed to arrive in nine minutes.

People evacuate in five.

The four-minute window is crucial.

At this hour of the night, there are only a couple security guards and a handful of janitors, making clearing the building easier—seven minutes at the very latest if our prior test runs prove to be correct.

Blaze fishes my burner phone out of my pocket and drops it into my hand. It's one of the old-style phones where I need to press the number three twice to get the letter *E*. I push the device back toward her and I'm momentarily struck by how beautiful she looks as the shadows curve along her face. "Make the call."

She shakes her head and returns the phone to my hand. "Your revenge is your own."

"Fine," I say, grabbing another burner and passing it to her. "I'll call if you send the email."

"Look at us, so domesticated," she teases. "But we both know I'm the one who makes the calls in this relationship." Artificial light glows against her soft skin when she unlocks the smartphone and scrolls until she locates the draft, anonymous email waiting to go out to every Ivy League university and major press agency in the country.

The timer goes off on my watch, sending a line of anxiety down my spine. She casts me a hesitant look. "Are you ready? There's no going back from this."

I've always been certain about the two things I want in life: I want Blaze in every way there is, and to bring the Osmans down. I have no intention of backtracking into the past, where the rest of my family sat on thrones while they made me hide behind them. Out of sight, out of mind.

They'll be able to see me now.

The whole world will.

My heart beats erratically in my chest, and I have to take a deep breath just to get the words out. "On the count of three?"

A smile splits across Blaze's face. "Wait. On three or after three?"

"Three," I say, and push the Call button at the same time Blaze rushes to click Send.

"You're meant to count down, asshole," she hisses while staring at the silver building. Neither of us utter a word as we wait with bated breath as the first ring chimes through the air. Her hand drops to my thigh, and she digs her nails into my muscles hard enough to make me grunt.

The line rings again, and still, nothing happens.

By the third ring, Blaze lets go of my leg.

At the fourth, she swings around to look at me with an accusatory glare.

"Did you fuck it up?"

I hold the phone up defensively. "I did exactly as the instructions said. I checked it—"

She jumps into my arms with a scream as orange, black, and vermillion explode into the sky with a thunderous boom. Alarms blare all around, and sirens start up from every corner of the city, dousing the surrounding buildings in a chorus of yellow, red, and blue. The flames go up in plumes of gray, mixing it into the navy sky, scattering ash in every direction the wind will carry it.

My family's livelihood is quite literally up in flames.

Fuck, if that isn't a sight to see.

Their research, their facilities, their income. *Gone.* They barely recovered from the information release two years ago. There's no bouncing back from losing their main facility. Finding a substitute and replacing everything they need to continue production would take months. And what happens to their staff during that time? Their shareholders?

I smile to myself. My family wanted to be in the limelight and keep me in the shadows, and they succeeded.

My cock hardens as I watch the fire roar.

"Holy shit!" Blaze giggles, clapping her hands as the light from the fire makes the golden threads of her hair gleam.

Her sterling-blue eyes find mine, burning just as brightly as the day I decided I wanted her. She may not have started my fascination with flames, but she was the first fire I fell for, and she'll be the last one I ever want to see.

"Now *that's* how you make a motherfucking bomb." She laughs— *God*, I'm addicted to the sound of it.

I smirk down at her, relishing in the heat that fans our way. "Are you impressed?"

She purses her lips, twisting them to the side with a shrug. "I've seen better."

"Liar."

Her tongue flicks out, and I zero in on the glistening trail she leaves behind on her plump lips. She shrugs noncommittally. "I guess it's a little hot." A grin spreads across her face. My cock strains against the zipper of my jeans every time I glance up at the fire, and it's near impossible to think when she rubs her bare legs against my own.

I clear my throat, reminding myself that ruining my parents' lives isn't where the line ends. "Did you send it?"

She checks the burner phone and shows me the screen. Right there in black-and-white is an email titled *Kiervan Osman: Plagiarism Scandal.*

My brother's college and every university he has any hope of getting into for his graduate degree will find evidence of all the copying and pasting I've done for him over the last five years I was playing his bitch. A lot of the references in his assignments were wrong or made-up. Past students' assignments which I stole paragraphs from. Everything is in that email. I changed the words just enough so his school's software wouldn't pick it up. Maybe he should have put some work into his assignments rather than submitting them without batting an eye.

Now, his own college will see the fraud that he is. So will every news agency chomping at the bit for another Osman scandal.

A semester before graduation too.

How rough.

Maybe he should have given me all the money like I asked, and at least he'd have a bachelor's degree to his name before losing his future by our father's side.

A year from now, Osman Pharmaceuticals will have no choice but to be liquidated. My parents will become social pariahs, and they'll scramble to salvage the pieces of their life. But nothing will be able to save them. Their company barely survived getting hit by the information release. There's no way they'll survive this blow.

Kiervan, on the other hand? He'll be unemployed, known for

being the slimy piece of shit he is, and he won't have the money to buy his freedom. He'll become a broke outcast, just like our parents. Forced to live in the shadows, just like I was.

Me? I'll have my degree and the girl of my dreams by my side. Admittedly, we had to balance my revenge out, of course. Even though I legally changed my last name to Aydin, my granddad's first name, I can't be the only one in the family who wasn't targeted. So the shitty house we were renting and my *beloved* car that I couldn't give a shit about both fell victim to an arson attack.

Tragic.

Fire trucks screech to a halt in front of the burning building. Men and women come spilling out, grabbing ladders and pulling hoses, screaming orders at each other left, right, and center.

"To the fall of House Osman." Blaze cheers by tapping the corner of our burner phones together.

Tonight, we're finally free. There's no family to torture us. No past that threatens to drag us back beneath the depths. From here on out, it'll always just be us. Everyone who's ever wronged us will have paid the price.

I grab a fistful of her hair, forcing her head into an upward angle and kiss her with every inch of my soul. She moans against my lips, and the combination of the crackle of flames with her saccharine voice makes me sink my greedy fingers into her flesh.

"I couldn't have done it without you," I break apart long enough to say. It's tempting to close my eyes, so there's nothing but the feel of her against me. Not only is seeing the way Blaze looks against the flames priceless beyond measure, but she's also otherworldly.

My grip tightens in her hair as I covertly reach for the box hidden within the pockets of my jeans. Her lips don't stop moving against mine, hungry with need as if I'm the only source of oxygen she can get. Taking her left hand that's clutching my shirt, I slide a ring onto her finger.

She's always been mine, but now she has a ring she'll never need to steal from me.

Blaze breaks the kiss, snapping her attention to the silver band around her finger and the black sapphire stone sitting in the center. Her lips part as she stares at the ring for three agonizing seconds. Then a ghost of a smile plays on her lips.

"You know you're meant to ask, right?"

"It wasn't a question." A smug grin pulls at my mouth.

"What if I want to say no?"

Reaching into my pocket, I grab the industrial-strength super glue I needed for the bomb. "I wouldn't recommend that."

Her jaw drops, and she snatches the glue from my hand. "You can't just 'no takesies backsies' a marriage proposal."

"It wasn't a proposal either. Because that implies there's an answer to be given."

Blue eyes glimmer with mischief as the light from the fire creates a halo around her copper hair. Her palms press against my chest to shove me back onto my elbows, and she straddles me in the little black skirt that does absolutely nothing to keep her warm.

A shiver runs down my spine as she trails her left hand up my chest, my ring sitting proudly on her finger, glinting against the fire. "You know... I did something special for you to fully commemorate and celebrate your night."

"And that is?" My voice comes out hoarse and gruff like I haven't used it in weeks.

Blaze leans forward to brush her lips against my ear, careful not

to block the flames from my sight. "I'm not wearing any underwear."
She pushes me back down before I get the chance to find out if that's
true.

A growl of frustration threatens to rumble out of my chest as
her potentially bare core grinds against my jeans. I silently curse the
thick material because I can't feel the heat of her pussy skating along
my cock, only the mind-blowing pressure. This woman makes me
fucking mad.

"Patience, lover boy." Clicking her tongue, she rocks back on her
heels to create distance between us. "That's not all."

If Blaze doesn't tell me in the next three seconds, I'm getting her
on her back and fucking her. I'll be fine with not finding out her next
surprise because the alternative is that I die from blue balls.

Slowly—*so fucking slowly*—she crawls down my body, coming
to a stop as she reaches my knees. Then she twists around, giving
me her back before she lowers her chest to the blanket between my
spread legs. I almost choke on a breath when her skirt pulls up over
her ass, presenting her sweet pussy to me, and the glow-in-the-dark,
customized butt plug with three words in block lettering: *Kohen's
Little Whore.*

Fucking hell.

She's the most ridiculous person I've ever met, and I'm completely,
utterly, madly in love with her.

And she's all mine.

I keep glancing between her ass, the moisture glistening on her
cunt, and the fire that's raging against the water hoses. Blaze shakes
her ass in my face, and my dick almost pops the damn zipper open.
"Take a picture. It'll last long—"

I dive forward, turning her words into a cry of pleasure that drowns out the wail of sirens. She arches her back, pushing her pretty little pussy against my face as I flatten my tongue to her clit. The muscles in her legs spasm when I push my tongue into her entrance, lapping up her juices like it's dessert. The moan that tears out of her next has me whipping out my cock to relieve the pressure, and white spots dance in my vision as soon as I fist it, releasing a strangled groan.

I need to fuck her now; if not I'm coming in my hand and screwing it up for the both of us.

Shifting onto my knees, my fingers slip inside her warm heat, and I abandon my dick to prod at the butt plug. I curse under my breath when she writhes from the pressure of the metal and my two fingers inside her. "Your pussy's so fucking tight. How do you think you're going to take my cock, huh?"

Blaze whimpers, bucking into my hand as the muscles in her core convulse. I slowly ease the plug out, teasing her with it as I pump it and my fingers into her at the same time. "Does my little whore like that?" She fists the blanket instead of answering, and jolts forward when I pinch her clit in punishment. "I asked you a question, Blaze."

Beyond the roar of the flames and the sound of the sirens, she says what always ignites the beast born and bred for her. "I think you could do better."

I pull my fingers out her core, grinning at the sound of her growl of protest. With one clean thrust, I slam my cock into her, making her lose her balance. "Jesus."

Fuck. My eyes damn well roll to the back of my head. Her pussy chokes me without a plug. With one? Any second now, I'm going to die from asphyxiation.

The next slam of my hips has her reaching out in front of her like some divine being might help her escape. "What did I say about mentioning another man, Thief?" I grunt, gripping her hips as I drive into her.

"I don't know," she says, biting back a guttural moan. "Why don't you remind me."

The corners of my lips tip up as I pull out of her completely. She whips around to slice me with a venomous glare. "Is that reminder enough?"

I slap her cherry-tattooed ass and twist her long red hair around my fist. With my free hand, I rip the buttons from her top, then twist her nipples between my thumb and forefinger before grabbing hold of her waist to keep her still.

"Are you sorry?" I tease, kneading her tits and pushing the tip of my cock inside of her before pulling back out.

Blaze growls in frustration and shoves her hips against mine. "Shut the fuck up and fuck me."

"Apologize," I say simply, gliding my cock along her pussy to watch her squirm.

She slaps my thigh. "I'm going to kill you."

I tap my length against her entrance. "Last chance."

"Fuck you, okay? I'm so—" Her words die on a scream as I fill her with a single drive of my hips. Blaze meets me, thrust for thrust until her legs give out and she comes with a feral cry, tightening around my cock so hard I'm sure it could break. I don't let her go even when she soaks the blanket with her squirt, then falls limp as she strangles my cock with another scream.

She's so fucking perfect. It's hard to believe she's even real.

My balls tighten as she comes a third time, cursing my name to the heavens as she slaps around the picnic blanket like she's trying to find something to kill me with. Electricity jolts through my veins, making a rabid snarl tear past my lips, pumping her pussy full of my release. It doesn't seem to stop. The combination of the flames and the plug forces me to slump down onto her as she milks me for every single drop.

I roll onto my side, taking her with me. Blaze squirms on my cock in an attempt to get away, but all it does is make her gasp. "You're hard again?"

Chuckling against her hair, I stare out at the evidence of my family's downfall and hold on to the girl who's always worn her emotions on her sleeve, and showed me how to fight even when I kept getting pushed aside. I hold on to the first person who ever chose me.

I was never scared about falling in love with her. I was always angry because I thought I'd only get to do it once. But every day, I fall again. Every day, I fall a little harder.

I don't know what I'm doing. But as long as I'm with her, I could be doing anything.

She's my flame. My everything. My Blaze. And there's nothing more beautiful than fire.

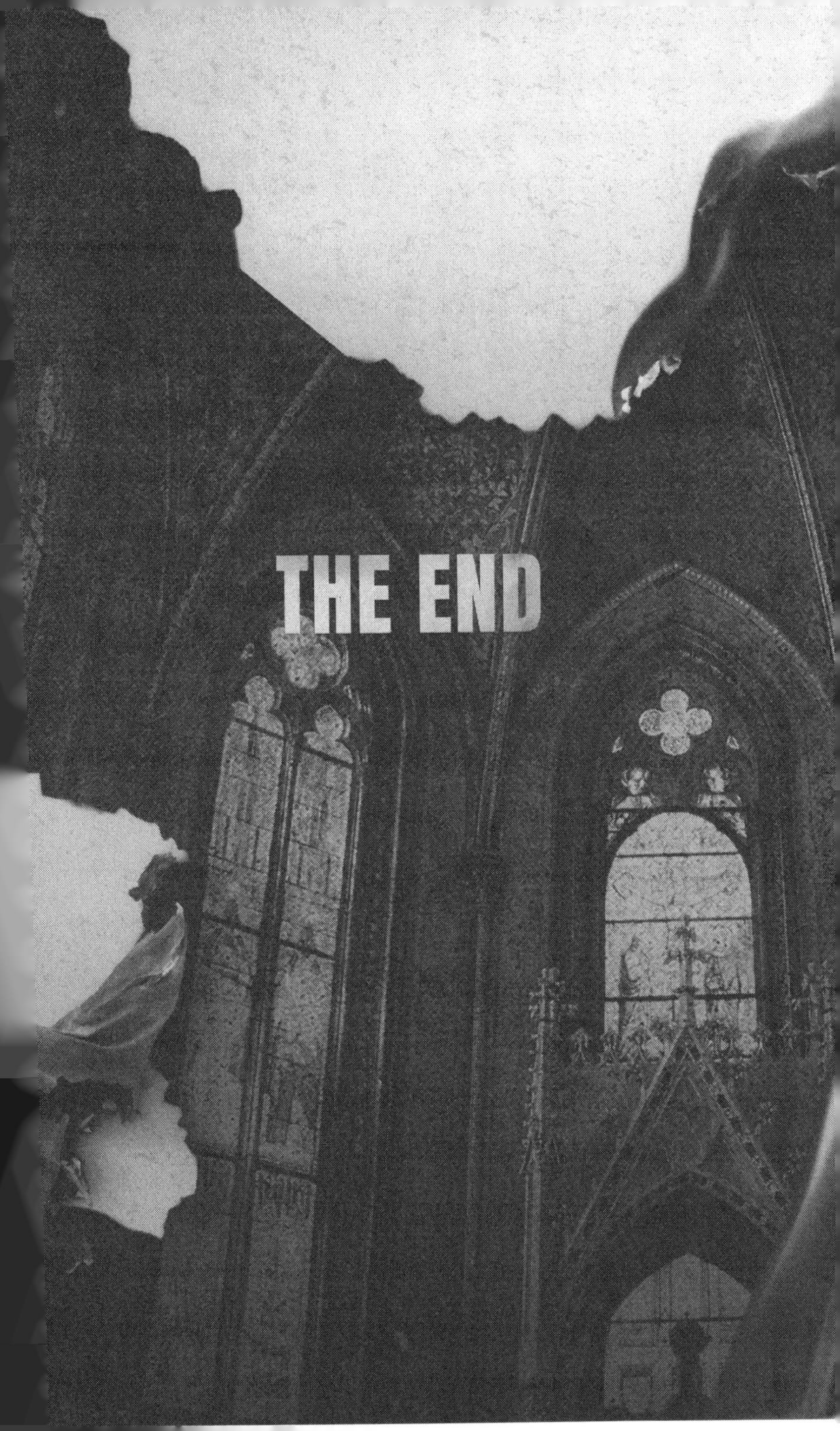
THE END

APOLOGIES

To all the Kyle's in the world, I'm sure you don't *all* punch walls and drink *Monsters*.

SPECIAL THANKS

Firstly, thank you to Hozier for coming up with this banger:

"All you have is your fire
And the place you need to reach
Don't you ever tame your demons
But always keep them on a leash"

Some of you came to this book after reading *Death's Obsession*, and you might be asking what on Earth you've just read, and why is it so different to *Death's Obsession*?

In answer to that, this book is dedicated to the readers who are sticking by me and my 'fuck around and find out' writing style.

This book wouldn't have happened for each and every reader who has showered me with nothing but love and support as I 1v1 my imposter syndrome. My street team has been so phenomenal with their unending enthusiasm for everything that I come up with.

To Kyle (who was speaking on behalf of all Kyle's), for approving on my 'Kyle' segments within the book.

Eve, you're a goddamn whiz. An absolute beast. You and Sam (#spidermonkey) have helped my ass more times than I can count with your amazing ideas and guidance. I honestly wouldn't have done it without you.

My super duper amazing friend and PA Tyla is probably part of the reason I haven't gone completely insane. You kept me in check and made sure I didn't drop the ball. Thank you (and Leigh Rivers) for enabling my unnatural obsession with a real life man.

Kiza, for always picking up Twilight references in every bloody thing I write. I can't help it when I grew up reading vampire/werewolf romances on Wattpad. It's engrained into my brain.

To my sister Patricia, I know you'll never read this or any of my books so that we can keep looking each other in the eyes, but thank you for answering my fifty million questions about what is or isn't medically possible. Thanks for being our family's designated family doctor.

Brynne Weaver... Jesus Christ you're the top dog. Your insanity (and writer's juice) kept me fueled. #deadlinebuddies even though I didn't make the deadline.

Genevive, your continuous support over my impulsive choices has resulted in this book. You're absolutely brilliant to brainstorm with.

Special thanks to my beta readers, Kat King, Rainelyn, Liberty, V, Nicole, Jennifer, Lauren and Nika. You guys were the absolute best. If it weren't for your feral comments and kind words, I would have had substantially more breakdowns if not.

To my alter ego, thanks for being Blaze 2.0.

Thank you to Haley for whipping my blurb into shape, and for always being so damn accommodating (I owe you a drink. This is NOT up for discussion). And Nessa for being such a cool editor.

My dog, Kylo. Your cuddles were phenomenal, but pawing at me every five seconds to throw the ball was less than helpful.

My other dog, Stan, thanks for only giving me the side eye whenever I come to you for emotional support. Kylo... buddy, dropping the ball on my face won't stop me from crying. A+ for trying though.

MORE BY

Death's Obsession

Skin of a Sinner

ABOUT THE AUTHOR

From an early age, romance author Avina St. Graves spent her days imagining fantasy worlds and dreamy fictional men, which spurred on from her introverted tendencies. In all her day dreaming, there seemed to be a reoccurring theme of morally grey female characters, love interests that belong in prison, and unnecessary trauma and bloodshed.

Much to everyone's misfortune, she now spends her days in a white collar job praying to every god known to man that she might be able to write full time and give the world more red flags to froth over.

Made in the USA
Middletown, DE
30 May 2024

55053969R10288